The
Mad Season

Kirsten Langston

The Mad Season
First Edition Copyright © 2012 Kirsten
Langston All rights reserved.

The Mad Season is a work of fiction. Any similarity to persons living or dead is purely coincidental. Names, places and incidents either are a product of the author's imagination or are used fictitiously.

ISBN:978-0-9885380-0-9

My eternal love and gratitude to Bob and Kathleen Langston, Paul Rivas, Bridget Langston, Jillian Robertson, Amelia Gonsalves, and Jessica Schultz. I extend my heartfelt thanks to Randy Mordecai for his time and talent and to Kyle Martinez, my brilliant editor, I simply cannot thank you enough for your kindness, keen eyes and encouraging words.

For Paul

Blessed is the man who does not walk in the counsel of the wicked or stand in the way of the sinners or sit in the seat of the mockers. But his delight is in the law of the Lord, and on his law he meditates day and night. He is like a tree planted by streams of water, which yields its fruit in season and whose leaf does not wither. Whatever he does prospers.

Not so the wicked! They are like chaff that the wind blows away. Therefore the wicked will not stand in the judgement, nor sinners in the assembly of the righteous.

For the Lord watches over the way of the righteous but the way of the wicked will perish.

Psalms 1:1-6

The Mad Season

Chapter 1

Aris had grown up poor. She grew up with turned-over dresses and clothes from secondhand stores. She did not really know about money until she moved to the city and she met John Prince. She could smell the money on him. She saw it glinting in his black eyes; she heard it in the inflection of his speech.

"We're going to be late," John warned her, as he checked his hair in the mirror. He flicked a stray hair neatly into place. He watched himself in the mirror as he spoke. Aris' violet eyes darted over and met his in the mirror.

"I'm going as fast as I can," she said, putting more mascara on her lashes.

"No, you're not," he countered. He examined her briefly in the mirror and nodded, apparently satisfied. Then he checked himself again and straightened his collar.

"Maybe I should wear the other shirt?" he asked himself. "Are you sure you want to wear that, Aris?"

Aris glanced down at herself. "You don't like it?"

"I didn't pick that out, did I?" John asked.

"No," she said hesitantly. "Do I look okay?"

John shrugged. "We don't have time for you to change anyway," he said.

"I'll be ready in a few minutes," she said.

"Hurry up," he murmured to her before he pinched her ass and went into the bedroom to change his shirt.

Sometimes she felt as if she were wearing a costume, taking part in a huge farce. How could this be her life now? The dress she was wearing cost more than she was willing to admit. She thought briefly of the little house in the dusty valley. If only Gram could see her now.

Aris' memories tasted of gin and ashes. Her mother, Laura, smelled of things that made Aris' stomach roil: vomit, gin, cigarettes, urine, desperation, and cruelty. Life with Laura was made up of sweaty nightmares and grasping, clammy hands. Childhood was a patchwork of jagged, scraping fingernails, flicks of hot ash, strange men calling her "honey" and Laura's high-pitched, drunken cries. When Aris was very young, Laura would tell her she was sick and the nasty-smelling stuff in the plastic bottle was medicine. "Mama needs to take her medicine." Aris was five when she realized Laura wasn't drinking medicine. She knew that when her mother started acting weird, it was because the stuff she'd been drinking made her drunk. She was not sure what drunk was exactly, but she knew it meant strange men in the trailer and Gram heaving sad, disapproving sighs. Drunk meant her mother fixing her with a muddy gaze, hands lashing out in anger and a thin-lipped mouth spewing foul confessions, wistful declarations. She knew when her mother went out, she was going somewhere to get drunk.

Laura's mood swings were swift and frightening; it seemed no matter how hard Aris tried to stay out of sight, Laura would find her. Her mother started drinking in the late morning and by noon, if she was still at home, she would be unbearably drunk; she would seek Aris. Laura screamed unintelligible words; she called Aris names.

She used to yell at Aris, "You goddamn thing, you ruined my life," plead with her, "Don't you understand? You never should have been born."

Many times, after a day of heavy drinking, Laura collapsed on the sticky stained floor of the trailer, urine running down her bare leg. "Oh, Christ," she moaned. "Christ," with her head in her hands, her eyes full of angry, unshed tears. "I had plans. I was going to get the fuck out of here. I was going to be someone, have something, but you ruined it. You fucked it up."

Following these diatribes, Laura's hard, muddy eyes softened and her lips quavered. She'd scoop Aris up in a suffocating hug and place loud smacking kisses on her face. Laura left big wet spots on her pale cheeks and forehead. At first, Aris basked in these overblown displays of affection, but as she got older, she began to hate them. She hated being so close to her mother. She detested being enveloped in Laura's sweaty, acrid embrace. Aris smelled the booze coming out of her mother's pores. She wrinkled her nose in distaste at the noxious fumes coming out of her mother's mouth.

Aris learned to avoid her mother when she had been drinking. She could tell her mother was intoxicated by the way she walked, the way she crooked her fingers at her. Many nights, Laura would feed Aris a hot dog or a TV dinner and then tell her she was "going to the store real quick," which usually meant she was going somewhere to drink.

When she was four, Laura got a trailer cheap from some friend of hers and she moved it onto the dirt lot beside Gram's little house. Aris had not wanted to go inside of it. Laura pulled her through the yard to the door of the blue, striped trailer.

"Will you shut the fuck up?" Laura yelled at her red-faced, crying daughter.

"I don't want to go in there," Aris said between sobs.

Laura smacked her hard across her butt and Aris stopped crying suddenly from the shock. Gram was following behind them, saying ineffectual things to Laura.

"Just let her go, Laura," Gram pleaded. "She can stay with me for a little while until she gets used to it."

"No."

Laura was obstinate and that night their pitifully meager possessions were moved into the trailer. Aris watched Gram's house outside the window, jealous of the warm, gold light that filtered through the lace curtains. Laura pulled her away.

"Get used to it, kid."

The trailer had not been cleaned out by its last occupants and Laura didn't bother to clean it either. It was small and filthy and smelled of old booze and dirty ashtrays. There was a cooking area that Laura rarely used, a small living room with a fold-out couch where Laura slept, and a tiny bunk bed behind a curtain where Aris slept. The first time Laura left Aris alone in the trailer, Aris panicked.

Aris awoke, and realizing her mother was not in the trailer, ran in a blind panic out into the pouring rain. Her tiny fists flailed against Gram's back door until she opened it, startled.

"Mama's gone," Aris said between hiccoughs as tears mingled with the rain on her face.

Gram pursed her lips grimly. She put Aris in a hot bath and waited for Laura to come home. She waited for three days.

Gram looked up from her knitting as Laura pushed through the tired door of the house. Her brown eyes were sunken into her pallid face. Her mouth hung in a dolorous, thin-lipped line. Her knees were knobby below her denim miniskirt; her pink, lacy tank top was stained. Laura took one look at her mother's face and shrugged. She walked to the kitchen and poured herself a cup of black coffee. Aris was on the floor, watching cartoons.

"Ain't she supposed to be at school?" Laura asked.

"She gets out of preschool at two. You should know that," Gram said. The reproof slid through the living room to the kitchen doorway. Laura sagged against it like a worn-out doll.

"Whatever." Laura shrugged again.

Gram opened her mouth but Laura raised her hand. "Spare me the lecture. My friend went to the hospital and she needed me. I don't want to talk about it. Besides, she can take care of herself," Laura said, gesturing to Aris.

"She's four years old! She can't be left alone like that!"

Laura drank deeply from the cup of cold coffee.

"Give me a break. She's fine. Look at her."

Laura gestured to the little blonde girl.

Gram's eyebrows dipped low in a frown.

7

"What if some kidnapper had come along?"

Laura waved her hand at her mother. "Please, in the valley? Give me a break. There was an emergency, Ma. What the fuck was I supposed to do?"

"Do not use that language in my house."

Laura shrugged, "Can you keep her for a minute? I need to shower and run over to Francie's house for something."

Gram sighed. "I guess so."

When Aris started school, she carefully compared herself to the other children. She learned quickly that she did not want to be different or stand out. To be different was to be a target; Aris realized she would rather be invisible. After her first day at school, she came home and instructed Gram to bathe her thoroughly. The other children did not have hair that smelled like the sweat of bad dreams; they didn't come to school in torn clothes with streaks of dirt across their faces. She assimilated quickly but beneath her unemotional and hushed demeanor, her insecurities rankled like little bugs.

As Aris got older, Laura's absences became longer and more frequent. The first time Laura was gone for a week, Gram got a phone call, then she took Aris over to the neighbor's house and got into the mint-green Cadillac. When she returned, Laura was with her. She could barely walk, she was so drunk. She was screaming at Gram, who was pulling her by the arm.

"Come away from the window, dear," Mrs. Nelson said, gently pulling Aris back.

Aris knew that when Gram took her to Mrs. Nelson's yellow house and got into the mint-green car, she was going to get her mother. One August day, the relentless sun hovered over the valley. The white wall-phone rang, and Gram put down her needlepoint and went to the kitchen. The call was short.

Gram came in and took Aris by the hand.

"I need you to go to Mrs. Nelson's house for a little bit."

"She's not home."

"What?" Gram looked down at Aris.

"She's in Monterey with her son, remember?"

"Oh, right," Gram murmured distractedly.

"What about the Spencers?" she muttered to herself. "No, no, they're at the pool. I saw them get in the van this morning."

Gram, her brow furrowed, looked down at Aris.

"I think you have to come with me," she said resignedly.

"Okay, where are we going?" Aris asked.

"To get your mother."

Aris' violet eyes were very round and she said nothing. She was going to see the bad place where Mama got drunk.

They drove to an area of town Gram called "the bad part." The streets were littered with garbage. Most of the storefronts were boarded up, empty. They drove slowly past signs that read Everything Must Go! and Store Closing. They passed houses sitting awkwardly behind chain-link fences; rusted cars on blocks were perched on the yellowed, dying lawns. At one house, Mexican children, their brown skin glistening, played naked in the sprinklers. Even with the windows rolled up and the air conditioning on, Aris could hear them shrieking.

They passed a few places with darkened windows, neon signs hanging over the door. Gram pulled in front of one. She glanced around. Two bikers stood out front smoking.

"Aris, you're going to come with me, honey."

Aris looked at her grandmother, fear darkening her eyes.

"It's okay, honey. It will only take a minute. I can't leave you alone in the car in this neighborhood. Come on," she said, unbuckling Aris' seatbelt.

Aris looked up at the brick building. There was a sign on the front.

"Red's," she sounded out.

Gram looked surprised. "You sure are learning a lot at school."

Gram took Aris' small, delicate hand into her tanned one and they walked toward the black door. Gram pushed it open. Immediately, Aris recognized the smell of old cigarettes and booze. It smelled like her mother. Her eyes adjusted to the dim light.

There was a big, square bar in the middle of the room, surrounded by stools. A fat man stood behind the bar. He spotted Gram and nodded.

"Laura, your ride's here!" he called out.

"Eh?"

Aris heard her mother's voice, but she did not see her.

"Thanks for coming down, Mrs. Dunn. I sure hate to do this to you," the fat man said apologetically.

"That's fine, Kenny," Gram said firmly.

"She's been in here for three days straight and she's not doing too good. Got into a fight with Celia last night and now she comes in this morning with this trucker-" he spotted Aris, broke off.

"Well, hey there, honey," he said with loud jocularity. "How you doin', honey?"

Aris stared up at him, said nothing. He smiled widely; Aris looked down at the dirty red carpet.

"Ma?"

"Time to come home now, Laura," Gram said.

Aris looked to her left. There she was, sitting on a stool in a black pleather miniskirt and red tank top. Laura had a tall, clear drink in front of her and a man with a long beard next to her. Aris noticed his white shirt was dirty. He had his hand on Laura's thigh. There were thick, black crescents under his stubby nails. He eyed Aris speculatively. His eyes were dark and ugly, and he had a cruel twist to his fleshy lips. Laura's hands fluttered up to her face and then settled back in her lap. Her fingers rested on the dirty hand that gripped her thigh.

"She ain't going nowhere," the man stated.

Laura laughed harshly. She picked up her drink and turned her back to her mother and daughter. There was a big tear down the back of her top.

"Laura," Gram said.

Laura turned quickly, murder in her eye.

"What?" she yelled.

"Laura," Kenny said warningly.

"What, Kenny!"

Laura jumped off the stool.

"You bring my kid in here? What the fuck are you thinking?" Laura screamed.

"It's time to go," Kenny said.

"Shut up, Kenny. Ma, why the hell would you bring her in here? What's the matter with you?"

She took a big drink from the glass, spilling some on her faux suede ankle boots.

"Laura, it's time to come home."

"No," Laura said sulkily.

"Yes," Kenny said firmly.

"Hey, she don't wanna leave," the man said.

"It's not up to her," Kenny said.

"Fuck you, asshole!"

The man got up from his stool and slammed his hands on the bar.

Kenny didn't move. "Either she leaves now with her mother or she leaves in ten minutes with the cops. And you can go with her," he added.

The man looked at Laura, snorted, and sat back down.

"Let's go, Laura," Gram said.

Laura looked around regretfully and started to walk out the door.

"Hey!" Kenny called.

Laura turned.

"You can't take that with you," he said, gesturing to the glass in her hand.

Laura looked at it and with a deft twist of her wrist, deposited its contents in her mouth. She slammed the empty glass on the bar.

"Lord, I never seen a woman drink that much gin at once," the man cackled.

Laura followed them to the car sullenly. She did not speak for the duration of the ride. When they got back to the house, Gram opened the door to the car and gestured for Aris to get out of the back seat.

"Can I run through the sprinklers, Gram?" Aris asked, thinking of the brown children shrieking in the August heat.

Gram nodded, her eyes clouded.

"No, kid, you can't," Laura said shortly as she stumbled out of the car.

Aris, brows furrowed, looked at her mother, but said nothing.

"Laura," Gram said.

"What?" Laura muttered. "She wanted to play in the damn sprinklers then you shoulda left me where I was."

"What has that got to do with Aris?"

Laura smirked.

"She's gonna sit with her mama in that stinking trailer. She's gonna get her mama a cold glass of water and then we're going to take a little nap. She don't need to be outside. It's too hot for playing outside."

"Laura, you are simply being cruel for the sake of being cruel. If you're mad at me, you don't need to punish Aris. There's no reason for her to sit in the house with you."

"It ain't a fucking house, Ma. It's a fucking tin can, piece-of-shit trailer. If I say she needs to stay inside, then she needs to stay inside. She's my kid!"

Laura teetered around the car to stand in front of Gram. She grasped Aris by the shoulders and jerked her backward. Aris stumbled over her own feet as her head came to rest against the black pleather skirt.

Gram pursed her lips. "How about you both come in the house? I've got the air conditioner running. It'll be nice and cool and you can take a nap there."

Aris could feel her mother's hesitation as she considered this proposal.

"Fine. Better than being in that shithole trailer anyway."

Aris hated living in the trailer. It was hot in the summer and cold in the winter, and it was always dirty. It smelled of cigarettes and vomit. She understood that they had to live there because of something called welfare. Welfare was very important to her mother and if they lived in Gram's house, they couldn't get it. Once a lady from the welfare place came looking for Aris and her mother. She'd been in Gram's house watching TV when Laura had come running through the back door.

"Hurry up, kid. That bitch from the welfare office is here. Get your ass out of this house!"

She grabbed Aris roughly by the arm and jerked her toward the back door. As they came around the corner, a woman with mousy hair was getting out of a gray car.

"Hey, Mrs. Thompson! How are you?" Laura called out in a jovial tone. Aris glanced up at her mother, perplexed. She'd never heard her mother speak to anyone that way before.

Aris started to look forward to her mother's prolonged absences. When Laura disappeared, relief flooded Aris' heart. Then she could go stay in Gram's tidy, warm house. The furniture was worn and some of it was shabby, but the house was always clean and smelled sugary. It was a sharp contrast to the space she shared with her mother. The dishes were always done after meals, and Gram put her in a bubble bath every night before she put her in the brass bed in the guest room. She'd sing her one song, off-key, before she switched on her night light. Aris didn't have a night light in the trailer; Laura claimed it kept her awake.

Gram walked her to the bus every morning, whether Laura was home or not. She mended Aris' clothes, and when Aris got hurt, it was Gram who she ran to. Gram took Aris out into the garden that was her pride and taught her the names of all the herbs and flowers. She would scoop up the earth in her tanned hands. "Good soil here, Aris. That's why there are so many farms."

Aris dreaded the time when her mother would finally reappear. Laura would yank her from her grandmother's house and take her back to the weed-filled lot.

"Welfare needs to see you live here, kid. You know?" Laura grinned at her. "If they think you don't live here, we could lose all our money, kid."

Aris nodded and dutifully followed her mother to the sloppy, slovenly trailer. She came to understand that without her, there would be no money for the "medicine" her mother craved so desperately.

As Aris grew older, Laura began to disappear for longer and longer periods of time. She came back at least once a month for her checks and food stamps; her cheap shoes slapping the pavement heralded the end of bubble baths and the brass bed. Laura's reappearances cast a great shadow over her daughter's contentment. At the sound of her voice, Aris' heart skipped a beat.

"Are you ready yet?"

The hand on her shoulder startled Aris out of her reverie. She shrugged off John's hand and smiled thinly.

"What?" he asked her.

"Nothing," she said out of the side of her mouth as she put the white hat on her head.

"I don't think you need a hat," he said to himself in the mirror.

"I don't want tan lines for the wedding. I'll look weird in the pictures."

"The wedding is months away; any tan you get will be faded by then," John said as he reached for the hat.

"It goes with the dress," Aris said primly as she clamped her hand over the hat.

John laughed, revealing his straight white teeth.

"Okay, babe, okay. I get it. You like the hat."

"Don't you?" she asked him.

"Sure," he said offhandedly. "Why not? Can we please go now? We are so late and my mother will be pissed."

Your mother will probably be pissed anyway, Aris thought. John's mother had yet to warm to her, but then, Janice didn't really seem to warm to anybody.

It was three weeks into April, and the weather had yet to become that threatening heat that engulfed Napa in the summer months. It was only a whisper, a lilting perfume on the breeze. Soon, sweat would run down backs and children would beg to go swimming, but not yet.

The car moved up the gravel drive of the house in Napa and Aris felt the butterflies rise up into her stomach. She put her hand on her stomach and tried to quell the mad fluttering. The white house loomed in front of them and Aris resisted the urge, as she always did, to compare it to Gram's house in the valley. She tried not to think of the dirty trailer on the dusty lot.

Aris was grateful as John reached out his hand to her as she stepped out of the car. They walked past the luxury vehicles parked on the long, gravel drive and Aris felt her feet dragging.

Prince children, of different ages and sizes, ran over to them while the adults looked on in amusement. John was a favorite among the younger children; he was always willing to organize a game, and he lavished attention on his young cousins.

The adults reluctantly got to their feet and trotted over to John and Aris. Soon, the family was swarming about them like wasps, and Aris felt John drop her hand. She stifled the urge to flee from the group. The air in front of her was full of hands, arms, and faces with rapidly moving mouths. The butterflies stabbed in her stomach and Aris clenched her fists.

There were too many people, too much movement.

She stared past the family, beyond the lawn to the pond. The green water was flat and stagnant. She imagined running down the hill screaming, leaping into the pond and leaving the wasps behind her to hover uselessly over the water. God, what would they do then? What would John do then? But Aris stood still, smiled politely and cocked her head in a birdlike manner while she watched everything as if it were happening in slow motion.

The swarm closed in. Aunts with disapproving smiles swooped in to kiss her on both cheeks; uncles with disarming eyes crushed her small breasts with eager hugs. Aris feigned happiness and thrust out her hand repeatedly to show everyone The Ring.

The Ring went to her knuckle and cost John a small fortune; Aris would not have picked it out herself. The Ring, so named because she could not think of it as an ordinary ring, was a square-cut diamond set in platinum. It was plain; the only thing remarkable about it was its size. It weighed her hand down. She kept her lips closed carefully around her crooked teeth, turned up the corners of her small, pouty mouth, and nodded at the polite oohing and aahing of the Prince family.

Beyond the group, sitting in her chair under the shade of the old weeping willow, called Astoria's Tree, was Astoria herself. She watched the melee with cloudy eyes, wondering what all the fuss was about. She smiled at the sight of her family. Her thin, white hair moved in the breeze. Astoria Windham-Prince, the great matriarch of the Prince family, watched the shaking hands and pursed lips depositing kisses on the air, and she wondered how her grandson John ended up with such an awkward girl. This Aris, this odd, young woman with the strange name. Astoria did not know her family; Astoria did not know where she came from or who her people were. Perhaps she had no people.

Astoria's watery blue-green eyes flicked to the nurse at her side. Now she was a lovely girl, Irish, clearly from good stock. That's what her father used to say: good stock. Astoria smiled at a sudden memory, so vivid, she felt as though it had happened yesterday: Barty Windham, his gray hair sticking out in little tufts on the side of his head, as it always did at the end of the day, putting his palms flat on his desk in the threadbare study.

"But is he from good stock?"

Astoria could hear the sound of his tremulous voice so clearly. He had been trying to sound forceful, but Barty never could sound forceful. He had been referring to Astoria's sister's future husband. He certainly had not been referring to Johnny Prince, the man Astoria had married. Johnny Prince was not from "good stock" and Barty knew it. Barty just didn't care.

Where was she? Oh, yes, she thought, the Irish girl. Her nurse was a sweet girl. Astoria liked the weekend nurse most of all; she was the youngest and the kindest and her hands were never cold. She placed a hand on Astoria's shoulder now and asked her if she needed anything. Such a polite girl. Astoria shook her head; she needed nothing. She was old.

She had never been a vain woman, quite the contrary. When one had no looks to speak of, well, she supposed vanity escaped one. Still, she stopped looking in mirrors years ago. She was going to be ninety-nine years old. She supposed she should be proud of her age, but she was not. To be as old as Astoria was to live in a prison. Not even able to go to the powder room by herself anymore! Astoria flicked her blue-green eyes sideways, as if to say bah, but she did not say anything. She rarely spoke anymore. There was no reason to, not really. Astoria had learned over the years that people were going to do what they wanted and she had no power to stop them. Her children were going to do what they wanted. Her husband had always done what he wanted and her grandson, John, was going to do a foolish, foolish thing and marry this odd young woman who had no place in the Prince family.

Aris slipped clumsily through the maze of arms and smiling faces until she found herself on the outside of the crowd. In her attempt to make a quick getaway, she failed to see Sarah at her elbow. Voices mingled with one another in a bubbling din, but Aris had no trouble hearing the whispery voice of John's sister.

"You are so late," Sarah observed with an enthusiastic smile on her face.

"I suppose I'm going to get court-martialed," Aris said dryly.

Sarah laughed harshly, without humor, and pulled her sunglasses down over her black eyes. John's older sister tossed her long, brown hair; she bared her teeth in a counterfeit smile. Aris could not deny Sarah's beauty, nor her unyielding grip on her youth. Her high and smooth forehead spoke of endless Botox injections and chemical peels. It was no secret how she kept her face so youthful. The evidence was in her unmoving forehead and her tightened eyes.

"We stayed in Napa last night," Sarah said.

"Uh huh," Aris said noncommittally.

"Perhaps you and John should consider that next time," Sarah said helpfully. "I mean, it's not like you have a job."

Aris frowned.

"You know, so you don't have to get time off or anything," Sarah clarified brightly.

Aris simply stared at her.

Sarah smiled at her again, her white teeth flashing in her chalky face. She eyed Aris up and down as they walked side by side across the wide lawn.

"What a lovely dress," Sarah said, a little too emphatically.

Sarah was wearing stylish shorts and a billowy, silk tank top. Next to her, Aris looked like something that tumbled out of the Great Gatsby. She was wearing a white knee-length frock with a lace overlay and pearls. Let's not forget the hat, Aris thought to herself. Now she saw why John had tried to get her to leave the hat at home. The dress was bad enough, but the hat made the whole outfit look ridiculous. Aris felt a rush of anger but pushed it down. It would not do to rise to the bait Sarah was throwing out. The last thing she wanted was to make a scene at a family party; Aris suspected Sarah was looking for just that, something else for her and the rest of them to chew on.

"Thank you," Aris said to Sarah, as she kept her eyes on the neatly cut, green spears of grass in front of her.

Marie, John and Sarah's cousin and Sarah's partner in crime, ran over to join them. The Whisper Sisters, Aris called them. Without fail, at any gathering, they would be off in a corner, clutching glasses of white wine and whispering furiously about the attendees. Marie had long, light-brown hair and sly, dark-blue eyes. She was thin to the point of an eating disorder, her cheeks gaunt, her limbs long and ropy.

"Aris," Marie grinned, her veneers gleaming in the sunlight.

"Marie," Aris said.

Marie grabbed her arm and laced it through her own. "My goodness, Where on earth did you get that dress?"

Marie laughed loudly; Aris tried in vain to remove her arm.

"I was just telling Sarah you would wear something interesting, and you did!"

"Yes," Aris agreed grimly.

"Of course, it's a little inappropriate, but we won't hold that against you," Sarah said, smiling at her.

Aris opened her mouth to reply, but could think of nothing to say. She shut it with a snap and Marie and Sarah exchanged a look.

"I haven't seen this infamous ring yet. Let me see," Marie demanded, sharing another look with Sarah.

Aris sighed, fully aware of what they were up to, but she had no idea how to stop it so she thrust out her hand obligingly and The Ring winked proudly in the sun.

"Oh," Marie said, shocked.

"I know," Sarah said knowingly.

Well, Aris thought, at least the three of them could agree on something.

"Whose idea was that?" Marie asked Sarah, who looked pointedly at Aris and shrugged.

Aris pulled her hand away from Marie and cut across the endless lawn; the green blades quivered in a breeze that lifted the small hairs on the back of her neck. The smell of the unmoving pond came wafting up the hill.

Sarah and Marie ran to catch up with her. They flanked her, ready to bat her between them like two cats.

"Oh, my goodness," came a gushing voice. "Oh. My. Goodness," it repeated, and Aris felt hands grab her from behind.

Marie sighed impatiently. "Hi, Mom."

Aris felt the hands squeeze tightly around her middle.

"Let me see it. Let me see it," the voice demanded and Aris turned around to face Morgan, John's aunt and Marie's mother.

Morgan pushed back her bushy, red hair, and winked one large, dark-blue eye at Aris. Her alabaster skin glowed golden in the light of the sun. She was a pretty woman, with delicate features and a small, red nose. She usually teetered around family parties in a flowing dress and towering heels. She always had a half-full glass of bourbon in her hand and a ready grin. Aris waited for the dangerous mixture of six-inch heels and alcohol to bring Morgan down, but it never did. No matter how drunk she was, she never removed the heels. Her ice cubes clinked in her glass as she fixed her blue-black eyes on Aris.

She grabbed Aris' hand and pulled it toward her.

"Oh!" Morgan did not hide her surprise.

Aris tried not to grimace. It was obvious the Prince family thought she was a gold digger already, but The Ring made it so much worse. She didn't really like it, but hadn't wanted to offend John. He had been so proud of it.

"Don't you love it?" he'd asked her as he put it on her finger. "I had it made especially for you. I told the jeweler that everyone had to know you're my girl. Everyone will see this and know you're a Prince!"

Except it hadn't really worked out that way. It seemed like the size and gaudiness only accentuated that she was, in fact, not a Prince. Most of the women of the family wore understated jewelry of very high quality. The Ring was neither understated nor of high quality.

"Why didn't you go to my jeweler?" Janice demanded when she saw it.

Aris flushed and looked away.

"Did you pick this out?" Janice asked her angrily.

"No," Aris said, surprised that her voice was as steady as it was.

Janice whirled on John, who looked confused.

"You picked this out?" she asked, making this sound like garbage.

"Yeah, why?" John asked, hurt in his eyes.

"Why didn't you go to my jeweler?" Janice asked.

"I didn't think about it. Jaime and Ken both got their rings from this guy. I think it's nice."

"Nouveau Riche," Janice said ominously.

"What?" John asked, his brow furrowed.

"Nothing. If this is what Aris wants, then this is what she shall have," Janice said, effectively dumping responsibility for The Ring in Aris' lap.

Uncle Gus and Aunt Minnie approached the little knot surrounding Aris. Minnie glanced down at The Ring, and her brown eyes narrowed.

Aris had little experience with the Prince clan as a whole. She had only met the aunts and uncles a few times. They were always politely distant. There was a sense of expectation when she was with them, as if they expected her to say and do all the right things, but were almost delighted when she said and did all the wrong things.

Aris swallowed, shifting under the expectant gazes of Morgan, Gus, and Minnie, Gus' wife.

"Now, someone told me you two were planning to go to Italy for your honeymoon," Morgan said, tactfully ignoring The Ring.

"Yes," Aris said. "I've never been."

"It's just beautiful," Morgan said. "When Rick and I went, we had the best time. I just loved those gondolas."

"Bah." Minnie waved her hand, as though batting away a bug. "Those are so touristy. I went to Florence and Venice and hated it. I went to Tuscany and took a three-week cooking course. Of course, I didn't like Tuscany all that much either."

"You don't like anything," Morgan said dismissively.

John had informed Aris of the long-standing feud between the two women after Morgan hosted one of the Prince family parties. Morgan and Minnie had gotten into a terrible row, which began as polite hissing, and ended with Minnie, her face red and her jaw working furiously, hustled out of the door by John's uncle, J.J. Gus made a stammered apology to Aris, as he hugged her profusely.

John wasn't sure how the feud began, but it had been going on as long as he could remember. They only once had ever come close to blows, John told Aris: Christmas, 1989. Minnie said something, no one was quite sure what, and Morgan lost her temper and charmingly, but angrily, hurled a porcelain figurine at Minnie's feet. Minnie reacted by charging Morgan, and probably would have slapped her if J.J. had not stepped between them.

Minnie stood between her husband and Morgan, though it was clear she wanted to be near neither. Minnie's breasts were huge; there was no other way to describe it. She was in the habit of pushing her chest out, like a barnyard hen, when she was upset or angry, which, it seemed to Aris, was quite often. Her face was lost in a sea of fat and wrinkles, like a grumpy Shar Pei. Her lips and nails were painted a bright garish red. Her black hair was cut close to the scalp.

"Can't imagine why anyone would want to spend all that time in Europe. As if we didn't have good things to do here in the U.S. of A. Europe, bah."

"Minnie, stop being so negative. Aris doesn't want to hear all your rubbish," Morgan chastised.

Minnie drew in a sharp breath, puffed out her chest and put her red-tipped, fat hand to her chest as though mortally wounded.

"Well, if she didn't want to hear it, she shouldn't have asked."

"She didn't ask," Morgan snapped.

Morgan looked at Gus, who was busily shoving pasta salad in his mouth. Seeing she was going to get no help from him, she shot Minnie a nasty look and turned to Aris again.

"Anyway, darling, I hope your boss is being flexible about the wedding planning. These things can be so time consuming. Forgive me, dear, but I simply cannot recall what it is you do."

"I'm not working at the moment."

"Ah," Gus pushed out before forking another sizable bite into his mouth. He nodded approvingly.

"What?" Minnie asked, irritably.

"Babies," Gus said around the food in his mouth.

Minnie looked at Aris with her oddly shaped brown eyes.

"Is that so?" she asked.

Aris was startled.

"Actually," she began.

"For God's sake Gustav, will you stop smacking your lips together like that! You're like a cow chewing cud."

"Minnie," Morgan hissed. "Aris was speaking."

Minnie ignored both Aris and Morgan and looked expectantly at Gus. Gus looked ashamed, but he didn't make any effort to lower the volume of his chewing.

Minnie raised her hand, and for a moment Aris thought she was going to slap him, but she patted the back of her spiky, black hair instead and turned her disapproving eyes on Aris.

"Well?" she spat.

"No, having a baby wasn't really in our plans at the moment."

"Then why aren't you working?" Minnie asked rudely.

Morgan looked appalled. Gus had run out of food and was now staring at the empty china rather forlornly.

"I'm a temp and I'm just between jobs right now."

"A temp," Minnie snorted.

Marie and Sarah shared a knowing smile.

"Yes, well," Aris started, feeling the need to explain herself. "I'm going back to school in the fall to get my masters. It didn't make sense to get a full-time job."

"Not as long as my brother is able to support you," Sarah said, her tone sincere, her eyes anything but.

Morgan smiled a drunken smile and nodded at Aris amiably.

"What are you getting your masters in?" Minnie demanded.

"Art history."

"That sounds like a great, big waste of time to me," Minnie commented.

Morgan shot Minnie a glare.

"How's Rick?" Aris asked Morgan.

Morgan's husband was fifteen years her senior and he had just recently had a stroke. He was in a nursing home, learning how to use his right hand again. He hated it, but had to stay there while Morgan had the house outfitted for his needs.

Morgan shrugged. "Hates the world, wants a drink, wants his cigars, decent food. He's miserable. I can't wait until he gets home."

"At least he gets a vacation from you," Minnie said under her breath.

"What was that?" Morgan snapped.

"I've got to go," Aris said urgently, without elaborating.

Morgan waved her off with a smile. Minnie, looking disgusted with the entire party, glanced away. Gus stepped closer to Aris. His inky eyes, nearly lost in the fleshy folds of his eyelids, twinkled. He put his fat hand to his graying hair. It was falling out, which he tried to remedy with the deepest comb-over Aris had ever seen. He gave a suspicious amount of hugs, and Aris had a feeling one was coming her way.

"Guess I'll get myself more food. You're going in that direction, right Aris?" he asked as he put his hand on the small of her back.

Aris danced away and smiled nervously.

"I was going to head to the powder room first."

"That's the same direction, up toward the house," he said jovially, glancing at his wife.

"I'm going toward the front to see if John is on the front porch."

"Oh." Gus' fat face fell in disappointment for a moment, and then he screwed it up in a smile. "Let me give you a hug of congratulations."

Before she could protest, Gus had wrapped both arms around her in a forceful hug that crushed her against his large breasts. She pulled away immediately.

The old house was turned out for the family reunion. This was the second reunion Aris had been to and there seemed to be no difference between this year and the last.

The large garden at the back of the house was a boisterous mass of flowers: delphiniums, hydrangeas, roses, lilies, and other flowers Aris did not know the names of. Multicolored Chinese lanterns hung between the trees nearest the porch. These would be turned on at seven p.m., and not a moment before. On the porch were white wicker chairs and glass-topped end tables that no one ever used. The expansive lawn was strewn with chairs and chaises and blankets. Simeon barbecued neared the back of the house, perfuming the air with the mouthwatering, smokey smell. Geraldine was busy loading the buffet table with delicate desserts, large salads, and baskets of freshly baked bread.

Aris walked the lush lawn toward the porch. The air was churning with too loud laughter and the high-pitched screams of children; she stifled the urge to cover her ears. Geraldine was on her way out of the back door with her hands full of bowls.

Aris quickened her pace so she could open the door for her.

"Thank you, young lady." Geraldine nodded.

"No problem," Aris responded.

Geraldine was a small woman; her caramel skin was unlined, even though Aris knew she had to be at least seventy. Her white hair was pulled back in a ponytail. She had a proud face; perfectly arched white brows hung over wide, shrewd eyes. She and her husband, Simeon, had been with "Miss Astoria" since the seventies. She was the housekeeper, and Simeon was the groundskeeper, "not the maid," Geraldine would remind everyone. "I cook the meals and tend what needs tending, but I ain't no maid."

She did not altogether approve of Aris, and Aris knew it. Still, Geraldine was always polite to her. She deposited the large bowls of potato chips and dip on the already overladen table that rested on the side porch.

"Enough food here to feed an army, but I guess that's what Miss Astoria has, isn't it?"

Geraldine was muttering more to herself than to Aris, but Aris nodded anyway. She looked out at the oak and willow trees that dotted the grounds; she watched the children zig-zag in a game of tag. She studied the countless cousins talking, laughing, and quietly getting drunk.

"Hey babe," John called out as he approached her.

Aris leaned over the white porch railing as she looked down at him on the lawn. His face was all-American, clean, and handsome. He had a plate of food in his hands. "Barbecue's ready to eat. It's really good!"

He smiled at her; his teeth were blinding white and perfectly straight. Aris loved his smile. He was unusually rumpled looking and there were grass stains on his impeccably ironed shorts.

"What did you do to yourself?" Aris asked.

John glanced down, his dancing, black eyes momentarily showing confusion.

"Grass stains," he smiled. "There's a game of football going on in the front yard. I guess we got a little too into it." He shrugged his broad shoulders.

"The hazard of a former Stanford quarterback," Aris supplied.

"Exactly."

The family began to line up on the porch as Simeon carried a platter of meat from the back of the house toward the tables. The porch was quickly invaded by a suffocating crowd of people. Aris backed away into the house. The family took their plates and spread out on the great lawn. They gathered in little clusters as the sun sank sleepily. Aris walked the halls of the house, loving the smell of the old wood in the dying light of the sun. She could hear the clanking of the dishes as the maid loaded the dishwasher. The sound of the party was muted inside the house, which was fairly empty of people. Aris used the bathroom and considered hiding in the house for a while; she finally resigned herself to her social obligation and dragged her feet toward the front door.

Astoria saw him before anyone else saw him. She watched the family around her, thinking placidly that Morgan was drunk, again. But there you had it, Morgan just did what she wanted. Never mind what people might think.

Never mind that her husband was in a rest
home. Never mind that that daughter of hers,
Marie, was clearly... What did they call it? She
had... Astoria groped for the word. Bulimic.
That's what it was! That girl didn't eat. Astoria
had never seen her eat! Not since she was a
child, anyway, but that was years ago.
Sometimes, it felt like days ago. Astoria noticed
movement on the porch. She slanted her blue-
green eyes toward it. It was not Geraldine.
Geraldine, who had worked for her for so many
years, was like her best friend instead of her
employee. But, no, it was not Geraldine. This
was a man. A big, graceful, handsome man. He
looked so much like her deceased husband,
Johnny Prince, that Astoria stifled a gasp and
wondered if she was seeing a ghost or if she had
died and he was coming to bring her to the other
side. A gesture he made checked her; it was not
her dead husband standing at her porch railing.
It was her grandson, Rhys. Astoria tried to
remember the last time she saw him and
couldn't. He must have been a teenager; she
knew it had been years.

As she made her way out of the house,
Aris looked across the lawn to the pond, where
John Junior, J.J., paced, mobile in hand. Aris

knew, from the pictures in the old house, that J.J. used to be a handsome man, but his once-handsome face had melted into itself over the years. High cheekbones had become jagged peaks on either side of his face. He was a very serious man; when he turned his shrewd, black eyes on Aris, she fought the urge to turn away. Although he was nearing seventy-one, he had not one gray hair on his head. They had never spoken much past polite small talk.

Aris knew that his tall, thin wife, Olivia, was no doubt wandering the estate in search of her husband. J.J. made a second career out of avoiding her. It was extremely rare to see the two of them in the same place at the same time, even in their own home. John informed Aris after a party one night that it was common knowledge, to everyone but Olivia, that J.J. had been cheating on her for years with a mistress he kept in Chinatown.

"You're joking," she said.

"No, babe," John said. "Honestly, I'm not sure if he's ever been faithful to her."

Aris looked at John and wondered if it was a philosophy he shared.

"Aunt Olivia doesn't seem to mind it."

"But you said she doesn't know about it."

John shrugged. "Either way, she's not getting hurt."

Although it was not nearly warm enough, a few of the older children were swimming in the pond. Parents stood at the water's edge, yelling for their children to get out of the water before they caught colds. There were so many cousins she could not keep them all straight. It was even harder to remember all the children's names. The only one she could remember was Tinsley, Sarah's daughter. The child was going to be a flower girl in her wedding. When Tinsley found out who she was walking down the aisle with, she threw such a terrific tantrum that Aris actually envied her.

"I will not, Mother!" Tinsley yelled in Sarah's face.

"Yes, you will, young lady!" Sarah stamped her foot.

"Mother, you are disgusting," Tinsley said, adopting her mother's habit of emphasizing certain words.

"How dare you!" Sarah yelled. Aris stood back, embarrassed. Janice flashed a grim smile.

Tinsley, rather vigorously, objected to holding hands with her younger cousin, the second flower girl, Ophelia. Aris was not sure who Ophelia's parents were, but apparently she lacked in home training; she was a frequent nose picker and occasional booger eater.

Tinsley streaked passed Aris just then, obviously on her way to the pond. Her father, Paul Hodge, slightly overweight and balding, was huffing behind her, calling her name. Aris suppressed a smile as she imagined the fight Tinsley would put up trying to get into the pond.

Sarah hissed out a breath. Her narrowed eyes were unblinking as she watched the figure on the porch. Leaning on the porch rail of the great white house was a man. He should have looked dwarfed by the house behind him, but he did not. She shaded her eyes.

"Is that who I think it is?" she asked Marie.

Marie looked in the direction Sarah was facing and took a swift drink of wine.

"Oh my God."

"I cannot believe he is here." Sarah's words came out staccato.

Sarah sucked the dank, pond-smelling air through her straightened, whitened teeth and let it out in a rush.

"He has a lot of nerve, doesn't he?" Sarah fumed. "Who the hell does he think he is?"

"Ooh, people are going to flip out!" Marie exclaimed delightedly.

Aris walked briskly up the hill; the light had faded and April thrust its cool arms around the estate, carrying with it the regal scent of roses. She wished she had brought a sweater. She wrapped her arms around herself as she reached the front porch; the moths were starting to gather around the hanging porch lights. Aris looked at the shadowy faces for the familiar one of her fiancé.

As she opened the door to the house, she almost ran into Disby. Disby's real name was Diana. Aris didn't know why they all called her Disby. At the age of forty-nine she was the youngest of Astoria's children. She was very tall and willowy and had short gray, hair. She reminded Aris of a nun.

"Are you enjoying yourself?" Disby asked Aris.

Aris nodded.

"I don't think you've met Rhys yet," Disby commented, beaming.

"No," Aris replied.

"He's Helen's, you know. He's been away for years. She's terribly happy to see him."

"I'm sure," Aris said politely.

"Are you going in?" Disby asked.

"I was looking for John," Aris said.

"He's around by the pond with his mother."

"I was just there," Aris said, perplexed.

"I just saw him out of the study window." Disby glanced down at Aris' hand. Her eyes widened but she said nothing.

Aris nodded politely and walked away.

Aris backtracked and went around to the back of the house. She was headed down the hill toward the pond when she felt a heavy gaze on her back. She turned around and looked up at the house.

In black, he lounged, antithesis to the spring. Blue-black hair hung down past his chin and lay across his golden, deeply tanned skin. It was dark; Aris could barely see his features. He was little more than a silhouette. He was sitting on the side porch, in the white wicker chair, the furniture no one ever used. No one else seemed to notice he was there. His hands rested on the white railing as he looked out at the crowd. His face was turned toward her. Aris looked away.

The children were lining up to kiss her crepe cheek. Astoria simply referred to them all as "children," whether they were her own grown-up children or her grandchildren or her great grandchildren. They were all just children, really. Disby had begged the little Irish girl to let Astoria stay up, but the nurse would not allow it. Astoria was feeling tired and wanted to lay down anyway.

"There's my Rhys. He looks like my husband."

The nurse nodded.

"He's good stock," Astoria said informatively.

John and his betrothed stepped up to her. Astoria eyed the girl's dress.

"That dress is too big on you," she said. "You must ask Geraldine to take it in."

Aris nodded.

She thinks I'm old and I don't know what I'm talking about, Astoria thought.

"John, you must be sure and speak to Geraldine," Astoria said as he bent low to kiss her cheek.

He nodded condescendingly.

Oh, forget it, Astoria thought as the nurse helped her up from her chair. She eyed the ostentatious ring on the girl's finger. It looked like something her husband would pick out for one of his painted women. She loved John as she loved all her grandchildren; he was a good boy, but she could tell he thought himself superior to other people. His head was turned by the flashy, the vulgar and though he was certainly "good stock," it was evident the boy hadn't any good taste. He reminded her of Johnny, her husband.

Aris watched as the red-haired nurse led Astoria away slowly. Her phone rang in her purse. Aris checked the number but didn't recognize it.

"Must be about work," she said as she answered.

"Hello?"

"Aris, that you? It's your Ma, kid. I heard you was getting married."

Aris drew in a swift breath; her heart skipped a beat. John was watching her. Aris backed away from him. She had not heard her mother's voice since she was ten years old. It still sounded the same. Raspy, drunken, contemptuous.

"Kid, you there?"

Aris quickly shut her phone.

"Who was that?" John asked, coming toward her.

"Wrong number." Aris tried to smile.

John didn't know anything about her mother or the way Aris had grown up. Laura had stopped being a part of her life so long ago that she never thought to mention her to John. When he asked, Aris said her mother took off and Gram raised her. John accepted this explanation and never asked any more questions about her family.

Hearing Laura's voice drew a cold mantle over Aris' shoulders. It reminded her of where she had come from and how different she was from these people, this world. Joining John's family would be like sticking her hand in a hornet's nest. As the rich and pretty, black-eyed family flapped and clucked around one another and everyone surreptitiously watched everyone else, Aris watched the Princes, and wondered if she were prepared for the sting.

Chapter 2

Astoria spent most of her days in dreams. She awoke from her dreams in the morning, held them in her pocket until afternoon, and spread them before her eyes until evening. She liked her dreams better than real life. They all thought she was senile, and maybe she was, partly. The truth of it was, she had lived too long, and she found her memories better companions than her nurses or Disby. She still knew who everyone was, even if she forgot the occasional name, and she still knew who she was; Astoria considered this to be quite an accomplishment. At her age, most people, well, how many people were as old as she? Not a lot, she decided, but the ones who were, most likely didn't know who they were or where they were. Astoria knew her house well; she had lived in it for so many years. She never forgot where she was: Johnny Prince's country estate. That's what he liked to call it. Ha! It was

a house, hardly an estate. Luckily, he hadn't
gotten his hands on it, so it was decorated
tastefully. Johnny Prince. He wasn't a dream.
He was never a dream; sometimes she felt him
sitting right beside her.

Johnny Prince had come from a wildly
rich family on the East Coast. He was decidedly
not "good stock." Astoria knew he had made all
of his money bootlegging and climbing into bed
with crooked politicians and Mafia bosses. He
never knew she knew; Johnny thought he got
away with everything.

He blazed a hot trail to the West Coast
and landed in the gilded lap of San Francisco
where he found his seventeen-year-old bride. In
the bosom of the very old money, very old-
world family of Barty Windham, Johnny found
Astoria.

Astoria Windham knew she was no
beauty. She was flat chested, short, and wiry.
Her red hair was not worn bobbed, but was long
and stick-straight down her back. Her facial
features were all small, save for her very large
blue-green eyes. This gave her the appearance
of an owl. She also knew Johnny Prince did not
love her; he married her for her social standing
and her family name. Barty had no money to

speak of; her parents were broke. Creditors had been calling. Then the good Lord saw fit to place the charming, philandering, egotistical Johnny Prince on the Windham doorstep. Her father had been overjoyed.

Johnny spotted her at one of the many gatherings of San Francisco society. Dressed in evening clothes, his black hair slicked back with pomade, Johnny prowled these parties looking for suitable business partners and unsuitable sexual partners. He had a penchant for seducing beautiful, young girls from prominent families. He didn't think Astoria knew about that either, but she did. He managed to seduce half the girls she went to school with.

She wasn't even supposed to be at the party, but her best friend, Ester Shaub, wouldn't take no for an answer. Astoria had been curious, but scared. She knew there would be drunken people at the party and she did not like drunken people. Astoria was not usually allowed at these kinds of parties. Her mother and father were extremely religious Catholics who believed young people's parties were dens of sin.

Astoria was staying with the Shaubs while her parents were in Europe. Her father was trying to find investors for his latest business venture. Barty and Gail Windham had no connections left stateside. Everything Barty invested in, every business deal he'd ever had, had gone sour. No one reputable would speak with him, so he'd gone to London, where his reputation had not yet been soiled.

The night Astoria met Johnny, he had been trying to seduce Ester. Ester was from a well-to-do family that had spot in the social register and a huge San Francisco mansion, but not much money. Ester was sixteen and beautiful. Her skin was the kind of alabaster white that seemed to glow. Her enormous, green eyes were framed with heavy, black lashes. Her blonde hair was bobbed and she used rouge with abandon. Astoria would not admit it, but there was jealousy buried deep in her heart. Everyone always stared at Ester; no one ever looked at Astoria.

At twenty-three, Johnny Prince was handsome and he knew it. Black, almond-shaped eyes and high, beautiful cheekbones were his greatest assets, but his hair and his mouth were his conceits. His mouth was generous, pouty, pink in his brown face. He was truly vain about his hair. He wore it slicked back with a deep side part. Johnny may have been coarse and crass, without an ounce of true class, but he was rich and he carried himself like he was rich. He had managed to convince more than one person to trust him simply by flashing his engaging smile. Women and men alike nearly swooned at his feet. Business associates and lovers allowed themselves to be seduced by Johnny Prince and his can't-lose attitude. His swagger was unparalleled, his good looks legendary. When he walked into a room, everyone knew it; the place would swell to contain him, as though ordinary walls could not hold him.

When Astoria spied him coming through the doors of Bunny Longworth's house, her stomach flipped over. She had never seen a man so handsome, so confident.

Astoria crept over to the edge of the room, nearly blending in with the wallpaper. Johnny walked into the Longworth foyer. She watched as he handed his black overcoat to the maid, who accepted it with a curtsy. The foyer was gloomy, covered in dark wood paneling.

"Johnny Prince!"

Bunny Longworth was a matron of forty-five. She had never been a great beauty, but now she was grotesque. Her eyelashes were not her own, anyone could tell, as they were affixed on her eyelids far above her natural eyelashes, which were sparse. Her thick, black eyebrows were drawn on, the left much higher than the right. Her mouth was a cautionary tale of too much rouge.

"No rouge for you," the mothers of San Francisco society would tell their daughters. "Do you want to look like Bunny Longworth?"

"Bunny," Johnny smirked, his white teeth gleaming. "How are you, gorgeous?"

"Never better, Johnny, you handsome devil. Now don't you try to steal all my dances tonight," she coquetted. "I'm spoken for, you know."

Johnny grimaced, but tried to hide it quickly. "I'll just have to be a gentleman and let the others have their turn."

Bunny put her hand on Johnny's arm.

"Well, I could be convinced..." she trailed off suggestively.

Johnny removed her hand from his arm and moved away. "Phillip! There you are!"

Johnny walked into the parlor, gliding right past Astoria as if she weren't even there.

Phillip lounged against the sideboard. "Pour you a drink?"

"Gin," Johnny said.

"How'd it go with Bunny?" Phillip guffawed.

"Her make-up is so thick, she's going to have to scrape it off with a pen-knife."

Astoria stayed behind him as he sauntered across the room to Ester. Astoria watched as he leaned against the wall and put his face close to Ester's. She could hardly blame him; Ester was very beautiful. Astoria cringed inwardly as Ester led Johnny over to her.

"Have you two met?" Ester asked brightly.

Astoria shook her head and seemed to fade even more into the wallpaper.

"No," Johnny said politely.

"Johnny Prince, this is my very best friend, Astoria Windham."

Astoria put out her hand, which was cold and slightly damp. John took it in his own and looked her over as if she were a horse he was going to buy.

"Barty Windham's daughter?" he asked.

Astoria nodded.

"I see," he said as he continued to assess her.

Johnny worked very hard to charm Ester. He was unfailingly polite to Astoria, when he remembered she was there. Still, she felt uneasy around him. He had an aura of danger and a carelessness he did not bother to hide. He also drank quite a bit. By the time Astoria was ready to go home, Ester and Johnny were both heavily inebriated.

When her parents returned from Europe they had no investors, no prospects, and were faced with becoming destitute. On a particularly gray and rainy day, grim-faced and silent, they collected Astoria from the Shaub house. When they arrived home, her mother sent her into the kitchen to make a pot of tea. While Astoria readied the tea service, she heard her mother, quite upset, addressing her father.

"This is all your fault!" Gail hissed. "What are we going to do? You'll have to get money from one of the boys or one of the girl's husbands. Someone."

"I already did. I can't ask for any more. Gail, we need a miracle."

"There's no such thing, Barty. Why are you such a failure? Oh! When I think of all the years, scraping together, making sure no one knew. Trying to maintain an air of respectability while you traipsed from one failed deal to another. Trying to mask my shame. I won't do it anymore, Barty. You need to handle this. Do you hear me?"

"Gail, there's nothing more I can do, short of pawning your jewelry," Barty said weakly.

"I have already done that, Barty! How do you think we got to London? Magic?"

Astoria lifted the kettle off the stove and poured the hot water into the teapot. She placed milk and sugar on the tray. She felt sorry for her father. She knew he tried his best; it wasn't his fault things didn't work out.

"Thank God the rest of our children are out of the house. Thank God we only have to take care of Astoria. Of course, God forbid she wants to get married. You couldn't give her a decent wedding even if you wanted to," Gail said shortly.

"She's not as attractive as the other girls and we have nothing to offer but our name. It'll be a while before she's married, Gail," Barty said wearily.

Astoria put a hand to her mouth and willed tears not to fall. She got out cups and saucers quickly.

"Hush," Gail whispered loudly.

"Oh," Barty said, startled. "Quite right, my dear."

"Can you go to the bank?" Gail asked.

"We're mortgaged to the hilt, Gail. We have nothing. We need a miracle," he repeated.

When Johnny Prince showed up on their doorstep, Barty thought it was divine intervention; he hadn't cared that Johnny wasn't good stock. He had not extensively interviewed Johnny as he had her sisters' husbands. No, he simply signed her over, like a piece of chattel. In Astoria, Johnny had a ticket to every society drawing room in San Francisco. Respectable doors that were previously closed to him because of his rakish reputation would be open.

The first time Johnny Prince called on her, Astoria did her best to feign interest. She was exceedingly polite to him, but did little to encourage his advances. He was very handsome and he made her terribly nervous, but, in truth, she had no interest in the man, no matter how charmingly he presented himself. Despite her polite reserve, he kept coming to see her. She behaved cautiously around him; she knew her parents were in favor of the union, and she was loathe to reject Johnny outright, but she didn't want to marry him.

After four weeks of stiffly receiving him in the sad little parlor, her mother took Astoria aside and gave her some firm instruction.

"Astoria, this man is interested in you, and yet, I've noticed you do very little to encourage him."

"Mother, I'm afraid Mr. Prince isn't a very Godly man," Astoria said slowly.

"What do you mean?" Gail asked sharply.

"I have heard things, that's all," Astoria said quietly.

"You know better than to pay attention to idle gossip," Gail admonished swiftly. "I'm going to be very plain with you, Astoria. Mr. Prince is very interested in you. I think," she declared triumphantly, "he might want to marry you."

"Marry me?" Astoria was aghast.

"It is our first good fortune in years," Gail said briskly. "He's extremely wealthy. You would never have to worry about money again. You would always have new dresses and fine things. You will never have another opportunity like this. You must take advantage of it."

Astoria lowered her face until the red curtain of her hair fell over it. Gail put her hand under Astoria's chin and lifted her head up, piercing her blue-green eyes with a hard stare.

"I don't like to say it, but you are a rather plain girl and you will never get a man like this again. This is your only chance. Our only chance. If Mr. Prince doesn't marry you, we'll all end up in the poorhouse."

The weight of her parents' financial responsibilities settled itself firmly on Astoria's bony shoulders. Each morning she would wake from harsh dreams and the enormity of what was expected of her would make itself known once again. Finally, to save her parents from financial ruin, Astoria agreed to marry a man she barely knew and didn't like.

To celebrate their engagement, Johnny commissioned the house in Napa. He also bought a house in San Francisco. It was an old Victorian, built in the 1800s. He felt owning such a piece of property further solidified his newfound respectability. Astoria privately disagreed with him, but she kept this opinion to herself.

On their wedding night, Johnny accidentally hit her. He had been terrifically drunk. The reception took place in her parents' house. Johnny had overridden Gail's objections about serving alcohol. Champagne and whiskey flowed unendingly, much to Gail's shock. The party brought about the unnatural pairing of old San Francisco society with Johnny Prince's raucous friends. It was a painful combination of the venerable and the vacuous. Gail was pale with embarrassment; Barty was red-faced with too much whiskey and desperation. The party quickly became a shrill and swift-moving shriek. By the time Astoria and Johnny left for the hotel, most of her parents' friends had left in a quiet shush of furs and evening capes. All that was left were her reproving family and Johnny's feral playmates.

They entered the room at the St. Francis and Astoria quickly avoided Johnny's embrace by locking herself in the bathroom. She was shaking at the thought of getting in the bed with him; Johnny didn't bother to hide his amusement.

"See here, just come out of the bathroom and get in the damn bed, Ester," he laughed.

"Astoria," she corrected softly.

He laughed. "Shit, I meant Astoria. Come on out here, honey. It won't be that bad."

She'd been in the bathroom for half an hour, getting ready. He was getting impatient; she could feel it growing on the other side of the door. Still, she could not bring herself to open it.

"I'll be out in a second," she called.

"That's what you said twenty minutes ago," he muttered.

Finally she opened the door. He was lounging indolently on the bed. He looked terribly handsome.

"Ah," he said in anticipation.

Astoria stood where she was, unable to move.

"You sure have a pretty little gown on there, don't you, honey?"

It was a lacy confection Ester had gotten for her. "He will love it, Tori. Believe me, I know!"

Johnny approached her, a lecherous smile on his tanned face. He came close and gathered her in his arms, kissing her thin, tight mouth quickly.

"Let's see what's going on under this thing," he slurred rudely as he started to pull up her gown while his other hand inched up to her breasts.

Astoria started to pull away in fear, only to find she couldn't. She was stuck.

"Damn, what the hell?" Johnny looked down her gown. "Damn lace is caught on my cuff link, I think."

He reached between their bodies to untangle it and Astoria stiffened. He laughed.

"You're as skittish as a young filly. Jesus Christ," he murmured. He pulled, but to no avail. Finally, he wrenched his hand away from her chest. The next thing she knew, she was thrust back against the wall and her eye was throbbing.

"Shit, did I hit you?" he asked, drunkenly.

Her eye felt like it was going to bulge out of her head. Johnny laughed at the look on her face.

"You're going to have a shiner, I think. Christ, everyone will think I beat you on our wedding night."

He was amused. She spent the next few weeks being feted by friends and family, trying to hide the bruise on her face.

"You're wearing as much face powder as Bunny Longworth," Johnny laughed at her.

During their brief courtship, he was unfailingly charming and extremely courteous, but once they were married, he was different. Johnny was capable of mad furies that came on like lightning and would disappear just as quickly. He drank liberally, cussed routinely, and had little regard for her feelings. She was startled at their first dinner in the Victorian when he suddenly got up from the table. He gave her a perfunctory kiss on the forehead, grabbed his hat and coat, and left without a word to her. This became a way of life. He would usually come home for the evening meal, but sometimes he did not. Astoria grew used to eating alone at the polished table. He would go out every night, and sometimes, he wouldn't come home for days. He would inevitably appear one morning at the breakfast table, a smile on his face as he absentmindedly kissed his wife. He behaved as though nothing had happened, and Astoria did not ask questions for fear of bringing on one of his black moods.

Astoria didn't become pregnant easily. One night, in the fifth year of their marriage, Johnny became enraged. He had been gone for days. He came home, drunk and angry. He stormed up the stairs to the master bedroom and flung open the door.

"Get up!" he screamed over her bed. "Goddamn it! Get up!"

Astoria woke with a start and leaped out of bed, thinking there was a fire.

"Come here!" He grabbed her by the arm and started pulling her out of the room and down the stairs. Johnny dragged her all the way down the street to her parents' house. He began banging and pounding on the door. When her bewildered father answered the door, Johnny shoved Astoria at him.

"Defective," he spat.

Barty Windham drew a sharp breath.

"You come here in the middle of the night, banging on my door, waking the entire house! Are you out of your mind, young man?" Barty's bushy, gray eyebrows drew together and he stamped his slippered foot.

"You shut up," Johnny ordered. He pointed his finger at Astoria accusingly. "I paid for her. I paid for this house. I paid for the clothes on your back and the food in your pantry and you sold me bad product."

John turned tipsily and began to walk away. Astoria stood quietly in the dim light of the foyer in her father's house and said nothing as she watched her husband disappear into the darkness.

He did not come for her the next day, nor the day after, and she was afraid to go home. She had no clothes or toiletries; she had no money, only the nightgown that she had worn to bed two nights before.

She stayed at her parents' house for two weeks without a word from Johnny. On the morning of the fifteenth day, he came for her. He came, she knew, not because he wanted to, but because he had to.

Astoria overheard her father and mother talking the morning before.

"The things he's doing, my God, Gail! Do you realize what kind of man our daughter lives with?" Barty cried. He was shuffling round the mahogany dining table in the elegant dining room. He was still in his pajamas and robe; his gray hair stuck out in tufts around his partially bald head. Her mother sat calmly at the head of the table, drinking coffee. She was already dressed in a severe, black frock; her faded, red hair was scraped back into a bun.

"He's stopped paying the bills, Barty. She's got to go back to him."

"He won't!" Barty said passionately. "He won't take her back. He said she can't get with child. Meanwhile, he's fathered at least half a dozen bastards at half a dozen whorehouses in the city."

"Barty!" Gail was shocked.

"I'm sorry Gail, but it's true. That's what set him off the other night. The whole damn town knows. He got some poor little whore in trouble and she tried to get rid of it and died. He went on a three-day drunk and then came home and dragged his own wife out of his house in the middle of the night. Now he won't let her come back home because she can't get with child. Everyone knows!" he yelled shrilly.

Astoria shrank back against the wall, wondering why she was surprised. Surely she knew somewhere in her heart he wasn't being faithful.

"What are we to do?" Barty cried, bereft. "Where are you going? Gail?"

Astoria heard the creak and rustle of her mother rising from her chair and her voice came closer as she answered, "I will take care of this, Barty."

Astoria did not know what her mother did, but the next day Johnny showed up at the door with roses and a smile.

Finally, after eleven years of marriage, Astoria produced their first son. When John Junior was born, Johnny Prince declared himself the proudest man in San Francisco and promptly disappeared for five days. When he returned he told the maid to pack Mrs. Prince's bags. Astoria, who thought she knew all her husband was capable of, was again surprised. He sent her to Napa, permanently. At first, Astoria was quite put out, but she learned that she much preferred to live apart from her husband. After that, it was rare that she saw the inside of the San Francisco house. Johnny would appear in Napa at odd times, always unannounced, and stay for short periods.

Astoria bore nine children in rapid succession. It felt like she was barely finished nursing one when another would come along. After J.J. came Gustav, named after some distant German ancestor of Johnny's, then Samuel, who died of a fatal hole in his heart when he was only nine days old. Astoria mourned the child for months until Johnny came in from San Francisco and shook her by the shoulders violently.

"You still have two sons who need your care! Snap out of it, Astoria!" he yelled.

He stayed for two weeks, watching her go through the motions of raising their children until he was satisfied she was finished grieving. By the time he left, she was pregnant with Helen.

Johnny was disappointed with their first girl and didn't bother to hide it. Helen was an ugly, mewling child. Red faced and toothless, she bore a striking resemblance to his Aunt Lucy, a woman he'd once deemed "too ugly to look at."

Then she had Michael. Her sweet, gentle Michael.

J.J. was very clearly Johnny's son. He was Johnny's pride, and from the moment the boy was born, Johnny groomed him to be his successor. Gustav was a whiny, sickly child; Johnny did not care for him. Helen had been a difficult baby, always crying, and was an even more difficult child. Helen was plainly terrified of Johnny, though, and rarely spoke in his presence. Michael was, though she hated to admit she had one, her favorite. From the beginning, she and the boy had a special bond. Michael was all hers in a way the other children were not. He was a handsome boy who grew into a handsome young man. He favored his father physically, but he had a light and gentle manner that could have only come from Astoria. When he died in Vietnam, a piece of Astoria died with him. They picked his draft number and Johnny had tried everything he could to get the boy out of it. He offered bribes to everyone: congressmen, people on the draft board, everyone. He was going to smuggle Michael out of the country, but Michael had talked him out of it.

"You're always talking about duty and country, Dad. You're in favor of this war, or at least you were."

He ran his fingers through his short, brown hair.

Johnny sighed. "Son, boys are dying over there. I won't have you be a name on a list. You are too young to understand! I won't have your body blown to bits or have you come home one of those goddamn zombies that kills himself! I won't have it!" he thundered.

Astoria was crying.

Michael went and died three weeks after he was deployed.

Janice was next; she was the last child Johnny had really paid attention to. She'd been a pretty baby who came out of the womb with a full head of black hair. Johnny had fallen in love with the girl; he showered such affection on her, Helen glowered with jealousy. Janice and J.J. were his obvious favorites. It was as if he picked from the litter the two that reminded him the most of himself; the other children he received with vague affection. The last three girls Astoria bore without fanfare, Diana being the last; the doctor had called her a "change-of-life baby." Johnny had not been present for the births of his last two children and Disby was no exception. He was in Hong Kong on business when Jane was born, Paris with a mistress when Morgan was born, and stuck in a meeting when Disby was born.

"Sorry," he said as he sailed into the hospital room, roses in hand. "I tried to get out as soon as I could. I just made ten million dollars," he said triumphantly.

"I just had a baby," Astoria said.

Astoria and her children lived in the house in Napa, only going into the city for holidays. Astoria attained a quiet dignity in her middle age, which continued to the present. Her homely face softened with motherhood and her blue-green eyes were lit with the joy of her children. She took on a soft glow that even Johnny noticed. She left behind the shyness of her childhood to become a thoughtful and encouraging woman who trailed the faint perfume of lavender wherever she went. She found her happiness in her children.

Astoria knew Johnny lived an entirely separate life. She had no illusions about what he was doing in San Francisco. He had a large group of rich friends and an unending supply of mistresses. Astoria knew what he got up to in the city, she always had, but she chose to ignore it.

Johnny aged well, his handsome face only becoming more so as the years rolled by.

His recklessness and rowdy behavior continued into his late fifties, when he finally curbed his lust for women, drinking, and good times. It was around this time he gained a new appreciation for his wife. They treated each other kindly and affectionately, the courteous distance of their youth replaced by a mutual respect. However, he found some of his progeny disappointing and didn't hesitate to show it. He was forever trying to instill a backbone in Gustav and trying to get Astoria to "fix" Helen.

"Take her to the goddamn beauty parlor! There's no need for her to have one big goddamn eyebrow when they can just pluck it! She looks like a monkey!"

Astoria tried to calm him, but he would not be calmed. He paced the study in San Francisco with a fierceness.

"I'm serious, you need to do something. Get the mustache waxed at least!"

"She's nine years old," Astoria protested.

"All the more reason to handle it." Johnny waved his scotch at her. "Before she gets embarrassed," he added.

He would take Gustav hunting in the redwoods and the boy would whine and cry about everything. He never had these problems when he took Michael or J.J.

"Goddamn kid acts like a little girl," Johnny complained to Astoria. "He's such a whiny little sissy."

Their last trip had been disastrous. They had driven into the Sierra Mountains to go fishing for the weekend.

"It's cold. I got water in my boots and my feet are wet," the fat little boy squeaked out.

Finally, Johnny lost his temper and slapped Gus across his plump, red cheeks. The boy had been too stunned to cry and Johnny never took him anywhere again.

When Janice was born, Johnny doted on her. Astoria felt a pang of jealousy in her heart, to see the way he carried on over Janice. He used to bring her into the city with the nanny for days at a time and show her to everyone. He brought her everywhere: parties, business meetings, even to supper clubs. As Janice grew into a young girl, Johnny stopped spending so much time with her. His precious, young baby had turned into a terror of a three-year-old, and he was not equipped with the patience to handle her. Still, everyone knew, she remained his favorite daughter.

Johnny had affection for his family, even love for his wife and children, but to the day he died, they remained little more than an afterthought. Astoria and Johnny bumped along through wars and deaths and babies and affairs which she knew about, but of which she never spoke.

Johnny died of a heart attack, collapsed on the floor beside his desk at his downtown office. His family mourned him deeply. Johnny Prince had not been an ideal father. He didn't come to first communions or dance recitals, he frequently missed birthday parties, and he rarely gave his children any acknowledgment other than a pat on the head and a distracted smile. It was rare for him to turn his attention to his children; he had invested time in J.J. and was frequently delighted by Janice, but they were like toys to him. He would pick them up when he felt like it and put them down when he got tired of them. His other children were victims of his absentee parenting, which consisted of issuing edicts and paying tuition. Still, when he passed away, when his vigor and vitality were no longer a part of their lives, they entered a painful period of grief. Astoria was keenly aware of his absence and would often find herself crying out for him in her sleep, something she had never done when he was alive.

Astoria relived these moments from her life, sometimes wishing she had said or done something differently, sometimes wondering what her life would have been like if she had been allowed to marry for love. There was a man, a long time ago, a man Johnny Prince never knew about, and she dreamed of him too. And her Michael. She prayed soon she would see her Michael. Would Johnny Prince be waiting for her? Doubtful. Astoria laughed shortly, causing the nurse to look up from her magazine.

"It's nothing," Astoria smiled.

Chapter 3

The azure sky sparkled and the dry California
heat undulated through the golden hills like a
fevered plague. Aris twisted in her sleep,
unwilling to awaken. She'd had bright and
tortuous dreams the night before, but could not
remember what they'd been about. The phone
by the bed rang, and she groaned and squinted
her eyes against the dazzle of early spring.

"Hello," she groaned.

"May I speak with Aris, please?"

Aris stifled the urge to throw the phone
against the wall.

"Speaking," she said, her voice a
squeaking hinge.

"Are you still sleeping?" the voice
asked, sounding incredulous.

"Um hum."

"It's late."

"How late?" she asked, as she stretched languorously. "Who is this?"

"It's ten and this is Rhys, John's cousin."

Aris sat up.

"What do you want?" she asked rudely.

"I have something for Johnny. He said to call you and have you come and get it. I can't really get away right now."

"What am I? Fed-Ex?" Aris muttered.

"Excuse me?"

"Nothing."

"Maybe I should call back when you're awake," he suggested, laughter in his voice.

"I'm awake," she wrapped her long, blonde hair around her hand.

Aris waited.

Rhys, the man from the reunion, Helen's boy, who had been away so long.

"So, do you want my address?"

"Let me get something to write on," Aris said reluctantly.

He gave her his address and told to her to come by anytime. Aris hung up, feeling unsettled. His voice had been sexy, teasing.

Aris called John.

"Your mysterious cousin called," she said abruptly when he answered. "I need to pick up a package from him."

"Yeah," John said absently. "I thought," John said, "since you don't do anything all day, you wouldn't mind. I'd do it myself, but I'm busy working. He can't put it in the mail for some reason."

"Oh," she said.

"Listen, Aris I would love to stay on the phone and chat but I'm in the middle of something right now."

"Oh, sure," Aris said, but he had already hung up.

She thought of the difference between her conversation with the two cousins. She thought about that teasing, sexy voice and measured it against John's brusque tone. Rhys. Aris shook out her hair as if to clear him from her head, but he clung inside like dirt in a cobweb.

"Get a grip on yourself," she said aloud.

The phone rang again.

"Jesus Christ," she said. "Now what?"

"Hello?"

The person on the other end coughed loudly and then said, "Aris, goddamn it, you're starting to make Mama upset. Now I know we ain't seen each other in a long time, but if I have to I'll show up on your doorstep. I bet them rich people you got yourself tangled up with would love to meet your Mama!"

The stench of Laura rose before her, as if she were four years old again. Booze, cigarettes, a strange man's cologne. Aris hung up before her mother could say anything else. She didn't know what else to do. This was the second time Laura had called her in a month. She knew her mother wasn't going to give up. She didn't even know how Laura had gotten her number. Laura knew about the wedding; no doubt she knew about the wealthy Prince family. Aris was, quite thoroughly, petrified. She had feared this moment since the day her mother left her. Laura had returned.

On her seventh birthday, Gram took Aris to the Five and Ten and bought her a little blonde doll that had real eyelashes and eyes that opened and closed. Aris named her Bonnie. She had a pink and white dress and she had a pink and white bottle to match. There was real milk in the bottle.

Aris and Gram had pancakes for breakfast that morning and a package came from Uncle Kirby, who was in Oregon. It was a purple My Little Pony. Aris watched Gram bake her a chocolate cake, dutifully licking the spoon Gram handed her with faux solemnity.

Her mother had been gone for two weeks. Around dinnertime Laura came in the house riding a cloud of cheap perfume.

"Hey, Ma? Where are you?"

"Back here, Laura," Gram said tiredly.

Laura came clacking into the blue and yellow kitchen in her cheap flip-flops.

"Damn September's hotter'n anything in this damn valley," Laura commented as she slid into a chair at the worn, wooden table.

Gram and Aris stared at her.

"What?"

"Laura, you got any idea what today is?"

"Yeah, Saturday. Why?" Laura reached over into Aris' plate and snatched a green bean.

"It's Aris' birthday today."

Laura's eyes widened.

"Oops!" she said grinning. "I just got my days mixed up, that's all."

Laura pinched Aris on the arm. "A pinch to grow an inch!"

She laughed coarsely.

Aris clamped her mouth shut. She pushed her plate toward her mother, who tucked in with gusto.

"Aris! This is your favorite meal," Gram said.

Aris shook her head. She wasn't hungry anymore.

Aris brought Bonnie with her wherever she went. Every time it was her turn for show and tell at school, she brought Bonnie until the teacher tactfully suggested to Gram that Aris bring something else next time. Bonnie slept with her in the brass bed at Gram's and she pulled the little doll close in the dark trailer at night when the creak of the door would awaken her. Heavy male footfalls stomped up the steps, and she heard a stranger's sleazy tone. While she listened to the words slipping and sliding around on an oil-slicked tongue, Aris cringed at her mother's husky responses and throaty chuckles. As Aris listened to the clink of glasses and the tinkle of the slow, steady outpouring of another anesthetizing drink, she clutched Bonnie and dreamed of being somewhere else.

When she was nine, her mother disappeared for longer than a month. The welfare lady came looking for Laura and found Aris in front of Gram's house. She was digging for worms to transport to the garden in the backyard. Gram said the worms made her plants happy. She told Aris she was doing her a valuable service by finding her worms.

"Where's your mom?" asked the lady. She was a new one. Mrs. Thompson didn't come around anymore.

Aris shrugged, unwilling to look at the woman.

"Is your mother home?"

Aris shrugged again and picked up a long, pink worm. She let it squirm in her palm, liking the feel of it.

The lady sighed huffily and made an impatient gesture.

"Are you all by yourself," she consulted a clipboard in her hand, "Aris?" she pronounced it Arris, like a pirate.

"Can I help you?"

Gram came out on the front porch.

"Yes, I'm looking for," the lady consulted the clipboard again, "Laura Dunn?"

"I'm Mary Dunn, Laura's mother."

"Well," the woman looked around in obvious disgust, "I'm from Social Services. I'm here to do a home visit."

"Laura's not here," Gram said firmly but politely.

The lady glanced at the trailer. "Is that her residence?"

Gram nodded. Aris watched the worm as it inched a wet trail to her wrist.

"Does Arris reside with you or there?"

The lady gestured to the trailer.

Gram started to speak and then stopped suddenly.

"Would you like to come in?" she asked the lady. "I just put on a nice pot of coffee and I made blueberry muffins. They're Aris' favorite."

Aris glanced up as the woman wrinkled her nose and then nodded curtly. As the two women walked through the house, Aris shadowed them outside, watching them through the windows. She hovered outside the open back door as they sat at the kitchen table.

"Mrs. Dunn," the lady said as she took another bite of the muffin. "These are delicious. I have to have the recipe."

"Call me Mary," Gram said warmly.

"Call me Eleanor," the lady smiled. She was older and dowdy, with salt and pepper hair and harsh, no-nonsense lines in her face, but Aris thought she looked pretty when she smiled.

"So, where exactly is your daughter?" Eleanor asked.

"That's what I wanted to talk to you about," Gram began. "Aris? Jesus, Mary, and

84

Joseph, you're likely to give us two old women heart attacks lurking around out there like that."

Aris instinctively stepped back into the shadows.

The two women smiled. "It's too late, girl, we've already seen you. Come in here and get a muffin and be on your way putting those worms in the garden."

Aris obeyed grudgingly, holding her squirming captives in one hand as she reached for a muffin with the other. They waited until she was out of earshot to resume their conversation.

A few weeks later, Laura appeared at the door of the green and white stucco house. She'd changed her hair; it was white-blonde, a cloud of spun sugar. Her muddy eyes were bleary and old mascara was smeared beneath them. She was wearing a cheap, red pleather skirt and matching jacket.

"Mama's home," Laura said matter-of-factly as she tried to pull open the screen door. The door held fast and Laura frowned.

"Hey, kid," she called to Aris, who was playing Barbies on the blue rug. "Come and open this door," she ordered.

Aris obeyed, crossed the little room and undid the lock on the door. Laura stepped into the house, her purple, fringed purse swinging in her hand. Aris eyed her mother speculatively. She knew Gram had been up to something. In the last few weeks she'd had meetings. She met with some people Eleanor brought over, and she met with Aris' teacher and principal, and she met with a man called James Irwin Esq. Aris thought Esq was the weirdest last name. She knew something was going on but she wasn't sure what. After two months with Gram, Aris couldn't control the taste of disappointment in her mouth and the fear that wound itself 'round her middle.

"You miss Mama, kid?" Laura asked her, grinning widely so Aris could see all the missing teeth in the back of her mouth.

"Yeah," she said quietly, because she knew this was what her mother expected to hear.

Her grandmother came back from the kitchen.

"Laura? That you?"

She wiped her hands on a yellow dish towel and came into the small, cozy living room.

"Yeah, Ma. Came to get Aris. What you been up to, kid?" Laura leaned over Aris with a leering smile on her face. Aris smelled the sour stench of alcohol and cigarettes.

Gram crossed the living room quickly and gestured for Aris to leave the room. Aris watched them, intrigued.

Her grandmother stepped in front of her.

"Where you been at, Laura?"

"I been to Los Angeles," Laura said haughtily. "With my new boyfriend. My new boyfriend has an apartment, with a pool. Wouldn't you like to go swimming every day?" she asked Aris.

Aris nodded, eyes downcast.

Laura patted her hair and pulled a pack of cigarettes from her purse.

"He's gonna take care of us, kid. He's a real cool guy."

She sat on the plaid sofa and fumbled in her bag for a light. Aris stared at her mother's bared white thigh.

"Laura!" Gram said sharply. "Don't even think about lighting that thing in my house."

"Like you didn't smoke when I was a kid, Ma."

"I mean it, Laura."

Laura sulkily threw her cigarette back in the purple purse.

"Me and Aris are moving to Los Angeles," Laura announced abruptly.

Aris' alarmed eyes flew to her grandmother.

Gram took a deep breath. "You might be, but Aris isn't."

Laura laughed, her hands fluttered up to her chest and then settled in her lap. "Give me a break, Ma."

"I'm serious. You been gone almost two months. A lot can happen in two months, Laura."

Red blotches started appearing on Laura's neck and crept up to her face.

"What the fuck you been up to, Ma? You trying to take my kid? Is that it? Please," Laura scoffed. "Nobody's gonna give her to you. They don't take kids away for no reason."

"You think I don't have a reason?" Gram put her hands on her slim hips.

"Ha! What? The house is dirty? I like a drink every now and then? She's clean, she eats, she goes to school."

"You're too late. If you take that child out of this house, it'll be kidnapping."

Laura jumped up from the plaid couch. "What the fuck! I will take her. She's mine! My new boyfriend says he loves kids! She'll be happy with me! We're starting a new life away from this shithole town!"

Gram stood firmly as Laura threw her arms out in wild gestures.

"If you leave with Aris, I will call the police and they will lock you up for a very long time," Gram promised.

"Well, aren't you a sneaky little bitch," Laura said appraisingly. "Going behind my motherfucking back to steal my fucking kid." Laura laughed and Aris started at the ugly sound. "I never wanted her anyway. You know I never fucking wanted her anyway."

Aris, used to such declarations, didn't even flinch.

"You leave this house, Laura. You leave and you don't come back," Gram said menacingly.

Gram was quiet, so quiet Aris could hardly hear her. Her arms were stiff and still at her sides; her hands clenched into fists, as though she were restraining herself from hitting Laura.

Laura glanced around the room wildly, her eyes coming to rest on Bonnie, who was perched on the orange easy chair. Her arm snaked out and snatched the doll.

"Fuck you and fuck this stupid fucking doll."

With a grunt, she pulled off Bonnie's head and presented it to Aris with a flourish. Aris did not raise her hands to accept the broken doll and her mother stared at her hard for a minute before tossing the two pieces of doll on the floor like garbage.

"Fine. Fine, you take her." Her mother turned and stumbled out, slamming the screen door behind her. "And you can keep the little bitch!"

Like a weed in a cracked sidewalk, Aris grew, fragile and always in danger of being stepped on. She grew up frugally and relatively happy, but she was always waiting for her mother to jump out of the shadows and grab her and drag her back to whatever gin-soaked life she'd created in L.A.

Unlike her mother, Aris was an exceptional-looking young woman. She did not have the heavy face and sunken eyes that plagued Laura; instead, she looked like her grandmother, whose blonde hair was the envy of women half her age. Aris and Mary shared delicate features. Aris had a heart-shaped face that framed her petite lips and expressive violet eyes. Gram called them "Liz Taylor" eyes and said she got them from her great-grandmother. "She was a beauty, Aris, she surely was."

After Laura left, Gram sold the trailer and they painted the guest room green, Aris' favorite color. She finished junior high and entered high school with the same objective she had in kindergarten, to remain invisible. She made few friends, and the ones she had weren't close. She simply couldn't bring herself to be like the other girls at school. Aris found them silly, with their empty-headed giggles, hair tossing and mad flirting. Aris was awkward by nature and tried to hide it by keeping her eyes on the ground and her mouth closed. She rarely spoke in class, preferring to draw odd pictures on the inside of her notebooks.

The public high school boasted one hundred graduating seniors. They were the children of farmers and town folks. They were simple kids; most knew when they graduated they would be going to work on their parents' farms or going to work at the local bank. Few had plans to go to college. Aris was one of those few. She did not particularly want to go, but her grandmother would have it no other way. In an uncharacteristic move, Gram took her to "the city," as she called it, to buy her clothes for college.

"I'm only going to the community college," Aris protested.

"I know," Gram said, "but from there you will go to an even bigger college. You need new clothes anyway. When was the last time you had new clothes?"

"We don't need to go to the city; it will be so expensive. I can get clothes at Maggie's Dress Rack, or even Target."

"No," Gram shook her head, blonde hair now streaked with white. "No, Aris, we are going to have a real girls' weekend in the city. You've never even been to the city and that's a dirty shame."

"I'll have to get the weekend off work," Aris said in protest.

"Aris, sweetheart, I want to do this for you. Take the weekend off and don't even think about spending your own money either. This is all on me."

Aris got up off of the plaid sofa and, as she walked away, her violet eyes bright, she called, "Okay, Gram. Thanks."

The mint-green Cadillac pulled out of the dusty valley and they began the journey to "the city." As she drove, Gram sang "We're Off to See the Wizard." Aris smiled; Gram had been doing that for as long as she could remember. The drive was long but Aris did not sleep. With great interest she watched the scenery go by in long, blurry streaks. The land changed from farms to nothing to towns to farms again. Finally, they crossed a bridge and she was in another world. The buildings of San Francisco loomed over them as Gram drove through the crowded streets.

"I've never seen so many people all at once," Aris commented. They all looked busy, somber, and important. Aris was impressed.

Gram parked the car in a garage and they headed up to put their bags in the hotel room. It was the first time Aris had stayed in a hotel and, although it could not have been regarded as one of the nicer places near Union Square, she was enchanted.

"Gram, little shampoos!"

"Oh?"

"Yeah, that's neat," Aris giggled.

Aris was overwhelmed by the city. Union Square was full of people. Maybe thousands. The thought almost made her ill. So many people. Aris felt hopelessly gauche. The girls walking around were so stylish. She tucked her head down and tried not to meet anyone's eye.

They had dinner in a fancy restaurant near the hotel. Both dressed up; Gram insisted Aris wear her new dress. It was short and purple and Aris loved it. She was fascinated with the smallest details of fine dining. The extra forks delighted her. When they sat down and the waiter laid her napkin in her lap, she stifled a giggle.

"Why do they do that, Gram?"

"I'm not sure," she replied.

"It's so funny. I mean, I know how to use a napkin."

On the drive back to the dust and dry heat of the valley, Aris was suddenly aware that there was a world beyond the one in which she lived. There were more than farms and dirt and the sons of farmers. This thought made her curiosity and fear rise simultaneously.

Rhys studied the painting before him. Aris, Johnny's girl. Her voice had been raspy from sleep; it was like something sweet melting, like butterscotch, caramel. Slow dark molasses coming out of that mouth. He looked at her lips in the painting; he had not really done the small, pouty mouth justice. He'd called Johnny because he had to get rid of the thing. He'd never intended to paint it, let alone give it to Johnny, but he couldn't keep it here. He was sick of her staring at him. He wondered what she would say when she saw it. He thought

briefly of his cousin. What would Johnny think
when he saw it? Would he be able to see the lust
dripping from her eyes? The way he'd painted
her had not been intentional; he had not done it
consciously. It was almost as if she appeared on
the canvas like magic: violet eyes and a
beckoning hand, those long, ungainly limbs
infused with a coltish grace. When Rhys stepped
back to look at it, he had been slightly shocked.
It did not look like the young woman he saw at
Astoria's house, that lovely, yet awkward girl,
so clearly unsure of herself. No, he thought as
he looked at the painting, this was a woman who
could put you on your knees, and keep you
there.

Chapter 4

Aris pulled another dress over her head and the attendant began to do up the buttons. Aris didn't like to think about the wedding. It was something that seemed to have taken on a life of its own. They had only been engaged for a few months when Janice asked them about setting a date.

"Why don't you wait a while?" she asked them at dinner.

Dinner with Janice was usually an uncomfortable affair for Aris. Janice criticized John as though he were still a little boy, and she treated Aris as if she were an old habit, something that must be broken and disposed of.

"No," John said, wiping his mouth and gesturing to the waiter. "I want this sewn up before next year."

"Sewn up?" Janice asked with a sidelong glance at Aris. "She's not a court case, John."

"This is rare. I ordered medium-rare," John informed the waiter. "Re-fire it," he ordered.

The waiter nodded and whisked the plate away.

"Don't ignore me, John," Janice said sharply.

"I'm not," John said, sounding petulant.

"Listen," Janice began. "You two don't really know each other all that well, but these things can be remedied with a nice, long engagement. What do you think, Aris?"

Aris looked up from the plate in front of her.

"Um, yeah," Aris said cautiously. "Why not?"

A small, cold smile formed on Janice's face. "There, you see?"

"She's only saying that to please you," John said.

Aris poured herself more wine. Janice watched her and frowned.

"That's absurd, John."

"She is," he insisted, and Aris felt her face grow hot. "See, look."

"Now, John," Janice began, iron in her tone, "I think we all agree here. There's no need to rock the boat."

John gritted his teeth. "I am not rocking anything, Mother. I don't like you interfering with my plans. Aris and I have spoken about this and we agree; we would like to get married as soon as possible."

Janice glanced at Aris, who took another swift gulp from her wine. The waiter returned.

"I hope this will be to your satisfaction," he said to John, who ignored him and cut into the steak. John waived the waiter off, without looking up.

"Thank you," Janice said to the man. "What is wrong with you?" she asked her son.

"Nothing. I just don't know why you are being so odd about this."

"I am not being anything," Janice said imperiously. "If that's what you want then I will take care of everything."

Aris mentally shook herself. Was Janice saying she was going to plan their wedding? She took another gulp from the wine glass, earning an unmistakable look from John. Janice reached out and put her hand over the top of Aris' glass.

"That's enough, darling, people will start to talk."

In fact, Janice had decided to plan her wedding and Aris was too shy to say anything to her future mother-in-law. When she mentioned it to John, he waved her off.

"She's paying for it, just let her do what she wants," he advised. "She's going to get her way in the end, anyway. You don't know my mother, I do. It's best to let her have her head."

Aris pulled the white lace away from her body. She hated it. She could hear Janice and Helen and Jane, John's aunts, chattering outside the dressing room. Where was Kristin? She promised she would be in town; she swore to Aris she was going to be there for the fitting. The Ring glittered maliciously as one of its prongs caught in the lace. Aris swore under her breath. The chattering stopped.

"What was that?" Janice called to her.

"Did you say something?" Jane called gaily. The clerk had brought them all champagne. Janice made sure Aris only had one glass. "Don't want anyone getting the wrong idea."

"No." Aris gritted her teeth as she carefully pulled The Ring away from the lacy froth covering her flat bosom.

Aris peeked through the tiny part in the red taffeta curtains. The three women sat in a semi-circle in front of the dais. Helen was extremely overweight and dressed mostly in caftans and long, ugly, voluminous skirts with matching tops. She was adorned with copious amounts of silver and turquoise jewelry. Her mouse-colored brown hair hung in her beady, black eyes; she was the only female in the family to have a rather thick mustache settled above her ill-shaped mouth.

"I just can't believe my Rhys is home," Helen was saying nervously.

"Yes, we're all so glad your Rhys has returned," Janice said lightly.

"What a lovely surprise for you!" Jane trilled.

Jane was twice divorced, and to the shock of the family, was currently dating a man who was the exact age of her youngest son. "At least," Janice had whispered to Aris once, "she has the good taste not to bring him to any family functions." After her second divorce, Jane dyed her graying hair platinum blonde and lost twenty-five pounds, and, being afflicted with the same nose as Helen, she had her nose "fixed." She lifted her champagne with elegant fingers and sipped it.

"Have you been to his new place yet?" Jane asked tipsily.

"Not yet," Helen said, distinctly uncomfortable.

"I'm sure your invitation got lost in the mail," Janice said silkily.

"Why? Has he invited you, Janice?" Helen sounded jealous.

Janice was watching the red curtains impatiently. Aris suppressed a shudder. Her future mother-in-law was like a poisonous lotus blossom. Her face was stamped with the evidence that she had once been a searing beauty. She was no longer young, her skin no longer elastic, shiny perfection. Janice retained some semblance of youth by subscribing to the same school of thought as Sarah. She wrestled and peeled and needled her age into submission. The effect was a peeled-back, pushed-out, hard, wrinkle-free face. Her bobbed, black hair was threaded with long, distinguished white streaks. Only her hands betrayed her age. They were long, thin, and heavily veined; the blue lines streaked across the thin, white skin with abandon.

"No, of course not, Helen," Janice said placatingly. "I'm sure he'll invite his mother before he invites anyone.

"I've been invited," Aris piped up from behind the curtain and immediately cursed herself.

"What?" Janice sounded alarmed.

"You?" Helen sounded disappointed.

"Why would he invite you?" Jane asked, puzzled.

"I'm picking up an engagement present," Aris called quickly. She inexplicably felt guilty.

"Oh, yes, of course," Helen said. "Jan, what about the ceremony?"

"I'll design the whole thing," Janice said. "Aris doesn't seem to have any preferences and I told John someone has to run the show here. Someone has to get this done and do it right."

The attendant gave Aris a little push and she stumbled out of the red curtains.

"Here's dress number three," Aris said.

Dress number three was a frumpy poof of lace that made the Great Gatsby dress she had worn to the reunion look fashionable. Helen's choice.

"Oh!" Helen teared up and hefted her great bulk off the love seat. "Oh!" she said again as she reached out to Aris.

"This is the dress," she declared rhapsodically.

Jane and Janice exchanged glances.
Helen approached Aris, her arms outstretched.
Her immense girth led her to perspire and the
reek of body odor wafted from her armpits.

Just then Kristin bounded in shrieking.

"I made it!"

Helen was so shocked at Kristin's
appearance that she let her arms drop and sat
swiftly back into the love seat.

Kristin was Aris's best friend. They met
in college and lived together for quite a few
years after college. Kristin caused quite a stir
wherever she went; Aris thought the Prince
women were going to need medical attention.

Kristin was tall, almost five foot nine, a
gorgeous shade of cocoa and covered in tattoos.
Her hair was short and purple, which only added
to her shocking appearance. Kristin dressed in
outrageously fashionable outfits and had a
mouth like a trucker.

"She's the maid of honor?" Janice hissed
to Jane. "She'll ruin the entire wedding."

Helen's mouth hung open.

Kristin was oblivious to the reaction she
caused; she usually was. She bounded up to the
dais and wrapped Aris in a hug.

"I haven't seen you in so fucking long!"

Kristin had recently moved to New York to join an up-and-coming internet news site. Aris felt her absence keenly.

Kristin pulled back and assessed Aris.

"Jesus Fucking H. Christ. Who the hell picked this out? This has got to be one of the ugliest dresses I have ever seen."

Helen blanched and Janice looked angry enough to hurt someone.

"This is so not you. No, no, no. You need something classic, but with an edge. And none of this lacy shit. Leave it to me!"

With that she dashed off into the sea of white dresses leaving Aris behind to smile wanly at the glowering women.

Astoria grimaced as the fat nurse waddled away from her bed. She did not like the nurse, with her mismatched eyes and her frumpy uniform. She was the mean nurse. Astoria told Disby time and again to dismiss her, but Disby never did. Astoria would have to do something about that. Disby had never had any backbone, not even when she was a girl. Astoria was forever prodding her into doing things. It was odd, Astoria thought, that the girl had never gotten married. Oh sure, that business about the hysterectomy was no good. It scared off the young man Disby was seeing, Biff or Bill or whatever his name was, but Astoria never liked him anyway. After that Bill or Biff broke the engagement and Disby stayed home all the time, like an old woman. Now, Disby was close to really being an old woman. She was going to die in this house, without ever having done a thing; Astoria was convinced of it.

"Mrs. Prince, I told you it was time to get out of bed. Are we starting to forget things?"

No, Astoria thought, we aren't. The nurse waddled up to the bed and started to pull Astoria out of it. Astoria pulled out of the woman's grasp, wincing at the sagging, wrinkled flesh on her arms. Sometimes Astoria forgot how old she looked.

"I'm quite alright," Astoria told the fat nurse.

"We don't look alright," the nurse said cheerfully. "Are we having some trouble getting out of bed?"

"No, I'm just thinking," Astoria said politely as the woman started to pull on her again. "I'll get up when I'm ready."

"Now, now, Mrs. Prince. When we say that, we usually stay in bed all day long and that's not good for us!"

"I've never stayed in bed all day in my life!" Astoria said indignantly.

A struggle ensued as Astoria pulled away from the woman's tight grip.

"Now, Mrs. Prince. I think we're not telling the truth, are we?"

The nurse smiled condescendingly at her. Astoria threw up her long-fingered, liver-spotted hands.

"Nurse," Astoria said, her voice wavering only slightly. "You are dismissed."

There! She had done it. Astoria smiled a thinly disguised triumphant smile. The nurse stared at her; the corner of her mouth turned down.

"You can't dismiss me," she argued, pulling on Astoria's arm. "You didn't hire me."

"I may not have hired you," Astoria said in her very best imitation of her late husband. "But I pay your salary and, what's more, I can fire you!"

The nurse pulled harder on her arm and Astoria resisted her as much as she could.

"You need to get out of this bed!" the nurse insisted.

"You need to get out of my room," Astoria told her. "No, out of my house!"

"I'll call Ms. Prince," the nurse threatened.

"Good! Call her!"

The nurse began to pull harder; she was getting quite rough.

"You're hurting me," Astoria told the woman, through gritted teeth.

"I am not!"

There was a scramble and the next thing she knew, Astoria was on the floor. She landed with a thump and looked up at the nurse, her blue-green eyes on fire. The nurse opened her mouth and gave a little scream.

"Mrs. Prince!"

Astoria was still in shock when Disby came running in. Disby looked at her mother, laying on the polished wood floor and then she looked at the nurse.

"She fell out of bed," the nurse said, wringing her plump hands and backing away from the scene.

Ha! Astoria thought as her hip and leg began to throb. She was pulled out of bed and deposited on the floor in a heap! Like a dog!

"Mother, are you okay?" Disby said alarmed.

Astoria gritted her teeth as the pain tore through her. "My hip."

"Oh my God. Nurse, call an ambulance."

Chapter 5

Tinsley's birthday was going to be unbearable. She was probably the only eight-year-old Aris knew who could boast the attendance of San Francisco City Council members at her birthday party.

She did not want to go to the party that afternoon and was dragging her feet around the small house like a petulant child.

"Aris, we're going to be late, again," John had reminded her patiently. He tapped his Breguet watch as he watched her apply her make-up.

Aris shot him a look in the mirror. "I'm going as fast as I can. Did you get the gift? I put it in the spare room."

"Yes, I have the gift. I have car keys in hand. You look beautiful. We need to go."

Aris applied her mascara quickly. "Okay, ready."

John appraised her. "You're not wearing that, are you?"

That was a green, strapless sundress. Aris shook her head.

"I guess not," she murmured.

John inclined his head toward her in a pleased gesture. Aris went to the dresser and pulled out a pair of black shorts. John had bought them for her. She slipped them on and pulled a white blouse out of the closet. The shorts were a little short, but so what?

John was waiting in the car. As Aris slid in the Mercedes, he glanced at her.

"Those are a little short, don't you think?"

"Do you want me to change again?" Aris asked him, clenching her fists.

John shrugged. "I didn't tell you to change the first time."

When they pulled up to Sarah's house, Aris stifled a groan. Sarah and Paul had a contemporary house built in Sausalito. Janice went out of her way to mention to everyone that building a custom house was "so gauche." The house was all glass and wood; huge windows showed views of the bay. The house, built to Sarah's exact specifications, was sleek and modern. Her decorator kept the design theme, which was stark white with heavy chrome accents, throughout the house.

Now, standing at the door, Aris balked inwardly when she heard the humming din coming from inside the house: a hive of bees, stingers at the ready. The door swung open and Paul Hodge favored them with a tired smile. His reddish-brown hair circled his head and fell too long around his ears. The top of his head was completely bald and, from the pinkish glow, it looked as if he'd been spending much of the party outside. He solemnly shook John's hand and grinned at Aris. Paul's teeth were long and his ears were too big, giving him the unfortunate appearance of a middle-aged rabbit.

"Imelda was supposed to be on door duty, but there was some kind of potty emergency in the downstairs bath," he said. Aris realized he was apologizing for answering his own door.

She and John crossed the threshold and she was enveloped in the special mix of family and society. Inside the house, it was hot and busy. Aris noticed Tinsley had more adults than children at her party; Sarah had invited all the "right" people.

As they stood in the foyer, Aris looked up at Sarah's Bleckner looming over them on the wall. Its starkness suited Sarah. When people commented on the painting, Sarah would wave her hand dismissively and say, "Oh, that."

Aris' fingers plucked absentmindedly at the hem of her shorts as she observed the scene before her. The house was overcrowded. Cocktails in hand, feathers spread like peacocks, the guests preened for one another.

The main living room was white on white. Overstuffed, white sofas dominated the space; there was a white rug on the light hardwood floor, white marble surrounding the fireplace. The only accent color was small touches of chrome here and there. It was cheerless and cold.

With the crush of people, it was at least ten degrees warmer in the house than it was outside, and Aris felt sweat bead up on her forehead. Sarah spotted them standing in the foyer and made her way through the crowd, a showy, faux exasperated smile on her face. Her brown hair was pulled back into a bun and she was wearing a trendy outfit of blue silk. A long rope of pearls hung from her white neck. She stepped to Aris and John, her eyes quickly taking in Aris' outfit.

"Hi," Sarah said in her whispery voice. "Aris, don't you just look like a little ball of sunshine. Of course, I don't have the gall to wear such short shorts. Good for you."

Sarah wrinkled her nose at Aris and gave her a feral smile.

"Thank you, Sarah," Aris said, not knowing what else to say.

Sarah lifted her black brow at Aris in amusement as she fingered the white pearls absently. Her usually dead eyes sparkled at the thought of prey. Sarah gestured with an elegant hand to a pile of gifts in the other room, at the foot of the white piano.

"You can just put it with the rest. Unfortunately, the mayor couldn't make it, but Senator Woolsey is over there, John," Sarah threw an arm toward a gray-haired man in the corner of the living room.

Someone called Sarah's name loudly and she flicked her black eyes at Aris before waving and dashing gracefully across the room. Aris and John placed their gift in the large pile that had amassed at the foot of the white piano. A large vase of freesias sat on top of the baby grand. The room was empty save for Paul Hodge and some men who seemed to be business associates gathered in a knot in the far corner, engaged in a heated discussion. The men glanced up as they entered the room and Aris felt an embarrassed smile spread across her face. Paul Hodge pursed his lips in a silent belch and ducked his head again. They exited quickly and walked through the maze of people into the wintry living room. Disby was seated on the sofa next to Helen. John leaned down to give them both a hug. He looked expectantly at Aris, who followed suit, holding her breath as she hugged Helen. When she leaned into Disby's hug, she noticed Disby smelled of cigarette smoke. The combination of the rank odors of the two women and the extreme heat inside the house had her stomach roiling.

Helen smiled genially at them both, and Aris stared at her tiny yellowed teeth. They looked like the teeth of a cat who had a two-pack-a-day habit.

"You're always so stiff," complained Helen, her beady, black eyes sizing up Aris shrewdly. Aris forced her breathing to slow as she willed her stomach to calm down. She imagined for a moment vomiting all over Sarah's pristine white-on-white living room.

"She's fine, Auntie Helen," John assured as he squeezed Aris' hand and smiled at her. Aris smiled back wanly. "Nerves."

Aris looked at him sideways but said nothing.

"So delightful to see you both," Disby said formally as she patted her steely hair with one hand and smoothed her long, denim skirt with the other.

Aris nodded. "Yes, it's lovely to see you," she said, equally formal. Wave after wave of heat rolled over her, and she prayed she wouldn't throw up. Aris closed her eyes.

"Have you been to Rhys' place yet?" Helen asked her.

Aris opened her eyes and tried to focus on the small, black hairs feathering Helen's upper lip.

"What do you mean?"

"To get your engagement present," Helen said, clearly eager to pump Aris for information.

Aris shook her head.

John, Helen, and Disby all looked at her expectantly.

She dug in the back of her mind for something that would satisfy them. All she wanted to do was get outside into the fresh air.

"I'm hoping to get out there sometime this week."

"Oh," Helen said, disappointed.

"Rhys. That child was so much trouble," Disby said. "A nice boy, very smart too. I suppose the adoption gave him some problems."

Helen glowered at her.

"Helen and her husband, Ben, well," Disby stopped. "Ben's no longer with us. They adopted Rhys when he was just a baby. I suspect he never got over not really belonging to the Prince family."

Helen and John stared at Disby. Aris tried to hide her surprise. Rhys looked like the rest of the Prince family; she never would have guessed he was adopted.

"Anyway, he's fine now," Disby finished lamely.

Aris nodded politely as sweat rolled down her cheek. She looked up at John, who glanced down at her and gave her a distracted smile.

Aris stood there in a moment of awkward silence, then Disby trilled a high-pitched giggle.

"Now, I hear the wedding plans are coming along smoothly," Disby commented.

Aris tried to smile.

"We should see the birthday girl," Aris said, pulling again at the hem of her shorts.

Helen, with much effort, pulled herself out of the deep cushions of the sofa and held out her arms.

"Come here, Aris. Let me look at you."

Aris groaned inwardly. Helen grasped her by the arms and sized her up. She smelled of sweat and bad perfume. Aris tried not to gag.

"Those shorts are too short," Helen said to John. "Mother won't like it if she sees Aris like this, and you know she already has her doubts."

John nodded. "I told Aris the same thing about her shorts, but she didn't have time to change."

Helen held Aris in her arms; Aris wanted to yank herself away from the overweight woman but she stood still and waited for the appraisal to be over. Helen sniffed delicately and dropped back onto the sofa.

Suddenly, she was free; she sucked at the hot air, gasping for a breath. John put his hand on the small of her back and guided her through the throng of people.

"I need to get some fresh air," she said to him.

John glanced down at her.

"You were a little rude to my aunts," he said blandly.

Aris looked up at him.

"I think I'm going to puke."

John frowned at her.

"I'm really hot. I just need to go outside for a minute."

John nodded and pulled her through the living room.

The back of the house was wall to wall windows, which provided an excellent view of the San Francisco skyline. John grinned and slapped high-fives with old friends and flung one-armed hugs around family members as Aris did her best not to openly cringe away from the suffocating crowd. They made their way through the kitchen toward the back of the house. Outside the sunroom was a balcony. Aris burst out of the glass door with such desperation that several people turned to look at her. She took great gulps of air and tasted salt. She felt her pounding heart slow down and her nausea subside.

There was a set of stairs that led to the patio below. Sarah's home was all house and no yard. Aris thought of the many days of her childhood spent in the backyard, digging in the mud. She wondered what Tinsley did in the diminutive bricked-up patch of land that served as their backyard. There were no scattered toys, only some outdoor furniture and a fire pit. The bay provided a cool breeze that swept through the small yard.

Aris noticed Morgan tipsily swaying on her high-heeled sandals. She smiled and wiggled her fingers at John and Aris. John waved back, but Morgan had already turned her attention back to Jane and the person sitting beside her. He was an older gentleman with bushy eyebrows and a graying beard.

"Who's that man with Jane?" Aris asked John.

"Haven't you guessed?" Marie was lounging behind them on the low brick wall. She leaned haughtily in white pants and a white tank top. Her brown hair was back in a ponytail. She thrust out her concave, flat chest and gestured toward Jane with her glass of white wine. She walked up to stand beside Aris and John.

"That's her beard," Marie giggled.

"What do you mean?" Aris asked.

"Aunt Jane was dating that kid. He was twenty-two. The family got tired of her indiscretions," Marie said laughing. "It was just so embarrassing. So now she's dating this guy, Barney or something. At least, she keeps him around for public events."

At that moment, Morgan tottered over to them, her dark-blue eyes over-bright.

"Hello, my darling daughter," she said walking up to Marie. Without waiting for an answer, she turned to John and Aris.

"Hello. I've just been talking with Jane's beard."

"Hi, Auntie Morgan." John leaned in to kiss her white cheek.

"Anything interesting?" Marie asked.

Morgan nodded and took a long drink of bourbon. Marie crossed her arms impatiently.

"What is it?"

Morgan leaned into the three of them, effectively fumigating the area with her breath and said conspiratorially, "Her beard has a beard!"

Morgan collapsed into laugher; Marie looked at her mother, disappointed, and walked up the stairs. Morgan turned to Aris.

"My goodness, that's a lovely outfit. Those shorts are nice, a little too short, but very nice."

Morgan smiled and John shot Aris a glance.

John and Aris wandered the house, saying hello to everyone. J.J., in a rare occurrence, was standing by his wife's side. Olivia inclined her blonde head at Aris and John.

"John, Aris, how are you?" she asked, her voice laced with spurious warmth.

"Great, Aunt Olivia. How are you?" John asked as he shook his uncle's hand.

Olivia smiled viciously. "I see your sister has invited that lesbian woman who's always making trouble at City Hall."

Aris cocked her head.

"You know the one I mean; she's always making huge issues out of things that nobody really cares about. I have nothing against lesbians. For a while I thought our Gracie was a lesbian. Of course, she isn't, but I didn't have a problem with it when I thought she was. Did I, J.J.?" Olivia asked her husband.

J.J. nodded brusquely and pulled his mobile from the case on his belt. Olivia continued in her eager voice, "Anyway, I guess she owns some school or her daughter goes to the same school as Tinsley or something," Olivia rolled her eyes. "I see Rhys isn't here, though why I expected him, I don't know. He never was one for the family functions. Have you met him yet, Aris?"

Aris shook her head. "Not really."

Olivia frowned at her.

"He's always been such a bad boy. The trouble he caused. Why, I will never forget the time Helen came back from-"

J.J. cleared his throat meaningfully.

"Anyway, let's talk about your wedding!" Olivia said quickly, sounding disappointed. "How exciting. I don't know if anyone could top our Jennifer's wedding, though. Of course, Aris, you weren't here for that one. John, were you in that? I can't remember."

John shook his head.

"At least you didn't decide to get married in Mexico. Isn't that a Third-World country, J.J.?"

Olivia glanced at her husband, who had his phone to his ear. He shrugged his shoulders, talking swiftly, as he backed away from them.

"I mean, my God, I can't believe Trina did that. Then to get divorced two years later.

Pregnant, no less! Poor Jane must have been beside herself. I don't know how she could have handled it. I really do not. Wasn't the guy she married significantly older? I can't remember. Do you?"

Aris shook her head.

"Yours will be fine, anyway. I heard Janice is planning the whole thing. Is that true, Aris?"

Olivia continued without waiting for a response.

"Of course, after what she did at Sarah's wedding, I can't believe you'll even let her near yours. Oh, you weren't there were you, Aris? Sarah wouldn't let her near the thing. She wouldn't let her mother, who was paying for the whole thing, mind you, have any say in anything. Sarah picked everything. An evening wedding at the de Young Museum. No priest; at least Trina had a priest. All that bizarre food! So what does Janice do as an act of revenge? She shows up wearing the most outrageous couture gown, done to the nines, takes her time sashaying down the aisle. She was the talk of that wedding. She outshone her own daughter and she knew it! Your mother is something else, John. I wouldn't like to get on her bad side. Aris, I've seen her eviscerate people. It's difficult to watch. Remember Ben? The things she did to him-" Olivia broke off as Janice sauntered up to them

"Olivia, shouldn't you be looking for J.J.?" Janice asked, a sultry smile skimming over her face.

Olivia laughed tightly. "I can never keep that man by my side for very long!"

Janice nodded lazily, quirking her black eyebrows as the corners of her mouth turned up slightly.

"I suppose I should go grab him. We need to go anyway," Olivia said as she began to walk away.

"John, darling, how are you?" Janice cooed.

"Fine, Mother."

"And you?" she turned to Aris.

"I'm great," Aris said as her hands hovered nervously in front of her chest.

Janice ignored Aris as she scanned the room.

"Oh hell, here comes Jane and that horrible guy she brought. Ugh. Have you met him?" she asked John and Aris.

Both shook their heads.

"Run the other way, darlings. The man is not normal. Why Morgan told her to get a beard is so completely beyond me!" Janice shook her head as she practically sprinted across the room.

They spotted Astoria in a high-backed, wooden chair in a corner of the living room and went over to say hello. She was smiling her vague smile and her eyes looked tired. The smell of lavender water wafted over to them.

Astoria had been in the home for a while. She wasn't sure how long. She had broken a few ribs and fractured something in her leg and almost broke her hip. The bruise on her hip was completely black. At the hospital, they told Disby even with 'round-the-clock nurses, it would be impossible to care for her at home. Astoria didn't believe them.

She didn't like the home. It was full of dying people. Every day, it seemed the coroner was parked outside, picking up another resident. Astoria was going to die in that place. She begged John Junior to take her back home, but he shook his head at her. She told Janice to find out what accommodations needed to be made for her at the house, but Janice said it just wasn't possible. The people that worked there were condescending and some were downright rude; the place smelled of disinfectant, like a hospital, and the residents were all sick and complained all day. Astoria wanted to get out. When the doctor said Disby could take her to the birthday party for a little while, Astoria had been ecstatic.

Now she was here, parked in her wheelchair in the corner, all alone. Young John and that girl were here, standing in front of Astoria as if she weren't even there. Astoria just wasn't sure about her. The girl seemed like a dreamer, as if she didn't have both feet on the ground. She always kept her mouth closed when she smiled. Seemed a little untrustworthy, like she was hiding something. Of course, she could be ashamed of those crooked teeth.

Astoria was hot and tired, and she wanted to go home, her own home; it was time for her pain pill. The doctor had her on a strict schedule. She craned her head around, looking for Disby. Where was that child? Astoria wanted to go outside and sit in the sea air; she wanted her pill and a cold glass of ice water. Where was Rhys? He wasn't at this party. Astoria recalled vaguely that he had spoken to her at another party recently, before that nurse had pulled her out of bed. She had told him it was nice to see him after all the time that had gone by and he smiled and kissed her on the cheek.

"I thought you were my husband, Johnny, come back to life," she said to him, and he laughed. When he laughed, he didn't look like Johnny so much. She saw his eyes drift toward young John's odd girl. Oh, dear, Astoria thought at the time.

"Let's do cake, Sarah!" Janice ordered.

Ah, it must be little Sarah's birthday, but Astoria was unsure as to whose house she was in. It certainly wasn't Janice's house. Janice had gotten the old Victorian when Johnny died. Astoria was glad; she hated the house. She knew her husband kept his painted women there. All those women. She didn't like the way Rhys looked at that Aris; Astoria had seen her husband look at women that way before.

Heads swiveled toward Janice and Tinsley. Sarah, who was loitering in the hallway with a handsome man, threw up her hands at her mother and rolled her eyes. She slipped into the kitchen, presumably to prepare the cake. John left Aris to talk to someone across the room. Aris stayed near Astoria, who was silent in the cacophony of shrieking laughter and low rumbles of male amusement. Aris observed the family: the hands hidden in pockets, the jovial greetings that masked long-standing grudges, the casual sparkle of diamonds and the contemptuous wrinkling of silks, the sudden flashes of white teeth and the glittering black eyes.

Sarah appeared in the doorway with a three-tiered, white cake, eight candles flaming across the tiers.

Janice started the crowd off singing "Happy Birthday" as Tinsley watched her mother waltz the cake across the room to her. Aris looked around, but didn't see frumpy Paul Hodge anywhere. Tinsley took a great breath and blew out her candles. The guests cheered, and Sarah carried the cake back toward the kitchen.

"How did she carry that heavy thing all by herself?" Aris heard someone ask.

"Cardboard," came the reply. "Everyone gets a cardboard version these days."

Aris moved toward the kitchen in search of water. She crossed over the hardwood floor of the great room and onto the black and white tiles of the kitchen.

Sarah and Marie were in front of the wine fridge, pulling out a bottle of white wine.

"Goddamn whisper wine," Aris muttered to herself.

"Aris," Sarah supplied a fake smile, and Aris twisted up the corners of her own mouth, careful to keep her teeth covered.

"Beautiful party," Aris murmured.

"Yes," Marie threw out.

"Thank you." Sarah waved her well-manicured hand, as if to say, oh, that.

"How are you?" Marie asked Aris, her eyes lit with malice.

"Fine," Aris said, waiting for Marie to bait the hook and get it into the water.

"I hear Rhys invited you to his house," Marie commented.

Aris nodded, "Yes, to pick up our engagement present."

Marie threw back her head and laughed.

"It's a little odd that he invited a practical stranger to his place, instead of a member of his own family, don't you think?"

Sarah nodded and looked challengingly at Aris. "I certainly do."

"Did you want some wine, Aris?" Marie asked.

"According to Mother, all you want is wine," Sarah said laughing. "You don't have a problem, do you?"

Aris looked at Marie's emaciated body and asked, "How many calories are in a glass of that?"

Sarah's mouth dropped open. Marie shifted uncomfortably, her dark-blue eyes snapping. Before she could reply, John came in the kitchen.

"So this is where my girl is," he exclaimed as he threw a possessive arm around Aris.

"We were just talking about Rhys," Sarah commented.

"Yeah?"

"God, remember when he left? I thought Helen was going to lose her mind," Marie said.

"So, what happened?" Aris asked.

Sarah shrugged.

"I bet he was on drugs. Major drug habit, that's my guess," Marie said emphatically.

"Nah," John shook his head.

"Morgan thinks he was in a cult," Sarah said scornfully.

"Anyway, he's reappeared after God knows how many years, and did you know he's like a famous artist or something?"

"What?" Sarah's eyes bugged out.

"Seriously," Marie nodded and drained her glass. "I googled him."

Sarah shot John a look and rolled her eyes.

"He's shown all over Europe."

In the midst of the conversation, Aris realized for the first time since she had been acquainted with the Prince family, she felt included.

"I cannot believe you googled him. Jesus, Marie," Sarah shook her head.

"What! I can't believe you didn't."

"You knew him best, John. What do you think? Is it plausible he's really an artist?" Sarah asked.

John held up his arms and backed away, his dark eyes twinkling. "I have nothing to say."

As John began talking with some other cousins across the kitchen, Sarah resumed speaking.

"There goes Uncle Gus. I can't keep him away from the buffet table. I told Paul we needed to have waiters passing the hors d'oeuvres but he thought it would be 'too much' for an eight-year-old's birthday party. Now frigging Gus is eating all the food!"

"Have you seen Aunt Minnie? She's wearing a red, white, and blue striped baseball cap," Marie said, refilling her wine glass.

Aris listened to the two women banter and gossip, and thought desperately of something witty to say. Aris opened her mouth to speak, and Sarah, who had been leaning against the granite counter, pivoted subtly until her back was to Aris, effectively shutting her out of the conversation. Sarah and Marie continued their speaking as if she were not there. Aris stared at Sarah's bared back and pressed her lips together as she shook away her tears.

On the way home Aris glanced at John; he looked tense.

"What?" she finally asked.

"Nothing," he said in a petulant tone.

"John?"

"I don't know what was wrong with you today."

"What do you mean?"

"You were rude to my aunts, rude to my sister, and the way you ran outside like that, people were looking at us."

Aris sighed deeply. "I'm sorry if you feel that way."

John slapped the steering wheel with his palm.

"That's not a real apology. You're only apologizing for how I feel, not for what you did."

"I didn't do anything," Aris protested.

"You're going to have to learn how to be a Prince," John said grimly.

Aris was stung.

"Do I stick out that much?" she asked in a small voice.

"Yes!" John exclaimed. "I can't believe you wore those shorts."

"You picked these shorts out!"

"They're not appropriate for Tinsley's party."

"You mean I'm not appropriate for Tinsley's fucking family."

John flinched. "I didn't say that."

"Like hell you didn't."

"I don't want to fight," John said.

"Obviously, you do. While we're at it, let's talk about the way your family treats me."

John frowned. "I don't know what you're talking about."

"Oh, come on. Your mother doesn't even trust me to plan our wedding! Every time I turn around someone is correcting me, watching me, waiting to catch me doing something!"

"They're just trying to help you! So am I!"

Aris stayed silent.

"If they're critical of you, it's because they love you. Just like me."

Aris didn't think so.

"If you say so."

"I think you're really sensitive. Honey, I'm sorry. It's true. You are in a different world now, and you didn't have the training and upbringing we all did. We're just trying to catch you up."

"Forget it," Aris said tiredly.

Once home, Aris walked through the door, exhausted by the events of the day. John grabbed her and pushed her gently against the wall. She had no desire for him, but the darkness obscured his face and, for some reason, this excited her.

Chapter 6

Aris drove to a large warehouse in a town she'd never heard of. She never came out to this part of the Bay Area; even with the GPS, she got lost. She circled the industrial area, an abandoned metropolis of large brick buildings, looking for the address. All the buildings looked the same: two or three stories of brick, large windows, wooden and metal cargo doors. Some places had the doors open and, as she drove slowly by, Aris saw white-hot weld sparks. She finally realized she'd passed his building twice and parked the white BMW beside a blue door with a black handle. As she exited the car, the dull heat stole over her. She felt languorous, despite the nervous flutter in her stomach. She lifted her hand and knocked at the small, wooden door. No one answered. Aris stepped back. It was hotter and drier than Larkspur; there was no breeze from the bay to cool things off. She was reminded of her grandmother's house in the valley.

The still heat hovered; her hands fluttered briefly with nerves. The place seemed deserted. She knocked again. This time the door opened immediately, giving her the impression that he had been there watching her through the peephole for some time.

Rhys stood at the door, clad in a pair of black jeans and nothing else. His hair hung in his eyes; he braced himself on either side of the door. Aris was struck by his nakedness. He had a tattoo on his chest of a skeleton riding a horse; she looked at the sinister grinning thing and inwardly shuddered. His blue-black hair fell to his chin, framing an elegant forehead, and black, winged brows crested above flashing, green eyes. He had an aristocratic nose and high cheek bones. His face was all angles but not his mouth. He had a pretty mouth, full lips, with an arrogant twist. She unhurriedly took in his broad shoulders, just like John's, and his beautiful long neck, like a woman's. Aris stared at his long fingers, artist's fingers; his hands were covered in paint.

She knew he was staring at her and she did not want to meet his eyes. Her gaze fell to the ground like a failed high-wire act. Rhys moved from the doorway; he swept back a graceful hand, an invitation.

He did not speak as he followed her up the dark stairs. He was aloof, as if he'd never spoken to her before. She felt strange coming into his home; unconsciously, she slowed her feet.

The light was dim. Aris could barely see; she could feel the heat of him behind her. The dark and narrow stairs opened up to a large loft. It was full of light; windows littered the high walls on either side. A large, unmade futon dominated the room; in it lay a long, white body capped with luxurious black curls. Aris started.

Rhys walked around her into the room.

"Katrina," he pointed with his lean, tanned arm.

Aris nodded, embarrassed. The place was bare. The floor was light-colored wood. The walls were exposed brick and blonde-colored wood. To her left was a small kitchen area. The large room was punctuated with various bookshelves packed with books. She did not see any art.

Rhys stood and watched her. He crossed his arms over his chest; Aris watched his tattoo jump with his heartbeat.

"Where is it?" she asked him rudely, her arms fluttering up to her chest like two sick butterflies.

"What?"

His voice was deep, sonorous. Aris sighed.

"Listen, I'm obviously here at a bad time. I can just come back."

Rhys shook his head.

"It's fine."

"So?" Aris prompted.

"What?"

Rhys smirked, as though he knew he was making her uncomfortable and he liked it. The figure on the bed stirred.

"Come on," Rhys gestured for her to follow him.

Aris hesitated, feeling that if she did follow him, she would be lost, somehow. She shook herself mentally. There was another set of stairs by the kitchen. Rhys started down and Aris reluctantly followed.

Aris stepped on the bottom stair with a thunk and looked around. It was considerably darker on the lower level of the place. She looked around the shadowy room. It was huge. She could see the shapes of various canvases scattered about the place. There were some odd pieces of furniture in the room as well. Rhys pushed open the large doors on the backside of the building; light flooded into the space. She was surprised to see a small stream running rather close to the building.

"It's here," he said, gesturing to a large canvas wrapped in paper.

"I don't think that's going to fit in my car," Aris said.

"No?"

"No."

"I have a truck, but there's no way I can get it to you any time soon."

"That's okay," Aris said quickly. She was eager to leave this strange place.

Despite her reluctance to be there, Aris peered into the dark corners, looking at the canvases. His art was deep, soulful, rebellious. She took a step closer to one of the larger canvases.

"This is amazing," she said to him.

Rhys watched her closely with hot eyes. Suddenly he laughed and shrugged.

"I mean, they said you were an artist, but I wasn't sure if it was really true."

"They?"

Aris looked away from the painting long enough to see his raised brows and amused smile.

"Your family," she clarified.

"Ah, yes. My family. Well, they would know," he said, laughter in his voice again.

There was a long pause.

"It looks like you just paint them and toss them down here," Aris said moving on to another painting.

"Pretty much," he said.

"You need someone to organize this," Aris murmured.

"I don't have the time for it," he said. "I guess I could hire someone."

Aris didn't reply. John had failed to mention his cousin was so talented. Maybe the family never treated him as one of their own because he was adopted. The thought made Aris look back at Rhys who was patiently watching her.

"I'll do it," she offered. The minute she said it, she felt something break inside her, as if something more important had just been decided. She shrugged it off. "I mean, I can do it for you. If you want it done."

Rhys regarded her solemnly.

"Why not?" he asked.

Aris waited, wondering why she had just offered to help him.

Rhys nodded and headed back up the stairs.

"Now?" he said over his shoulder.

"Why not?" she muttered.

Aris stared at his retreating back. Despite her unease, her fingers itched to get into the paintings and the ink and charcoal prints piled on the old desk. After several long moments, she turned to the room and began poking around in the piles of papers and canvases.

"It's closer to the bay than you would think."

Katrina was on the stairs. She was astonishingly white. Her face was unlined and her eyes were tip-tilted and brown. Her long, black hair cascaded down her back in a tumble of curls. Clad in baggy shorts, black garters and stockings, and a white tank top, she looked terribly exotic. There were rhinestones at her neck and wrists. Aris involuntarily glanced down at herself. An old tank top and cut-offs.

"Katrina," the woman held out her bejeweled hand.

"Aris."

Aris reached for her hand and had a sudden flash in her mind's eye of Rhys and this woman rolling around in his bed. A flush crept up her face.

"You can get a breeze with these doors open. Listen, it doesn't really matter how you organize these; most likely it will be redone at the gallery, eventually."

Aris nodded, slightly miffed that this woman was giving her orders.

"Are you putting all of these in the show?" Aris asked.

"I'm not sure. Rhys doesn't really have a cohesive theme; he usually never does. I'll have to see everything and pull out what I want."

"Oh, have you been together long?" Aris asked nosily.

Katrina stared at her for a beat. "I've never shown him at my own gallery before, no."

That was not what Aris meant.

"I was at gallery in New York that showed his work a few years ago. I wanted to stay here and go through them, but Rhys is a very private person."

She spoke of him as if she knew him well, but Aris got the impression that she did not really know him at all.

"Rhys is not like most artists; he doesn't need his hand held. He doesn't care if he shows or not. He paints, he creates, and then he forgets about them and they end up in dark, lonely corners."

Aris wondered if the women in Rhys' life suffered a similar fate. Katrina looked as if she was wondering the same thing, then she glanced down at Aris' hand.

"Oh, I see you are engaged," Katrina said, her eyes showing visible relief.

So, the bombshell had been threatened by her, Aris thought. Interesting. She glanced down at The Ring. It glittered unabashedly in the bright light.

"It's very..."

Aris willed her to fill in the blank.

"Nice," Katrina finished benignly, smiling a white, toothy smile and stepping around Aris. She sauntered out the large back doors and Aris found herself watching her go.

Katrina disappeared around the corner, and Aris turned back toward the vast room. There were stacks of paintings leaning against the walls. There was a drafting table, a few scattered arm chairs, and piles of papers lying here and there like snow drifts. The paintings ranged from large canvases to small hand-painted daguerreotypes in hammered tin and copper frames. She resisted the urge to look up and instead crouched on the floor beside a pile of papers.

The day unravelled quickly, and before Aris realized it, it was three o'clock. She cleared her throat and looked up at the light-filled second level. She did not see any movement above. She knew it would be rude to leave without saying goodbye, but she did not particularly want to see Rhys. She went up the stairs with a light tread. The place was empty; Rhys was not there. It smelled of cold coffee and soap.

Aris pulled her purse a little closer to her body and sprinted down the stairs to the blue, wooden door.

"Where's the gift?" John asked as he came through the door.

Aris was unpacking the bag of Chinese food she bought for dinner.

"What gift?" she asked absently.

"Didn't you go to see Rhys today?"

"Yeah. The painting was too big to fit in the car. I had to leave it there."

John frowned as he checked his reflection in the mirror in the hall. He smoothed out his already-smooth hair.

"I wonder why he didn't mention that it was oversized."

Aris shrugged.

"The temp agency call today?" he asked her.

"No, why?"

"I thought maybe you had a job today."

"Why would you think that?" Aris asked.

"You didn't cook."

Aris looked up from the food she was spooning onto a plate.

"What?"

"I mean, you usually only get Chinese when you're working."

"I am working."

"For who?"

John came up behind her and put his arms around her. He nuzzled her neck and his hands crept up toward her breasts.

"Your cousin."

His hands stopped.

"Rhys," Aris clarified.

"You?" John asked, incredulous.

"Yes, me," Aris said, annoyed.

"What on earth could he have for you to do?"

"I was an art history major, remember?"

"So what? He had a couple of Monets for you to study?"

John pulled away and she could feel his annoyance.

"John," Aris said in a placating voice.

"Okay, what are you doing?"

Aris turned around. John was leaning against the counter with his arms crossed. Outside, rain threatened. The clouds were dark and hovered low.

"Cataloguing some of his work for him." She said it lightly.

"You must have been there a long time if you didn't have time to cook my dinner," John observed.

"I wasn't there that long," Aris hedged.

"So how does this work? The two of you going through his crap?" John asked her huffily as he took the plate from her hands and sat at the kitchen table.

Aris bristled at John's terminology.

"No."

Aris had intended the plate she'd fixed to be for herself. She pulled out another plate and started spooning out more food.

"What then?" John asked, his mouth full of food.

"I didn't even see him all day. I was in a storage space; he was in his loft or something. We don't work together."

John's black eyes softened slightly.

"Watch out around him, honey," he warned.

The skies opened at that moment and a hard rain pelted the roof. The sound was like machine gunfire.

"Why?"

John shrugged.

"He's kind of," John paused and thought, "predatory."

Aris laughed and felt her face redden. "You think he's going to seduce me?"

John regarded her, stone-faced. "I didn't say that. That's not what I meant. He would never do something like that."

"So?" Aris prompted.

"He's just, Rhys is, well, he was very strange. He's one of those people who can sort of, turn your head."

"I don't get what you're saying."

John sighed heavily, as he usually did when he was frustrated with her.

"I'm sorry, John, but I really don't get what you're trying to warn me about."

"Just be on your guard with him, okay?"

"Sure."

"Please let me know if you're going to be working late again. I don't like eating take-out all the time."

Chapter 7

Laura Dunn sat on the toilet of the old trailer she shared with Old Max. Old Max was how he had introduced himself to Laura when they met that night on the beach in Santa Cruz. Old Max was an old hippie. Time had suspended him somewhere between sixty-five and seventy, though he might have been older or younger; his flaccid, gray skin hung in great folds around his lanky bones. His face was deeply lined, gaunt, and drawn. His eyes were frequently threaded with red, due to his excessive marijuana habit. He had a scraggly, gray beard and long, smelly, gray hair, which he tied back with a string.

He had a habit of leaving his false teeth out for days. Laura would find them in odd places, like in the cereal cupboard or on the back of the toilet. He never bothered to clean them before he shoved them back in his mouth.

He preferred to wear threadbare, tie-dyed shirts and never failed to have a faded, old army jacket thrown over his shoulders.

Laura inched her jean skirt higher up her thighs and felt the hot splash of urine on her thighs as it puddled in the stained toilet. She drummed her stubby nails on her leg as she waited. She heard Old Max in the sitting area of the trailer, fussing with his Mason jars. She examined herself in the faded mirror across from the toilet.

Though she failed to recognize it, Laura had not aged well. She was underweight, her breasts hung, two slack pouches, above her rib cage; hovering over her prominent collarbone was a heavy face like a walnut, brown and wrinkled. The whites of her muddy eyes had yellowed; many of her teeth had fallen out or turned brown. She had the classic face of an alcoholic: bloated, red nose, broken capillaries all over her face. Her thinning hair was an over-processed mass of white-blonde cotton candy. Despite only being forty-six, Laura looked old, used up. She never lost her penchant for wearing overtly sexual, tacky clothing.

Laura got up off the toilet just as Old Max led his dealer, a stocky twenty-year-old blond kid, into the trailer.

"Hey!" Laura yelled as she hastily pulled down her skirt.

Old Max ignored her, but the kid gaped.

"Next time shut the door," Old Max muttered in his deep voice.

"The door don't work, Old Max. You were supposed to fix it ages ago!" Laura bellowed.

Old Max waved his hand at her dismissively. He gestured to the kid to clear a space off the green couch and sit down. The kid jerked his blond head, indicating he would stand. Old Max shrugged.

The stained and sagging couch was covered in Laura's and Old Max's dirty clothes. The floor of the trailer was littered with broken bongs that Old Max said he was going to fix, but never did. Plastic TV dinner trays, half full of old food, were stacked on the floor. Flies buzzed in and out of a large hole in the window screen. The whole place reeked of dirty bong water and rotting food.

Laura reached for her pack of cigarettes and lighted one.

"Get out of here with that shit," Old Max commanded.

"Fuck you," Laura muttered.

"Whassat?"

Laura smirked. Old Max was half deaf.

"You're smoking," she pointed to the joint in his hand.

"This is good smoke; that crap you smoke kills people," Old Max said.

Laura opened the door to the trailer.

"This better?"

"No, get outside."

"Gimme your phone," she demanded.

Laura stepped from the broken steps of the trailer and laughed abruptly. She'd spent years running from that tin-can piece of shit in the valley and look at her now, right back where she started.

Laura dialed the numbers she had memorized. It was a 415 area code. Laura knew that meant money. She could smell it; Aris had it, all Laura wanted was a little piece. All she wanted was what she deserved.

"The number you have dialed is no longer in service."

The fucking kid had changed her number. Fine, if that's the way she wanted to play it. Fine. Laura had gotten an address from that fancy private eye she hired. It was funnier than hell, how she found out about Aris. Someone left a San Francisco newspaper at the diner Old Max liked to go to on Sundays. He was thumbing through it when Laura spotted a picture of Aris. She looked just like Laura's mother used to. Laura would have recognized her anywhere. She'd grabbed the paper from Old Max's hands.

"What're you doing?" he asked perplexed.

"Nothing."

She hadn't said a word to Old Max. She didn't want to share anything with him. She took what was left of her disability settlement check and hired the P.I. She knew where Aris lived; now if she could just get off this damn mountain.

Laura made a sound of teenage frustration and kicked at the dirt. Old Max had hauled the trailer up to the mountains of Sonoma County last September. They'd been staying in Santa Cruz, but there had been a misunderstanding with his dealer and they'd had to get out quick. Specifically, Old Max owed his Santa Cruz dealer five grand for a couple of pounds of weed and had neglected to pay. Old Max swore he'd been shorted and refused to pay full price. Laura thought he'd done something with the weed. She'd been with Old Max for about four years and he had the strange habits of a former meth addict. He would frequently hide or bury drugs and money and then forget where he put it. So many nights, she'd awakened to the sound of a shovel hitting the hard-packed earth and peeking out the window, she'd see Old Max, his skin hanging from his arms like bat wings, surrounded by shallow holes in the moonlight.

She sucked viciously at her menthol cigarette, ignoring the panoramic view of the lush, green Sonoma Valley below. She wondered idly how she'd managed to end up here. She heard Old Max in the trailer, trying to talk the kid down on his price. It was the same thing every time Old Max got more weed. Laura was sick of Old Max, sick of being buried in the bucolic hills of Sonoma County. She deserved better, and she was going to see that she got it.

When Laura left the Merced Valley at the age of twenty-six, her head was full of liquor and dreams. She'd gone to Los Angeles with Sammy Two-Step to become a movie star. Sammy's real last name was Kowalski, but he thought Sammy Two-Step sounded more Hollywood. Laura thought it sounded stupid. Sammy told her he was a heavyweight in Hollywood. He knew everybody. So she followed him there, her desperation palpable, intent upon finding the glamorous life that she was sure awaited her.

Laura didn't realize Sammy Kowalski knew all the Hollywood big shots because he was a two-bit, star-fucking drug dealer. He lived in a tiny apartment in the San Fernando Valley. When he said he was going to get her in the movies, he meant porn.

Sammy had extensive contacts in the porn industry and he thought Laura was perfect porn material. In the end, with a team of people waiting on her, in the bathroom of a mansion, Laura had chickened out. She sat in a bedroom, naked under a cheap sateen robe, eyes heavily ringed in kohl, and knew she wasn't going to be able to perform.

"Hey, baby? What's wrong? Everyone is waiting."

Sammy caressed her bare thigh with his gold-ringed hands. The backs of his hands were covered in black hair.

"I can't do it," Laura told him, ashamed.

"What do you mean? Everyone is waiting. You said you were okay with this. You can't back out now."

"I'm sorry," Laura said genuinely.

"What the fuck am I supposed to tell Dan? You know, he's a good friend of mine."

Laura shrugged.

"Maybe we just start off nice and easy. What do you say? No big commitment, just a little kissing at first?" he cajoled.

Sammy was born to persuade women to do things they didn't want to do; it was a talent he'd cultivated to his advantage. Laura felt guilty for letting him down.

She shook her head and stared at the rose carpeting beneath her feet. Soon after, Sammy began using his persuasive talents in a new profession, as a pimp. Laura quickly left his place and stayed with his friend Donnie for a few months. She found living in Los Angeles more difficult than she'd thought it would be. She bounced from man to man like a drunken ping-pong ball. The women she met did not like her; she had no friends. She held down menial jobs in fits and starts. There were times where she found herself sleeping on church steps and in homeless shelters because the man she'd been living with kicked her out.

Ever since she left the green and white stucco house, she'd been subject to the whims of a man. The men she chose were always the same type of man: rough, loud, swaggering braggarts. She was consistently attracted to what her father would have termed the lowest common denominator. Sometimes she would go into a bar, find the best-dressed, most successful-looking guy there, and then get to his house and find his living room full of stolen car stereos.

Each relationship she found herself in mirrored the one before it. She started out loving and pliable, but she was unable to control her unremitting mood swings. She craved drama as much as she craved alcohol and would often pick fights with people out of boredom. Her boyfriends tired quickly of her mercurial disposition, and she repeatedly found herself unceremoniously dumped, gently pushed away by the fatigued hands of men who had enough. She treated most of the people in her life the same way she had treated her daughter: with a peculiar mix of affection, abuse, and absentmindedness.

Los Angeles sucked Laura up in its glittering arms, and then spat her out, a dried husk; her dreams got lost in the daily shuffle for survival. From Southern California, she moved up to Oregon, where a girlfriend got her a job as the night manager of a Motel 6. It was then that she began writing the letters to Aris. They were filled with dreamy platitudes and half-formed apologies. She never sent them, but kept them at the bottom of a drawer in her small apartment. Laura continued to drink heavily, and occasionally indulged in a part-time meth habit. She got fired from Motel 6 for her frequent absenteeism, and she left Oregon, with its long, tree-lined stretches of road and snowy winters.

She made her way back down to California and found herself the subject of a religious conversion at the age of thirty-two, thanks to a man named Timothy Tulkin, a Mormon who swept her away to the bosom of his family in Salt Lake City, Utah.

Without a proper education and little work experience, she found herself well-suited to working odd refinery jobs. The companies expected little of her, and no one seemed to care if she drank so long as she did not do it on the job. She met Timothy Tulkin in a refinery in Richmond. He was a rep for a valve company and, despite the rumors of her promiscuity circling the refinery, he spotted her in the parking lot and asked her to dinner.

Laura enjoyed seeing herself through Timothy's eyes. He was a naive and gentle soul who thought Laura was a sweet, misunderstood girl that simply needed a good man to stand beside her. Laura wore demure, flowered dresses and limited herself to one glass of white wine at dinner. Timothy was smitten, and Laura went to great pains to control her emotions. She knew, if she tried hard enough, she could be the woman he already thought she was.

She cleaned her apartment and stuffed her letters to Aris in the bottom of an old suitcase. She dyed her hair back to its natural dirty blonde and took special care not to bite her nails. Timothy was devoted to his religion, which, Laura was disappointed to learn, had many rules.

"What do you mean I can't drink or smoke?"

Timothy took her hand eagerly. "We don't believe in using addictive substances."

"Uh huh," Laura said suspiciously. "Do you think I drink too much?"

"No, but if you really want to get married, then you have to convert and, honey, you can't convert if you drink and smoke."

Laura considered this. Timothy grasped her hand earnestly and peered into her face with adoring blue eyes.

"Laura, darling, I want you to come home and meet my parents and family. I've been waiting for a girl like you."

"Timmy," Laura said carefully, her head swimming with visions of herself as his wife.

Laura shook her head. Timothy Tulkin removed his hand from hers and stood up from the couch.

"Think about it. When you make up your mind, I'll be here, but I'm going back to Salt Lake in a few weeks..." he trailed off.

"Oh, honey," she bleated. She was loathe to disappoint him. He straightened his cardboard-colored suit, ran a feminine hand through his sandy hair, and gave her a perfunctory kiss before he left.

She spent the next three days nursing several bottles of gin on her fold-out sofa bed. She got out the letters to Aris and read them over and over. Timothy did not know she had a daughter. Of her family, she told him next to nothing. She told him her mother was still alive and living in the valley, but they didn't get along. She failed to mention her fifteen-year-old, violet-eyed daughter. She found herself on the cusp of becoming a Mormon bride; she longed to leave behind the days of uncertainty and fear. She knew Timmy was her ticket out, and she was enchanted with the woman he saw when he looked at her. Timmy held the promise of a life she had never known she wanted and, in those three gin-permeated days, she imagined herself, neat and smiling, growing silver-haired on an old, white porch. The image was so seductive that Laura managed to convince herself to marry him and move to Utah.

She tried, vainly and desperately, to contort herself into a diminutive and respectable wife. Her days in Salt Lake City were numbered, but she would not admit it. Timmy's family were kind and nonjudgmental, but they treated her as one treats a stray dog, as if she might bite their long, white fingers unexpectedly.

Timothy Tulkin bought a small, yellow house on a quiet street and Laura swept the front porch with pride. Little by little, over the course of the year, Laura's careful facade began to fracture. Timmy was leaving her for the first time since they had been married.

"Can't they send someone else?" she whined as he packed his bag.

"No," he said patiently. "This is my job, sweetheart. If I didn't have to travel, I wouldn't have met you. Remember?"

Laura shrugged and twisted her hands in her lap.

"What will I do without you for six whole weeks?"

"Laura, you'll be fine and if you need anything, my mother or sisters or the ladies from church can help you. You won't be alone."

"Timmy," she said. "I don't know if I can do this."

He came to sit beside her on the bed. "Of course you can. I'll call you every night and be back in no time."

"Can't I go with you?" she asked.

"Laura, the road is no place for a lady."

"Hey, I used to work in the very same refineries you're going to!" Laura's voice pitched higher and her hands rose up to her mouth.

"To this day," he said innocently, "I have no idea how you got there. You don't belong in places like that. You belong here."

His tone was final and Laura felt her desperation leak out of her, replaced with her incessant need to please.

On a Tuesday in May, as Timothy left his wife standing forlornly on the front porch, he felt a tug of foreboding, which he ignored.

That Sunday, Mrs. Natalie Tulkin, Timmy's mother, called Laura and asked her if she wanted a ride to church. Laura, who had a bottle of gin beside the bed and a half-smoked pack of cigarettes on the bedside table, demurred, claiming illness.

"How about I stop by with a nice pot of soup?"

"No thanks, Mom," Laura said, her throat hoarse from smoking. "I wouldn't want you to catch this."

The next week, she demurred again, this time citing a stomach ailment.

"I think she's pregnant," Natalie said excitedly, when she hung up the phone.

Laura was, in fact, not pregnant. She had her tubes tied in Oregon after her second abortion. She had failed to tell her husband this, and he and his family were under the impression she was able to have children. Laura saw no point in correcting them.

By the third week, Laura had dried out enough to make it to church with the Tulkin family.

"Something's wrong," Natalie whispered to her husband. "She really does look ill."

"Pregnant women sometimes do," he mused.

By the time Timothy came home from his travels, Laura had hidden emergency packs of cigarettes and bottles of gin around the house.

She began going to the store, the bank, the gas station, and coming home drunk.

Timothy was unaware that her daily sojourns were the obvious fabrications of a practiced alcoholic. She began to behave erratically; he thought she was upset because she hadn't conceived yet. He suggested counseling at the church. Laura scoffed at him.

"There's nothing wrong with me, damn it!"

Timmy winced. "Please, don't swear."

"Gimme a break," she rolled her eyes.

For the better part of that autumn Timmy did everything he could to placate and diffuse his wife. She had become volatile and demanding. Her anger, so carefully hidden from him in the past, gushed forth from a seemingly inexhaustible fount. There were times where he cowered before her blind rages, and he was ashamed.

One day, he discovered a pack of cigarettes in the garage and confronted her.

"Those aren't mine," Laura said baldly.

"Then whose are they?"

"How the hell should I know?"

"Please, don't swear," he said timidly.

She rounded on him.

"Why don't you leave me the fuck alone!"

Timmy stepped back and ran his hands through his sandy hair, a gesture he often made when he was flustered.

"Laura!"

"Gimme a break," she rolled her hard, mud-colored eyes at him.

"I don't know who you are anymore! I don't know what to do!" he cried in anguish.

His bashful, needy bride had become a baleful, violent stranger. He was at a loss.

Laura's marriage ended in early January, when Timmy found a half-drunk bottle of gin hidden in the linen closet.

"Are you going through my stuff?" she asked angrily.

"We can get you some help, Laura. We can fix this."

"I ain't broken, Timmy. I'm sick of your shit. 'Don't cuss. Don't smoke. Don't drink. Don't fuck with the lights on,'" she mimicked rudely. "I'm over it."

"What?"

He sank on the bed, unable to speak.

"I love you, Laura. I want a family with you. Let me help you," he pleaded.

Laura looked down her nose at the pitiful spineless thing on the bed wondering what she had ever seen in him.

"Forget it," she said harshly, grabbing the bottle of gin from his limp, delicate hand. "I really am over it."

She left Utah that night in Timmy's Range Rover, the glowing tip of her cigarette jutting from her mouth. She followed her ill-fated marriage with thirteen years of odd jobs, crude men, and sour-tasting mornings, writing sad, self-pitying letters to a daughter she had abandoned.

Laura ground out her cigarette and glanced through the dirty and torn screen into the trailer. Old Max was trying to show the kid his specimen collection. Old Max collected dead bugs. He kept them in Mason jars which lined the kitchen counter. Laura hated them; she didn't know what anyone needed with a jar full of dead beetles.

The screen door opened and the kid came out, taking a big breath. Laura smirked and patted her stiff, white-blonde hair.

"What's the matter, kid? Does my fucking house smell?' Laura said rudely.

The kid nodded as he walked to his car.

"Yeah, lady," he said succinctly, "your fucking house does smell."

"What the fuck do you even know? You thieving little shit!" Laura screamed. "You charge him twice what you charge everyone else for your shit weed!"

He turned around.

"What the hell?"

"You heard me, you little asshole. How dare you insult me!"

Laura advanced on him; he was standing in front of his car with his fists clenched.   Old Max came slowly out of the house, his shoulders hunched under the green army jacket. He stood on the top step and surveyed the scene.

"Laura, what's going on out here?"

"This little shit is a liar and a cheat, and he's pissed that I called him on it,"Laura screamed.

"Dude," the kid held up his hands, " this bitch just started yelling at me."

"Bitch! Old Max is going to kick your fucking ass!"

The kid looked at the gray, old man and laughed. "Sure he is."

Laura glanced at Old Max, who was standing on the step with his arms crossed.

"Fine, goddamn it! I'll do it myself!" Laura said.

At this, he laughed harder.

"Yeah, you look like you've seen a few fights. That how you lost all them teeth?"

On a scream, Laura charged. The kid grabbed her quickly and restrained her. He threw her to the ground.

"That's it, man. Fuck this shit. You want any more weed, you ain't getting it from me," he said as he got into his car. "Call someone else."

Laura looked up at Old Max; she was covered in dirt and spoiling for a fight.

"What the fuck! You can't even defend me?"

Old Max shrugged and watched the kid's red car speed down the road, leaving little eddies of dust in its wake.

Laura snorted in disgust and peeled herself off the ground. Her bottom was covered in nettles and dirt.

"Goddamn it," she muttered.

Chapter 8

Aris returned to Rhys' the next day. She knocked at the blue door and waited. She heard him thundering down the narrow stairs and he opened the door.

"What do you usually do?" he asked over his shoulder as he led her up the stairs.

Katrina was in the kitchen making coffee.

"Good morning, Aris." Katrina favored her with a toothy smile.

"Good morning," Aris said, trying not to stare. Katrina was wearing panties and a tiny lace tank top that was almost see-through.

Rhys sat at the table and lighted a cigarette. Katrina wrinkled her nose.

"God, I wish he wouldn't do that inside."

Rhys ignored her.

"You didn't answer my question," Rhys said, his green eyes on Aris.

"Oh," Aris started. "I've been working at various temp jobs, you know, usually administrative stuff. Nothing very interesting."

"For how long?" Katrina asked.

"About a year or so. Before that it was another administrative job. My degree wasn't very useful, I guess."

Aris shrugged; she was uncomfortable talking about herself.

"What was your degree in?" Rhys asked her.

"Art history."

"So, at least you know what you are doing down there," Katrina said.

Rhys frowned.

Aris felt like she was intruding on what looked like a cozy, domestic scene.

"I should get down there," she offered.

"Want some coffee?" Rhys asked her as she made her way to the stairs.

"No, thank you. I don't really care for coffee."

As Aris picked her way down the stairs, she heard Katrina ask Rhys if he wanted breakfast.

"No," he answered, sounding aloof.

"What are you doing today?" she asked him.

Aris stopped on the stairs, cocked her head and listened.

"I don't know. Why?"

"I thought we could do something together."

"I'm busy," he said. "Maybe you should put something on; you embarrassed her."

"No, I didn't," Katrina snapped.

"You wanted to make it evident you slept over," Rhys said lightly. "You have. Now I think it's time for you to go."

"What?" Katrina asked, sounding shocked.

"You wanted to make sure Rhys was going to be a good boy. If you were a dog, you would have pissed on me."

"Rhys! What are you talking about?"

Aris could hear the desperation in Katrina's voice, and the guilt.

"It's time to go, Kat. I'm not interested in these games."

Aris turned to go down the stairs. She shouldn't be listening to this.

"I don't know what you're talking about!"

"Yes, you do."

Aris got to the bottom of the stairs and realized she could still hear them. She cringed.

"I can't believe you are doing this to me!"

"How would your girlfriend feel if she knew what I've been doing to you?"

"How dare you bring that up? You don't even know her."

"I don't really know you," Rhys said lazily. His tone was not harsh, but it was very matter-of-fact. His implacability must have infuriated Katrina.

There were stomping sounds, Katrina was gathering her things. The sounds came closer to the back stairs.

"No," Rhys said mildly. "You can go out the front door. I won't have you bothering her with your petty shit. Go home to your girlfriend, Kat."

"Fuck you, Rhys Prince. You're unbelievable."

Aris heard Katrina clatter down the other set of stairs and the blue door slammed. She listened, but there was no sound from the loft above. She set about to work.

A few hours later, Rhys came down the stairs.

"Hey, you should open these backdoors and get a breeze in here. It's getting hot already."

Aris nodded.

"Listen, I'm going away for a little while. Only a few weeks but you can still come by. I'll leave you a key."

"Are you sure you want me here alone?" she asked, thinking about what a private person Katrina said he was.

Rhys laughed and the sound was lovely. "What are you going to do, rob me?"

"Well, no, but I could start snooping in your stuff."

Rhys waved his hand, a flash of ink and silver rings.

"There's nothing in here to snoop."

Astoria looked at the man who brought her the tray. He didn't speak much English.

"No, thank you," she said to him. "No, gracias."

The man deposited the tray on the table by the bed and left. Astoria sighed. Geraldine brought her lunch most days, but nobody here seemed to remember that. Wailing started up out in the hall; it was Mrs. Perkins again.

The nurse came into Astoria's room.

"Mrs. Perkins is at it again," she said to the air, as if Astoria couldn't hear her.

"Excuse me," Astoria said, hating the sound of her tremulous voice.

The nurse ignored her and pulled her wheelchair around.

"Let's get you up and out of this bed. Maybe you can have lunch outside today."

"No, thank you. I don't want that lunch and I don't care to eat outside. My friend Geraldine is coming with my lunch."

The nurse continued to ignore her and started to lower her bed down so Astoria could slide in the chair. Astoria wondered if anyone even heard her. The wailing grew louder. Several people were trying to reason with Mrs. Perkins, who, in Astoria's opinion, was beyond all reasoning.

"Come on, honey. Let's get you outside."

Something in Astoria snapped. "I am not your honey and I have already told you I don't want to eat outside."

The nurse backed away, hurt and anger in her brown eyes. Geraldine appeared in the doorway.

"Oh, excuse me," the nurse said.

Geraldine nodded regally; the nurse slipped past her.

"I'm so glad you're here, Geraldine."

"I can't stand this place," Geraldine muttered as Astoria got into the chair. "Listen to that old woman wail away like a little baby. I saw her in the hallway. Ain't nothing wrong with that woman."

Geraldine settled Astoria at the little table by the window and sat across from her.

"The sooner you get out of here, the better."

"I agree," Astoria said.

"I brought you some leftover barbecue. Simeon made it the other night."

Astoria clapped her hands together. "Oh, goody. Did you bring the cards too?"

"I certainly did."

Astoria opened the container before her and the delicious smell of barbecue wafted toward her.

"They won't let you eat this stuff here. You should see the slop they bring me for dinner. As if you turn a certain age and your taste buds dry up and die. They ought to be shot, these people. Taking away dignity like they do. All 'sweetie' and 'honey' and 'dear.' I am not a child!" Astoria said forcefully.

Geraldine nodded. "I know, Miss Astoria. They older you get, the worse people treat you. Should be the other way around."

Astoria was so glad Geraldine was here. Now she knew why so many people died in these places; it wasn't because they were old. It was the way they cut you off from everyone and everything. Your whole life is gone and replaced with strangers that call you "honey" and "sweetie." There's no choice in what you eat or where you go; it's all decided for you, as though you were a child.

"I am not a child," Astoria said again.

"Miss Astoria," Geraldine began.

Astoria wished she would drop the "Miss," but it had been so many years now and besides, it was almost like a joke between them. "I should call you Miss Geraldine," Astoria said once.

"Damn right you should," Geraldine had replied and they had gone into peals of laughter.

"I don't mean to trouble you. I know you're in here getting well."

Astoria gave a snort. "If that's what you want to call it. They're trying to kill me."

"John Junior was out at the house last week. I was there late to train the new maid. He had some men with him."

"Men?" Astoria asked. "What do you mean?"

Geraldine shook her head. "I don't know. They had on suits. They toured the property. They had a survey guy out there too."

Astoria pondered this.

"What can he mean having a surveyor out there?"

Geraldine regarded her silently.

"Maybe he's thinking you're not coming home."

"That's a terrible thing to say!"

"I know it is. I'm still saying it. Somebody has to."

"Did Mr. Johnny leave you that house?" Geraldine asked. "I mean, do you own it outright?"

"Yes," Astoria said faintly.

"Then there shouldn't be anything to worry about," Geraldine said.

"Right," Astoria said tremulously. "Right."

Rhys had been gone for two weeks. He said something about settling his affairs in Europe and Aris thought that sounded so exotic. She went to his place about once a week and did some work. She had no real inclination to be there when he wasn't, something that sounded warning bells in the back of her head, but she willed them to silence. The painting he was gifting to her and John was still there in the storage space, leaning against an old desk. It was wrapped in paper.

At the end of the second week, Aris peeled back a little corner of the paper. Blue background. She peeled back a little bit more. Sweat ran down her back in tiny, hot rivulets.

Violet eyes, not unlike her own, stared back at her. They were hot, lusty eyes, the eyes of a woman who knew precisely what she was and what she wanted. Aris pulled away the paper completely. It was her.

Her body was folded over itself, her legs barely covering her breasts as she reached out to the viewer. Her limbs were long; there was a grace to them that she did not actually possess. Her mouth was screwed up in a clever, knowing smile. Aris had never smiled like that in her life. Her long, blonde hair tumbled down her back in sexy tangles.

Aris tilted her head like a little bird and stared at this woman who was supposed to be her. John would hate this painting. He'd take one look at it and stow it away in the rafters in the garage. Aris heard a noise; the blue door was opening. She quickly covered up the painting.

"Aris? I'm home. I didn't want to scare you," Rhys called from the top of the loft.

"Hi," she said lamely.

He thundered down the back stairs and landed before her. He took in her flushed face and sweaty back.

"I think you'd better take the rest of the day off," he said. "It's too hot to work anyway."

Rhys pushed open the back door and took her hand in his own. Aris resisted the urge to twist away from him like a little kid. He led her to the back of the property to edge of the stream.

"Why don't you wade in a little bit? I think it would do you some good," he offered kindly.

Aris shook her head dumbly at him.

"I'm fine."

"Please," he said. "For me."

Rhys crossed his eyes and grinned. Despite herself, Aris laughed. Then she thought of the woman in the painting and her face reddened again.

Rhys noted her flush.

"I don't want to have to drag you in," he said flashing his teeth at her.

"Okay, okay."

Aris stepped out of her flip flops and gingerly dipped her foot in the water. It was cold and lovely.

She stifled a happy sigh. Rhys heard it, though, and laughed at her.

"You can thank me now," he said teasingly.

Aris kept thinking about the woman in the painting. Is that how he saw her? Is that who he thought she was?

He materialized next to her, the stream rushing around both their calves.

"It's great, huh?" he asked her.

Aris tried to meet his green eyes and failed; her hands fluttered at her sides. She nodded mutely.

"I thought you'd be done by now," he said casually.

"I'm sorry," she said, instantly upset at herself for dallying for the last couple of weeks.

He laughed. "It's no big deal. Kat will be coming to collect soon, though."

"I'll get right on it," Aris promised as she turned to step out of the stream.

Rhys grabbed her arm and his grip was hot on her skin.

"Hey, calm down. Jesus, you are a bundle of nerves. No more work today; take the rest of the day off."

He still held her arm.

"Okay," she said staring down at the hand gripping her skin. It was clean of paint and ink; the silver rings caught the light.

He reached out with his other arm and drew her deeper into the water. "Just stand still for a second, Aris."

So she stood next to him in the cool water and counted down the seconds until she could get away.

As she drove home, Aris couldn't stop thinking about Rhys and his hands on her, and his hot green eyes.

Men should always beware when a woman suddenly changes her hair. It signals a change in the brain, the heart. When Aris came through the garage door John looked up from the computer. His face immediately froze in an O of surprise.

"Your hair," he said.

"I cut it," Aris said nonchalantly.

It was short. She felt like Mia Farrow in Rosemary's Baby, exposed and a little garish.

She could see John was almost sickened by the lack of hair.

"It's really short."

"I know," she fingered the back of her head. "I was just walking past a salon and decided to just get rid of it."

"Why?"

"I didn't want the weight of it anymore," Aris said as she walked over to him. I didn't want to look like the woman in the picture, she said to herself.

"But the wedding," he protested.

"What about it?" Aris asked confused.

"What are you going to do? It's too short," John said stiffly.

Aris shrugged. "You sound angry."

"I am angry."

"Why?"

"You look ridiculous."

Aris' hand fluttered up to grab a lock of shorn hair. John shook his head at her.

"Hey, it's your hair," he said. "Do what you want to it. I'm only the one who has to look at you all the time."

"You're being silly," Aris murmured.

"Whatever," he said. "Somebody from the temp agency called. I think they have another job for you."

Aris fingered her hair absently. "I'm working for Rhys right now."

"That wasn't supposed to last all summer, was it?"

John pushed away from his laptop and rose from the granite breakfast bar.

Aris turned away from him without answering and went to the mirror in the front hall. Her blonde hair was too short and she looked like a young boy. Her eyes were enormous and luminous. Her mouth looked more prominent. She was not even sure that she liked it, but now nobody would confuse her with the woman in the painting, not Rhys, not John and certainly not Aris.

"Aris?" he called from the kitchen.

She didn't answer him, but stared at herself in the dim light of the hall. She almost didn't recognize herself.

"Aris?" John called again, his voice closer.

"What?"

John approached her and placed his heavy hands on her slim shoulders. He looked at them in the mirror. His black eyes pierced hers and he rearranged his face into a mask of understanding.

"You think moving a bunch of paintings around is a job?"

"Is that what you think I do all day?"

"Quite frankly, I don't know what you two do all day!"

"What the hell does that mean?" Aris whirled on him.

"Nothing, nothing. Calm down."

John methodically massaged her shoulders. He leaned in and spoke softly into her ear. "I've told you, you don't need to work. I have more than enough money. We can have a house three times the size of this one. It's not about money. I just want to see you settled and happy."

"I am happy," she said.

"You're restless. I can see it. It's not healthy. It's like you're waiting for something."

He paused, nipped her earlobe.

"I think I know what it is," he said, nibbling her neck.

"What's that?" she asked petulantly.

"A baby."

Aris wrenched away. "What?"

John smiled condescendingly.

"What are you talking about?" she asked.

"B-A-B-Y," he spelled, grinning.

"I know how to spell it, thank you," she said drily. "What on earth would make you think I want a baby?"

John heaved a sigh, "Every woman wants a baby. It's built into you biologically."

"What makes you think I want a baby right now?"

John shrugged.

"No, really, why on earth would you want to knock me up now? We aren't even married yet."

"Knock you up? Do you have to be so crass? It's not appealing when you talk that way. You sound-"

"I sound what? Poor?" Aris laughed.

"Uneducated."

"Jesus Christ, John!" Aris exclaimed, her voice rising.

"Alright," John said placatingly. "But think about this: we're not getting any younger and I want to be able to play ball with my son. Most of the guys that are my age at work have kids that are five or six. We're behind the curve."

"I wasn't aware there was a baby curve."

"I just want to give you what you need."

Aris studied her fiancé with shuttered eyes. She was not sure what she needed.

Chapter 9

She met John at work; she had been his administrative assistant.

"He goes through them quickly, you mustn't get too settled in," Marjorie, her gray-eyed, gray-haired supervisor told her.

Aris followed Marjorie down the hall. The law offices of MacDonald Dempsey & Porter had a distinct style: gray. The walls were gray; the floor was a darker gray. The filing cabinets were gunmetal gray.

Out of pure fate, Aris had worn a gray suit. As Marjorie led her down the gray halls, Aris briefly pictured herself taking a running start and catapulting out of the gray-framed windows.

"This is Mr. Prince's office. You'll be working out of it."

Marjorie knocked, waited, then pushed open the door.

"He's not here right now. I believe he had a breakfast meeting. You can use that," Marjorie pointed to the empty, round table to her left.

"Okay." Aris mustered a sickly grin.

"There's no phone and no computer," Marjorie said, sounding quite satisfied.

Aris nodded.

"You mustn't ever use Mr. Prince's telephone or computer without his permission. Am I making myself clear?" Marjorie studied Aris as if she were a grubby little kid.

Aris nodded again.

"Speak up!" Marjorie barked at her.

"Yes!" Aris said loudly.

"You can organize those until Mr. Prince gets here," Marjorie said, gesturing to a mass of files on the floor.

Marjorie flicked one last disdainful look at Aris and left the room.

Aris sat at the table and started to organize the files; she was almost finished when the door opened.

John Prince was so handsome that her breath caught. He was young, younger than Aris had imagined. His suit looked expensive; his briefcase probably cost more than her car. He wore his money well; it showed in his smile, his confident eyes.

"Who are you?" he asked in mock fright.

"I'm your new admin," Aris informed him.

John laughed. His eyes strayed to the mirror on the wall above her head. He assessed himself. Satisfied, he turned his black eyes back to Aris.

"What's your name?" he asked as he walked over to his desk.

"Aris Dunn."

John's lips quirked.

The phone on the desk rang. John answered it and his laughter rang out. Aris watched him from her lowered lashes. He was tall and well built. His black eyes danced as he spoke to whomever was on the phone.

Aris let her eyes wander over him. He was broad-shouldered; his suit, no doubt, hid a flat stomach. John settled into his desk and Aris finished up the files.

"Excuse me," she said to him. His head was bent over his desk.

He didn't look up. "What?"

"I'm finished with those files. What should I start on now?"

He looked up, his eyes showing disbelief. "You're finished?"

Aris nodded.

"The last girl I had said it would take her two or three weeks to get that done. The one before her couldn't alphabetize for shit," he said bitterly. "You finished it in one morning."

Aris nodded again.

"Well," John sat back in his brown leather chair. "It's eleven-thirty. Why don't you go to lunch?"

The people at the office all seemed to belong to the same club. It was a club of wealth and privilege and Aris didn't know how to get in. She was not even sure she wanted in, but she didn't like feeling like an outsider; it made her feel conspicuous. The women all had expensive clothes and fine, delicate jewelry. Beside them, Aris felt cheap. Her ill-fitting suits and faux pearls made her feel silly, like a little girl playing at something.

Aris tried to ignore John's effect on women. When John Prince walked down the hall, heads popped up in cubicles, eyes followed him closely, cheeks stained red, and mouths stretched in silly grins. She tried not to notice the way he looked at her, as if he couldn't figure her out, but he was going to do his best.

His black eyes followed her when she walked; she could feel them. He always had a grin for her. He tried to tease her, sometimes, about silly things.

"Aris, you'd better stop that," he said in a warning tone.

Aris looked up from the document she was proofing.

"Stop what?" she asked, somewhat alarmed.

"Stop working so hard. You never leave this room," he said easily, laughing at his own joke.

"Oh," Aris blushed.

"Why don't you go see some of the other girls in the office? Trade make-up secrets, or whatever it is you girls do. Get out of here," he suggested.

"I don't trade make-up secrets," Aris said drily.

"No, a girl like you doesn't need any make-up," he said absently.

At least once a week, Aris would come in to the office to find some kind of offering on the table for her: a jelly donut, an apple, business cards with her name on them.

"Thank you," she'd say lamely to John.

He'd grin, very pleased with himself.
Aris wondered at the small gifts. Was he hitting
on her? He didn't act like he was. John treated
her very courteously; he teased her, but he never
crossed the line into romantic territory. He was
good-natured and easygoing. Everyone at the
office liked him. Aris was rather in awe of him.
John Prince was everything she'd never known,
everything she never would be: rich, charming,
ambitious. She became more aware of him as
time went on. His office seemed to shrink, the
walls getting smaller and smaller until Aris felt
like she was pressed up against him.

Every day, Aris tried not to become
distracted by his spicy scent. Over her papers
and reports, she eyed him hungrily. He was
always dressed immaculately, hard muscles
bunching under crisp, white shirts. Dark-brown
hair cut close to the scalp framed a face meant
for a Roman coin. His features were straight,
pure male, all-American. He was the football
star who wouldn't date her; he was the man at
the bar who wouldn't deign to buy her a drink.
He was everything she never had.

The weeks dragged on; summer shifted
into autumn. Aris became a part of the
inevitable office rhythm. Each day promised
gray walls, gray carpeting and the hours filled

with endless and repetitive tasks, punctuated by harsh barks from Marjorie's thin lips. Her only reprieve was John Prince.

Socially, she never really found a place in the office. Everyone seemed to already know everyone else and there was no place for a girl from the Merced Valley with crooked teeth. The women ignored her and the men mostly did the same. Sometimes, Aris would see a burgeoning attraction in someone's eye, but it was quickly squashed. She didn't appeal to these people.

The lights of San Francisco were dimmed by the pallor of descending winter, and the Christmas Season announced itself amid a flurry of rainstorms.

"Are you coming to the Christmas party?"

John Prince lounged in the doorway, his black eyes quizzical.

"I wasn't planning on it."

"I think you'd better go, Aris," he said. "Did you get my suit from the cleaners?"

His eyes were on his own face as he looked at himself in the mirror.

"They delivered it," she said. "It's on the back of the door."

"Great. We don't look kindly on employees who skip the party," John informed her.

"Oh," Aris said. "I don't really have anything to wear."

The party was at the St. Francis. It was supposed to be a really fancy dinner. Aris pictured herself there, wearing an inappropriate dress and talking to no one. That sounded horrible.

John smiled at her.

"We're all getting the rest of the afternoon off. I'm sure you can rustle up something."

He grabbed the suit from the back of the door.

"I'll see you tonight."

Aris opened her mouth to tell him she still wasn't sure about going, then closed it again. He was already gone.

Aris spent money she didn't have on a dress she hoped was appropriate. Fueled by Kristin's enthusiasm and a glass of wine, Aris went to the party.

The ballroom was beautifully decorated; white flowers and ice sculptures littered the tables and a band played quietly in the background. Aris looked down at her dress. She bought something black, conservative, and she was woefully underdressed. The men had on dark suits, some even wearing tuxedos; the women were in gauzy, floaty dresses or glittering in sequins.

"Aris."

John's voice, Aris turned. Her breath hitched. He looked so gorgeous. He smiled down at her and Aris imagined him taking her hand and leading her off to the dance floor, leading her off to a better life.

"I'm so glad you could make it," he said politely, even coldly.

Aris' brow furrowed over her violet eyes. "Thank you," she said formally.

"This is my girlfriend, Chloe."

A beautiful, icy-looking blonde stepped forward and held out an elegant hand to Aris.

"So, John tells me you work for him," Chloe said dismissively.

Aris shook the woman's hand; Chloe withdrew it quickly.

"John, there's Tommy Dempsey. Let's go say hello."

John nodded and walked off. Chloe speared Aris with one last disdainful glance.

"What is she wearing?" Aris heard her say incredulously to John before they moved off.

The party was dismal. Aris was seated at a table with Marjorie, who made it a point to tell Aris that her dress "wasn't very party-like." Aris sat through the dinner and the raffle; she watched John and Chloe from the corner of her eye. They sat at a table with all the senior partners. John was on the fast track; he would be a partner in no time. Chloe smiled and laughed and looked altogether too poised. Aris felt a wave of jealousy. How stupid she had been, wondering if John was hitting on her with all those silly presents. Why on Earth would he want Aris when he had someone like Chloe? Aris felt a furious shame envelop her and, murmuring goodnight to those at her table, she got up from her chair. They barely noticed.

She struck out of the ballroom as if there were a fire at her back.

"Hey!"

Aris looked back. John was running to catch up with her. She waited, her face red.

"Are you leaving already?" he asked.

"I'm not feeling well."

"Oh." His handsome face showed concern. "Listen, before you take off."

Aris waited.

"I wanted to give you this," John pulled a plastic card out of his wallet. "I should have gotten you a Christmas card but I didn't have time."

Aris took the card from him. It was a gift card to a very upscale spa.

"Oh, thank you," Aris said. "I didn't get you anything."

"What do you get the guy who has everything? Right?" he laughed easily. "I thought you could go and get your nails done or something," he said as he eyed her hands.

Her hands fluttered up to her chest of their own accord. Aris had the urge to cover her nails.

"Chloe says it's a really chic place. She goes there once a week."

"Oh."

John shifted his weight. "I guess you were right about not having anything to wear," he said looking at her matronly black dress.

Aris was mortified.

"Thank you for this," she said, raising the card up.

"I hope you feel better," he said sympathetically.

Aris watched his retreating back as he went into the ballroom. Chloe, in her ice-blue dress, was waiting for him in the doorway. She made an impatient gesture, then shot Aris a superior look.

Christmas came and went. Aris went to the valley, feeling little satisfaction in being there. Gram's cozy house felt stuffy; the worn furniture grated on Aris' nerves. She went back to the city quickly, back to the city and the shining beacon that John Prince had become.

John was talking about hiring her directly, instead of through the temp company. He still left something on the table for her: a cold drink, a fortune cookie, once he left a paper origami bird. Aris took it home and hung it from her ceiling. It dove and swung over her head at night. She lay in bed and dreamed of John Prince, of being the beautiful Chloe.

Around spring, John came to work late. He removed his sunglasses to reveal a shiner.

"Oh my God!" Aris exclaimed. "What happened?"

John favored her with a tired smile. "I got into a bar fight."

"What?"

It was so unlike her image of him that she had trouble believing him.

"What really happened?" she asked him.

"No, really. Chloe dumped me-"

Aris' heart soared and she heard a rushing in her ears.

"So Jaime and Ken, you know, from the office, took me out."

"And you got into a bar fight."

John nodded. "I don't want to talk about it anymore," he said swiftly.

Aris nodded.

They were working on a hard case and it was not unusual for her to stay late. Aris worked the long hours without complaint.

"Do you need me late again tonight?" Aris asked him, noting the shiner was almost healed.

"Yes," he said brusquely, without looking at her. "You might as well plan on dinner here."

"Okay."

Around six, Aris asked John what he wanted for dinner.

"Whatever," he said dismissively.

"Chinese or Italian?" she asked him.

John looked up, his eyes tired. "You know what. I know the best Italian place, just around the corner from here. Let's go there, get the hell out of this office."

Aris was surprised.

"Sure," she said, her heart pounding. Of course she was being silly, this wasn't a date.

They went down the street two blocks and were soon seated in a dim Italian restaurant.

"You never leave the office for lunch," John commented as he opened his menu.

"No," Aris said. She saved money by bringing her lunch. She ate in the office while John went out.

"That's too bad; there's a lot of nice places around here," he said.

"Yeah," Aris looked around. "This place is great."

John half-smirked.

"What?"

"I used to meet Chloe here for lunch; she hated it."

Aris fingered her menu.

"You should get the Pomodoro," John told her.

Aris followed his advice. They stayed at the restaurant for at least two hours. They laughed and talked. Sometime during the middle of the meal, John stopped treating her like an employee.

"How did you come by your name?" he asked her.

Aris winced but decided to tell him the truth. "I was named after the cat."

His black eyes bulged. "What?"

Aris nodded.

"That's a new one."

Aris blushed.

"I like it," he said earnestly. "What about your family?"

"What about them?" Aris sipped her wine.

"Do they live around here?" he asked.

"I don't even live around here," she sidestepped.

"Where do you live?" he asked.

"Oakland."

John leaned forward until he was inches from her. "I'd really like to see your place."

Aris felt herself go limp. Was he propositioning her? If she accepted, tomorrow would she find herself a fool out of a job? John pulled back.

"I'm sorry," he said contritely. "Too much wine. I didn't mean to scare you."

"No, no," Aris said quickly. "I just didn't expect-"

"Me to sexually harass you," John supplied.

Aris laughed. "You aren't."

"Are you sure?" he asked her intently.

"I am sure."

"But you don't want to show me your place?"

"Not right now," Aris said pertly.

John laughed. "I have a great idea. I have to go to this thing this weekend. Some benefit. Would you come with me?"

Aris balked, remembering the horrible Christmas party.

"I have a better idea, why don't you come over for dinner instead?"

"Ditch my charitable obligations?"

Aris nodded, her heart in her throat.

"Aris is a bad girl," he said, reaching up to finger one of her golden curls.

She blushed.

"I like it."

His voice was mellow, dreamy. Aris felt her body tighten in response. John grinned at her and she smiled back. And just like that, she held John Prince and his secluded glittering world in her freshly manicured hands.

For the next few months, Aris suspended John over herself, like the paper bird he had once given her. She worshiped at the altar of John Prince and he seemed to revel in it. She was desperate for those shiny, black eyes on her.

Aris loved his flirtatious and easygoing manner. His ready smile and unending supply of confidence amazed her.

"When am I going to meet this guy?" Kristin asked, annoyed. She was laying on Aris' bed, thumbing through a magazine.

"Soon," Aris promised.

"You guys have been dating forever and I haven't seen him one time," Kristin flopped onto her belly. "I wish we still lived together," she sighed dramatically. "I love Oakland."

Aris said nothing; John hadn't liked her apartment in Oakland. He'd asked her if she was going to move soon.

"For what that temp company is billing you at, you could get a nicer place in San Francisco, or close by anyway."

He wrinkled his nose at her bohemian little neighborhood. He blithely ignored the homeless people begging in doorways. He found her place to be too small. "I feel like I'm suffocating in here. Don't you feel closed in? It's so small."

"I don't get half of what they bill me out for," she said. "I like to send a little money to my Gram, that's why I don't have a nicer place."

"Well, you deserve one," he said, putting his arm around her and drawing her close.

Aris looked at Kristin and wondered if John would like her.

"How about we all go out to dinner one night this week?" Kristin suggested.

"Um."

Kristin studied her face. "You don't want me to meet him."

"No," Aris said quickly. "That's not it."

Aris tried to put Kristin off as long as she could. She managed a few more months but finally, in September, she had run out of excuses.

Kristin was hosting a charity event and she wanted Aris and John to come.

"Didn't you say he was kind of rich?"

"Yes," Aris admitted.

"Great, come to the drag show and have him spend some big bucks at the auction," Kristin said, flashing her bright smile.

Aris had been vague about the all male drag revue when she told John. It was probably going to be pretty rowdy. She wasn't sure if John would like it. She mentioned it to him, hoping he would say no, but he didn't.

"We have to go and support your friend, don't we?" he said easily.

For the past few months, they'd been spending all their time together. She hadn't met any of his friends and he hadn't met hers. They'd stayed in the cozy cocoon of new love, barely even noticing the passing of time.

"Besides, I'd love to meet a friend of yours," John said.

"I haven't met any of yours," Aris countered.

John frowned.

"What?"

Was he keeping her from his friends on purpose? The thought hadn't occurred to her until then. Maybe he was ashamed of her; maybe she was just some girl to sleep with and nothing more.

"Nothing," he said. "It's just that-"

"What?"

"I can't really tell anyone I'm dating you."

"Why not?"

She was crestfallen. Her paranoia was justified; he was ashamed of her.

"Because of work. You would lose your job for sure. I can't say what they would do to me."

Relief washed over her in clean waves.

"I can ask to be placed somewhere else," she offered.

"No, no," John said quickly. "Don't do that."

"Why not?"

He paused. "We don't really know what this is, Aris. I would hate for you to lose this great job. Marjorie is warming up to the idea of getting you on full time."

"Yes, but I feel weird working for you," she said. "It would be better if I moved on anyway."

John frowned at her again. He was displeased with her.

"Promise me you won't do anything yet."

The night of the show, John picked Aris up from her apartment.

"Kristin is meeting us here," Aris told him.

Kristin ended up being an hour late. John was angry.

"What kind of a person does this?" he fumed.

Aris did her best to placate him. Kristin finally showed up. When Aris opened the door, she tried not to groan. Kristin was wearing an outrageous outfit; her hair was three different colors. Her multiple piercings and tattoos stood out in relief.

"Sorry babe," she said to Aris. "You know how it is."

Kristin stepped into the small living room and John eyed her up and down. She was dressed in a pair of gold tights, short-shorts, and a green shirt that read, Fuck You. I'm Irish. Her make-up was garish. His eyes showed shock and then disgust, which he covered up quickly with a bland look.

"You're late," he said to Kristin.

"You must be the mysterious Mr. Prince," Kristin said, putting emphasis on the mister.

John kept his hands in his pocket.

"You're nothing like I pictured," he said.

"What did you picture?" she asked, grinning slightly.

"Someone more like Aris, I guess," he said dully.

Kristin turned from John to Aris and said, "Listen, I'm really late, so we have to leave, like, now."

Aris nodded and grabbed her purse.

"I think we'll sit this one out," John said smoothly, as he grabbed Aris' hand.

Aris did nothing. She stood there as Kristin narrowed her eyes at them. She wanted to protest but part of her thought John was right, Kristin had left them waiting for an hour and now she was demanding they leave right away.

"Aris?" Kristin quirked a brow at her.

"John's got an early golf game tomorrow," Aris said. "If you had been on time, maybe we could have made it."

"John has an early golf game," Kristin repeated.

"I'm sorry," Aris said feelingly.

John smirked.

Kristin looked at them both for a second and then bounded out the door.

"Are all your friends like her?" he asked when Kristin was gone.

"Like what?" Aris bristled.

"So colorful."

"She's pretty much my only close friend."

John nodded, his eyes thoughtful.

In November, Aris shyly asked John if he would like to meet Gram. She hoped Gram and John would get along better than Kristin and John.

"The infamous Gram?" he grinned, and she felt an answering smile curve her lips.

When they pulled up, Gram came out on the little white porch, shading her eyes with her hand. Aris quickly assessed the house: peeling white paint, weeds growing in the cracks in the walkway. She glanced at John. If he had any objection to the little house, he hid it well.

"Come on in, kids; I got some cookies fresh out of the oven for you."

John grinned and loped up the path to the porch.

"Chocolate chip?" he asked.

"You betcha," Gram said with an answering smile.

The three of them sat around the kitchen table, drinking milk and eating cookies. The conversation flowed easily and John seemed to be at home in the tiny green and white cottage. Aris let out a breath. John took both ladies out to dinner at the local diner. Aris watched his face for telltale signs that he was disgusted with the greasy spoon, but it was well shuttered. After, they went home and watched an old movie on TV.

Aris studied Gram as she watched the film. For the first time, she realized Gram looked old and fragile. Her white hair was piled on top of her head; her face was pale and deep lines were etched in her sagging skin. She was still a good-looking woman, but she looked tired. Aris wondered if it was such a good idea for her to be so far away from Gram.

The next morning, John slept late. Aris got up and went out to the garden; she knew Gram would be out there. She liked to have her coffee first thing in the morning on the back porch. A stifling fog hung over the barren yard.

"This winter is going to be a long one," Gram commented.

Aris sat across from her at the little outdoor table. Mist filtered through the cold air.

"Gram, I was thinking," she started.

"No," Gram said stoutly.

"You don't even know what I'm going to say," she protested.

"Sure I do," Gram sipped her coffee from her chipped, blue mug and gazed levelly at her. "You think I should move to the city, or worse, you should move back here. Well, save your breath. I wouldn't have you. You don't belong here, Aris, any more than I belong in the city.

"I can see you're having trouble getting around," Aris said. "You're all alone out here. If something should happen, I'd never forgive myself."

"What do you think is going to happen? I'm going to fall and break my hip? I'm going to have a heart attack in the garden? Honey, I'm seventy-five years old. My days are numbered whether you live here or somewhere else."

"Don't be so morbid, Gram!" Aris exclaimed.

Gram rolled her eyes. "I'm just stating the facts."

"Don't," Aris said with a small smile. "You sure you're okay?"

"Aris, I'm fine. I'm not alone. I'm probably out more than you are. I always have people coming over. Just had a doctor's appointment last week and I'm in better shape than most women my age. You don't worry about me, you hear?"

"Okay, Gram," Aris said, resigned.

"Now," Gram said, leaning across the table. "Let's talk about this boy you've brought to meet me. You met his family? He treat you well? You like him?"

Aris tilted her head and thought a moment. "No, I haven't yet met the family. Yes, he treats me well, and yes, I like him."

"You love him, Aris?" Gram asked quietly.

Aris closed her violet eyes, her sooty, black lashes making crescents on her cheeks. She was lucky; unlike many blondes, she had dark eyelashes and she never had to draw in her eyebrows. In truth, she was not entirely sure, but if it wasn't love, it was certainly the closest she'd ever come. She opened her eyes and said, "Yes."

Gram regarded her with shrewd eyes, but said nothing.

They returned from Gram's house and Aris was in high spirits.

"That went well," she said.

John glanced at her. "Did you think it wouldn't?"

"I was worried," she admitted.

John laughed. "You're always worried. How could I not love Gram?" he asked.

"How could she not love you?" Aris asked.

John softened. "She's a sweet, old lady," he said. "I can see why you send her money every month. She doesn't have much does she?"

Aris was silent. So he'd noticed the worn furniture and peeling paint.

"You know what we ought to do?" he asked.

"Hmmm?"

"We should hire someone to go out there and paint the house. Inside and out."

Aris said nothing. Gram would hate that. "Maybe.'"

John cut his black eyes to her. Aris shifted uncomfortably in her seat.

The following Monday, Marjorie called Aris into her office.

She was seated at her steely, gray desk, her hands folded in front of her.

"Have a seat, Aris. I'll make this quick."

They were going to hire her permanently. It was finally going to happen; Aris hid a grin. That meant a hefty raise.

Marjorie leveled her gray eyes on her.

"Mr. Prince is very impressed with your work," she began. "He seems to think we should take you on a permanent hire."

Aris nodded. "It's been a pleasure to work for him."

"I'm sure it has."

Marjorie cleared her throat and then continued. "Yes, it has come to our attention that you and Mr. Prince are involved in a romantic relationship."

Aris stared at Marjorie blankly.

"That's against company policy. I'm afraid we have to let you go."

Aris sank back into the chair. What was going to happen to John?

Marjorie watched her, superiority gleaming in her eyes.

"We don't tolerate this kind of behavior here at MacDonald, Dempsey & Porter. We simply do not. Furthermore, I have taken the liberty of informing your employer, San Francisco Staffing, and they will no longer be using your services."

Aris gaped at her. The last was said with relish and Aris realized the old woman had been waiting for something like this. She disliked Aris from the start.

"On a more personal note, I think you are disgusting. You'll never get ahead by sleeping your way to the top."

Marjorie wagged her bony finger at Aris.

"That is all," she said dismissively. "Pack your things and go."

A fierce anger rose up in Aris; her throat burned with it. She squashed it down.

"What will happen to John?" she asked. Maybe she could do something to help him; she wanted to make sure he didn't get fired.

Marjorie looked down her hawkish nose. "That's really none of your business."

Aris got up from the chair. "Please, if there's anyone I can talk to, this wasn't his fault."

"Stupid girl, nothing will happen to him. He's a Prince."

Aris slipped out the door and made her way to John's office. People watched her bustle down the gray halls and she wondered if they knew. He was not there when she returned and she thought about waiting for him but spied Marjorie watching her from across the hall. A knot of women had gathered around Marjorie's doorway. They all watched Aris gather her lunch bag and the couple of possessions she'd brought to work: a coffee mug, a small pot of African Violets.

"These temps, why do they bring anything? They're called temporary for a reason." Aris ignored the women in the hall as she left the office.

"She must've thought she was hot shit, sleeping with him. As if John Prince would ever think about someone like her seriously."

Aris felt her face grow hot with tears and she wondered where John was. She left several messages with him; when he finally called her back he had been unconcerned.

"Yeah, MacDonald called me while I was at the deposition this morning. Gave me some bullshit speech and told me to 'keep it in my pants.' It's no big deal," John laughed.

He laughed.

"Everyone thinks I was trying to sleep my way to the top and they said that you'd never take me seriously. For Christ's sake, John, I am out of a job."

"You're upset." He sounded surprised.

"Hey, we don't all land on our feet, John Prince."

He was silent. "Didn't you tell me not that long ago that you'd be able to be placed somewhere else?"

"She told the staffing company. She said they didn't want to use me anymore."

John swore. "That uppity bitch."

Aris felt a small beam of satisfaction go through her.

"Call them," he said. "She might've just been saying that."

"Maybe you're right," Aris said, hope flaring.

"A Prince never takes no for an answer, honey."

"I'm not a Prince," Aris said.

"Maybe you should be," John suggested.

Aris was silent.

"Hey, I've got to go, but I will be over after work, okay?"

"Okay," she said in a small voice.

"Aris, stop worrying," he ordered. "Everything will work out."

The staffing company didn't return any of her calls; it was their way of saying they didn't want her anymore. She decided to take some temporary holiday work at a department store. John had not been happy.

"You're better than that," he said. "You're smarter than that."

"I don't have a lot of choices right now," she said.

"We could move in together," John suggested.

"I don't know," she said.

"My girlfriend should not be working retail. It's bad for our image," he teased.

"Girlfriend?"

John pulled her into his lap.

"Of course."

Aris beamed.

Chapter 10

Aris was getting ready for a party in Napa. She examined her red dress before she slipped it on. It was one of the few pieces of clothing that John had not picked out. She pulled a face. John laughed at her nervousness and told her it was just practice before the big leagues. It was her first official public duty as John's fiancée.

"What is it again?" Aris asked as she ran her fingers through her hair.

"The Prince family is being honored for their charitable contributions to the community," John said as he slipped on his tuxedo jacket.

"Where is it being held?"

"The vineyard, but we'll end up back at Granny's house," John said.

"Granny's not there," Aris said.

"No, Disby still lives there though."

"Sad, about your Grandma," Aris said.

"You're thinking about your Gram?" John asked.

Aris nodded. It had been too long since she had visited Gram and she promised herself she would go see her soon.

"Do you like the dress?" Aris was careful to check with him after the debacle of the too-short black shorts.

John nodded. "Too bad your hair's so short though. That dress would look great with your hair curled and piled on your head."

Aris shrugged.

"I went to the safety deposit box today," John said.

"Oh?"

"I pulled these out for you."

John presented her with two black, velvet boxes. One contained a glittering diamond necklace and the other, a matching bracelet. She'd never seen anything like them. There were so many diamonds; both the necklace and bracelet were extremely heavy.

"They're Mother's, but she said you could wear them tonight."

Aris accepted the jewels with shaking hands.

As John and Aris drove up the long drive, she lifted her hand to the back of her head and pulled slightly at the ends of her hair, the pain waking her up. The front of the house was littered with long limousines; they looked like shining, black beetles idling before the graceful, white house. She stepped onto the drive; the penetrating heat slapped her with a suddenness that made her jerk back and long for the icy interior of John's car. The house sat calm and silent while the anxious, idling limousines waited. Aris knew the calm was misleading. She could sense the electric chaos zipping through the house. As if to prove her intuition, Tinsley came tearing out of the front door with a scream.

"I won't! I won't! I won't!" Her pretty blonde hair trailed behind her as she made a dash from the porch to the wide front lawn.

Janice was not far behind. She had outdone herself in a gold, lame couture gown. Aris raised her eyebrows at the sight of her. Janice was walking as fast as she could after the running Tinsley; her spiked, black heels clearly made the endeavor difficult.

"Young lady, come back here!" Janice screamed after the girl. Tinsley looked back once and stopped on the lawn a few feet in front of John and Aris.

"I won't do it!" Tinsley stamped her feet in indignation as her face screwed up in disgust. "That's gross!" she said, chastising her grandmother, and then she ran.

Aris was biting the inside of her mouth to keep from laughing. John noticed and sent her a warning glance. Janice was on the porch, staring after Tinsley, her jaw set in anger. She grabbed one of the pillars to steady herself and then spotted John and Aris.

John walked up the porch steps and Janice threw up her arms.

"Honestly, John! What kind of parents are Sarah and Paul? Sarah had no problem performing duties such as these when she was Tinsley's age. That child is a hellion! I simply cannot abide by it!"

From behind Aris, a frisson and then: "Is she ready for her close-up?"

The whisper in her ear sent feathery tendrils gliding across her skin. She did not have to turn her head to know it was Rhys. He smelled of mint and soap and clean soil drenched in fresh rain.

The torrid heat licked at her bared neck.

Rhys stayed to her left, hands in pockets, and watched the scene on the porch. He was close enough for her to feel the warmth from his body, and Aris stiffened with awareness. Janice was ranting and John was patting her back. The door swung open. Sarah came onto the porch; she tapped Janice on the shoulder. Janice turned around and Sarah fixed her hematite eyes on her mother.

"Why is my daughter running through this house like a wild person? Mother, what did you say to her?"

Janice was all smiles and lash fluttering. "Nothing."

Sarah showed her teeth and thrust her white chin out. "Don't you lie to me! Tinsley came running through the backdoor and locked herself in the powder room. What did you do?"

"Nothing! It's just..."

"What?" Sarah said sharply.

"Well, I told her that when we went onstage to get the award, it would be nice if she gave Mr. Thompson a little kiss. That's all." Janice shrugged her shoulders dismissively.

Sarah's face twisted. "Mother! How could you? Now I'll be lucky if I can get her to go at all!"

She turned on her heels, her floaty black dress swirling around her calves, and charged through the door. "Paul! Paul! Where are you? Did you get her out of the bathroom?"

John turned to Janice and he looked at her, chagrined. "Mom, don't you think that's a bit much for a kid her age? Mr. Thompson has Bell's palsy."

Janice sniffed and smiled slightly. "Oh, John. Children these days are so antiseptic."

Rhys began to walk toward the porch steps. Aris felt a void where he had stood. His black suit fit him perfectly. He loped up the stairs and grabbed Janice by both shoulders. "Nonsense, Johnny Boy. Why in the world would kissing an old, liver-spotted stranger with half his face falling down be scary for a eight-year-old?"

He grinned, his mouth a sudden explosion of perfect, white teeth.

"Rhys," Janice said primly, shrugging his hands off her shoulders. "When you put it that way, perhaps that's a bit much for Tinsley."

She turned to go inside and Rhys stepped forward and kissed her on the cheek. Janice was unsure how to handle the sudden affection. She nodded and walked away.

John looked down on Aris from the porch. "Honey, you coming in?"

Aris ascended the steps, aware that they were both watching her. The door swung open and Sarah thrust herself onto the porch.

"Well, isn't this the scandal! Thanks to Mother, my daughter is refusing to even go! Who's going to stay home with her? I can't believe this!"

Sarah stopped long enough in her rant to upbraid Aris.

"What on earth are you wearing?" she said disgustedly. "What did you do to your hair?"

Rhys glanced at Sarah, snorted in derision. Sarah lifted her hand dismissively. "I see someone lent you the diamonds."

Aris made no answer.

"I'm rather surprised you're wearing them. They don't really suit you-"

"She can watch Rin Tin Tin," Rhys interrupted as he chucked his chin toward Aris.

"Huh?" Aris asked dumbly.

"You. Aris. You can watch Tinsley." Her name in his mouth sounded like something sweet, something to be savored.

"Why doesn't Paul watch her?" asked Morgan as she tumbled out of the front door, followed by Disby.

"Because Paul has to be with me, that's why," Sarah said exasperated.

"The child might feel better having her father with her. I mean, she doesn't really know

Aris all that well," Morgan slurred and Aris realized she was drunk.

"No, Aris is fine," Sarah waved her hand at Aris in her, oh that, gesture.

"All settled. Come Morgan, let's get in the car." Disby practically dragged Morgan off the porch and onto the front lawn. Aris watched Morgan walk across the lawn in her towering Louboutin heels, thinking she was so drunk, surely she couldn't make it across the uneven grass to the gravel drive without at least stumbling. She and Disby were holding hands; Morgan never faltered.

The family began to pour out of the house like blood from a gushing wound. They were laughing and chattering as they headed across the lawn to the drive. Aris noticed J.J. was not among them. Helen looked odd, wearing a billowy organza dress and clunky heels. Jane was elegant in black. Gus was guiding her onto the lawn while Minnie, looking put out, followed behind them in a shapeless, ivory, sequined dress. Paul Hodge, dowdy in his ill-fitting tuxedo, came out with Janice on one arm and Sarah on the other. Marie, rail-thin and pale, came through the door and gave Aris a once-over before her lower lip trembled in humor. Aris turned to John.

"How long will you be?"

John grimaced. "These things can sometimes run a little long, and they're serving dinner, but we planned on dessert here."

"Okay."

Aris reached up to kiss him, aware of eyes on her back and knowing exactly to whom they belonged.

Still the horde came through the door, cousins upon cousins, and John got swept up into them. Finally, the door shut with a bang and Aris was alone on the porch. The late afternoon pulsed with the sweltering heat. She watched them all gather themselves into the waiting cars. The trees began to toss restlessly. An uneasy breeze swept the barren porch and Aris shuddered. She was glad not to be going. Janice and Sarah lowered themselves into the car and Paul Hodge scrambled in after them. Before he got into the waiting limo, John sought her out, raised his hand to her. Aris raised her own in a gesture of farewell and turned to go inside without waiting to watch him drive away.

"Tinsley? It's Aris. Where are you?"

Aris heard no answer, and the great house seemed to give a tired sigh. She walked further back into the dim heat and heard no noise.

"Where are you, honey?"

Silence stretched before her; she walked down the hall toward the back study.

Tinsley was there on the couch, small and blonde. Aris went into the room and sat next to her. She had a sudden memory of her childhood, the sickening stench of cigarettes and gin, and her mother's too-tight hugs.

Tinsley twisted herself into a little ball.

"You? They left me with you?" Tinsley cried incredulously. "I don't even know you!"

Aris was unsure of what to say to the child. She had a valid point; she did not know Aris that well.

"Um, I think I have some gum in my purse," Aris tried.

"So what!"

"How about we go exploring?"

"What do you mean?"

"Uh, let's check out the attic."

"Why?" Tinsley demanded.

Aris thought quickly, but nothing came. "Why not?"

Surprisingly, Tinsley seemed to accept this.

"Okay, let's go." She reached for Aris' hand and Aris was startled at how small her fingers were. Glancing out the window, she saw something moving: tall, lean, golden skin, black hair. Outside, the long branches of the willows swung. The green pond rippled uneasily. Her red dress was clinging to her; sweat trailed a cold hand down her back.

"Come on." Tinsley tugged on her hand impatiently.

Aris kicked off her shoes and they padded slowly to the stairs.

Second floor. "What's that noise?" Tinsley asked.

Aris heard it; it sounded like a bird or something.

"I'm not sure. Let's go."

Third floor. The noise was more insistent. Tinsley's feet slowed.

"What if it's a ghost?" she asked, alarm in her black eyes.

"That's silly," Aris said.

"What if it's Grandpa?" Tinsley asked in a stage whisper. "Grandpa Johnny as a ghost."

Aris imagined Johnny Prince hanging around the attic, like Banquo's ghost. She shook herself.

"Don't be silly. Grandpa's in heaven," she said firmly.

Attic stairs. "I don't want to go up."

"It's fine," Aris said as she imagined bats circling the rafters. "It's probably nothing."

"I don't want to go," Tinsley said stubbornly.

Suddenly, the attic door opened, causing Tinsley and Aris to jump and cry out.

"Jesus Fucking H. Christ!" Aris screamed, using Kristin's favorite epithet.

"Sorry, I didn't mean to scare you guys," Rhys said as he stepped out of the darkened doorway.

"You!" Aris exclaimed.

"Who are you?" Tinsley asked confused.

"I'm your cousin Rhys, and you're Rin Tin Tin."

"No one calls me that!" Tinsley exclaimed, delighted.

"I just did."

Tinsley screwed up her face. "Were you making that noise up there, trying to scare us?"

He glanced at Aris and laughed. "No. I was up there looking for something."

"Did you find it?" Tinsley asked.

"Nope."

"We're going exploring," Tinsley said, as Rhys looked Aris over with hot, green eyes.

"You cut your hair," he said to Aris quietly. He reached out with his hand and fingered a short, blonde lock. Aris shivered.

"Aunt Minnie said she looks like a Haight Street dyke," Tinsley beamed.

Rhys raised his eyebrows, amused. He removed his fingers and Aris quelled the urge to pull him back to her as he stepped past them.

Aris and Tinsley entered the attic, Tinsley holding onto Aris' hand tightly. The attic was hot and filled with late afternoon sunlight, the dark corners lit up. Aris shuddered, despite the heat. A window was open at the far end of the attic and a rack of old clothes was swaying with a breeze.

"Here's the noise we heard," Aris said as she walked to the window to close it. She crossed the floor, hot, with her mind full of ghosts. Once at the window, she looked out, taking in the emerald grass, the stale, cloudy pond, the trees moving in a virulent breeze.

Aris thought of Rhys and her stomach fluttered briefly. The breeze coursing through the window became more insistent, as if to mimic what was happening inside her. From somewhere below, a door slammed. Aris jumped.

"Let's get outta here," Tinsley suggested.

"Good idea," Aris agreed.

Aris and Tinsley got some frozen dinners and settled down in the study, and Tinsley fell asleep watching TV. Aris was unsure of what had happened on the attic stairs. She didn't want to think about it. She wrapped her arms around herself; even though the heat sat on her skin like a persistent bug; she felt a chill. She blindly watched the television, praying Rhys did not reappear. She sat next to the sleeping little girl, tensed, waiting for Rhys to walk through the door or appear like a specter outside the window, but she didn't see him again.

About two hours later, she heard cars coming up the driveway. Footsteps on the front porch drew her back to reality. The house, so still for so long, suddenly filled with noise. Tinsley awoke with a start. She sat up and rubbed her eyes, looking around, disoriented. Aris tried to smile at her.

"Aris, how sweet of you and Rhys to volunteer to stay with Tinsley. Though I daresay, it shouldn't take two of you to watch one child."

Janice was standing perfectly framed in the doorway of the study. She bared her teeth in a malicious smile.

Aris stuttered. "Um, well, I'm not exactly sure. I mean, Rhys didn't volunteer. Just me. I did."

Janice nodded. "He was here with you, wasn't he?"

"Yeah, I guess. I mean, I saw him, but he wasn't-"

Janice ignored her. "Tinsley, you look like you just had a nap!"

The eight-year-old nodded. "I did. A long one. I'm hungry," she said. "I want everyone to call me Rin Tin Tin now!" Tinsley declared as she hopped off the green, velvet sofa and scampered off in search of food. Janice wrinkled her nose at the declaration and turned to Aris.

"The ceremony was lovely, Aris. It's such a shame you couldn't be there. It was breathtaking. Mother was pleased, I think, and the place was packed. You know, the Prince family has done a lot for this community. Since you came from rather humble beginnings, I'm sure you can appreciate that."

Janice sat neatly beside Aris on the arm of the sofa; she looked ready to spring up at a moment's notice.

"Rhys is Helen's only son," Janice said with a funny smile. "He's very unusual, kind of a troublemaker in his youth. He disappeared years ago."

Aris nodded again.

"What about you? It's a shame you never even left the house tonight, after borrowing the diamonds."

Janice gave her a look, black eyes snapping. "John tells me you're going back to school. Maybe you should consider getting a job," Janice suggested lightly. "A real job."

"Uh huh," Aris said, her head cocked to the noise in the hall.

Morgan glided into the room, her bushy, red hair a cloud around her red face.

"There you are Jan! J.J.'s mistress is here," Morgan said bluntly.

Janice got to her feet at once. "What do you mean?"

"Just what I said."

"Does Olivia know who she is?"

"I don't think so," Morgan said haltingly.

"As long as Olivia doesn't know," Janice said.

"Everyone else knows! The press is here!"

"If J.J. wants her to leave, he'll tell her to leave."

"Aris. I didn't notice you there," Morgan said brightly. "I didn't see you at the dinner. Where were you?"

"I stayed here with Tinsley."

"Oh," Morgan's eyes raked over her. "Where did all your beautiful blonde hair go?" she asked, disappointed.

"I cut it," Aris responded, her hand automatically going to the back of her head and stroking her soft hair.

"Why ever would you do such a thing?"

Morgan came over to the sofa and put a heavily ringed hand to Aris' head. "All that beautiful hair, gone. What a damn shame."

"Yes, Morgan, it's a tragedy of the first degree," Janice said drolly.

"It is," Morgan argued drunkenly. "Poor thing looks like a boy."

"She does not," Janice said dismissively.

John came into the room swiftly. Before he could make it to the sofa, Morgan pulled back her hand and cried, "John, I cannot believe you let your fiancée cut all that beautiful hair! What were you thinking?"

"Auntie Morgan, Aris doesn't need my permission to get a haircut," John said, placing his hand on the top of Aris' head.

"I bet you don't even like it," Morgan said slyly.

Aris looked at the three Princes towering over her, felt the heavy weight of John's hand on her head and immediately got to her feet.

Morgan craned her neck to look outside. "What on earth is she doing? That new maid is putting slices of cake on bread plates! Doesn't she know any better? Where did Disby find her?" Morgan asked as she hurried out of the room.

"Cake on bread plates, what a fucking tragedy." A voice, low and husky, came from the doorway.

Rhys stepped into the room; the air around him shimmered with manic energy. Janice frowned.

"Here we are, one big, happy family," he said.

"Yes, we are," Janice said, looking at her nephew with piercing eyes. "We missed you at the ceremony, Rhys."

He shrugged. "I decided to stay here and take a nap. I didn't think anyone would notice."

"I did."

He shrugged again.

Janice squared her shoulders. "Excuse me, there are some people I need to say hello to."

Rhys grinned at her retreating figure. He clapped John on the back.

"Are those banquets as boring as I remember?" Rhys asked John.

"Worse," John said, laughing. "We should have a drink in the grapes, for old time's sake," he said to Rhys without sparing Aris a glance.

Rhys nodded. "Why not?"

John made to leave with Rhys, then turned, as though he suddenly remembered his fiancée.

"Honey, do you want to come with us?"

Rhys did not look back, but kept walking toward the door. Once he reached the doorway, he stopped and waited, keeping his back to them.

Aris glanced at his broad back.

"You two go ahead," Aris said. "I'll just freshen up."

"Okay," John said as he loped away.

Aris sat down on the green sofa to pull on her shoes. She noticed a blister forming on her big toe.

"Damn," she whispered. Aris shrugged and decided to go barefoot.

She walked through the narrow hallway to the large living room. The picture windows faced Astoria's garden, lit by hidden lights. The flowers were really starting to bloom; pinks and reds and orange crushed together in a riotous mass.

The house was stuffed with people. The loud buzzing of conversation hummed in her ears. She didn't know anyone there. She spotted J.J., drink in hand, surrounded by men in black and gray suits. Probably people from his office. A beautiful Asian woman hovered near his elbow. Must be his mistress. Disby was seated on the blue sofa between two handsome older men. She looked distinctly uncomfortable.

Aris felt her stomach rumble and decided to get some cake. She settled herself outside under Astoria's tree. The evening breeze swept across the green grass and Aris watched the stars come out. She kept her eyes downcast, trying to discourage anyone from speaking with her. From time to time she scanned the grounds for John and Rhys, but she didn't see either of them.

She was tired and ready to leave. She left the old willow and went to find John. She walked gingerly around the grounds, mindful of her bare feet.

Aris had finished her tour of the front and back, and resigned herself to the fact that she would have to go back inside to search for John. She came in through the kitchen door. Geraldine and Simeon were both in the kitchen directing a handful of unfamiliar maids in their duties.

Aris slipped past the hustle and bustle as quickly as she could, earning an exasperated look from Geraldine. She entered the front parlor; the people inside were all dressed in black, a murder of chattering crows. Aris started to glance down at her red dress, then stopped herself. The air was thick with the heat, clogged with smothered emotions. She felt like she was suffocating.

"There you are!" Jane was to her left, her champagne-colored hair dazzling, her black eyes sparkling. "I didn't see you at the ceremony," she commented.

"I stayed here with Tinsley," Aris explained as she spotted Rhys behind Jane speaking with a man she didn't know.

"You're wearing the diamonds," Jane commented, fingering her own elaborate emerald necklace.

"Yes."

"They don't really suit you," Jane said, puzzled. "I'm not sure why."

Jane grasped the elbow of a gentleman to her right. He turned. It was the man with the beard Aris had seen her with at Tinsley's birthday party. Graying brown hair hung around his ears; over his eyes hung thick and bushy, gray eyebrows. He had dark circles under his eyes, sunken cheekbones and a melting jawline. His mouth was obscured by his close-cut, graying beard. He was a portly man; he looked awkward in his tuxedo.

"Have you met Bernie?"

"No, I haven't," Aris said politely, her eyes surreptitiously darting around the room, looking for John, avoiding Rhys. Her eyes settled on a gentleman who had to be Mr. Thompson. It was evident he had Bell's palsy. He was indeed covered in liver spots and possessed a lopsided and thin mustache settled above his fleshy lips. No wonder Tinsley didn't want to kiss him.

Bernie held out his hand.

"Pleased to meet you, young lady," he said, peering over the top of his tortoiseshell glasses.

Aris grasped his sweaty hand in her own, pumped it a few times, and tried to pull away, but he held fast.

"You are whose daughter, now?"

"No one's. I mean, I'm Janice's daughter-in-law. Almost."

Bernie nodded, still clutching her hand.

"You have eyes like Liz Taylor. I bet you get that all the time," he grinned, small teeth coming to rest on his lower lip.

Aris forcibly pulled her hand out of his.

"I get it a lot," she affirmed with a wan smile. Rhys was still talking to the man, but his green eyes were locked onto Aris.

"Yes," Bernie mused, stroking his beard and eyeing her speculatively. "That's quite a ring there."

Aris glanced down at The Ring. She wanted to pull a Sarah and say, "oh, that?" but she couldn't bring herself to do it. Jane looked on, clearly embarrassed by the size of The Ring.

Minnie was steamrolling her way through the crowd, using her enormous bust as a weapon, headed right for Aris. Gus was chugging behind her like an old train engine.

"Aris," Minnie said curtly.

"Minnie, hello."

"Harrump," Minnie said.

"Hello, hello Aris. So good to see you, we were just looking for John. Can't seem to find him. Minnie's looking for a lawyer," Gus said eagerly, eyes on the dessert table, his hands reaching out for Aris' arm.

"Oh?" Bernie asked, his right eyebrow raised.

Minnie spared him a glance.

"Who are you?" she asked rudely.

"Minnie and Gus, this is my friend Bernie," Jane said smoothly.

"Pleased to make your acquaintance," Gus said, sticking out his fat hand.

The two men shook hands vigorously. Minnie looked on impatiently.

"Where's your fiancé?" she asked Aris.

Aris shrugged. "I was just looking for him myself."

She could feel Bernie's eyes on her; her face began to turn pink.

"I need him to recommend a good lawyer. I'm suing the idiot who rear-ended me last week," Minnie declared.

"Did you cut your hair?" Gus interrupted.

"Damn it Gustav! I was speaking! What is wrong with you? Don't you have any manners at all?" Minnie exploded.

Gus looked appropriately shamed, and shut his mouth with a snap.

"Of course she cut her hair! Just look at it; she took about three feet off."

Gus looked at his feet and mumbled something unintelligible.

"Where are your shoes?" Helen asked, coming up behind her. Aris caught a whiff of her fetid body odor and unconsciously held her breath. "You can't walk around barefoot, there's press here."

"I was getting a blister so I just left them off for a while," Aris explained, resisting the urge to glance at Rhys again.

"Humph," said Minnie. "That's because you wear cheap shoes."

Aris looked at her.

"Cheap shoes and all those diamonds," Minnie said sourly.

"You need to put your shoes on," Helen said, baring her stumpy, yellow teeth. "It's tacky."

Jane leaned in conspiratorially. "She's right darling, you should probably go put your shoes back on. Get a Band-Aid for that blister."

"You know, it's a shame to wear such cheap shoes with the diamonds," Helen said to Jane, who nodded.

Tinsley came up behind Aris and ducked around her legs to peer curiously into the group.

"Hello, little one," Bernie said as he bent down with an ingratiating smile.

"Jesus Fucking H. Christ! That's a big booger up there in your nose," Tinsley observed.

Rhys, who was just close enough to hear, suddenly laughed out loud, causing Jane, Helen, and Minnie to look at him reproachfully. He ignored them and shot Aris a meaningful glance before he walked away.

"Uh," Aris said, trying not to laugh.

"Where is Sarah?" Minnie fumed as Aris stole away.

She went to the study and grabbed her purple heels and her purse, muttering to herself. "I will put my shoes on when I'm damn good and ready."

"No time like the present," Rhys said from behind her.

"Oh!" Aris started. Her hands started to shake slightly.

"Sorry," he said politely. "I didn't mean to scare you, honey." He tossed the endearment out lazily at her feet.

"That's okay," Aris said as she sat on the sofa to put on her shoes. Rhys pulled off his jacket and tie and sat elegantly in the brown wingback chair in the corner. He studiously rolled up the sleeves of his white shirt and yanked open three buttons. Aris got a glimpse of a smooth, brown chest. Her heart danced as she bent to pull on her shoes.

"Guess you're damn good and ready," he commented.

"Guess I am," Aris said. "Do you know where John is?"

"Looking for you," Rhys said, taking a sip of the amber liquid from the crystal glass in his hand.

"Oh," Aris said, her heart starting to hammer in her ears.

"Welcome home," he said.

Aris was unsure of how to respond, so she said nothing. Rhys didn't seem to expect a response anyway. She stood, unsteady in her shoes, her blister throbbing faintly.

"Aris. I've been looking for you," John said as he stepped into the room.

"I'm ready to go," Aris said without preamble.

"No," John said shortly. "We can't leave this early. People would be angry and insulted."

"I'm tired."

Rhys watched the exchange without bothering to disguise his interest.

"Another hour," John said. "Don't be difficult."

Aris sighed.

John grasped her arm and propelled her out of the study. Aris winced as her shoe rubbed against her blister.

"See you, man," John called to Rhys.

Behind them, Rhys made no answer.

Chapter 11

A few days after the party, Aris returned to Rhys' and resumed her work. The large double doors on the front of the building were open, and Aris called out as a mild breeze ruffled the papers inside. No one answered, so she set about to work. Around one, she pulled an apple out of her bag and perched on the brown leather chair. She ate quickly, wondering where Rhys was; she had not seen or heard him all day. The idea that he was lurking around the building, surreptitiously watching her, had a hot flush creeping up her neck. She was rifling through more papers when she heard his heavy tread on the stairs.

"It's too hot," he said. "You should stop for the day."

She looked up, caught momentarily in his green eyes.

He was again in jeans, with no shirt. His hands were covered with red paint. Aris glanced down at them.

"I usually paint up there. Better light."

"I should be finished in a few days." It came out nervously, and his elegant brow furrowed. A strange tension began to build and dip and sway between them.

Aris swallowed hard.

The heat rolled over her swiftly and she gave a mirage-like shimmer and felt cold sweat drip down her back. Rhys closed the gap between them quickly and reached out his hand. He closed his fingers around her arm; she watched his silver rings glint in the glitter of the sun.

"You okay?"

Aris nodded. The pressure of his arm felt like a vise. It was hot, wet with paint. She closed her eyes for a moment and thought his elegant and intricately carved rings were no match for The Ring.

Rhys pulled her closer to him.

"Maybe you should sit down for a minute."

"I'm fine."

"Yeah, you look it."

He maneuvered her with ease across the floor until her legs hit the back of a chair.

"Sit," he ordered softly, and pushed her gently into the waiting chair.

Aris tried to get up and he pushed her back.

"I'm fine, damn it!"

Rhys laughed at her.

He crouched down beside her, his face close to hers. His skin was surprisingly smooth, almost poreless; his emerald eyes were a mix of concern and amusement. His pretty mouth was twisted in a wry smile. He was too close; Aris wondered what it would be like to kiss him and flames licked at the inside of her thighs.

Rhys looked at her and his smile widened, as if he knew what she was thinking. Aris fought the urge to smile back, knowing he watched the battle in her face. Laughter bubbled up in his throat and he cut off a quick chuckle.

"Just sit there for a minute, alright? John wouldn't be too happy if I sent his bride-to-be home with heat stroke."

John.

His name was like a cold rag thrown in her face. Aris suddenly wished to be home.

"I'm fine now. I really am." She could hear the panicky note in her voice.

Rhys got up and backed away. His eyes were quizzical, but he said nothing.

"Come with me," he ordered.

Aris got up from the chair, her limbs were shaky.

"What?"

Rhys assessed her with his green eyes.

"I don't want to go back in the creek," she said petulantly.

Rhys laughed shortly.

"No. I have a better idea. Let's play hooky."

"What?"

Rhys grabbed her hand. It felt like an electric shock; she pulled her hand away quickly. He laughed again. "Trust me. Come on."

He grabbed a T-shirt slung over a nearby chair and pulled it over his head.

"Come on," he said again.

Aris followed him warily. He led her out to his truck and opened the passenger side door for her. She balked. "Where are we going?"

"Surprise," he said shortly.

Aris hesitated. "All the doors and windows are open in there. Anyone could come in and steal all those lovely paintings."

"Let 'em," he said. "Who cares?"

247

Aris jumped into the truck and watched Rhys shut her door and get into the driver's seat.

"Where are we going?"

"Some place cool."

She was keenly aware of him as they drove. The air was pulsing between them; she watched his hands on the steering wheel and felt something akin to hunger. He drove slowly into town and parked in front of the old movie theater.

"We're going to the movies?" she asked incredulously.

"Yep."

Aris looked up at the marquee. "We're going to see Red Dust?"

"Perfect movie for a hot day."

"You're a little odd," she commented as he bought their tickets.

Rhys laughed at her. "Air conditioned, baby."

The minute he called her baby, something shifted inside of her. She was acting like she was on a date. She was acting like she wasn't wearing that God-awful Ring. Aris carefully reigned herself in and rearranged her face into a more remote expression.

"I'll buy the popcorn," she offered coolly.

Rhys looked at her, his green eyes searching.

"Whatever you say."

They were the only ones in the theater. They sat through the movie, munching stale popcorn. Aris studiously avoided looking at Rhys in the flickering light. She wondered what she was doing. She felt the heat of him; her legs shifted. Despite the air conditioning, sweat ran down the back of her calves, rivulets slipped between her small breasts. She was waiting for him to grab her. She wanted him to. Her body was in a state of readiness, expectation, but he did nothing, said nothing. Aris put her hand on the armrest between them. She sighed deeply. Rhys reached out slowly; Aris fixed her eyes on the screen. He put his hand on the armrest next to her, then his fingers brushed hers. Aris felt an electric zip go up her arm. His fingers were warm and gentle; they brushed again, then rested against hers. They watched the rest of the movie like that. When it was over, Aris couldn't meet his green eyes. She felt like she'd just cheated on John. They drove back to his place in silence and Aris convinced herself that they were just sharing an armrest and nothing more. He didn't even know what he was doing; he wasn't even aware of his effect on her. She was the one who was making something out of nothing.

When they exited the truck, Aris went straight to her car.

"I didn't realize how late it was," she said hurriedly. "John will be upset if his dinner's late."

Rhys' black brows crested in disbelief.

"You're not really the June Cleaver kind of girl, are you?" he asked, watching her closely.

Aris shrugged and jumped in her car. "Thanks for the movie," she called.

"Take care, Aris."

She drove off; her name hung in the air. Aris, no longer a name, became a candied delicacy he'd thrust in the air between them.

When she stepped through the door at home, she expected to feel an immediate sense of normalcy, but she did not. Instead, she fought the urge to cry.

Something was going on between Rhys and that girl with young John's gaudy ring, Aris. Astoria knew it. She told the nurse she had to make a call to her daughter Helen, but when they brought her the phone, she couldn't remember Helen's number. Astoria didn't want to call any of her other children; she wanted to speak to Helen about this. After all, she was the boy's mother.

Astoria had seen it the night of the ceremony at the vineyard. The doctor at the home let her out for the whole night. Astoria felt like a sailor on shore leave. The home had her in bed by nine o'clock, usually. They liked to give her pills to make her sleep, but Astoria had stopped sleeping years ago. Some people, when they got old, slept more; some slept less. Astoria slept maybe one or two hours a night. That suited her just fine, but they didn't think so at the home. They kept telling her she needed her rest, and she wanted to tell them she'd have plenty of time to sleep when she was dead. They didn't like you to talk about death at the home. Ha! As if the residents weren't dropping like flies every day.

They allowed her to go to the ceremony in her wheelchair, and Astoria was excited to be back at her house for the party afterward. Geraldine wheeled her around the party for a little while. All the people were so surprised to see her.

"There, you see that?" Astoria asked Geraldine.

"Mmm hmmm, I sure do see that!"

Astoria was waving her hand toward Rhys, whose green eyes were locked on Aris as if she were the only person in the room.

"That's dangerous," Astoria said.

"Simeon used to look at me like that," Geraldine commented. "Mr. Johnny ever look at you like that?"

"Good Lord, no," Astoria said. "She's young John's girl. Not Rhys' girl."

The two women watched as Aris flicked her eyes at Rhys and then reddened and looked away.

"Yessir, that sure is dangerous," Geraldine agreed. "Damn dangerous."

Astoria patted her friend's hand. "I've missed you so much."

"You sure you're gonna get out of that place?"

"Of course I am," Astoria said indignantly. "They're just waiting for my fracture to heal up."

"Okay," Geraldine said, sounding dubious.

The two women watched as Rhys left the room. Aris quickly followed.

"Do you think-" Geraldine began.

"If they're not yet, they will be soon," Astoria answered.

"Mrs. Prince?"

The nurse was talking to her. Astoria snapped out of her reverie.

"Yes?"

"This is Dr. Millen. He's going to take over while Dr. Thompson is on vacation," the nurse explained, gesturing to the man beside her.

He was short and squat, with black, oily hair and a stiff, black goatee. Astoria disliked him instantly. He looked smug and superior. In Astoria's experience, that was never a good thing.

"Mrs. Prince, I've been looking over your chart and I think we can do better than this."

He spoke into his mobile as he scrolled through it.

"You know," she said. "It's more effective, when you are speaking to someone, if you actually look at them."

The doctor looked up from his phone and stared at her for a moment, then he shot a pointed look at the nurse.

"Yes, I think we can do much better," he said, ignoring her.

"Nurse, I'd like you to give Mrs. Prince this combination of meds instead. Dr. Thompson must be slipping," he said briskly as he wrote something on Astoria's chart. He was out of the room before Astoria could say a word. The nurse looked after him with shining eyes.

"He's the best on the staff," she informed Astoria. "You're lucky to have him."

"Why is he changing my medication?" Astoria asked the woman.

"Don't you worry about that, dear," the nurse said as she exited the room.

Rhys awoke from the dream with sweat lingering on his brow. The sheets were twisted around his legs, as if he'd been wrestling with something. The dream, the nightmare, was already fading. He could only remember hazy images. He shook out his hair and got out of the bed. The air was hot around him; the fan did little to cool off the place. It just pushed the hot air around.

He went downstairs and pushed open the door to the creek. The moon was high; silver light blanketed everything, like snow. He rubbed his face with his hands. Aris. The name, the syllables, glided over his tongue. He wanted to feel her, to taste her. Rhys didn't think about anyone or anything else. She was like poison, pumping through his blood. He put his feet in the cool water and breathed in. She was the poison, she was the antidote. If he'd ever wanted a woman this much before, he couldn't remember it. He waited for her to finish the damnable job she was doing with his paintings. His patience was reaching an end-point though; he was not going to be able to play the good boy much longer. A few more days and he'd never see her again.

John wasn't happy.

"What do you mean, you're not finished?" he asked, his face getting red. "It's been weeks."

"I know," Aris threw out, wondering how she would placate him. "I didn't really do enough work while he was gone."

"Why not?" John asked nastily as he tied his tie. He watched himself intently in the mirror.

"I don't know," Aris admitted. "No motivation I guess."

"This is getting ridiculous," John said as he yanked on his coat. "Finish it today," he ordered.

Aris gazed at him.

"I'm serious, Aris."

"Okay, John," Aris whispered.

Aris drove to Rhys' house, thinking this would be the last time she would see him alone. Her heart slid down to her stomach; she felt a heaviness settle on her shoulders. Then guilt bloomed inside her chest. John was right, she was drawing it out. Her loyalty was to John, not his strange, magnetized cousin.

So why, she asked herself, did she feel more comfortable sitting on the floor of Rhys' place than she did in her own house?

She remembered the first time she met John's friends. They weren't people from the office. They were rich. Aris never had any real idea about John's money until she met his friends. They were all poker-faced, swaggering men, with wives and girlfriends that looked like fashion models. Approval was meted out in small doses. Aris had been so nervous.

"Stop worrying," John chided her.

She looked at her new clothes. John had taken her shopping. They went to small boutiques, places she'd never even heard of. Everything was tailored.

They were going sailing with a group of people. "I've known them since grade school. Oh Aris, you know how it is. You all go to the same schools, end up working at the same places. It's a small world."

Rory and Cynthia met them at the dock. Rory was a tall Nordic god. Cynthia was short, with nervous hands and darting eyes.

"The doctor put me on something new," she told Aris as they walked down the dock. "What are you on?"

"Nothing," Aris said, feeling as though she should have been on something.

Cynthia shot her a look of disbelief.

"Let's go below, you can meet the other girls."

Aris dutifully followed as John and Rory slapped high fives with the other men. Below the deck, four women sat around a table in a semi-circle.

"This is John's new girl, everyone," Cynthia called to them. "Her name is Paris."

"Aris," Aris corrected shyly.

Cynthia leveled a look at her. "Really?"

"Yes."

"And you're dating John Prince?" one of the women at the table asked.

"Yes."

All the women laughed and Aris forced herself to join in.

"If you land him, it certainly won't be a misnomer," a blonde said.

"This is Bella," Cynthia said, pointing to the blonde. "Xanax."

Aris furrowed her brow as the other women laughed.

"Greta," Cynthia pointed to a brunette. "Klonopin."

"Elisa. Plain old Paxil for me." Another blonde extended her arm.

"I'm Chottie," said a brilliant redhead. "ETC once upon a time ago, now my doctor has me on something I can't even pronounce. What are you on?" she asked.

Aris stared at her, wondering what she should say. Were these women serious?

Cynthia laughed. "She told me nothing! Isn't that hilarious?"

The women laughed again and Aris threw them a tiny smile. She was careful to keep her mouth closed.

"Get Erin a drink," Chottie ordered.

"It's Aris," Aris said quietly, but nobody was listening.

Aris sat in silence while the women around her chatted, comparing dermatologists and psychiatrists.

"Do you work?" one of the blondes asked. Aris thought it was Elisa.

"I work at Nordstrom," Aris said.

The women regarded her silently.

"Really?" Cynthia asked, disbelieving.

"Yes," Aris felt as if she had stumbled into a well-hidden hole.

"Are you smart!" Chottie trilled. "Why have a big career when you're waiting for John to marry you? Good idea."

"Doesn't your father help you out, though?" Bella asked.

"My father-" Aris stopped. "He's dead."

The women clucked and made sympathetic noises and someone poured more wine.

"I bet your mother doesn't hardly give you a penny," Cynthia said. "Did your dad leave everything to her?"

My God, Aris thought. They think I'm one of them. They think I'm rich.

They took her silence for assent and everyone clucked and sighed some more.

"Don't worry," Chottie said, chummily. "You'll be married to John soon enough."

Everyone laughed and Aris tried to join in.

"I think it's a wise decision, not getting your teeth fixed," Chottie said to Aris. "It gives you character."

"But if you want to," Chottie continued, "I'll give you the name of my dentist. He did my veneers and Bella's too."

Afterward, when they had gone home, Aris asked John how long he had known them all.

"Years," he said briefly. "You passed, by the way. They loved you."

"I didn't know it was a test," Aris said.

John laughed. "Aris, when isn't it a test?"

Aris said nothing.

"It wouldn't matter though," he said, putting his hand on her thigh.

"No?"

"Aris," he said intently. "You're my girl because I want you to be. It doesn't really matter what anyone else thinks."

Aris had fallen in love with him in that moment, really fallen in love.

Now John Prince was becoming a ghost in his own house. That beacon, John's bright light, which she used to hold so dear, shrank into obscurity. When Aris saw him, she saw through him, and behind him was Rhys. Rhys, whose light burned brighter and hotter than anything John could ever produce. Chilly foreboding kissed her on the back of her exposed neck, and Aris brushed it off like a bothersome insect.

She arrived at Rhys' brick building and parked the car. She got out reluctantly and knocked upon the blue door.

"Hello? Rhys?"

His name rolled out on her tongue and she savored the taste of it for one moment. She listened, but heard only silence.

"It's Aris. I'm coming up."

She pushed at the blue door; it was unlocked. As she came up the stairs, the large bed came into view. She saw at once he was in it. He was asleep, covered only by a white sheet. It rode low on his hips; he obviously wore nothing. Aris stared for a moment. He opened a lazy green eye; the smell of him, earthy, minty, sex, invaded her nostrils. She said nothing, but started to make her way across the wood floor to the other staircase. She knew he watched her as she crossed the room.

He'll turn your head.

She remembered John's warning and steeled herself. He was turning her head.

The afternoon sun swelled in the sky, and the heat rippled. Aris had the doors open, but the breeze was slight. She had not seen Rhys all day, which pleased her. When she thought of him, her hands shook. Her disappointment at her own inability to control her feelings was palpable. Her body was a taut string, and Rhys held both ends. As the days washed into one another, he pulled at both ends of her with practiced hands.

Aris told herself she was being ridiculous, then she thought of his strong-looking, paint-stained hands and forcibly pushed back a tide of warmth. For days, she'd slid into the white BMW, ignoring the stretching attraction swimming lazily in her stomach. She had to finish the job today. She had to get away from him.

"Mom, it's really very simple," John Junior was saying. Astoria tried to focus. He was the only one who ever called her "Mom." The others always called her "Mother."

"The vineyard backs up right to the house. They want the whole thing."

Today was not a good day for Astoria. The new medicine Dr. Millen put her on was terrible. Astoria didn't like it; it made her fuzzy. She heard someone mention the word dementia. Astoria knew she was not demented.

"You can't," Astoria said, upset to realize the sentence came out slurred.

"Mom, are you okay?" John Junior asked, concern lacing his tone.

Astoria nodded drunkenly.

"Maybe it's time you go," the nurse suggested as she came in the room. "Mrs. Prince needs her rest."

Astoria wanted to bellow. She did not need her rest; it was just the medication. Her son was plotting something; he looked like his father when he was plotting. Astoria was familiar with the look in his black eyes. All her children had that peculiar glint when they were trying to get away with something.

Astoria tried to focus.

"John Junior" she said carefully. "You must not do anything. Do you understand?"

"Mom, calm down, everything will be okay. Nurse?" John Junior turned to the nurse, alarmed.

"She's okay. She's fine," the nurse said soothingly. "Doctor wants to see you before you go."

Ah! Astoria knew what that meant. They were going to tell John Junior there was something wrong with her head.

"Pills," she tried to say to him. It came out garbled.

"There, there, honey," the nurse said placatingly. "Let's get you into bed for a nice nap."

Nap? Astoria never napped. As old as she was, she never napped. She got tired; she liked to rest but she never slept during the day.

As the nurse got her into the bed, Astoria was aghast to discover her limbs wouldn't cooperate. She closed her eyes and heard footsteps.

"Is she out?"

It was Dr. Millen; Astoria recognized his clipped tones.

"Yes, she is," the nurse said.

"Doctor," John Junior's voice was hard.

"Yes, sir?"

Ah, Dr. Millen sounded a little bit deferential, didn't he? Astoria smiled or thought she smiled.

"What is wrong with my mother?"

"What do you mean?"

"What do you think I mean? She's incoherent. She's fallen asleep twice since I've been here and not realized it! She's having trouble remembering people's names. She wasn't like this last week."

Silence.

Astoria tried to open her eyes, but the lids were too heavy.

"Mr. Prince, your mother is in what we call the early stages of dementia."

Dementia! Not that business again.

"So suddenly?"

"It only seems sudden to you. I'm sure it's been going on for years."

"She was fine when she came in here," John Junior insisted.

Dr. Millen laughed a mean little laugh.

"You're not listening. I told you, it only seems that way to you."

"What are you doing for her?"

"Everything we can."

Dr. Millen's voice held a note of reassurance.

"Which is what, precisely?"

"We've got her on some great new meds and we're keeping her as comfortable as possible. Listen, these things often go quickly when you have someone entering the end stage of life."

"End stage," John Junior said faintly.

"Yes, that's right. I wouldn't expect her to last the month."

Astoria started to drift off; she couldn't help it. She struggled to open her eyes again.

"You're saying she's dying," John Junior said.

"That's what I'm saying. This quote unquote sudden onset of dementia is simply a precursor to death. It won't be long now. I suggest you say your goodbyes while she still knows who you are."

John Junior was silent. Astoria was hearing them as if they were in a dream.

"How long, approximately?"

"Oh, about two weeks, not much longer," Dr. Millen said nonchalantly. "I'm running late. It was nice meeting you."

Footsteps, then silence. Then John Junior was on his phone.

"We're moving forward," he barked. "Two weeks."

It was Johnny's voice. Her husband Johnny, making another of his hard-edged business deals. It was better if she stayed out of it, kept to the house and the children. Little Janice was barely out of diapers. Johnny said he wanted another boy soon. Astoria dreamed on as her son stole out of the room.

The heat circled her; her boyish body was drenched. Her shorn hair was sticking out like a halo. Katrina appeared at the big doors on the backside of the building.

"Hi, Aris."

Aris stopped shuffling the ink drawings in her hands and looked up. Katrina was framed in the middle of the two doors; the light and the blue sky were a perfect backdrop for her. Her black hair was piled on top of her head; she was bedecked in rhinestones again, blue this time. She had on a smart gray suit.

"Hi," Aris said.

"We're here to pick up."

Katrina sashayed into the room; her figure was a perfect hourglass. Aris looked down at her own boyish body.

The doors on the other side of the building opened. Two men were there with a large truck. They backed the truck up until it was partially in the building and began to load the paintings into the back of the van.

Katrina watched them. When they were almost finished, she turned to Aris.

"Shall I tell Rhys you came by?"

"No," Katrina tossed over her shoulder. "He knew I was coming."

The two men pulled closed the groaning doors, and Aris turned back to the papers in her hands. Aris felt the day stretch; it was almost time to go. She would not be back. She was glad she would not be back. She never wanted to see Rhys again, this strange man who made her heart beat like a tom tom. Yet, she felt a peculiar melancholy at leaving him, as if she were missing some secret puzzle piece or vital ingredient and Rhys would supply it to her, if only she stayed a little longer. She shook herself. They had barely said two words to each other. She was marrying his cousin. He'll turn your head. Stop it, she told herself.

She went upstairs for water. Upon reaching the landing she saw Rhys, stripped to the waist, a palette in his hands covered in shades of purple. He was standing in the middle of the room in front of an empty canvas.

He glanced up as she came in. Aris ducked her head; she did not want to see his bared brown chest.

"I'm almost finished. I just needed a drink," she said as she opened the small fridge. "Katrina was here, she picked everything up. I'm just tidying up down there."

Rhys waved his hand in a gesture reminiscent of Sarah's oh, that.

"I know."

He stepped back. Studied her.

"Come here, Aris."

She automatically took a step toward him, then stopped.

"Why?"

He just looked at her, one black brow quirked.

"Why?" she repeated, alarm rising in her stomach.

"Because," he said, exasperation leaking into his tone.

Still, she did not move.

"What for?"

"Just come here," he ordered softly. He was amused.

Aris put her water down on the small counter. She walked toward him; he held her gaze until she was next to him. She felt laid open and languid, as though she were melting. He held her violet eyes penetratingly, and she swallowed a gasp.

"Was that so hard?" he asked, condescension and amusement creeping into his voice.

Rhys looked at her and began to mix color. She watched him. His skin was smooth, brown. She looked down at his hands; they were long, capable looking, covered in ink and paint. She remembered the gentle, warm feel of his fingers resting against her own. Fire shot into her belly. He looked back up at her. Aris felt her breasts tingle, her body go liquid.

Rhys' eyes were dark with concentration. He leaned in closer to her. Aris pulled in a sharp breath. He reached up slowly, put a paint-stained hand on her golden cheek, and tilted her head up slightly. She felt a wet spot where he had smudged her cheek with paint. He peered at her. She felt naked.

Suddenly, he dropped his hand and turned away from her.

"I got it now," he said, and she was disconcerted to discover she was disappointed for some reason.

She went down the stairs slowly, dreamily. She was about to pull the back doors closed when she heard him running down the stairs.

It was not a slow seduction. He simply grabbed her, his arms encircling, rings flashing like lightning, paint-stained fingers pressing brutally into her sweaty skin. He pushed her against the wall, mashed her face into the cold brick. She was trapped in the quickening minutes, reacting so swiftly at his touch that he made a startled noise. With one hand, he kept her pressed against the brick, with the other, he pulled at her shorts. Then he stopped. It was only for a second, but Aris felt that second stretch until it broke. He took his hand off the back of her head and dragged it across the hot skin of her back, inclining his head until it rested gently against hers. She felt several urgent tugs at her shorts and panties. Her slim body jerked as air hit her bare skin. She faintly recognized the tinkle of Rhys undoing his belt. She closed her eyes and felt that first familiar shove of flesh into flesh. It was ugly and violent, and, as the first wrathful explosions wracked her, she heard Rhys behind her, make a sound of grim satisfaction.

Chapter 12

As the sun began its descent into the valley, Laura watched Old Max take a few bong hits, befouling the trailer with the stench of bad weed. As the night crept in, the smothering blanket of heat wrapped around the hills began to dissipate, and Old Max pulled his jacket tightly around his shoulders. He lifted his Mason jars from the kitchen counter and deposited the contents on the TV tray in front of him. Dead bugs littered the small, tin surface and fell on the dirty floor. Laura sipped gin from a green plastic cup and observed the old man without bothering to hide her disgust. She waited until he slipped into a deep sleep on the couch, dead bugs scattered about him, and she went to the small closet and pulled out a battered, blue, striped suitcase. Her letters to Aris.

Laura was seventeen when she got pregnant. She realized it one day in March. The valley was covered with a blank, impenetrable fog. Laura awoke in her mother's house, opened her eyes, and stared at the white, plaster ceiling. She felt off.

She had progressed quickly from sweaty teenage fumbling to lovers of a more sophisticated touch. She knew the father was one of those men who bought her bottles of cheap gin wrapped in a paper bag. Laura preferred men who were older, men who could buy her liquor. Sometimes she took a particular fancy to one, and when she had finished her plastic bottle of gin, she'd reach over across the bench seat of the truck and, with drunken and soulful eyes, put her hand on him.

Laura had not had an easy life in the pallid, fertile valley of California. At least, Laura didn't think she had an easy life. She had always felt put upon by her mother and father and failed to recognize the multitude of sacrifices they performed. From a very early age, she exhibited a proclivity for beastly tantrums, brisk mood swings and reckless behavior. She was a selfish child who grew sulkily into a selfish, boozy teenager.

Mary Dunn always thought she and her husband, Jim, had provided the best possible life for her children and that they would benefit from having advantages she and Jim had not had. Though she hated to admit it, both of her children were disappointments.

"Fuck ups," Jim said.

"Don't use that language," Mary admonished.

When Laura realized she was pregnant, the first thing she did was laugh. She barked out a harsh and amused laugh and turned her head to look out of the wavy glass at the thick fog swirling against the window. It obscured the trees in the yard and made Laura feel as though the rest of the world had disappeared. Her hands fluttered against themselves under the blankets and she forced them to be still and laughed again. Laura thought it was funny that she was pregnant. As the child grew in her belly, Laura's amusement grew. She'd look down at her rounding belly and chortle quietly. She did not bother to hide her pregnancy and she found her mother giving her strange looks at the dinner table.

"What, Ma?" she yelled exasperated.

"Nothing," Mary said worriedly.

It did not occur to Laura that one day the thing that was living inside her was going to come out. She came to think of her pregnancy as a sickness, not a prelude to a child. Both her parents continued to watch her at the dinner table, like she was an animal at the zoo, something to be locked up and feared, something that would bite. Laura found power and amusement in their fear of her.

Finally, when Laura was six months gone, her mother came into her room. She sat on the bed, her long, blonde hair pulled back into a serviceable ponytail.

"Laura, you got something to tell me," Mary said. It was not a question.

Laura shrugged.

Mary waited, her sherry-colored eyes impatient.

"Do I really have to say it, Ma?"

"You need to see a doctor."

"I already tried to get an abortion. I don't have enough money and besides, I realized it too late. They won't do it."

"Abortion?" Mary was flabbergasted. "You'll go to hell for even thinking it!"

Laura shrugged again, her heavy face made more so by her pregnancy.

"You need to see a doctor to make sure the baby is alright," Mary clarified.

"Whatever," Laura said sulkily.

Laura was prone to prolonged periods of melancholy; being pregnant made them worse. She would look at the small bump under her T-shirt and tears would start to flow from her mud- colored eyes. Jim looked at his daughter's obvious shame and hung his head in disgust. He stopped speaking to her.

In June, Kirby found out he wasn't going to graduate. He didn't have enough credits. He dropped out, and Jim kicked him out of the house.

Her brother was a strange and solitary boy who never seemed to form an attachment to the family. He was absent from most meals; even when he was a young child, he preferred the solitude of his room. When he hit his teens, he became involved in the burgeoning drug scene in the valley. His parents were mercifully unaware of his criminal activities. Laura knew he prided himself as an outlaw; she thought he was ridiculous. When Jim kicked him out, she followed him to his dingy, gray room as he packed a bag.

"Where will you go?" she asked.

Kirby shrugged, his dirty-blond hair swinging over his shoulders.

"Who's the father?"

"I was raped."

Kirby turned to her, his eyes penetrating.

"Who did it, Laura? I'll fuckin' kill him. Who was it?"

"Forget it."

"Like hell, I have a gun. I will fuckin' kill somebody. Give me a name."

She didn't know why she told him the lie, but she liked the feeling of excitement that poured into her veins. She liked the idea of her brother going crazy and killing someone to defend her honor. She hadn't expected Kirby to take such an interest, but she was delighted by it all the same. She looked down at her stretched skin; she couldn't wear her own clothes anymore. Mary had taken her to the Goodwill to find some maternity clothes.

"Forget it. I don't want to talk about it," Laura said dismissively, with a touch of martyrdom in her eyes.

Kirby left that night, Mary trailing sad tears in his wake, and Jim impassively watching TV in the orange easy chair. He returned around midnight, breaking in through the back window by the kitchen door, eyes wild, blond hair disheveled. Jim came running into the living room with Mary behind him. Kirby brandished his gun. Mary gasped.

Laura watched from the darkened hallway, her hands resting on her belly. Her father circled Kirby slowly.

"You want to come in here and shoot me, son? Is that it? Well, go ahead. I'm right here. Go ahead and shoot."

"I will shoot, old man. Don't think I won't!" Kirby said excitedly.

"Then fucking do it!" Jim roared.

"I will!" Kirby screamed back. "You're an excuse for a man. A piece of shit father. You let your daughter get raped! You kicked me out! Fuck you!"

Jim stood in the shadowy living room in his blue boxers and white undershirt and screamed for his son to shoot him. Kirby held the revolver on him with shaky hands. Mary jumped between the two.

"Kirby, you need to leave now," Mary said calmly.

"Huh?" he asked confusedly.

"It's time to go now," Mary said again. "Stop pointing that thing at me. I can't believe you brought it into this house."

Kirby lowered the gun slowly and backed toward the front door.

"Ma," he said uncertainly.

"Just go," Mary said tiredly.

Laura shuffled back to her bed as she heard her father and mother boarding up the hole in the window. No one mentioned the incident the next day, and that was the last time Laura saw her brother. The atmosphere in the house grew sallow and tired. Laura looked up one day and realized her parents were old. Her short and fiery father spent most of his time in the orange easy chair, smoothing back his wild, gray hair with a weathered hand. Her mother's beautiful blonde hair, hair that once won her a beauty contest and a free trip to Hollywood, was shot through with silver.

Their weariness invaded the walls and slunk about the floorboards, oozed into the floor grates and circled the sagging crown molding. She saw it in their muted eyes and bowed shoulders. The more they tucked their chins to their chests, the more attention Laura demanded from them. If her tiresome tantrums failed to garner a reaction, she would try tears. She deliberately broke her mother's porcelain figurines that decorated the curio cabinet in the living room, simply because she'd wanted to see her mother's mouth turn down in a tired mask of anger.

Being pregnant isolated Laura, and she blamed the child inside her. She looked down at her distended belly and silently hated the thing that had taken her cheap youth. This thing conceived in the dirty toilet of a local bar, with a man who smelled bad and drank whiskey. With a big, swollen belly, no one was buying her drinks anymore. No one was there for her to bum smokes from. There was only Laura, and the thing growing inside her.

When her pregnancy was advanced, in the heat of the summer, Laura would lie on the plaid couch under the window unit like a beached whale, issuing forth complaints until her father rattled his paper and left the room in a silent huff. Sweat poured down her back and throat and she wished for a cold beer. The thing kicked and Laura gritted her teeth. She was trapped in this fat body, a holding-pen for the swift-kicking little beast inside her.

Her father died a month before Aris was born, in the sick heat of August. He began complaining of headaches and one morning he woke up and didn't recognize Mary or Laura. The doctor pronounced his brain riddled with tumors; they could do nothing for him. Laura watched her small and spirited father succumb quickly to the cancer that ate his memories and robbed him of his senses. Mary awoke Laura each morning with the intent of taking her to see her dying father and, each morning, Laura would find an excuse not to go. Finally, Laura acquiesced and followed her mother sullenly down the dark hospital corridor.

"He won't even talk to me, you'll see," Laura told her mother knowingly. "He hates me."

When they entered the room, he thought Laura was Mary, and placed a gentle hand on her stomach. He had lost the use of his right side and reached out with his left. Mary had tears shining in her eyes. Jim Dunn died that night and five weeks later, Aris came.

Laura went into labor in the early morning, moaning and bellowing like a cow, and when the baby finally came, it was an ugly, pink, mewling thing. She named it Aris, after the cat. Laura thought it was hilarious. Her mother did not think so.

"You gotta give that child a proper name, Laura," Mary said. Laura had laughed at her.

"It's good enough for the cat, ain't it?"

"This is not a cat, Laura!" Mary had been appalled.

"Might as well be," Laura shrugged.

After three days in the hospital, Laura came back to her mother's house, took one look at the crib in the corner of her room and walked out. She walked out of the bedroom and down the hallway to the living room. Then she walked out the front door. She was on the sidewalk before she realized she still carried the baby. Mary followed her outside, her eyes questioning. Laura walked back up the porch stairs, oblivious to the peeling white paint. She handed her mother her baby and started down the sidewalk.

Laura thumbed drunkenly through her letters to her daughter and decided it was time to go see the kid. Maybe Old Max would let her borrow his car for a few days. Old Max awoke with a loud snore and Laura looked up impatiently.

"Go back to sleep, old man," she said tiredly.

"Huh?" he rubbed his eyes. "What're you doing? Whassat?"

Laura began to gather the crisp and yellowing letters.

"Nothing."

Old Max started to load up his bong in
the dim light.

"I was thinking, maybe it's time you
go," he said casually.

Aris stole out of the brick building
before Rhys could buckle his belt. He didn't try
to follow her. The sun was setting; the sky was
on fire. Aris realized she was going to be late.
She picked up her phone and called John as if it
were the most natural thing in the world. He
didn't answer.

"It's me. I finished today and I'm not
coming back. It's done," she said forcefully.
"Anyway, I'm running late. I'll meet you at your
mother's."

They were supposed to finalize the
wedding plans tonight.

"Well," Janice said as she answered the
door. "At least one of you decided to show up."

"John's not here?" Aris asked, relieved.

"No," Janice said swiftly. "He isn't and
you're late."

"I'm sorry."

Janice smirked as she led Aris toward
the dining room of the elegant, yellow Victorian
house.

"Do you know where he is?" she asked Aris.

"I think he's still at the office."

"Where have you been?" Janice asked her lazily. Aris heard, or imagined she heard, a thread of iron lacing the question.

"I've just finished up at Rhys' place."

Aris took her seat at the polished cherrywood dining room table. Janice sat across from her and pierced Aris with her black eyes. Aris felt her hands flutter up under the table and she willed them to still. Her face was showing everything. Janice knew. John would know. Everyone would find out. Panic sent waves of electricity down her nerve endings.

"Is that so?" Janice asked as she opened her laptop.

"Yes, you know I was working for him."

"I was aware," Janice murmured, looking uninterested. "You won't be going back there?"

"No," Aris answered quickly. Too quickly. Janice glanced up from her computer screen.

"Good," Janice said with finality. "Now you can focus on John and the wedding."

Aris nodded.

"Now," Janice began in her take-charge voice. "We have to decide on the floral arrangements for the tables. I know you mentioned hydrangeas, but I think they're too common and too large. What we are really going for is something elegant, understated. You probably don't understand, but understatement can sometimes be the exact statement you want to make."

"I really do like the hydrangeas," Aris began cautiously.

A key sounded in the lock and the door pushed open.

"You're late, John!" Janice called out.

"I know," he answered as he came into the room looking harried. His tie was askew and his briefcase hung from his fingers as if he would drop it at any moment.

"We were just discussing flowers. Maybe you can help with this," Janice said silkily.

"Sure," John said as he sat at the table and took out his mobile. He immediately began scrolling through his emails.

"Hydrangeas or something smaller?" Janice asked him.

John wrinkled his perfect nose. "Smaller," he said disgustedly. "I don't really like those big, showy flowers. Too much of a good thing."

John glanced up to meet Aris' violet eyes. "Right, honey?"

"Perfect," Janice said with a beam of satisfaction. "Let's move onto food, shall we?"

Aris eyed her husband-to-be and felt like she was looking at a stranger. His black eyes were intent on his phone. His dark brown hair fell over his forehead. Aris conjured up hot green eyes and then flushed. She pushed the green eyes, and the man to whom they belonged, out of her head. Her place was with John. She loved John.

"Listen, I've got to make a few phone calls," John interrupted his mother.

Janice stopped speaking and glared at him.

"You're interrupting me," she informed him.

John grimaced and looked like a twelve-year-old. "Sorry, Mother."

"Fine." Janice waved her hand at him. "Go. Aris and I will finish things. I don't want to hear any complaints about the food though. This is your time to give your input."

"I'm sure whatever you pick will be fine," John said, his fingers already scrolling through his contacts.

He left the room and Janice looked over the table at Aris. She looked as if she would swallow her whole. Her lips spread, revealing her white teeth. It was an approximation of a smile, yet it was not a smile at all.

"I know you don't like seafood all that much, but people will expect some kind of fish course, you know."

Aris nodded tiredly. She remembered the first time she'd met Janice. John took Aris out to a fancy dinner and afterward, he told her they were going somewhere special for dessert.

"Where?" she asked eagerly.

"It's a surprise," he told her, his black eyes dancing.

They pulled up in front of the yellow Victorian and Aris felt her stomach drop to her feet.

"Where are we?" she asked, fear turning sluggishly in her stomach. The filet mignon she'd eaten earlier turned with it.

"My mother's house," John grinned. "She said we should drop by for dessert."

Aris gaped at him. Meeting his mother was not something she'd wanted to do on the

287

spur of the moment like this. What's worse, John knew it; they'd had a conversation only a few weeks earlier.

"I want you to meet my mom," he said.

"I'm nervous," Aris admitted.

"Don't be," he chided her.

"I am. Let's plan something with her, okay? Like a lunch or something."

John laughed at her. "What are you so nervous about?"

Aris reddened. "What if she doesn't like me?"

John laughed again. "Oh baby, she doesn't like anybody."

Aris felt alarm. "You're not serious."

John cracked his neck and his eyes softened. "She's not that bad. She can be a tough lady, though. I don't think she's ever had a problem with any of my other girlfriends."

None of his other girlfriends had been poor girls with crooked teeth from the Merced Valley either. John's friends assumed she was one of them, in the rich club, and she did not bother to correct them, but Aris knew she couldn't lie to John's family.

They'd gone up the steps to the house and Aris swallowed her anger at John. Maybe he'd forgotten about her nerves. Maybe he thought this would be easier on her in the long run. Still, she didn't like surprises and he knew it. At the top of the stairs the door opened as if Janice had been watching them through the lace curtains.

"So," Janice said, baring her teeth. "This is your new girl."

"Aris," John said as he gave Aris a little push forward.

Aris stumbled in front of Janice and gave a little yelp.

"Happy to make your acquaintance, finally," Janice said.

Aris grasped the small, white hand Janice offered.

"Yes, me too," Aris said haltingly.

Janice withdrew her hand and leveled her black eyes on Aris.

"Are you nervous, darling?"

Aris shook her head.

"Your hand is hot and sweaty," Janice said as she led them into the house.

"Maybe a little," Aris admitted.

Janice tipped her head to the ceiling, like an animal scenting blood.

"John, I've gotten your favorite cherry pie from that bakery you like."

"Great," John said enthusiastically.

Janice waved her hand at him. She led the way through the tasteful antiques and expensive furniture. They all sat down at the dining room table. Janice sat at the head and gestured for Aris to sit on one side of her and John on the other. A maid came through the door.

"Would you like anything to drink?" Janice asked Aris.

"Water," Aris said, thinking, cyanide.

"Same for me," John said.

"Coffee," Janice said succinctly to the maid.

Aris had never been served by a maid in her life. She supposed it was just like being in a restaurant. John and Janice barely acknowledged the woman when she came back with the drinks and slices of cherry pie.

"Thank you," Aris told the woman, who nodded.

"So John tells me you work at the mall," Janice began. Aris wanted to crumple into a ball under the table. She glanced at John; he was eating his pie with gusto.

"Nordstrom," Aris supplied.

"Almost the mall," Janice laughed. "Why is that?"

Aris glanced at John again.

"Um, I got let go from my last job, which is where I met John, and I've been meaning to get my resume to another temp company but I'm making good money right now, so..."

Aris trailed off and Janice wrinkled her nose in obvious distaste. "I see," she said. "Do you not have an adequate education for more advanced work?"

Aris' violet eyes widened. "I have a degree from SF State."

Janice smiled coldly. "In what? Fashion Merchandising?"

John glanced up from his pie.

"Leave her alone, Mother."

Janice laughed loudly. "You act as if I'm grilling the girl. We're just having a cozy chat. I'm curious about your lovely new girl."

John smiled. "She's great."

Janice sat back from her pie; she'd barely touched it. "Then that's all I need to know, isn't it?"

Aris took a deep breath.

"Tell me about your family," Janice asked.

Aris cringed inwardly.

"Aris was raised by her Gram," John said firmly. "Gram is the sweetest old lady you'd ever meet. She reminds me of Granny."

"Where are your parents?" Janice asked Aris.

"They're dead," John answered, his black eyes alert.

"I'm sure Aris can answer for herself, John," Janice admonished him.

Aris' eyes swung from John to his mother, wondering if she should correct him or perpetuate the lie.

"Aris is quite an unusual name," Janice commented smoothly as the maid came in to refill the drinks. "How did you come by it?"

Aris looked Janice squarely in her cold, black eyes and said, "I have no idea."

John bit into another piece of pie and grunted in satisfaction. Aris was unsure if he was happy with the pie or her answer to the question.

"Are you in there?" Janice was asking.

Aris pushed her mind back into the present. She shook her head. "I'm sorry. My mind wandered."

"I was telling you I booked the three-piece for the ceremony. The one with that famous cellist, whose name completely escapes me."

"Oh," Aris nodded. "Great," she said lamely. Green eyes flashed in her mind and she suddenly felt hot hands grabbing at her again. Aris stood abruptly. "I really don't feel well. You don't mind if I go home, do you?"

"I certainly do," Janice said smartly. "But I suppose if you're sick, I can finish this up."

"Thanks," Aris said as she dashed out of the room. She passed John in the living room on his phone.

"I don't care," he was saying.

Aris waved her hand to get his attention. He shook his head and turned his back to her. Aris slipped out the door and tried to breathe.

Chapter 13

Astoria had lost track of time. She no longer remembered what day it was or who had been to visit her last. It was difficult to discern her dreams from reality. She dreamed Ben and Helen had come to see her, but he was dead, so she knew it couldn't be true. She thought Janice had been by, zipping into the room in dashing furs, riding a wave of Chanel and smoking furiously. Did they let people smoke in hospitals anymore?

Gustav and Minnie hadn't yet been to see her, of that she was sure.

Disby was there; she had been sitting beside Astoria for the longest time, weeping. Astoria saw her daughter as though she were a projection from a film. There was a gauzy curtain separating them and Astoria could not part the curtain to speak to her.

"He's made me leave. He told me you were..."

Astoria stared at Disby. He, who? Who was she talking about? Behind those thoughts, behind the fuzzy things she was trying to think of, was something she had once known. Something very insistent, something pressing. Someone that must be dealt with. Was it Janice? Janice and her indiscretions? It was so important.

"Mother, what are we going to do? I've moved in with Helen. He says he's having the house painted, but I know it's a lie! You've got to tell me what to do," Disby cried out passionately.

Astoria was reminded of her father, Barty. Disby was very much like him. She leaned in as tears ran down her daughter's face. Her eyes wandered down to the flowered coverlet that was settled over her. Someone had brought it for her. It was her very own. She liked it; it smelled of her lavender water. Astoria looked at her limp legs under the blanket. She had not been out of bed in what seemed like weeks. The nurses brought all her meals to her in bed. Geraldine didn't come as often. They said things when they were in her room, horrible things that Astoria didn't like hearing. "She's barely in there." "Won't be long now." "Mrs. Prince, can you hear me? She doesn't even know what's going on."

"Mother! They told me something terrible this morning." Disby paused as if she were wondering if she should continue.

Disby focused her small eyes on Astoria and Astoria suddenly realized what was so pressing. "Pills," she said as clearly as possible, which was not very clear at all.

"What?" Disby leaned in. "What did you say?"

"Pills," Astoria said more slowly.

"Pills?" Disby repeated, not understanding. "Is it time for your pills? Should I call the nurse?"

Astoria gripped the rails on the side of her bed. Her eyes were intense as she leaned in toward Disby.

"No more pills," she said in the horrible rasp that was now her voice.

Disby softened. "You have to take the pills. The doctor says they're helping you. Tell me what to do, Mother," Disby said.

The nurse swept into the room. "She needs her rest, Miz Prince.

Disby cleared her throat nervously and nodded. "I know."

"It's no good pressing her on things. She probably doesn't even know who you are."

Disby's tired eyes turned back to Astoria. Her face crumpled under the weight of the nurse's words.

"Disby," Astoria pushed out.

Disby smiled instantly. "Yes, Mother. It's me. Don't you worry. I'll figure this out myself."

"No pills. Tell Janice," Astoria said slowly.

"Nurse, she doesn't want to take her pills," Disby said tentatively.

"They all become a little bit uncooperative. It's part of the disease," the nurse informed her importantly.

"Oh," Disby said.

"Lie back, dear," the nurse instructed as she tipped the bed down. "Take a nap."

"No," Astoria said loudly.

The nurse looked at Disby, as if to say, see what I mean?

Disby looked ashamed. "I've been upsetting her. I should've been quiet."

The nurse looked at Astoria, whose agitation was becoming more evident. She shot a disapproving look at Disby, who blushed.

"We can just give her a little sedative," the nurse said. She left the room and quickly returned with a syringe.

"Oh," Disby started. She was afraid of needles. Astoria remembered the time they had to hold her down at the doctor's office so they could take blood. Poor little thing. Astoria patted her hand. The nurse came closer and Astoria was suddenly aware again of something very pressing, something prodding at her from the fog of her mind. It needed her attention. What was it? The nurse was picking up her wrist with rough hands. Astoria looked down at her flowered coverlet and the scent of her lavender water drifted up toward her. The house!

Astoria reared back from the nurse and her needle full of dreams.

"No!" she yelled.

"I'm going to have to call someone to hold you down, Miz Prince," the nurse warned.

Just like Disby.

"No more pills," she told Disby again.

Disby frowned as an orderly came in the room to hold Astoria down on the bed. Astoria lay very still as the nurse inserted the needle. "Not the house," she murmured as she sank into darkness.

"Did you understand what she was saying?" someone was asking in the dark.

"Not a word," another voice said.

"La casa," a man's voice said softly.

Around her, the darkness sighed and Astoria drifted away.

The blue door stared at her, as if it knew why she was there. Aris was not sure why she was there, but this smug, blue door seemed to. She felt like what had happened between her and Rhys was a dream, fuzzy and garbled, but she knew she had not dreamed it. She had felt the heat of him suddenly leave her when he backed away. She had heard the loud thunderclap of his zipper and the gentle tinkling of his belt buckle.

Anger and shame coursed through her veins, like hot whiskey. She didn't even know if he would let her inside, and, for a moment, she imagined herself banging with bleeding hands on the smug, blue door while he watched benignly from the solace of his loft. She lifted her hand to the door and it swung open before she made contact. He stood on the narrow bottom step of the gloomy stairs, his emerald eyes shuttered, his face impassive. The air was sticky with a wet heat; the sky was the color of ghosts. Earthquake weather, Gram called it. Aris pushed passed him abruptly and charged up the stairs.

She stood waiting in the center of the room and listened to him come slowly up the stairs. When he reached the top, he stopped and held up his hands as if in surrender. The hazy light filtered in the room, infusing it with a dreamlike quality. Rhys inclined his head toward her regally. She took a deep breath. Her arms fluttered at her side, like bugs against a window. She opened her mouth to speak.

"Aris," he said.

Her mouth was dry. She did not answer him. He came closer and closer, his bare feet making no sound as he crossed the wide floor to where she stood. He stopped, no more than a few inches from her, and looked down into her face.

His breath stirred her hair, and his hand reached out. She felt as though it were disembodied, as if it did not belong to him. He grabbed her left hand. The Ring glittered accusingly. Rhys grabbed it and started to pull it off her finger. The slide of his skin on hers was like an electric storm. The air between them crackled with it. Aris made an involuntary noise. Her head fell back suddenly. He dipped his black head and leaned his face against her yellow hair, inhaling deeply. She could not move. She stood in the murky room, and she let him put his hands on her; she breathed him in and exhaled her guilt.

She felt all that she was, all she had ever been, leak out of her until she was empty. She was nothing and he was nothing; they weren't even people, but two things, mad and desperate, locked in a stillness. She put her hands on his chest; her eyes were purple with need. She put her hands on the back of his neck and pulled his pretty mouth toward her own. When his mouth made contact, something exploded within her. She reached between them. He grabbed her hand and pulled it away, held it in his own as he kissed her. He was unhurried.

The heat swirled around them, and Aris felt her world tilt as she lay in his bed. She heard a muffled thunk as he dropped The Ring. Then he was on top of her; he was looking at her. His eyes were so dark. She reached for him again, and he pulled her hands away, held them loosely in his own.

"I will make you beg, Aris."

And God help her, she wanted to beg him. She would delight in begging him.

Laura smiled a crafty, sneering smile when she backed the car down the dirt road. Old Max wanted her gone, she was gone. She had spent the week stalling, trying to find where he'd hidden some of his money. She waited until he took his nap, and she'd take off into the woods behind the trailer, spade in hand. Finally, she found a ziplock bag with a few hundred in it. She grinned and slipped the money in her pocket. When she got back to the trailer, Old Max was awake.

"Where you been?" he asked suspiciously.

"Taking a walk. That against the law?"

"You ready to go yet?"

He had asked this every day for the last week. She usually told him yes and then waited for him to pass out or pull out his dead bugs and forget about her. This time she made a great display of packing her bags, hauling the blue suitcase from the closet.

"I'm ready," she said, knowing he had no intention of going anywhere.

Old Max looked perplexed.

"Really?"

"Uh huh."

"It's a little late in the day," he mumbled.

Laura lounged under his red eyes, surrounded by a rank cloud of smoke. She smiled and assured him he could drive her off the mountain first thing in the morning. Old Max smiled genially in return and slipped his car keys in his pocket before he went to sleep. Laura sat down on the filthy sofa and watched the sun shift in the sky. She waited until his breathing was deep and even, then she got up and gently removed the keys from his shorts pocket and stole out of the trailer. She pushed the old Camaro down the road, and when she was about a half-mile away, she hopped in and started the engine.

Now she was parked in front of her daughter's house. The sun had gone down, but the persistent heat crept slyly across the steaming asphalt and lingered in the tall trees. Laura parked the car on the street and sat there. No one was home. Laura sat and waited.

Aris pushed open the door to the grape-colored house and surreptitiously glanced around. The house was empty. She breathed deeply. Aris went to the patio and sank down into a chair. She didn't know what she was doing. She was miserable, yet she was happier than she had ever been. She'd gone to Rhys, she supposed, to tell him they could never see each other again, to beg him not to tell John. But when she got there, she became confused. Was that why she was really there? Is that what she really wanted? When they slipped into his bed, Aris told herself that was the last time, that was the last goodbye. Now she knew it wasn't. When John came home, she would tell him. She would leave him.

"And then what?" she asked aloud.

Then she would be out of a home; she had almost no money of her own. She'd have to go back to the valley and stay in Gram's house, or go to Rhys' place and ask him to take her in. Aris pictured Katrina being hustled out of his door and imagined she would encounter the same if she tried to stay with Rhys.

You don't even know what this is. You don't even know what he's doing with you, she argued with herself. It's something, she thought. So was John. He was something, a vicious voice reminded her.

She would tell him, she would. As soon as she had some kind of a plan. Or maybe it's just summer madness, another voice piped up. Summer madness, cold feet, maybe she really did belong with John.

If only she could call Gram, but Gram had a stroke that autumn. She couldn't even speak anymore. The months surrounding Gram's stroke presented themselves with unreal clarity. For the first time in her life, Aris was alone in the world. Alone, except for John Prince.

When John bought the house, the first thing Aris did was call Gram.

"Do you like it?" John asked her.

Aris looked at the lavender house. It was a small, neat, three-bedroom in Marin. The yard was full of greenery and well taken care of.

"Let's go in," the realtor suggested. She couldn't keep her eyes off John. Aris had almost gotten used to the way women looked at John with longing.

"This is cute," Aris said. It was the first house she'd seen that was more to her own tastes than John's. He preferred modern-looking places. This house reminded her a bit of Gram's house.

"Of course, it's closer to the bottom of your price range," the realtor was saying. "However, when Aris was describing what she liked, I knew she had to see this one."

John strode through the house as if he owned it already.

"Nice yard," he commented, looking out of the picture window into the backyard.

"You can't hardly get a yard this size in San Francisco," the realtor said knowingly, batting her lashes at him. She shot a smile at Aris.

"I think this one is calling Aris' name," the woman said.

John glanced at her. "Is it?" he asked, surprised. "I thought we discussed what we wanted. This kind of place isn't really our style," he informed the realtor.

They had not really discussed anything. John had copied her on an email of preferences he'd sent to the realtor. Aris was surprised he wanted to move in with her.

"I can't keep going to Oakland, honey," he told her. "Your place is too small. My lease is up. Let's do this."

Now John looked at her, waiting.

"It reminds me of Gram's house," Aris offered.

John glanced around again. "It's more updated than that, but yes, I see what you mean. If you love it, it's yours."

Aris' eyes widened. Was he serious, just like that?

"John," Aris began apprehensively.

He held up a hand and looked at the realtor. "Let's make this happen."

The day they were moving in, Aris received a phone call.

"Miss Aris Dunn?"

"Yes?" Aris asked, her heart thudding.

"This is the Merced County hospital. Your grandmother, Mrs. Mary Dunn, is here. I'm sorry to have to tell you this, but she's suffered a stroke."

Aris almost dropped the phone. She didn't remember calling John over, didn't remember him taking the phone from her hand and bundling her in the car. It seemed like she blinked and they were in the valley.

When they got to Gram's house, she walked in, and the smell of home filled her nostrils. She wanted to cry, but the tears would not come. The house was as Gram had left it. The paper from two days ago was spread across the plaid couch. Her favorite blue mug was outside on the table, with coffee still in it. Eerie fog wrapped itself around the house. The tree branches shivered, as though cold. It was like a movie set, staged and ready for the star to walk in.

John helped Aris make all the arrangements. She went through the motions like an automaton, not thinking, not feeling, just doing.

"You'll want to call your mother," John said.

"No," Aris said shortly. "I told you, I have nothing to do with my parents. I haven't since I was a kid."

"But Aris," he protested, "this is her mother. You have to call her."

"John, I haven't seen her since I was ten. She's gone. I wouldn't even know where to find her."

"How could she just give up her own flesh and blood?" John asked angrily.

"Believe me, John, I'm better off for it."

"Don't you have an uncle?"

"Yeah, Uncle Kirby. When I was younger he mailed Gram money occasionally, and he sent me presents. My mother told me he sold drugs and stole. She said everything Uncle Kirby ever gave me fell off the back of a truck. I didn't understand what she meant until I was older. I think he's in jail or something, John. I wouldn't even know where to find him."

John made a noncommittal noise.

Aris went to the hospital; Gram looked old and broken, her beauty queen hair almost totally white, her uncooperative limbs wrinkled. The doctor told Aris that Gram was conscious, but she couldn't move or speak. It might take years of therapy to get her to function somewhat normally. Aris was beside herself.

The last thing Gram had said to her was, "Aris, honey, don't you ever let anyone make you feel like you are less than them. You're not," she said emphatically. "You are a good person. If they can't see that, if John can't see that, then you don't need to be around those people. I don't care if they have all the money in the world. You hear me, Aris? I love you, honey."

That was the last time they spoke. Aris felt Gram's absence as keenly as if one of her own limbs was missing. She went through the motions of living; she went to work, she ate, she bathed, she kissed John goodbye in the mornings. The holiday season pressed in at a frantic pace with its grotesque flashing lights and too-loud laughter. She didn't notice any of it. Gram was making no progress at all in therapy. The most she could do was moan and move her left hand a bit. Aris was all alone; she felt it pressing in on her at night. John asked her if she wanted to sell Gram's house; she said she didn't want to think about it. He asked her if they should start moving out the furniture; she shrugged. He told her she had to at least clean out the closets. He was acting as if Gram were dead.

Three days before Christmas, he asked her what she was going to wear to Christmas dinner.

"What are you talking about?"

"To dinner, in Napa."

Aris was confused. "Huh?"

"N-A-P-A," he spelled.

"I know how to spell," she said absently. "Why are we going to Napa?"

"For Christmas."

He sat down beside her on their new sofa. She inhaled his spicy scent.

"You can't spend the holiday alone," he reasoned. "We live together now. What would people think if you didn't come with me?"

Aris wanted to tell him that the holiday didn't matter. She would go to the nursing home and hold Gram's hand all day long. She didn't care about Christmas.

"I don't care. I'm not really in the mood to party," she said wanly.

"I refuse to let you spend the day alone. You come with me. I'll make sure you have a good time."

Aris knew that eventually, someday, she would have good times again, but she didn't think it was going to be anytime soon.

"Okay," she said. It was easier not to argue.

Aris and John drove to Napa early Christmas morning after exchanging gifts. She'd gotten him a set of golf clubs he'd wanted; she'd been saving for months. He got her a pair of diamond earrings. She gasped when she opened the box; John grinned excitedly.

"I can take them back," he said teasingly.

"Don't you dare!" she said smacking him on the arm. She marveled at the sparkle they produced; she had never seen anything as clear as those diamonds.

"No, really, I can tell you don't like them. I'll take them back," he said as he watched her putting them on in the mirror. Her ears drooped with the weight of the stones, but she didn't care.

As the car crawled up the drive, gravel crunching beneath the black tires, the great white house loomed in front of them. Aris thought it was one of the most beautiful and welcoming houses she'd ever seen. John noticed her expression.

"You like it?"

"It's beautiful," she said emphatically.

The sun was high in the cloudless sky, but the air was cold. Aris felt the coolness biting her flushed cheeks as she got out of the car. The drive was lined with cars similar to John's: Lexus, Mercedes, SUVs. Everything was expensive, brand new, and shiny. They walked up the porch, and as John opened the door, Aris was bombarded by the din of the Prince family. People, drinks in hand, slipped in and out of rooms; children ran across the polished wood floors, only to be admonished by watchful parents.

As soon as they stepped through the door, they were surrounded. John was giving and accepting hugs and trying to introduce Aris to everyone. The space before her was filled with pumping hands and breathless kisses. She met so many people in the first ten minutes, faces and names melted into one another. Dancing black eyes, like John's, assessed her. She surveyed the crowd; the family was well dressed and jewelry winked conspicuously at wrists, ears, and necks. Everyone gleamed with the same polish and elegance she'd first noticed in John. She saw Janice eyeing her from across the room. She noticed an ancient woman sitting in an easy chair in the side parlor, watching the melee and smiling faintly. Someone grasped her arm. It was a redhead who smelled of bourbon. Aris heard the faint tinkling of ice and noticed the glass in the woman's hand.

"I'm Morgan, darling," the redhead said. "You must come meet Mother."

Aris let Morgan drag her through the crowd to the old woman in the chair.

"Mother," Morgan said loudly. "This is John's girlfriend, Paris."

"Aris," Aris corrected her quietly.

"Oh," Morgan said. "What an unusual name. Do you spell it with an H?"

Aris spelled her name.

"Hmm," Morgan contemplated, taking a long drink from her glass.

"Mother, this is Aris."

Aris extended her hand and noticed the faint smell of lavender clinging to the old woman.

"How do you do?" Astoria said in a tremulous voice.

"I'm good. Merry Christmas."

"And to you, young lady."

Astoria withdrew her spotted hand. Aris
felt a tug deep within her. She missed Gram
terribly. She searched the crowded house for
John but couldn't find him amidst all the people.
Children shrieked; adults spoke loudly over one
another, occasionally emitting loud barks of
laughter. Aris felt the world tilt slightly; she
needed fresh air. She looked around again for
John, this time a little desperately. Morgan had
left her side, and Aris was alone with Astoria,
who turned her cloudy eyes on her progeny,
forgetting Aris was there.

Aris looked about helplessly, then
squared her shoulders and began to move
through the crowd. The majority of the people
ignored her, but she could feel a few curious
glances spearing her as she walked. Finally, she
found John near the back of the house. There
was a den and another living room. This, too,
was crowded with people. He was in the white,
meaty arms of an obese, middle-aged woman.
He spotted Aris just as the woman began
rocking him back and forth, like a baby.

"Aris!" he called out as the woman
released him.

Aris walked over to them.

"Have you met Auntie Helen yet?"

Aris shook her head. "I don't think so."

"Come here and give Auntie Helen a big hug!" the woman ordered.

Aris hesitantly stepped into the thick arms held out to her. Instantly she was enveloped in a bone-crushing hug that stole her breath. She stifled a gag. Finally, the woman released her and Aris took a grateful step back.

"You're the first girl John's ever brought to a holiday party," Helen commented. "You must be something special."

"I hope so," Aris said.

John gave her shoulders a squeeze. "She is, Auntie Helen. She is."

Aris could not help but smile. A thin, dark-haired woman sidled up to them. She was wearing a huge diamond pendant on her black dress. She noticed Aris staring at it.

"My Christmas present from Paul," she said airily. "I see you also got something shiny," she said, gesturing to Aris' ears.

"Yes," Aris reddened, forcing her hands to stay at her side. "They're from John."

"I'm John's sister, Sarah," she said.

"Pleased to meet you," Aris said politely.

"Yes," Sarah drawled. "I'm surprised it's taken this long to meet you."

Sarah nodded as a man appeared by her side. He was overweight and unattractive. He opened his mouth and let out a small belch of air.

"Aris, this is my sister's husband, Paul Hodge," John said.

The frumpy man held out his thick, stubby hand. Aris grasped it and he belched again.

"Pleased to meet you," she said.

He nodded curtly.

"Paul, where is Tinsley? She hasn't said Merry Christmas to Granny yet."

Aris watched the man waddle away and she wondered how Sarah ended up with him. Sarah spun away as someone called out her name. Aris looked up at John; he was watching the scene with a contented smile on his face.

"Are you having fun?" he asked.

"Um," Aris said.

"Hello, John, have you seen J.J.?" a tall, blonde woman asked.

"He's in the back den, Aunt Olivia. At least, I think he is," John said to the woman, who touched Aris' arm briefly before she moved away.

"There you two are. You know, Aris, this is the first time my son has brought a guest to Christmas dinner. I certainly hope you are enjoying yourself."

"I am," Aris said to Janice, whose eyes went straight to the glittering diamonds on her ears.

"Sarah told me John gave you the most adorable earrings for Christmas."

"Yes." Aris fingered them unconsciously.

"Don't do that dear, you'll leave fingerprints on them," another blonde woman cautioned.

"Oh," Aris immediately dropped her hand.

"Have you met my sister, Jane?" Janice asked.

"No, I haven't."

"Yes, you did," Jane corrected her. "When you first came in."

"I'm sorry!" Aris blushed.

Jane waved her hand and turned back to the man she was speaking to. He was a big man, older, but very handsome. He had an unlit cigar clamped between his lips.

"That's Morgan's husband, Rick," Janice explained.

"Why aren't you with your own family for the holidays?"

"My Gram had a stroke."

"My, my." Janice clucked her tongue. "You poor, poor dear. What a terrible thing to have happen. John, you did the right thing by bringing her here. I can't imagine what you must be going through. Poor, poor Aris."

Janice spoke of Aris as if she were a stray puppy that John brought in from the rain. Aris cut her eyes to John, but he was looking at his mother in gratitude.

"You sit next to me at dinner, Aris. We must become very good friends," Janice said, smiling her disarming smile.

By the time dinner was served, Aris was tired, overstimulated, and ready to leave. John did not seem to notice her visibly lagging behind the crowd rushing to the tables. She was seated next to John and his mother, who, despite her promise of becoming good friends, ignored Aris the entire meal. Aris sat across from Sarah and Sarah's cousin Marie; each did a great deal of whispering, looking meaningfully at Aris and giggling. No one but John spoke to her during the meal, for which she was grateful. She had enough of the crowd. She was not used to such raucous holidays; she missed her grandmother and their quiet, cozy celebrations.

Winter was peppered with frequent visits to Gram, who showed little to no progress. At the end of February, Janice asked Aris to lunch, something Aris kept putting off until she knew she could put it off no longer.

"Any more refusals and I'd have gotten the idea that you were avoiding me," Janice chided her as they sat down.

The place was very posh; it was a mecca for the ladies who lunched. Aris had not known what to wear. John laughed at her.

"You don't really care about clothes. When we first met, you dressed like a schoolmarm. Now you're a mess trying to figure out what to wear!"

"Your mother notices everything. I want to be as close to perfect as possible."

"Wear that red dress I picked out for you. Red is a power color."

Aris looked at Janice now and quickly assessed her chic dress. Compared to Janice, Aris thought she was holding her own.

"I'm sorry, I've been busy," Aris said.

"Of course, retail is a very busy business," Janice said airily.

"I'm not in retail anymore," Aris informed her.

"Oh?" Janice laid her napkin in her lap.

"I've taken a place at another temp company."

Janice frowned. "That's a career choice that will lead nowhere."

Aris felt the blood rush to her face.

"I'm not sure what I want to do yet," she said defensively.

Janice called over the waiter and ordered a drink.

"There's nothing wrong with that kind of lackadaisical attitude, I suppose. Not everyone needs to claw their way to the top, after all. Of course, there are other ways to get to the top, aren't there?"

Janice sent Aris a sidelong glance and Aris wondered if Marjorie had somehow spoken to Janice. She imagined the steely-haired woman calling Janice up and telling her exactly how Aris thought she could get to the top.

Aris made her way through the lunch carefully, tiptoeing around Janice, always searching her comments for the land mines she hid so well. At the end of the meal, Aris was so tense, she could barely move her arms.

"You know," Janice leaned in.

Here it comes, thought Aris.

"I'm a little concerned that John bought a house."

Janice sat back and toyed with her water glass as she let this sink in. It became clear she was not going to elaborate, so Aris asked her why.

"My mother thinks you're living in sin." Janice gave a little laugh. "Of course, I've tried to explain how modern relationships work to her, but you know..." Janice trailed off. "John told me he's put your name on the deed. He bought you that house."

Aris started. She'd been unaware. She thought the house was his. Of course, she signed a few papers, but she hadn't known that she was part-owner of the place.

"I wasn't aware," Aris said.

"Come now," Janice trilled. "No need to act ignorant about this. Of course a girl like you would want her own house. Who wouldn't? I'm not blaming you," Janice said. "Or judging you."

Yes, you are, Aris thought.

"What woman in your place wouldn't do the same thing?" Janice asked lightly.

"You think I'm a gold digger?" Aris asked incredulously.

"Oh, that's a terrible term," Janice said offhandedly.

"Is that what you think?" Aris pressed, her eyes violet fire.

Janice sat back from her, surprise written on her face.

"What are you saying?" Aris asked her angrily.

"What I am saying, young lady, is that you have gotten all you can out of my son. He can't get married without a prenup and you won't touch a penny of the Prince money. The trusts are specifically designed to ensure things like that don't happen. So what I am saying to you, darling, is take your house and go away."

Aris reared back as though Janice had hit her. She looked around at all the ladies pleasantly lunching, then she looked back at Janice.

"You think I'm after John's money?"

Janice smiled. "Maybe. He's quite taken with you, but I've told him marriage is off the table."

Aris felt anger and beneath it, fear. He wanted to marry her. Did she want to marry him?

"Regardless of whether or not you actually are after his money, you've never had money. You grew up poor. You probably can't even separate John from the money. You might not even know if it's him you love or the life he can give you. It's a good life, darling," Janice said smugly. "But you don't earn it by sleeping with John."

Aris jumped up and knocked the chair back. The anger was moving through her at a fast pace; she felt her fist close and saw Janice's black eyes flick down to her hand. She flinched slightly and Aris realized Janice was afraid she would hit her.

"Sit down," Janice hissed furiously.

"No," Aris said loudly. "Listen, darling, I'm not after anything. It was John's idea to buy that house, his idea to put me on the deed."

Janice sat back in her chair, her jaw open. The other patrons of the restaurant, in the manner of polite society, were politely ignoring them.

"Sit down, Aris," Janice hissed.

"No," Aris crossed her arms. "I'm leaving. Thanks for lunch."

Aris returned home; she hesitated to mention the conversation to John because she didn't want him to start talking about marriage. She waited for weeks, but apparently, Janice didn't mention it either. For months, Aris waited for him to propose like she was waiting for a bomb to drop. She couldn't picture herself married to him, but at the same time she loved him and wanted to be with him.

One night he took her to a fancy restaurant on the bay and, after dinner, he slid a black, velvet box across the white tablecloth. She was afraid to open the box. She knew, now that he had pulled out the black box, that things would never be the same. She contemplated the box for so long before opening it; John cleared his throat nervously.

Finally, she opened it. There, nestled securely in the black velvet, was a huge diamond. Aris blinked slowly. The Ring was a promise of a new life, something alien and unfamiliar. She realized in that moment that she loved the feeling of dating the star quarterback, but she wondered if it would be the same if she married him. Maybe Janice was right, maybe she couldn't separate John from his money or his lifestyle. She felt a curious pull inside her. She looked up at his eager face; his black eyes were unsure, searching. She'd never seen John uncertain of anything. She couldn't stand disappointing him; she wanted so much to please him, and she loved him.

Aris took the ring out of the box and slipped it on her finger.

"Yes," she said.

Aris looked at The Ring as it lay sparkling on the floor beside the bed.

"He paid a lot of money for that thing, didn't he?" Rhys asked as he lighted a cigarette.

He was beside her, his brown skin streaked with sweat. He reached out a hand to her, and Aris turned into it eagerly.

"I guess," she said, not wanting to talk about John.

"Does he love you, really love you?" Rhys asked.

Aris paused. "What does it matter to you?"

"Why shouldn't it matter to me?" he asked. He was very matter of fact.

"I'm not sure I want to talk about this."

Rhys laughed at her.

"What do you think of the Prince family?" he asked her seriously.

"I don't fit in," Aris said instantly. "I'm not sure they want me to fit in."

"It bothers you," Rhys observed.

"Of course it does," Aris said. "Doesn't it bother you?" she asked, making the assumption that he did not fit in.

"No," he laughed harshly. "Not anymore."

"Is it because you were adopted?" Aris asked.

Rhys gave a funny smile. "Maybe."

"Don't want to talk about it?" she asked.

Rhys stubbed out his cigarette. "Yeah, about as much as you want to talk about Johnny."

"What are we going to do?" Aris asked, snuggling up to him.

He kissed her and his lips and tongue took possession of her. He infected her. She welcomed his hands, the tangle of his legs, his bare, hairless chest inches from her nipples. His breath, his eyes, his everything, she wanted it; she wanted to fuse herself to Rhys, drink him, eat him, become him.

"What are we going to do?" her words were muffled in his neck.

"I'll tell you what we're going to do," he muttered as he handled her roughly.

The summer stretched its legs and the heat came down like a rough sheet. The trees were still and silent; the asphalt baked under sandaled feet. The omnipresent sun sat high in the blue sky, its harsh rays hammering down on weary heads. Bodies dripped sweat and the air became thick with heat.

"Have you seen that thing parked outside?" John asked her.

Aris, barely registering he was speaking to her, nodded. The old Camaro had been there for a few days. Aris had hardly noticed it.

"Someone must have abandoned it," he fumed. "It's disgusting. This isn't that kind of place. This is a nice place and now some asshole has decided to ruin it with that piece of crap."

Aris shrugged.

"It could be a neighbor's," she suggested.

John laughed at her. "Why don't you go around and ask the neighbors if that's their car?"

Aris glanced at him.

"No one who's living here would have a car like that. It's a certain kind of person who has cars like that."

Aris narrowed her eyes. "What kind is that?"

John sighed. "I'm not getting into it with you. You know what I mean," he said impatiently.

Aris did know what he meant, and she thought of how many people in Gram's neighborhood had cars like that.

"What are you doing up so early?" John asked as he knotted his tie.

"Couldn't sleep," Aris yawned.

"It's too hot," John grimaced.

"I guess," Aris said as she shuffled out to the kitchen.

"Coffee?" John asked her as he came in behind her.

"No."

"What are you doing today?" John asked her.

Aris tried not to think of Rhys. "I thought I would go to campus and check out the bookstore, see if any of the books I need are in."

"You can just call," John said.

"I want to go see the campus," Aris said, annoyed.

"Fine. I'm just trying to help you have a more productive day."

"Well, you're not helping," she snapped.

"Whatever," John said, his black eyes hurt. "Take care of the abandoned car," he said as he sailed out the door.

Aris did not call the police as John suggested. In fact, she didn't even go near the car; instead, she threw on some clothes and left the house. As Aris drove past the rusty car, she craned her head to see if she could see inside.

She drove to Rhys' place, eager to get to him. These days she thought of nothing but Rhys.

"I don't understand," someone was saying. "She seemed fine just a few weeks ago."

"That's how these things work. I'm so sorry," came a sympathetic voice. "I know how close you two are."

"Lady, you don't know the half of it. If it weren't for Astoria Prince, I don't know where my life would have gone. She's taken care of me and mine like we were her own flesh and blood."

Astoria struggled to lift her head. Geraldine was here.

"There she is!" the nurse said brightly. "Look, honey, your friend is here."

Astoria nodded. She could tell by the look on Geraldine's face that she was shocked at her appearance.

"How you doing, Miss Astoria?" Geraldine asked gently.

"No more pills," Astoria said, but even Geraldine couldn't understand her.

"I don't know what you're saying." She shook her head.

"Pills," Astoria tried again.

"Honey, I can't understand you," Geraldine said. She cursed.

"It's better if you leave her be, she needs her rest," the nurse said.

"But she just woke up!"

"Sleep is better for them at this stage."

Geraldine disregarded the nurse and leaned in. "Miss Astoria, I gotta go to New Orleans for Katie's wedding. Simeon and I will be out there a couple of weeks. I'll leave the number of our hotel with the nurses here, in case you need me."

Astoria nodded.

"I wish to God Katie wasn't getting married right now. I don't want to leave you."

Astoria patted Geraldine's hand as Geraldine looked at her with worried eyes.

"Where were you?" John asked Aris as she came through the door, flushed and smiling.

"Finally got the engagement present," she said blithely. "Did you know the seats in the BMW folded down? I had no idea."

"Let me see it," John said.

"It's in the car," Aris said, gesturing to the garage.

John went to the garage and pulled the paper-wrapped canvas out. He laid it out on the kitchen table and stripped the paper off. Lusty eyes stared at him; he peeled more. A nude woman stared back at him. Blonde hair, violet eyes, long, graceful limbs. John laughed shortly.

"Is that supposed to be you?" he asked incredulously.

Aris shifted uncomfortably. "Yes."

"It doesn't look anything like you."

"I think it does."

"Well, yeah, it does resemble you, but the attitude is all wrong. I've never seen you look like this in my life. He really doesn't know you at all."

"I guess not."

John glanced at her.

"I don't really like the idea of him painting you naked either."

"It's not like I posed for it," she said, reddening. Her hands fluttered around her throat.

John frowned.

"You can't see anything."

"He has a lot of nerve, giving us this. We can never show anyone. We'll have to put it in the storage space. I can't have the partners at the firm come here for dinner and see a naked

331

portrait of my wife. It's completely inappropriate."

"I knew you would feel this way. I told Rhys, but-"

"You told Rhys?"

Aris nodded. "He said to take it anyway."

John nodded. "I don't want you going back there. People will start to talk."

Aris laughed shortly. "What people?"

"Just people," John said, as he turned back to his laptop. "Enough is enough."

He didn't like her going over there. It wasn't that he didn't trust Rhys, but there had always been something about his cousin that John didn't understand. And what he did not understand, he did not associate with, and he certainly didn't want Aris associating with it. He was grateful to Rhys for taking such obvious pity on Aris, offering her that fake job just to keep her busy and keep the family from talking about her lack of ambition. It was a nice thing to do, but there was a limit to how much time she could spend over there without it looking suspicious. John knew it and he knew Rhys knew it. Rhys had grown up in the Prince family, just like John; he knew what was acceptable and what wasn't. It was Aris John was worried about.

She was so gauche, so nervous. Sometimes, he couldn't stand it. He had been born with unending confidence and didn't understand people who were not confident. He had worked hard with Aris, even before they started dating, to make her into what he knew she could be, what she should be. The right clothes, the right job, a good manicure and haircut: These were necessary changes. It was imperative that she fit in with his friends and family. It wasn't because he was ashamed of her, he told himself, it was because he didn't want her to feel out of place or uncomfortable. He could feel her need to fit in from miles away. Aris was someone who didn't want to stick out or be noticed. She was, really, the opposite of Rhys. Rhys the black sheep; Rhys did whatever he wanted, whenever he felt like it.

"I'm serious," John called out to Aris' retreating back.

"Come here," Rhys ordered.

Aris laughed and tossed her short, blonde hair. "No."

Rhys lunged into the water. "Goddamn it, don't play the coquette with me. Get over here."

Aris kicked at him with her feet. The little creek rushed and whirled around them.

"Don't you want to put some clothes on?" Rhys asked her.

"No," Aris laughed.

Rhys pointed to the two buildings next to his own. "People work in there, you know. They can see you."

"I don't care!" Aris said. "I'm not coming back in until you get rid of it."

Rhys grimaced. "I can't."

"Why the hell not? I don't like it."

Rhys knew why she didn't like it. It was a painting of his own face, splintered and cut up into pieces. She hated it. When he showed it to her she ran out of the bed, stark naked, and jumped into the creek. She was laughing, but he knew it bothered her.

"Put it downstairs," Aris ordered.

"Get over here," Rhys countered.

"I don't like seeing you like that."

"I'm not finished," Rhys told her. "I'll move it when I'm done. I promise."

He waded into the water after her. "Come on, baby. Come back inside."

Aris splashed at him again, catching him in the face. Anger flashed in his green eyes.

"Don't play rough with me, Aris," he warned. "You'll lose."

She laughed at him. She'd never felt more free in her life. She never felt more powerful.

"No, I won't," Aris said confidently. "Not this time."

A shadow crossed his handsome face and Aris wondered if she had hurt him. Was he thinking of John? John. It was better for her if she didn't think about him either. She knew real feelings and people were involved. She wanted to believe she could escape this unscathed, but as the days wore on, the chances of that happening grew slim.

Suddenly, Rhys picked her up out of the water. They didn't even make it up the stairs before they started tearing at each other. Fucking Rhys was an act of violence. They grappled with each other like they were fighting their own demons. They swung fists and swore and whispered soft obscenities in each other's ears. This was so unlike anything she had ever had; Aris was enthralled. Rhys was sweeter and more intense than anything she had ever imagined. He was more fantastic and complicated than any man she could have ever dreamed up.

When they were together, the world shrank to Rhys: his eyes, his paint-streaked hands, the timbre of his voice. He was in her blood and she was unable to extract him. He lived inside of her.

John was a shadow; John was nothing. Rhys burned like the sun and Aris turned her face to him and bathed in the warmth.

As the days passed and summer became sluggish and steamy, Aris fell deeply in love. Sometimes she awoke in the night and went outside. The pavement was still warm, the night birds sang in the shadowy trees. Aris would sit on the sidewalk and tip her head back, still half asleep, and think, this isn't love, this is greater than love. This is something that hasn't even been discovered yet; this is what I have. This is all I have and it is all that matters.

Aris learned Rhys as though she were learning Braille, by touch, by feel. She ran her hands over his lean, long body and memorized every sinew, every bone, every pulse of a muscle she observed, stored away. She watched him paint, the flick of his elegant wrist, his brow laced together in concentration, the way his pupils dilated. She traced each line of the lurid tattoo he wore so gracefully. She put her hands in his black hair and told her fingertips to remember how it felt. Silky, soft. She put her mouth on him and tasted the salt.

He laughed at his own misfortune; he laughed at himself, and everyone else. Rhys was sharp, unable to stomach hypocrisy. If he felt any shame at their deception, he never mentioned it to her. They never spoke of the past or the future; neither wanted to remember the past and the future was too uncertain. They only spoke of each other, of their love of art, the beauty of the grotesque. They lived life swimming among great concepts and reveling in the details: love, death, art, beauty, pain, pleasure, the light at four o'clock, the shape of Aris' tiny toes, the flecks of gold in Rhys' eyes. Aris had never lived life that way; life was usually cluttered with the minutiae of living: dental appointments, traffic lights, mouse traps, gold watches. Rhys taught her there was something different. In the unbroken quiet of the hot afternoon, Aris asked him, "What are we going to do?" But Rhys didn't answer. Deeply asleep, he breathed hard as if he was running from something.

Chapter 14

John came home late, as he did almost every night. Aris was already in bed, asleep. This case was long and difficult and he was putting in more and more hours. He never saw Aris anymore; John couldn't remember the last time they sat down and had a meal together. He put his briefcase in his office and went to the kitchen to get some food. He opened the refrigerator; it was almost empty. John tried to swallow his anger. He didn't understand what she did all day. Why couldn't she go grocery shopping? John closed the fridge and started opening cabinets. These, too, were almost bare. John slammed the last cabinet and hoped the loud crack woke her up.

He grabbed a beer and sat down at the kitchen table. He looked around the slightly cluttered house. That was another thing! Why was the house messy? Aris had only two things to do, and that was clean the house and cook the food. For the last few weeks, she had done neither. John wondered if he should hire a housekeeper. As he downed his beer, a tiny seed deposited into his brain. What if she was with Rhys? John shook his head in disgust. He knew that was not possible. Rhys would never betray him and Aris couldn't possibly find Rhys attractive. John knew Rhys was attractive to most women, the kind of women who liked that mysterious bad boy crap. Women like that weren't worth much anyway, John thought; his cousin was welcomed to them. Rhys was everything Aris feared; all she ever wanted to do was conform and belong. John shrugged at the absurd thought, but it dogged him for the next few days.

The day he found out he had to go to New York, his heart plummeted a bit. He left the office early, hoping to take Aris out to dinner, but when he got home she wasn't there. John waited almost two hours before she sailed through the door. She looked happy, and, was John imagining, secretive?

"Where were you?" he asked her shortly as she came in the house.

Aris started. "Jesus. You scared me."

"Why are you so jumpy? Didn't you see my car in the drive?"

Aris shook her head. John tried not to wince at that horrible haircut.

"I don't know," she said. "I guess I wasn't expecting you to yell like that."

"I didn't yell," John told her.

Aris shrugged.

"Where have you been?"

Aris shot him a look. "The grocery store. Why?"

"Where are the groceries?" he asked tightly.

"In the trunk."

"Oh." John felt like a jerk. "I'll go get them," he said courteously.

John got the groceries out of the trunk and loaded them onto the granite countertop.

"You know," he said as he watched her put the groceries away, "I've been considering hiring a housekeeper."

Aris glanced at him.

"Why? I do all the housekeeping."

"You haven't been doing a very good job lately."

"I haven't?" Aris asked him. Did she sound slightly incredulous?

"No," John said baldly. "We're always running out of food. You don't go to the store when you should. We eat take-out way too much and frankly, the house is a mess."

"Oh," Aris said and flushed. "I'm sorry. I guess this lazy summer is getting to me."

"I can hire someone to do it," John said. "If you don't feel like it."

"No, no," Aris protested. "That would be a waste of money."

Oh, God, he wished she wouldn't talk like that! It made her sound so low-class.

"Don't say that," John instructed. "Nothing is a waste of money as long as it makes you happy."

"I am happy."

"Are you?"

John watched her closely.

"Of course," Aris smiled.

He had yet to bring up the teeth, but he wanted her to look pretty in the wedding pictures. Years from now, she would look at the pictures and hate her teeth. Maybe he would just give her veneers as a present, maybe for her birthday.

"I saw that Camaro again," John mentioned to Aris. Was it his imagination or did she stiffen?

"Did you?"

"Must be some neighbor's fix-it project or something. I saw it a few times in the area. I wish they'd keep it in their garage."

Aris frowned.

"I have to go out of town for a week or so," John announced.

Did she brighten at the idea?

"You do?" Aris asked, sounding surprised. "You never go out of town."

"In this particular case, we are dealing with international clients. We've agreed to meet in New York. Aren't you sad that I'm leaving?" John asked, watching her.

"It's only a week or so, right? I'll manage."

"Why don't you come with me?"

Aris paused. "I'd rather go to New York when we can spend time together. I'd just be in a hotel room, waiting for you all day."

"You wouldn't have to wait, you know. You could go shopping or out to eat or even, God forbid, sightseeing."

"I don't want to do those things without you," Aris protested.

"Fine," John said angrily. "Whatever you want. Sit around here and do nothing."

Aris left the house; the air was thick with heat and it was difficult to breathe. The Camaro was parked across the street again. This time, there was someone in the car. An old woman, with spun sugar hair, was smoking in the front seat. The smell of cheap booze and cigarettes rose unbidden. Aris turned to go back inside but it was too late.

"Hey!" a rusty voice called. It was the same tone Laura used for the welfare lady.

Aris leaned her head against the front door and refused to turn around. She recognized Laura's footfalls behind her. Funny, after all those years, it still sounded the same; it still meant the same thing to Aris, the end of peace and contentment.

"Don't tell me you didn't know it was me parked over there. I been watching you, kid."

Aris winced.

"Turn around and let me look at you," Laura commanded in a harder voice.

Aris reluctantly turned. Time had not been kind to Laura. She had missing teeth and dirty fingernails. Her clothes were absurdly inappropriate for a woman of her age. Her hair was falling

343

out. Laura grinned at her and held out her ropy arms.

"Come here, baby girl," she cooed.

Aris stared at her.

Laura's muddy eyes flashed in anger.

"What? You too good to give your own mother a hug?" she asked bluntly. "You think you're better than me? You ain't," Laura said shortly.

Her mother had not changed in the last twenty years. She was still a cold, desperate, and angry woman.

"What do you want?" Aris asked tiredly.

Laura laughed, a hard, husky sound. "I just wanted to see you, kid. I thought I could meet your fiancé. You know, I need a place to stay for a while and it sure would help me out if I could stay here. Am I invited to the wedding?"

Laura chattered at her as though nothing had happened, as if she hadn't been calling her and threatening her.

"You can't stay here," Aris said disgustedly.

"Yeah," Laura said as she lighted a cigarette. "You sure as shit do think you're better'n me."

Aris stared mutely.

"What a laugh," Laura said, but she did not laugh.

"Listen, I know we ain't seen each other in a long time. I know I ain't been the best mother, but give me a chance to make it up to you. That's why I'm here."

"That's why you've been calling me?"

Laura nodded excitedly.

"That's why you've been leaving me threatening messages alluding to blackmail?" Aris asked scornfully.

Laura's face fell. "I am having some financial trouble, now that you mention it. Kid, those weren't threats," Laura said unconvincingly.

Aris gave a deep sigh. Anger and pity mingled with old childhood fears.

"Wait!" Laura shouted. "Wait. I have something for you."

Laura shimmied back to the car and opened the trunk, which gave a loud screech. She came back with a battered, old suitcase and threw it with a thump onto the hood of Aris' car.

"Nice car," Laura muttered.

She opened the suitcase; mixed among short skirts and low-cut tank tops were yellowed papers.

"Wait, hold on a second. I got something for you. Something you can keep."

Aris watched her mother, puzzled.

"I don't want anything from you."

"Sure, you can have these. I been saving for you all these years. They're for you," Laura explained rapidly as she gathered the papers. She was rifling through the clothes and toiletries, grabbing wrinkled papers here and there.

"Mama," Aris said softly.

"Maybe this wasn't the best approach, you know, I guess, trying to get money like that. But I do need some help and if you know the whole story, then you'll help me."

Desperation with a tinge of craziness in her voice. Aris took a step back.

"Stop it," she said to Laura, who was still frantically searching the case.

"I said stop it. I don't care what your story is. I don't care, Mama."

Laura turned with the papers still in her hand.

"What?"

"I don't want anything from you," Aris said. "I won't give you anything either."

Laura's face fell, then she rallied.

"I will tell the whole world what a piece of trash you really are!" she screamed as she shoved the papers back in the suitcase.

"You have no idea who you're dealing with. You think you're such hot shit! You're no better than me!"

Laura shut the suitcase and hauled it off the car, scratching the paint in the process. She whirled and faced Aris. She was inches away and Aris could smell her rank breath.

"You listen good, kid," Laura said meanly, her muddy eyes hard. "You got a choice and you're lucky I'm giving you a choice. You either set me up nice or you brace yourself, because I will tell the papers everything about you and me. I will tell the hot-shit Prince family exactly who their golden boy is marrying."

Fear flashed in Aris' eyes; Laura saw it and smiled.

"See you around, kid."

Aris fled to Rhys and tried to put the whole scene from her mind. She did not know what else to do. Life was becoming a knot of others' wants and needs and Aris felt like she was at the center of it all, unable to quell the dangerously swollen tide.

John called when he could, but it seemed Aris never answered her phone. Instead, they left each other messages, playing phone tag. As the days went by and the case wore on, John felt tension growing inside him. He cut the trip short and flew home early. He did not call Aris to tell her. When he arrived in Larkspur, he expected to find the house empty and it was. The rusty Camaro was parked across the street again. John grimaced. He whipped out his phone to call the police. Enough was enough. He heard a sound like a whiny groan; something was emerging from the car. John shuddered. It was a woman, at least he thought it was. She was slight, with brown, wizened skin and spun sugar hair. She was dressed like a prostitute.

"Bet you're wondering where she is?" the woman hollered across the street.

John frowned. The woman lighted a cigarette and approached him. Up close, she was even more of a mess.

"Yeah, well, I know where she is," the woman continued in her gravelly voice.

"Who are you?" John asked disgustedly.

The woman grinned, revealing missing teeth.

"I'm her mother, Laura."

John took an involuntary step back. Surely, this couldn't be Aris' mother. This was some kind of joke.

"Too good to shake hands, huh, hot shit?"

"Please vacate my property immediately," John ordered. "You couldn't possibly be Aris' mother."

Laura laughed. "Ain't you the fancy lawyer! I ain't going nowhere."

"I'll call the police, Ma'am. I'm not sure who you are, but you can't be Aris' mother. Aris could never be related to someone like you."

Laura stiffened. "Like what, asshole?"

John wrinkled his nose.

"Oh yeah," Laura fumbled in her purse and took out her wallet. She thrust a picture at him. It was a little girl, maybe eight or nine. The violet eyes were unmistakable.

Laura laughed at him. "She's not good enough for you, even I know that."

John found himself nodding.

"She's fucking around on you," Laura said slyly. "Gimme some cash and I'll tell you where to find her."

Like a robot, John reached for his wallet and pulled out the money inside.

"Jesus Christ! You rich assholes!" Laura crowed. "Who runs around with six hundred bucks? Jesus Christ," she repeated.

"Tell me," John said, steely-eyed.

"Oh, sure, but first invite me in. I gotta pee," Laura demanded.

John grabbed her arms and squeezed.

"You're hurting me!"

"Tell me," he said again.

"Fine, fine. Just let me go."

She gave him an address. "Some good-looking guy too, real tough guy. Green eyes. I seen them out there. Seen him kiss her in the movies. I been following them for the last week," Laura bragged.

John turned from the woman, his black eyes far away. She barked out a laugh and sashayed across the street to the rusty car.

Aris was sleeping with his cousin. A dull knife slashed across his body; he felt hard, electric jealousy course through his limbs. He would kill them both. No, he argued with himself. It simply wasn't possible. There was no way Aris would prefer Rhys to him. Rhys might be a good-looking guy, but that wasn't enough to do it for Aris. Rhys was a loser and everyone knew it. He was adopted, for Christ's sake; he wasn't even a real Prince.

John went to their room and tore it apart looking for evidence, for a clue. He ripped open the drawers and pulled out a sketchbook. He thumbed through it. Aris sketched? Several shadowy pencil drawings crowded the pages. John ripped out page after page.

When he got to the industrial area where Rhys lived, John felt his gut tightening. He parked in front of the blue door and noted, with some odd satisfaction, that Aris' car, the car John had bought her, was parked out front. At the door, John hesitated. Then he twisted the knob; to his surprise the door gave way and swung open. As he mounted the dim stairs, the sounds he heard were unmistakable. He went slowly, stair by stair, praying he was wrong, knowing he was right. As he reached the top stair, the loft opened up before him. There was a large bed, low to the ground, and in it was his fiancée.

She looked like he had never seen her look: a warrior-queen, with mussed short hair and airy, graceful limbs. Her head was thrown back in passion. Beneath her was Rhys, brown, hard-bodied, gripping her hips, utterly savage.

It was Rhys who saw him come into the room. It was Rhys who lazily removed his hands from Aris' hips. He had not the grace or decency to look embarrassed. Instead, he wore a look of absolute pity. Aris' violet eyes flew open. They were purple with passion. When her gaze landed on John, she looked at him with a combination of pity and contempt. John, who the whole ride over had been thinking how he would kill them both, or at least beat Rhys bloody, turned and rattled down the stairs like a corpse.

Chapter 15

Although fondness of the drink ran in the family, John Prince was not known to be a drinker. Regardless, John Prince was drunk. He had been drunk for a week and he intended to stay that way. He sagged in the white wicker chair on the porch of the house in Napa and stared out at the dirty, green pond. He watched a dragonfly hover over the cloudy water. He ignored the sweat that ran down his sunburned face. He automatically tipped the beer can to his mouth, swallowing reflexively. The dragonfly buzzed away in a blaze of electric blue. He wiped his mouth with the back of his hand. His mobile lay on the glass-topped table next to him. The battery had, thankfully, died a few days before. He was glad; he didn't want to listen to the insistent buzzing of emails and voicemails. He was not sure if anyone knew where he was, and he didn't care if they did. He just wanted to stay drunk. He'd gouge out his own eyes if he could.

The hot afternoon settled around him, and he tipped the can back again. He did not know how long he sat there among those wicker chairs that no one ever used. He looked down at the smooth, worn wood of the porch, and when he looked back up, the sky was purple and crickets were calling to one another in the shadows.

He knew Disby was staying with Helen while the house was painted; it looked like the painters hadn't started yet. John didn't care who was there. He wasn't leaving.

The house had an abandoned feel to it; even though John had been staying there for a week, the house retained the empty feeling it had acquired when Disby packed up and moved to Helen's. Because of the painting, the staff had been given several weeks off; without them to perform the small tasks of dusting and weeding, the house had a slightly blemished appearance. The shelves and windowsills had a light layer of dust on them. Dust bunnies scurried across the floor when John walked, and the beautiful, old wood became marred with his dirty footprints.

Outside, the grass was too high and the garden hosted several tall and spiky interlopers.

John had gone over the edge and he didn't care. He only cared about staying drunk. He vaguely remembered a well-timed phone call to his assistant explaining he would be taking some personal time. He hoped he had not sounded too drunk.

John was passed out amidst the beer cans on the lawn, his skin reddening in the high July sun. The last thing he remembered was the black night sky and glittering spinning stars. That was how Disby found him. He awoke to her humming and her sandals slamming down on the porch as she made her way to the door. He opened his eyes and watched as Disby discovered his many empty beer cans on the porch. He rolled his eyes up to the sky. He was still drunk; the sun was too bright and burned his eyes. The day was already dry and heavy with choking heat.

"John?" Disby screamed, running over to the unmoving figure on the lawn. Her screeching was painful to him and he tried to sit up.

"Shh. Auntie. Quiet," he said, putting his finger to his lips. She was shocked at his disheveled appearance, but quickly tried to hide it.

"Hello, dear. What a..." Disby stopped for a moment as her eyes searched his face. He was gaunt, his eyes hollowed out in his face. He was unshaven and couldn't remember the last time he bathed. He knew he smelled.

"Surprise," John finished her sentence.

"Yes, very much so. I just came to get some things."

Disby was uncomfortable and edged away from him slowly.

John put his spinning head in his hands. He was going to vomit. He felt it rising in his throat. Disby looked around helplessly.

"What are you doing here?" she asked.

John shook his head.

"You can't stay here, dear," Disby informed him gently.

John waved her off.

John turned his head to the side and vomited, loudly retching. A stream of beer and bile poured out of his mouth onto the soft, green grass.

Disby turned away in distaste.

"Young man?" Disby continued to walk toward the porch, her nose wrinkled at the smell of either John or his puddle of vomit.

"Answer me, young man," Disby demanded.

John wiped vomit from the corner of his mouth with the back of his hand and then wiped his hand on his pants.

"I'm not leaving," he said.

Disby blinked and tilted her head, birdlike.

"What are you even doing here anyway? And in this condition? Where's Aris?"

"Aris is probably fucking cousin Rhys, that's where Aris is," John slurred.

Disby's eyes widened.

"Not leaving," John repeated emphatically.

Disby left the Napa house perplexed. She had never seen her nephew in such a state, and she was not sure what to make of it.

She let herself into Helen's house, her gray brow furrowed. Helen was in the kitchen making fried chicken, and Disby wrinkled her nose at the smell of hot oil. She didn't know how Helen could eat the way she did. Refined sugars and fried foods, it was a wonder she was still alive. Disby was a vegetarian. She carefully put her purse in the closet and surveyed the gaudy red and gold living room with a subdued wince.

"Disby?" Helen called from the small kitchen.

"It's me," Disby called out as she sailed through the kitchen door.

The kitchen was a pink nightmare. The walls were a pale pink, the countertops pink tile, and Helen had covered everything in hot pink gingham. Rhys called it the Pepto Palace.

"Where have you been?" Helen asked, wiping her hands on her soiled apron.

"Helen," Disby said dramatically as she poured herself a glass of iced tea. "You won't believe what I just saw."

"What?"

Helen jumped aside as grease splattered.

"I went to Napa to get a few things I had forgotten, and who should I find, drunk as a skunk, passed out on the lawn?"

"Who?" Helen turned around to face her sister, her beady eyes wide.

"John!"

Disby deposited herself in a kitchen chair and waited for Helen's reaction.

"What?"

"Uh huh," Disby nodded her gray head and took a sip of tea.

"No!"

"Yes," Disby said, nodding.

Helen stood there, looking at Disby, her face frozen in shock.

"What the hell was he doing there?"

"He said Aris has been having an affair!"

Helen shifted her bulk and waited for Disby to continue, ignoring the pops and hisses of the chicken on the stove.

"He vomited right in front of me."

"An affair with who?" Helen asked.

"Rhys."

Helen dropped her tongs on the pink tile and tears began to form in her black eyes.

"How could he do this to me?" she wailed. "After all I've done for him! This is how he repays me? I'll never be able to hold up my head again."

The smell of burning chicken filled the room. Disby got up and turned off the stove.

"I'm going to need one of my pills," Helen cried pitifully.

"I'll get them for you," Disby said, reaching for the bottle of Valium in Helen's purse.

"Oh," Helen wept as she sank to the floor. "Why must he cause me so much pain? Why must I endure such shame?"

Disby ineffectually patted Helen's broad back and realized she would have to call Janice and break the news to her. The thought had her trembling.

John knew the nights, smoldering with the hot embers of July. He knew the days, over-bright and sluggish with lurid warmth. Day and night piled on top of each other until they were one thing in his mind. He rattled about the still house like a wraith. He wandered the place like a forgotten ghost, trailing beer cans in his wake. The passage of time washed over him in unending waves. He did not know how long he had been in Napa. He did not care. He knew Disby had come, but he didn't remember when. Time became irrelevant to him. He only knew drunk and sleep, and that was all he wanted to know.

He drank until life became fuzzy around the edges and he was able to breath easier. On occasion he felt a hot wetness dripping on his hands and realized he was crying. Something had broken inside him. He felt it with each torpid pump of his blood; it sang hollowly in his aching bones. It twisted sharply in his gut. Bitterness filled him to the brim, eliciting short barks of humorless laughter from his chapped lips. He rarely ate and his clothes had begun to hang from his thin frame.

John arrived at his Granny's house in a blind stupor. He didn't know where else to go. He didn't want to go home; he couldn't set foot in the house. He couldn't bear the thought of facing his mother or Sarah's endless barrage of questions. Without realizing it, he drove to Napa. He let himself in, using the hidden key in the flower pot by the back door. The stale scent of lavender filled his nostrils as he went straight back to the study to the liquor cabinet. He drank every ounce of liquor in the house and, by the second week, had driven to town to buy cases and cases of beer. The old man at the counter assessed his purchases.

"Must be having a party!"

John dreamed of death. He frequently thought of hanging himself from the rafters in the attic, and even went up to there to see if they could hold his weight without breaking. He searched the groundskeeper's sheds for a rope and carried it around the property with him for days before abandoning it in the garden one night. When he dreamed, he dreamed of Aris and her violet eyes. He was plagued with visions of his cousin's silver ringed hands and the red paint streaked across Aris' body, like a bloody brand. He could never remember these dreams, but he woke shaking, hands groping for a beer.

Aris sat alone in the empty house. The heat pushed itself into her; it licked at her skin with a dull force. John was gone. She didn't know where he was, she didn't know if she cared. His silence, his absence, stung. She looked down at her red toenails, remembered the name of the polish, Harlot, and buried her head in hands.

For days after John had found them together, numbness coursed through her veins; her mouth was filled with the sour taste of deceit. John had been gone for a week at least. Aris did not know where he was; she did not care. When she slept, she would sleep in the easy chair; she dared not enter their bed. She wandered the hot house, a gray ghost, drifting among their things like a wisp of nothingness. She roamed the house, fingering items that used to mean something: the blown glass they'd gotten in Mendocino, the green vase he bought her from the antique shop in Sonoma, the pair of shoes he'd picked out for her in Paris, which she left so carelessly on the patio.

The guilt, the easy guilt, which she thought had made her affair so exciting, came crashing down onto her. She had willfully destroyed a man and a relationship and she had no idea why she did it. Did she love Rhys? She thought she did. Did she love John? She wasn't sure. Maybe Janice was right, maybe she couldn't separate John from his money and his lifestyle. Was that what she loved?

When John clattered down the stairs, Aris had breathed a sigh of relief. It was over. They were free. Aris looked down at Rhys; his face was shuttered. He plucked her off of him, as if she were weightless. As he dressed quickly, Aris sat in the puddled sheets, naked and stunned.

"You should go," he said to her.

That, she had not been expecting. It was the voice he had used with Katrina the day he told her to go. The coldness of his tone was like being slapped. Aris said nothing; she put on her clothes quickly and left silently. She had not seen Rhys since.

The days ran together like watercolors, with Aris suspended within them. It was as if life were indefinitely paused.

"Hey, Aris, your front door is wide open, for Christ's sake."

It was Rhys, his voice laced with his brand of frenetic energy. He appeared in the living room doorway, just as she was tearing down the hall to the bedroom.

"Aris?"

Aris could not answer him. She toppled headfirst onto the bed. The smell of John hit her. Rhys came into the room; she could feel his presence, the heat of him. She looked up from the bed, tears forming in her eyes. Rhys grimaced and closed the gap between them. He came to the bed and hauled her into his arms.

"Please don't cry," he said. "Please don't."

The words were tender and Aris curled into him.

She was not sure who began kissing who, but suddenly, they were kissing. Kissing madly, fiercely and Aris knew then, she would have done anything for him. She would have let him do anything to her.

Rhys pushed her back on the bed. His hot mouth roamed over her. A nascent consciousness fell over her. He was fucking her. Her arms circled him and her hands grasped at his firm flesh. Her nostrils filled with the spicy smell of John's cologne. Even as the spasms wracked her, she began to cry.

"Stop it!" she screamed. "Get off me!"

Rhys pulled back immediately. Aris reached down to her ankles and pulled up her panties. She wrenched herself up, sitting with her legs folded under her. Her face was flushed from crying, her eyes webbed with ruby. Her stomach clenched madly; she wanted to retch. Aris clutched the wrinkled bedspread with both hands and squeezed until her knuckles turned white. Aris began to beat on his solid chest with her small fists.

"What are you doing here?" she sobbed. Rhys stood impassively and let her hit him. "You told me to go and I left and I haven't heard from you in a week. Now you show up at my door and fuck me?"

Rhys grabbed her arms and pushed her lightly away.

"If that's how you want to play this, fine."

Rhys pulled on his pants and grabbed his shirt.

"I'm leaving."

"Leaving?" Aris' brows crested. "Are you kidding?"

Rhys' green eyes raked over her. "What do you think?"

"What if John had been here?" she asked him, her eyes smears of violet glittering in her pale face.

Rhys smirked. "I knew Johnny wasn't here."

"Why did you come here?"

Rhys studied her, emerald eyes detached.

"John knew, he finally knew, and when you could have me free and clear, you told me to get out!"

"He knew because he figured it out, not because you told him, Aris! You wouldn't tell him. I don't think you ever had any intention of telling him."

"I was afraid to!"

Rhys smirked again. "Why? Afraid you'd miss out on the free ride?"

Aris gasped. "You're disgusting! How can you say that to me?"

He leaned in the doorframe. She eyed his brown chest, the tattoo grinning at her. She hated him suddenly, hated him so fiercely that she could have killed him.

"Do you love me?" she asked him quietly. "I mean, this whole time, I thought you loved me. I thought-"

Aris stopped and looked at him, unwilling to further humiliate herself. Rhys tilted his head. He studied her with his piercing eyes; he stayed silent.

Tears began to pour down her cheeks.

"I am so stupid," she said to herself. "Oh my God, I am so stupid."

She couldn't even look up at him; she kept her eyes on the floor. To see the same pity in his eyes that he'd had for John, she couldn't stand it. He'd used her and she let him and she was so stupid; she hadn't known what was going on.

"What are you doing here?" she asked him quietly, still unable to look at him.

Rhys was silent.

"I said what are you doing here?" Aris screamed. "Get out of my house! You sick bastard! You destroyed my life and you did it for fun! For fun! You wanted to humiliate John! You wanted to flip off the whole goddamn family, and you used me to do it."

Rhys was taken aback; he threw up his hands and backed out of the room. Aris pulled her tank top down with such force that it ripped at the shoulder. She followed him, a woman possessed with bright, red eyes and hair like a golden halo.

"Look at me!" she screamed to his retreating back. "You had what you wanted! You tore John's guts out and you got to give the big 'fuck you' to your family. Why did you come here? Why come back to me now? Just to drive it home?"

She laughed maniacally.

Rhys turned to face her.

"Is that what you think of me?" he asked her quietly, angrily. His mouth twisted, his eyes were flat and cold. "If that's what you think, then I don't know why the hell I came here."

Aris let out a sudden howl, like a wounded beast. Rage and self-loathing mingled with mortification. She wanted to hurt or be hurt.

Rhys took her measure calmly, his green eyes flicking over her face with a glacial disregard.

"Shut up!" she screamed.

He started down the hall and dropped his shirt on the floor. He was moving quickly, taking long strides, trying to outrun Aris. She ran behind him and pushed him. She was a woman on the brink, nearly completely unhinged.

Rhys stumbled; that perfect physique, for a moment, crumpled. He turned swiftly so he faced her, Aris, the she-demon, all claws and teeth and burning eyes. He shoved her roughly against the wall. His large paint-covered hands pinned her there while her eyes lit with madness, and she laughed at him.

"What the fuck is wrong with you?" she whispered. "I hate you," she cried. "I hate you so much. You ruined my life."

"I ruined your life? Take some goddamn responsibility, Aris. You wanted out. You wanted out the moment Johnny roped you in! I was just a means to an end for you. You never said anything about love."

"But it was love!" she cried before she could stop herself.

"If it was love," he asked her quietly, "then why didn't you go home that first day and tell Johnny? Why'd you keep on sneaking behind his back? It was never love. Don't be a fool."

Rhys pressed her harder against the wall, his face inches from hers; his eyes, no longer cold, were green flames.

"It's so patently obvious you're jealous of John," Aris whispered viciously. "Poor adopted Rhys, never really fit in with the family. You were never a golden boy like John, but you had it just as easy as he did. You want to play black sheep and martyr? Please, you're pathetic."

"Shut up!" he yelled in her face, hands digging into her flesh. "You have no idea about my life. You have no fucking clue what you're talking about!"

Aris laughed meanly. "It's obvious everyone thinks you're trash. Garbage. Every single person in the family thinks so. You think I don't know about you? I know enough about you. You are garbage," she spat.

He released her shoulders then and stepped back from her. His eyes were anguished. His face was twisted in fury, his gorgeous, pouty mouth a snarl.

He started to walk away but Aris wasn't finished. She grabbed his bare shoulder; it was hot to the touch. He turned.

"What do you want from me, Aris?"

"I want you to hit me," she said it plainly, surprised at the words that came out of her mouth. She needed the pain she felt on the inside to be mirrored on the outside.

"I'm not going to do that, so go find some other guy to beat the shit out of you. It shouldn't be too hard."

Rhys sagged against the wall abruptly. Aris, suddenly aware of her body, wrapped her arms around her stomach. Fatigue draped over her and she simply shook her head. Rhys reached out to her, and she shied away.

"Don't touch me. You make me sick," she turned away from him. "I make myself sick."

John awoke and opened his eyes to stare at his big toe. It was covered in black hair. He wriggled it a bit. He was lying on his back on the porch. At some point, he must have dragged a   mattress outside because he was laying on one. He was stripped to the waist; he had put on his rumpled khakis again. He did not know what time it was. He was almost out of beer and he would have to go back to town to get more. The cloudless, azure sky hovered overhead. John watched a blue jay hop around on the lawn. It emitted several loud squawks that made him want to cover his ears. He heard the engine of a car coming down the drive. The gravel crunched under the weight of the tires. He closed his eyes.

He heard two car doors slam and then the sound of footsteps. The footsteps came closer and closer. He could already smell his mother's perfume. He recognized the click-clack of her clipped walk. There was someone with her.

"It's a good thing I've brought you," Janice said.

"Yes, well, maybe we should have brought some orderlies as well," said the man.

John opened one eye and looked at the pair before him. His mother stood at the foot of the mattress, not a hair out of place. She wore her distress in her black eyes and downturned mouth. Beside her stood a tall, trim man in his fifties. He was handsome, with gray hair and bright, blue eyes that twinkled. His face was without expression.

"John?" Janice said in voice he hadn't heard since he was a child.

"John, it's Mommy," she said.

John did not move; he just stared up at them with one dull, black eye.

"Dear God, Sidney, he's catatonic," she said, her voice rising in horror.

"I don't think so, Jan. I think he's just drunk."

The man leaned down toward the mess on the mattress.

"Hello, John. I'm Sidney. I'm a doctor. We'd like to get you somewhere more comfortable," said the man companionably.

John opened his other eye. He continued to stare up at his mother and Sidney.

"Darling, I had no idea you were this far gone. I would have come out here sooner."

Janice glanced at the doctor beside her. He was known for his discretion, and other family members had sought his help in the past. She stifled her embarrassment with a silly laugh.

John stared at his mother, wondering woodenly if she was really there.

"Don't want to go," John muttered.

"Yes, well, you don't have a choice. I'm certainly not going to let you stay here and drink yourself to death." Janice put her hands on her silk-clad hips.

"Why not?" John said grumpily.

"Young man, get up off that mattress," Janice ordered.

John waved his mother away.

"Young man," she said in a firm voice. "You get up off that stinking thing and come with me."

John tried to sit up and fell back upon the dirty, beer-stained mattress.

"Here, son, let me help you." Sidney leaned down to grab his arm.

John shook him off violently.

"Not your son. Don't have a dad. Do I, Ma?"

Janice's mouth dropped open when he called her Ma. Her black eyes widened.

"My mother is divorced. Did you know that?" John addressed Sidney. "He left her."

John jabbed his finger toward his mother.

"He. Got. Out." The words came out of his mouth staccato as he pulled himself up by the railing of the porch.

"That's enough, young man," Janice said imperiously. "I won't stand for that kind of talk."

John smirked as he leaned on the railing for support. He staggered past the two figures and into the house. The usually spotless kitchen was filthy. The smell emanating from the room was nauseating. Food wrappers and cans littered the butcher block counters and table. The wood floor was covered in muddy footprints and garbage. Pots full of food he had cooked and forgot about sat on the stove. The sink overflowed with putrid, brown water and dishes. Beer cans tinkled and clanked as John's feet scattered them. A black cat sat on the kitchen table, cleaning its paws. It hissed as Janice and Sidney came through the door.

"We don't have a cat," Janice whispered to Sidney.

"I know we don't have a cat, Ma," John yelled over his shoulder.

He walked over to the fridge and pulled out a can of beer. He leaned back against the fridge as he opened the can and took a long swig.

"I'm going to have to hire a cleaning crew to come in here and clean this. John, how could you do this to Granny's house?" Janice cried. "Where are the painters?"

"This is my cat," John said, as if he had not heard his mother. "Found him by the pond. He chases the things sometimes, but that's okay. If he catches that bird, we might have him for dinner," John grinned.

"I'd like you to go away now, please," he said politely. "I'm busy."

"No, John. You are coming with us," Janice began. Sidney put a hand on her arm.

"John, you either come with us or you go to jail," Sidney said as he slowly walked closer.

John smiled again.

"I'll put up a hell of a fight, Mister," he said in a John Wayne voice.

Sidney put his hand in his pocket as he came even closer. John threw his can of beer to the floor. The black cat jumped onto the stove top and began licking the side of a sticky pot.

"Stay away from me!" John screamed as he staggered back, his arms flailing as he tried to punch. He slipped on a puddle of muck and landed hard, limbs akimbo. Sidney pulled the syringe out of his pocket and plunged it into John's arm. The black cat jumped to the floor and ran out the door.

Chapter 16

"Damn you! I don't need this! I don't want to be here! Mother, get me out of here!" John screamed as the orderlies took him through the double doors at The Redwoods. Janice grimaced. Suddenly his face was replaced with Rhys' face and Aris was behind him, wearing her wedding dress, grinning happily.

Janice awoke from the dream, pale, sad, and alone in her bed. Rhys and Aris, it was simply not possible, but she had seen the predatory look in his eyes on that spring day in April when he appeared on the porch, like a ghost. She saw the way he watched Aris, but she convinced herself it was nothing. Now her son was locked up in a padded cell. Damn that Aris. She suddenly wanted a cigarette badly. She hadn't smoked in years.

Janice rose from the bed with a vigor that she did not truly feel; she was going to see her mother. When Janice got to the home, her mother was sleeping and she was unable to wake her.

"I want to see my mother's doctor," Janice demanded of the nurse at the front desk.

"He's busy right now," the nurse said importantly.

"I don't care if he's performing open-fucking-heart surgery. I want to see him. Now."

The nurse was so startled that she merely pointed to an office door in the hall. Janice knocked on the door and pushed it open.

Dr. Millen looked up and blithely assessed Janice. A perverted little smile played around his lips and he stroked his black goatee.

"Where's the fire?" he asked her teasingly.

Janice speared him with her black eyes.

"Who are you? You're not my mother's doctor."

"Who is your mother?"

"My mother is Mrs. Astoria Windham-Prince and you are not her doctor."

The man smiled condescendingly. "I am."

"No," Janice said through gritted teeth. "My mother's doctor is Dr. Thompson. I don't know who the hell you are."

The short, portly man drew himself up and stood. He was at least three inches shorter than Janice.

"I'm filling in for Dr. Thompson," he said to her breasts. "I'm Dr. Millen."

"What is wrong with my mother?" Janice demanded.

Dr. Millen glanced at his mobile as it pinged on the desk. He made a move to grab it.

"Do not even touch it," Janice told him. "I am here speaking to you and the very least you can do is be respectful enough not to get on your fucking phone."

The last words were said silkily. Dr. Millen glanced at the phone again.

"Very well," he said curtly. "What do you want me to say?"

Janice clenched her fists as outrage coursed through her veins.

"What I want you to do is tell me what is wrong with my mother? Why is she sleeping? She never sleeps during the day."

"First of all, she became uncooperative and I authorized a sedative. Second of all, I can't believe you people don't communicate with each other," the doctor said rudely as he glanced at the mobile again. "I've already told several members of your family that your mother is dying. She has dementia. She is at the end-stage. Now, please excuse me," Dr. Millen said as he shoved Janice toward the door. "I'm very busy."

Janice threw his hands off her arm. "Take your hands off of me. My mother is not dying. I've never heard a bigger load of bullshit in my whole life. If you've hurt her, if you've done something to her," Janice said threateningly, taking menacing steps toward him, "I will personally see you ruined."

The doctor puffed up. "Don't be ridiculous. Who do you think you are, coming in here and threatening me?"

Janice laughed in his face. "Millen, you said your name was? You're a moron," she stated.

The doctor's mouth opened and closed but he could make no sound.

"Since you seem to have no idea who I am, I shall tell you. I am a woman who does not abide negligence or laziness and I am a woman you do not want to cross. I am the daughter of Astoria Prince, and your poor care and obvious lack of training have hurt my mother. You're a shiftless idiot, Millen, and I'm going to see to it that you never practice medicine again."

With that speech, Janice whirled out of his office. He stumbled out into the hall behind her.

"Listen, Mrs. Prince. You don't know what you're talking about," he said rapidly. "I'm sorry if my diagnosis has upset you but that's the way it is. Your mother is very old. Quite frankly, she's lucky to have made it this far. You're overreacting."

Janice turned on him.

"I am going to sit with my mother, while I wait for my personal physician. He is going to examine her and I am more than confident that he will find evidence of mistreatment. While I wait for my physician, I'm calling Dr. Thompson and I'm calling Wayne Brody. You might recognize the name. He's the director of this facility. Start cleaning your desk, you fool. You'll be out on your ass in an hour."

The nurses in the lobby stared, openmouthed, as Dr. Millen scurried away.

"Our lawyer will be contacting you," Janice called after him. "Such careless mistakes won't be tolerated."

Janice waited beside her sleeping mother for her doctor. When she got Dr. Thompson on the phone, he apologized profusely. "Mrs. Prince, I am so sorry. I'm on vacation. I don't choose who replaces me when I go. The nurse faxed me your mother's chart and it appears after I left Dr. Millen changed her med combo quite a bit. That is what is causing this quote unquote dementia. We'll have to wean her off of them, of course. These pills are very strong and not something she can just stop taking. It will be a few weeks, but your mother will be back to normal."

Janice hung up the phone; she could hardly wait for her mother to return to her senses. She had to tell her something. A confession.

Janice had been a charming, black-haired, black-eyed little girl. From a very young age, she knew how to get her own way. Her father indulged her without restraint; her mother would step in delicately when she thought things were going too far. Janice was blithely unaware she lived a life of privilege. She believed all people were as happy as she, all people were as well provided for as she. As she grew up in the well-mannered house of her mother, her life was punctuated by visits from her father. He showered her with affection, and she basked in it. She knew, from the way Helen scowled at her, that he did not treat his other children as he treated her and J.J. They were different; they were special. As she grew into a young woman, her willfulness and wild streak grew broad and unfettered. She used her considerable charm to get her way and when she did not get her way, she reached for the crackling anger that was never far from the surface and unleashed it without restraint.

When she left for college, her father pulled her aside.

"Young lady," he said, smoothing his graying hair. "Most girls, like your sisters, are going to go to college, find a man and get married. You, my Janice, you are different. You were made for more. You and J.J. should be running my company, both of you. You major in business, like your brother did, and when you get out, I'm going to give you a job. You should have been born a man, Janice," he patted her hand and took a sip of his drink.

"You are more like me than any of the other children," he smiled affectionately. "I see so much of myself in you."

It had never occurred to Janice to consider the future. She hadn't given any thought to working for her father. It was not unappealing. She grinned and shrugged. If she didn't want to, he wouldn't make her. She knew that.

"I've had so many disappointments in my life," her father said.

Janice had a feeling he was peeling back some curtain and giving her a glimpse of himself, some secret part of him.

"But you, Janice. You are perfect. You would never disappoint me."

In her twentieth year, just before her senior year at Stanford, Janice went to Europe. She managed to convince her father that she would benefit from the cultural enrichment. Her family never traveled when she was young; her mother didn't like to leave Napa. Her father had been all over the world, but he went alone.

Janice and her friend DeeDee landed in London at the end of May, and Janice, aware that, for once, no one was watching her, immediately focused on having as much fun as possible. She had her fingers wrapped around the world, as though it were a little green and blue ball made simply to delight her. She instantly fell in with a fast and rich crowd of young and bored Americans.

They traveled the continent with abandon, crashing parties and lolling on beaches. Janice loved the men in Europe. They were dashing, foreign, and rich. They spoke with intoxicating accents and recklessly bought her presents. Janice wore her feckless youth with passion; she was saucy and charming and beautiful, and she knew it.

She was at a party in Venice with a group of Americans when she spotted a man staring at her from across the room. Janice knew she was pretty, and she was used to being stared at. But this guy was bugging her.

"Who is that guy?" she asked the Italian boy at her side. The boy had the face of an angel and sported so large a cock he was in the habit of whipping down his pants at parties just to show off.

"Who? The short guy?" the boy said in heavily accented English.

They both stared at him, as he, in turn, stared at them.

He was very dark and had a close-clipped mustache. His hair was long and silver, and he wore an earring in his ear, like a pirate. He was slight in stature, much shorter than Janice. He suddenly swept a low bow to them. Janice sniffed and turned her back on the man.

She heard a loud laugh from his direction. Then he was at her elbow. She looked at him, annoyed. He was older than her father, and there was a hint of craziness to his brown eyes. He began speaking in rapid Italian to her.

Janice rolled her eyes. "I don't speak Italian that well," she said curtly.

"Oh," he said jovially. "I switch to English for you, beautiful girl."

Janice cocked a brow expectantly.

"I am going to paint you, Bellissima!" he declared. "And you," he turned to Paolo. "You I am going to keep in my bed."

Paolo shrugged. Janice grinned.

His name was Count Mastorani. Although, Janice was sure he wasn't really a count. He seemed to be quite penniless, but he was a very gifted artist. He was old and small, but he was extremely energetic. He took Janice and Paolo to exciting parties and introduced her to a great many interesting people. He was a gypsy of sorts, always staying at this palazzo or that villa. He seemed to have no shortage of rich friends willing to take him in. Mastorani was like an overindulgent grandparent. He took great pains to introduce her to every young, eligible man he could find and seemed to delight in her affairs.

True to his word, Mastorani kept Paolo in his bed and painted Janice. He took them to his cousin's home in the countryside and boasted about his sexual prowess while he painted.

"Paolo is so beautiful, you think an old man like me cannot keep up with him, but I can, Bellissima! I am a bull! I cannot die, Bellissima! I will live forever!"

Mastorani opened a show in Rome at the end of June; he included a few nudes of Janice. Within three days she received a letter from her father at her hotel in Spain. The white envelope contained an article clipped from the San Francisco Examiner. The headline read, "Local Heiress Poses Nude." There was a small picture of her father in the corner. The envelope also contained a one-way ticket to San Francisco.

Her arrival at the Napa house had been cause for celebration. Jane, Morgan, and Disby spilled out in the yard erupting in high, feminine chatter as Janice emerged from the car.

"Jan!"

"We didn't know you were coming home!"

"I thought you were staying in Europe all summer?"

The three girls surrounded Janice, shrieking with excitement. Her mother, her faded red hair ruffling in the easy breeze, had come out on the porch and watched her with a smile on her face. The sun was just starting to set and the golden light infused the scene with a dreamlike quality.

Janice spent the first few days at home sleeping. She rarely woke before noon. She would get up and spend the rest of the day laying by the pond, sleeping. She knew her mother was worried about her. Every so often she would feel eyes on her and turn to see Astoria watching her. She started leaving the house and going for long walks among the verdant rows of lush grapes, simply to remove herself from her worried mother's line of vision. She wound her meandering way through the open fields, past the vineyards, sometimes on dirt roads.

"Hey!"

Janice turned, her long, black hair swinging across her back. "What?"

The man was half hidden in the grapes. He stepped out and nodded at her.

"You're trespassing."

Janice shrugged. "So?"

She studied him. He was wearing tight jeans, a white T-shirt, and a straw cowboy hat. His tanned face had a day's worth of stubble on it. He was handsome. High cheekbones dominated his face; an expressive and wide mouth twisted while she assessed him.

She smiled.

He did not return the smile, but looked her blatantly up and down. Janice knew what he saw without having to glance down: long, brown legs topped by scandalously short shorts, a trim, tight body, small breasts showcased in a tank top.

"Mm hmm, trouble, from the look of you," he said tipping his hat.

Janice shook her head as she laughed. A flash of white teeth.

"I'm not trouble. I promise."

"Uh huh," he said as he stepped back into the grapes.

Janice followed behind him.

"What are you doing?"

"Working," he said shortly.

"You own this place?"

"Nope," he said as he walked further into the row of grapes. "Just work here."

"My name is Janice."

"Of course it is," he said drolly.

"Don't you have a name?"

"Yeah, I'm too damn old for you and not interested besides."

"Long name."

He laughed. "My name is Nick."

"Pleased to meet you Nick," she said cheerfully to his back.

He turned and pulled his hat off. Thick, black hair tumbled down into his face. He squinted his green eyes at her.

"Janice, I think it's time for you to go on home."

"I think it's time you offered me a beer," she said.

"Are you even old enough to drink? What are you, about sixteen?"

Janice laughed. "I'm twenty."

Nick looked at her dubiously.

"Do you want to I.D. me?"

"No," he said slowly. "But I'm still too damn old for you."

"How damn old are you?" she asked, elegant brows arched.

"Thirty."

"I've had older," she said airily, waving her arm at a fly.

"I'll bet you have," he muttered. "Well, I'm not interested."

Janice laughed at him, struck a pose. "Of course you are."

Nick snorted again. "You have overdosed on confidence."

"Meet me for a drink, tonight, in town. Pink Elephant."

Nick put his hat back on and sighed.

"If I say yes, you'll get on home?"

"Sure," she chirped.

"Fine. Eight. Don't be late."

Janice turned and skipped away, her long, brown legs kicking up dust as she went. As she left the man, she was keenly aware of the butterflies in her stomach.

She sat at a dark table in the corner and sipped a screwdriver. Around nine o'clock she realized he wasn't coming. She had another screwdriver. Then she had another. She drove home quite drunk, praying her mother wouldn't still be awake.

The next day she took the car out to the vineyard where she met Nick. She pulled into the yard. He was standing by a barn, talking to an older man.

When she got out of the car, he said something to the man and loped over.

"What are you doing here?" he asked rudely.

"You fucking stood me up," she said slowly, her black eyes snapping with anger.

"Look, I told you I wasn't interested."

"Bullshit."

Nick sighed. He took his hat off and scratched his head. His thick, black hair spilled down to his shoulders.

"Okay," he admitted, "maybe I am interested. I just don't want any complications right now."

"I'm not complicated. I just came here to tell you that you are absolute trash and you make me sick," Janice smiled brightly. "Now that I've done that, I'm leaving. Asshole."

Janice turned on her heel and started to walk toward the car. Nick reached out and grabbed her arm. His grip was warm and strong. She looked down at his brown hand. He had long fingers, the fingers of an artist or a musician. She tried to shake him off but he held firm.

"You got a mouth on you, you know that?"

"Kindly let me go," Janice ordered through gritted teeth.

"Wait a second," he said, easing his grip.

"No," she said, and this time, she succeeded in pulling her arm away. She started back to the car; her sandaled feet made little puffs of dust as she stomped away.

Nick ran to catch up with her. He stood in front of the station wagon, blocking her way.

"I kinda like you, Janice."

"Congratulations. Now fuck off."

He laughed and stepped to the side, sweeping his arm in a welcoming gesture. Janice got in the car and sped off.

Two days later, she was taking one of her walks when a white truck pulled up next to her. Nick was inside. His shirt was off, and his muscular brown chest glistened with sweat. Janice swallowed as the butterflies began to flutter.

"Hey," he said, "want to go swimming?"

"Not with you." Janice countered.

"Come on," he coaxed. "I have a cooler full of cold beer and some sandwiches. As I recall, I owe you a beer."

Janice continued walking.

"You owe me more than a beer."

He drove slowly beside her.

"I guess I owe you an apology," he said ruefully and smiled.

Janice felt her heart leap when he smiled. She stopped and turned to face the truck.

"Get in!" he said, laughing.

"I'm waiting for my apology," she said haughtily.

"Of course you are. I'd better do it right."

He put the truck in park and got out. He came around to the passenger side and fell to his knees before her. He grabbed her hand and placed it over his heart. Janice stifled a gasp at the intimate pose.

"Janice, I can do nothing more than beg your forgiveness. I was so struck by your charm and beauty that I didn't know how to-"

"Oh, get up!" Janice shouted, laughing.

He grinned and opened the car door for her. "My lady."

Janice climbed in and watched him as he came around the front of the car to the driver's side. He didn't walk, he prowled. He swaggered. Each movement was an invitation. Everything about him made a woman want to swoon and be ravaged.

Nick drove her quite a way into the hills. "I have a secret spot," he said.
He stopped the truck at a small pond in a clearing. The pond reflected the green trees that hovered above it. The air was perfumed with honeysuckle. Nick leaped out of the truck and came around to open her door. Janice stepped

out, her blood singing. Sweat ran down the back
of her legs. She gave an unladylike tug at the
bottom of her shorts.

Nick pulled an ice chest out of the back
and placed it, and a blanket, under a tree. Then
he stripped off his jeans and ran down to the
pond in his underwear. Janice shrugged,
unzipped her shorts, took off her tank top and
followed.

"Ooh! That's cold!" she yelled.

Nick laughed and splashed her.

"Baby," he taunted.

"Ha!" she lunged at him, but he darted
away.

They swam for a while and then
emerged, streaming with pond water, to lie side
by side on the blanket.

"So Janice, you have a last name?"

"Prince," she answered, her eyes closed.

"Prince?" he said, alarm in his voice.
"As in Prince Group Vineyards?"

"I don't know. I guess."

"What do you mean you guess? Don't
you know if your family owns a vineyard?"

"My family owns a lot of things. Daddy
might have a vineyard. I know he has a lot of
land in Napa. Makes sense he would have a
vineyard."

Nick laughed derisively. "'Daddy might have a vineyard,'" he repeated.

"What?"

"Damn," he said ruefully.

"Damn what?" she demanded, opening her eyes.

"You're the boss's daughter."

Janice shrugged and closed her eyes. "Well, I have to be somebody's daughter."

Nick leaned up on his elbow.

"You honestly mean to tell me you had no idea that land I was working was your own."

"Nope."

"How can you not know what your Dad does? What he owns?" he asked, flabbergasted.

"Because he owns so damn much. What do you care? It's not as if he'll know some random field hand."

Nick shot up and started looking around for his clothes. Janice opened her eyes at the sudden movement. She raised herself lazily on her elbow.

"What?"

"I am not a random field hand, you ignorant little brat. I'm the head vintner at the winery. I make the goddamn wine."

"Oh," Janice said, nonplussed. "My mistake."

He started pulling on his jeans.

Janice got up and placed a hand on his arm.

"I'm sorry. I didn't know. Please don't get all pissed off."

He grunted.

"Shall I apologize to you?" she asked charmingly.

He sighed and buttoned his pants.

"Come on," she said coaxingly. "I'll get you a beer."

He allowed himself to be led back to the blanket and she opened the ice chest for a beer. She saw him eyeing her. She glanced down. Her yellow panties and bra were completely see-through. Her nipples showed enticingly through the cotton. Janice suppressed a knowing smile as her stomach flip-flopped.

He reached up and grabbed her at the waist and pulled her down on top of him. She had no time to think as he settled his lips on hers. They devoured with their mouths as their hands ripped at each other with an animalistic fury.

When the sun began to go down, Nick suggested they head back. Janice was reluctant. Nick was unlike any other guy she'd been with.

She told him to drop her at the top of the drive, out of view of the house. She didn't want her mother to know what she was doing. When she got into the house, she felt like her feet were hovering over the floor. She was awash in bliss, but the uncertainty of Nick's affection tickled the back of her throat.

"I was about to call the Sheriff," Astoria said as she ascended the stairs to her room.

"Sorry Mother, I lost track of time," she said absently.

Three tortuous days went by and Nick hadn't called her. She walked everyday; she haunted the dusty, quiet roads, waiting for the white truck to drive by. Each time she heard a car coming behind her, she held her breath. Finally, on the fourth day, after holding her mother and sisters hostage with her tension-filled gestures and harsh, snapping comments, she called the vineyard.

"This is Janice Prince. I need to speak to Nick," she realized with horror she didn't know his last name.

"Who's this, now?' asked the guy who answered the phone.

"Janice Prince," she said crisply. "Put Nick on the phone, please."

"Right away, Ma'am," he said, sounding confused.

Nick came to the phone.

"Janice?"

"Hi, thanks for calling by the way. It's nice to know you missed me."

"I've been busy," he said quietly.

"You're lying," she accused.

"Maybe I am."

"Why haven't you called me?"

"I don't know," he admitted. "Maybe we made a mistake. Maybe we should just chalk this up to summer madness."

"Summer's not over."

"No, it's not but-"

"Come pick me up after work," she cut him off.

"Janice," he started.

"Nick, come on. Don't resist," she said, laughing, appalled at the desperation she was feeling. "It'll only hurt more if you resist me."

Nick laughed.

"Irresistible, huh?"

"I am," she said seriously.

She waited for him in the waning light at the top of the drive, listening to the insects chirping in the bushes. She watched a few bees make lazy turns around the flowers that lined the top of the driveway. The white truck pulled up, and Janice felt her heart leap. His teeth flashed white in his tanned face as she hopped in the truck.

"Where are we going?" he asked her.

"I don't know. Let's go to your place."

"It's not much," he said.

"I don't care."

As she entered Nick's sparse cabin, Janice felt a strange shyness fall over her. It startled her.

"I told you it wasn't much. I don't live here full time. I'm from L.A. originally. I came out here to see if it was a fit. I might get a bigger place later."

"I like it," she said, fingering the worn couch.

The cabin was on a little hill, and the vineyard was spread below them. Looking down on the neat, green rows cresting the gentle hills, Janice felt like a goddess surveying her kingdom. Nick put his hand on her shoulder and she looked at the long, brown fingers before she turned to him.

Janice's summer, which she had anticipated would be like every other summer before it, took on a gilded quality. The sleepy and boring town of Napa was suddenly over the rainbow and everything was touched by magic. Life was beautiful, and she was grasping it with both hands and taking a bite out of it, savoring the lush sweetness of love in the summertime.

There was not a day she spent without Nick. She was so taken with him, and he with her, that they failed to notice their surroundings and would often discover they had missed a turn driving or that hours had gone by.

Nick talked to her about his passion: making wine. He'd studied his craft in Italy and France. He was cultured but down-to-earth. He was able to keep up with her, both physically and mentally. He made her laugh and was delighted with her sharp wit. When she left him in the early morning light, her skin always smelled like the soil. She loved it so much that she didn't want to bathe, lest she wash his smell off of her. One night she went home with his jacket and slept with it in the bed next to her. In the morning, she laughed at herself for doing such a childish thing.

Sometimes, she would sneak out and spend all night with him in his cabin. These nights were filled with laughter and intense passion. She found a freedom with him she had not realized existed. In such a short time, he knew her completely. She didn't have to be anything for him but herself. The feeling was electrifying.

The nights she spent without him were long. She spent those nights dreaming what their life would be like. They would get married and build a huge house in Napa. Her father would put Nick in charge of expanding the winery and she would be the toast of the entire wine-making world.

Janice followed Nick around the vineyard during the hot summer days. Sweat left trails down her back and between her petite breasts. She would watch Nick as he looked at her hungrily, and she knew it was only a matter of time before he swept her away to his bed. By the end of August, she was so entrenched in his life, she knew what he was doing at any time of the day or night. She had become accustomed to his routines and structured her life around him.

At the vineyard, he taught her about the soil and the grapes and the long process of making a bottle of wine. He loved what he did, and she envied him. He was happiest when he was walking among the twining emerald leaves. She spent many nights in his cozy cabin until she knew the place by heart. She could have walked there in her sleep she knew the route so well. She discovered a shortcut through her own backyard. She slipped into the grapes that bordered the back of the yard, walked a half-mile and made a sharp right. A few more yards and she would appear in his clearing.

She was the luckiest girl in the world. She was young, rich, beautiful, and in love. Life had attained a slow, dreamy quality, and Janice was bathing in it. Nick brought bottles of his favorite wines and had her taste them. He kissed her stained, purple lips. Most of their evenings were spent in a tangle of sheets in his bed. She always left before sunrise; she did not want to upset her mother.

The insistent heat of August bore down on them, day and night. The slow, dreamlike days gained speed. Janice realized she would have to return to school in a few weeks. She waited for Nick to ask her to stay in Napa; she waited for him to ask her to marry him. One night, laying in his low bed, listening to the nighttime noises outside his open window, she said she loved him. She was tired of waiting on him. She figured if she reassured him with her love, he would feel more comfortable with his proposal. The sheets were in a heap on the floor. They were sticky with sweat; she was cradled in his arms, despite the heat. She loved the feel of his warm, strong hands.

"I love you."

She said it without fear, without even a hint of uncertainty.

His hand, which was making slow circles on her stomach, stopped. He let out a deep sigh. She felt panic close over her heart. The insects outside seemed to get louder and louder, and still he said nothing. Janice was ready to leap out of bed.

"Janice," he said, his voice sad. "I love you too."

"You don't have to say it, Nick," she said hotly.

"No," he said, "it's true. I do."

"Then why do you sound so sad?"

She pulled away to look at him questioningly. His green eyes flickered briefly.

"It's just..."

"What?"

He shook himself.

"Nothing. Nothing, baby."

He pulled her back into his arms, where she snuggled happily. Before she knew it, August had melted into September and she was due back at Stanford. Nick still hadn't asked her to marry him or even to quit school to stay with him. Every time she brought it up, he was noncommittal or he changed the subject.

As she packed her bags, she tried to come up with a plan so she could stay closer to Napa, closer to Nick. It was only a matter of time until he asked her to marry him. They were in love.

Her family had noticed the change in her. Her mother saw her daughter's secret smiles and knew instantly her daughter had fallen in love. Her sisters learned quickly that Janice would agree to almost anything. Jane was borrowing her clothes constantly, and, when she was home, Morgan and Disby would beg her to do their hair or let them experiment with her make-up. Never had Janice been more agreeable.

Janice took her mother's station wagon into town to buy a few things from the drug store for school. Nick had called and told her he would have to cancel tonight, some sort of wine-making emergency. Janice was disappointed, but tried not to show it.

"That's okay. I have plenty to do here anyway, getting ready to leave."

"Okay, good. See you later then. I'll call you."

He sounded distracted.

Janice was coming out of the drugstore when she saw him. He was about ten feet away and heading toward her. He was with a blonde woman and two little kids.

"No," she said aloud. "No," she said again, insistently. But she knew; every inch of her hummed with the knowledge.

As he got closer, his green eyes widened. Shock, which he covered quickly, blazed in his handsome face. Janice was stock still in the middle of the sidewalk. They would have to go right past her. What was she going to do? Her brain begged her for a reprieve from the awful truth; maybe she was wrong? But she knew, inside her heart, she was not wrong.

Then they were there, on top of her, about to walk right past her. His eyes burned into hers. The blonde was talking in a low voice and one of the kids was saying, "Daddy? Isn't that right, Daddy?"

Oh, God.

They were just past her when something in her shouted out to speak.

"Nick? Is that you?" her voice sounded tinny, like it was not her own.

He turned. The first thing she saw was those gorgeous, high cheek bones he'd inherited from some Cherokee ancestor. They stood in relief in his brown face. Then the eyes. His bright, green eyes were flat, cold. She'd never

seen them this way. They were usually warm
and heavy with lust or dancing with amusement.
And the mouth. That beautiful, wide mouth,
with the slightly crooked teeth. It opened. He
spoke. It was just them. No one else here. Just
Nick and Janice, like it always had been. The
street, the cars, the sidewalk, all receded in her
mind until all was Nick and Janice and this
suspended moment.

"Janice! What a surprise!"

From the corner of her eye, she saw
movement. The blonde. Her hand snaked out
and grasped Nick's. Janice flicked her black
eyes to the woman. She was short, dumpy,
overweight. Her hair was long and hung in her
eyes. Her face was unremarkable.

Janice knew what the woman saw. A tall,
young beauty in her prime. Long legs and pert
breasts. She should feel insecure, Janice thought
blithely.

"Is this your family?" she asked calmly.

"Um, yes, it is," Nick said
uncomfortably.

Janice waited.

"Ah, this is my wife, Jaime, and our two
children, Mickey and Jenna."

"Pleased to meet you," Janice said
without sparing the woman or children a glance.

"How do you know Nick?" the blonde asked tartly, her eyes darting between Janice and Nick.

"I work for her father," Nick said quickly. "He owns the vineyard."

Janice stood still, did not speak.

"Um, well, we'd better get going. Bye, Janice. See you later." Nick gave a pathetic wave and pulled his wife down the street.

Janice did not know how she got home. She kept playing the scene over and over in her mind. Everything he had ever said or done was suspect. The summer's dreamy quality dropped away in an instant. Reality put its cold, demanding hand on her shoulder. She regarded everything dully. It was as if the world had lost its color. Everything was gray. She wished fervently for winter. The heat belonged to another time, another life. Nick's deception had broken something inside of her, and she would never again be who she was before. She had changed, irrevocably, and not for the better.

Chapter 17

Janice was at school for a month and a half before she realized she was pregnant. She spent October and November fighting morning sickness and wondering what she was going to do. Every time she thought of telling her parents she was pregnant, she heard her father's voice: "Janice, you are perfect. You would never disappoint me."

She knew she should get rid of it. She wanted to hate it. She prayed at night that the tiny spark of life inside her would simply slip out one day and take the need to make a decision away from her. She felt funny cramps in her abdomen and wished there to be blood in her panties, but this thing, Nick's baby, clung to her with determination. The spark, as she thought of it, wanted to live. At the end of November, Janice talked herself into it. She was going to get rid of it. It was a complication. It was unwanted. It would ruin her life. She went to a doctor who took one look at her and said, "Are you sure you want to do this?"

She wished the stupid man had never asked her that question. She slid off the exam table, shaking her head tiredly.

"Wait!" he called after her.

She kept going.

Once she chose to keep the baby, she was confronted with another decision. Did she have the courage to disappoint her father and break her mother's heart by keeping the baby? Should she give it up? Janice clung to the little spark fiercely. She was surprised to find herself so protective of it, so proprietary. The little spark was hers. It did not belong with strangers.

She went home for Christmas break. The family gathered at the house in San Francisco for the holidays. It was one of the few times during the year that found Astoria in the city. They would all sit at the huge dining room table, Johnny at one end and Astoria at the other, with their children between them.

The San Francisco house had Johnny Prince's touch all over it. The man, although blessed with good business sense, had terrible taste. The Victorian was outfitted with gaudy, gold wallpaper, gold fixtures, gold lighting; rich, red velvet adorned the windows. If it was shiny or sparkled, Johnny Prince wanted it in his house. He was like a child in that way. She didn't know how her mother could stand it.

Janice came home from Stanford a week before Christmas. She took up residence in the San Francisco house, since the Napa house had been closed up. It would remain shuttered for the last week of December. Johnny expected Astoria to attend all the holiday parties with him. Every year, for as long as Janice could remember, her mother would pack up the children and make the journey into the city. They would be divided among the rooms in the house. She would stay until New Year's Eve, returning to the house in Napa, children in tow, on New Year's Day. Johnny threw a huge party downtown on New Year's Eve. He had done so for years. He always sent his wife home at twelve thirty and had his mistress brought in at twelve forty-five.

Janice entered the old house and wrinkled her nose at the potted palms in the foyer. Something smelled horrible. Her mother came around the corner and threw her arms around her.

"You're home!"

Janice smiled wanly and nodded.

"You don't look so well," Astoria commented.

"I'm fine, Mother."

"Maybe you would like to go upstairs and lay down? I've put you in the blue room. By yourself."

Janice brightened. "You mean I don't have to share?"

"No," Astoria said smiling. "With Helen married and Michael..."

Astoria trailed off. Michael had only just died two years before in Vietnam.

"Okay," Janice said quickly.

Astoria always cooked a big breakfast for the children in the house on Christmas Day. Recently, J.J. and Olivia started bringing their kids over in the morning.

Johnny Prince awoke early on Christmas morning and started working in his office. Janice didn't think he had ever taken a day off. Even when they were little, they would have to pry him out of the office to open his presents.

Now that he had grandchildren, he was slightly more involved. J.J. and Olivia's four children were cute little babies who were growing into cute little children. Spoiled brats, in Janice's opinion, but charming nonetheless.

They would come just in time for breakfast. J.J. would take his place next to his father, and the two would discuss business to the exclusion of the rest of the family. Olivia would sit, her back ramrod straight, her hair a teased, blonde cloud around her head, and begin repeating society gossip to Astoria, who listened politely, but Janice knew she couldn't have cared less. Their four children, whose names Janice was constantly confusing, would be dressed in matching outfits. They banged their cutlery against the china and complained loudly about the food.

Gus and Minnie had five children that were all fat like their father and bad tempered like their mother. They would come soon after breakfast, all seven of them lumbering into the house, the floorboards creaking in distress. Gus would head straight for the kitchen in a thinly veiled attempt to scrounge whatever food might be left. "Just going to see Mother," he would say, his fat sausage fingers working nervously. Johnny barely spared Gus a glance when he came into the house.

Just before dinner, Helen and Ben came. They had just been married in what Janice thought was the tackiest ceremony she had ever had the displeasure to participate in. Awful, pink dresses and terrible, burgundy cummerbunds; Helen had inherited her taste from her father and the wedding reception had been a perfect reflection of it. Everything was covered in gold glitter: the flowers, the tables, the dance floor.

Dinner, which Janice remembered as being a very quiet and solemn affair from her childhood, was now a loud and raucous meal, thanks to her nieces and nephews. Her father did not seem to mind the noise, and her mother clearly reveled in it. Janice got a small twinge when she realized her child might one day join the fray.

Once dinner in the opulent and overdone dining room was complete, the family scattered around the house. Astoria and Minnie and Helen went to the kitchen to tend to the dishes. Gus and Johnny and Ben adjourned to the study to drink brandy and to talk politics and sports. The children retreated to various rooms in the house to play with their new toys.

Janice managed to corner J.J. alone on the porch. He was smoking a cigar, and she felt a wave a nausea wash over her. Although he was twenty years her senior, there was always a closeness between them.

"J.J.?"

"Hey Jan," he said, and she could tell he was smiling in the dark.

"I've got to talk to you about something. I need your help." Her hands twisted around themselves as she spoke.

"What?"

"You can't tell Mom or Dad. Okay?"

"Jan, aren't we a little old for this?"

"Shut up and listen," she said impatiently.

"Okay, okay, Jesus. What?"

"I'm in trouble."

"Yeah, what is it?"

"No, I'm in trouble," she repeated.

"Oh," he said.

"Oh!" he exclaimed, finally catching on.

"You need money to get rid of it?"

"No," Janice said slowly. "I don't want to get rid of it. I'm not even sure I can, at this point."

"Of course you can. How far?"

"I think four months, maybe five."

"What? Haven't you seen a doctor?"

"No," she said blithely.

"Jesus! What in the hell is wrong with you!" he shouted.

"Shut up! Do you want the whole fucking house to know? Damn it, J.J."

"Sorry," he lowered his voice considerably. "If you're keeping it, they're going to know eventually."

"I have an idea."

J.J. waited silently.

"What if I give the baby to Helen and Ben?"

"Hmmm."

"She can't have kids, they've been trying forever and, that way, I could still be around him."

"Him?"

"I think it's a him," she said, unconsciously placing a hand on her stomach.

"Not tell anyone?"

Janice nodded.

"That way everyone is happy. No one gets hurt, and I get to watch my baby grow up."

"It's not bad. It's a little crazy though, Jan," he commented, drawing hard on his cigar.

"Will you talk to Helen and Ben? They'll do anything you tell them to do. Ben's an idiot and Helen's desperate."

"All right Jan, I'll make it happen, but I don't like the idea of you all alone and pregnant at school. And we have to get you to a doctor!"

Janice smiled. In a way, she would get to keep her baby and she would never have to see the look of disappointment in her parents' eyes. They would never know of her shame and her loss. No one would ever see the pieces inside her, the part of her that Nick shattered. In the back of her mind, she cursed herself for being a coward. She'd never backed down from anything or anyone in her life, and she was backing down now.

"Helen and Ben can tell everyone they adopted," J.J. was musing. "You'll have the baby before you graduate from school. Of course, you can't come home for spring break, but that's not too unusual..."

Helen and Ben agreed to take the child, as long as it was healthy. Evidently, Janice thought, Helen's desperation only went so far.

Janice gave birth to Rhys Michael Prince in May of 1977. She'd managed to cover the pregnancy at school by wearing baggy clothing. It was the week during her final exams when she felt the first pains. She went to her last final, already feeling contractions. Her pregnancy had been relatively easy but her labor was not. She was in labor for almost two days. For the first day, they refused to let J.J. in the room. She'd called J.J. when the pain started and he made the drive with Helen and Ben. She hadn't wanted anyone but J.J. in the room with her.

"Get my fucking brother in here," she ordered the nurse.

The woman stopped. "That's highly unusual."

"I don't give a shit. Go get me my brother."

The nurse stared at her.

"Now!"

But J.J. didn't come. When the nurse came back a half-hour later, Janice asked her, "Where is my brother?"

"I told you it was highly unusual for family to be allowed in the room."

"You didn't tell him I wanted him here?"

"No."

Janice gritted her teeth as another pain ripped through her. She started pulling out her I.V. as she sat up.

"Mrs. Jones! What are you doing? You can't do that!"

The nurse was alarmed.

"If you won't get my fucking brother, I will go and get him myself," Janice said as cold sweat rolled down her face.

"I'll get him. I'll get him right now," the nurse promised, clearly fearful her charge might have the baby in the hospital waiting room.

On the second day, Janice was still in labor. The doctor wanted to do a cesarean, but she convinced him to wait another hour. It was in that hour that Rhys was born. That fierce little creature conceived in love, the only love she would ever know, came into the world with a loud cry in the midnight hour.

Rhys stayed with Janice for three days while they were in the hospital. Janice, much to the chagrin of the medical staff, had insisted he stay with her in her private room.

"Don't you want your rest dear? He should be in the nursery with the other babies," the nurse said, grabbing the edge of the plastic crib and starting to pull it away.

Janice grabbed the other side of the crib.

"No, I do not want to rest," she said through gritted teeth.

The nurse gripped the crib harder and tried to pull it away. Janice pulled back. She had not liked the nurse when she first saw her. She was short and squat, with a wrinkled, unhappy face and short, curly hair. The woman inclined her steel-gray head at Janice.

"Listen, I know you're giving him to that couple I saw in the waiting room. It's not good for you to spend too much time with him, you know."

At this, Janice wrenched the crib away from the woman, feeling a pinch in her abdomen as she did so. She smiled her sweetest smile.

"Get out of my room, and don't come back. Am I making myself clear?"

The woman's faded blue eyes snapped.

"Excuse me?"

"You heard me. You are dismissed. Put someone else on my room. I don't want you."

"What? What?" The nurse sputtered.

"Go!" Janice ordered.

The nurse backed out of the room slowly, shaking with anger. "Don't you dare try to breast-feed that child!" she called out as she opened the door. "He won't feed from a bottle if you do!"

Janice smirked at the woman and placed her son at her breast.

"I'll do whatever I damn well please," she told him. He looked sleepily up at her. She spent those three days marveling at his tiny toes, stroking his soft, black hair, loving it when his mewling cries interrupted her sleep. She craved the tug at her breast when she put him there.

On the third day, they were both released. She got into the blue wheelchair, knowing that Helen and Ben waited on the other

side of the door. The nurse placed him in her
arms and she clutched him tightly. Once she got
past that door, he would become someone else's
child. The nurse started to push her from behind,
and Janice stifled the urge to put her feet on the
floor and stop the chair. She was making a
mistake. J.J. saw the look in her black eyes.

"You can't change your mind now,
Janice. It's already been decided."

The wide, white door opened and Janice
wanted to scream. She clutched the baby even
tighter, for a moment thinking she could just
take him and keep him. Somehow.

Helen held out her beefy, white arms.

"Ben, just look at him," she cooed.

Ben nodded.

"Our baby," Helen said beatifically.

Janice swallowed hard. She was not
going to let them see her cry. She unlocked her
arms and passed her child to Helen, who
swooped him up. A sharp cry rent the air. Janice
felt her breasts tingle in response.

"What'd you do?" Ben asked, peering
into the blue blanket.

"Nothing," Helen answered, startled.

"He's hungry," Janice said.

Helen started to walk away with the
baby. Janice wanted to leap up and wrench the

screaming child out of her arms, but she kept perfectly still. J.J. put his hand on her shoulder.

"Ben! Ben! Come on," Helen called. "We need to get him home and fix him a bottle."

Janice sat in the chair and watched them walk away with her son, his wailing carving out pieces of her heart as the sound got further and further away.

Sometimes Helen missed her husband Ben. She didn't like to admit it, but sometimes she missed him. Sometimes she even missed living in Montana, away from the rest of the family. She picked up her phone and dialed the numbers she knew by heart. When he didn't answer, Helen wasn't surprised. He never answered her phone calls.

This scandal with Aris was the last straw for Helen. She never should have taken him. If she hadn't taken Rhys, maybe she could have kept Ben. The day J.J. came to her house, he made it all sound so easy, so smart. She signed papers, swearing never to tell where they had gotten the child and then one day, she had him. One day, he was simply there in her arms. Helen had loved Rhys so much.

Rhys was a loud and demanding baby. By the end of the first day, Helen was exhausted. All Rhys did was cry. He cried the whole way home from the hospital. Ben gritted his teeth, said nothing. Helen fussed at the child uselessly. It took her two days to get him to eat. He wouldn't tolerate being put down. Every time she placed him in the yellow bassinet, he would turn red-faced and wail at her.

"Now I know why women drown their babies in the bathtub," she said distressed.

Ben had not held the child since they'd brought him home. He peered into her arms and looked at the howling bundle and grunted.

"Oh, Ben! What am I going to do?"

"You'll figure it out," he said as he slipped out into the garage.

Benjamin Smith was a plain man, both in looks and beliefs. His face was long and homely, with a sleepy-eyed brown gaze. Everything about him was average, from his education to his mannerisms. He moved to Montana in his early thirties and had been there three years when he met Helen Prince one cool spring morning.

She was a plump woman, which Ben liked. Ben had always been attracted to women who looked like his mother. He liked their soft folds, their natural acquiescence. He liked the way Helen blushed.

After almost a year and a half, Ben decided to propose. He did it one autumn night while they were rocking on the porch of his house. The sky was scattered with winking stars. He tugged at his trousers and got on one knee before her. The ring he presented to her was a simple gold band with a pear-cut diamond chip in the center. It was plain, compared to the rings her sisters-in-law had, but Helen barely noticed. She gave a pig-like squeal before she jumped up from the rocker with a quickness that belied her great size.

"Now," he said, getting down to business. "We can't very well live here, in this old bachelor pad. You need something befitting a lady."

"When are you coming to California to look at places?" Helen asked.

"What in the hell are you talking about?" Ben asked startled. "You're moving to Montana."

"What?" Helen was astonished. "Why would I do that? I can't leave my family. They're all I have."

"You have me."

"Oh," Helen looked embarrassed. "Yes, that's true," she admitted.

"Helen," Ben said reasonably. "I have a business here. I can't just leave that. It took me years to build up the relationships I have with my customers. What do you have in California? Besides family?"

Helen hesitated.

Ben slapped his hand down on the porch rail. "Exactly!"

A silence filled the night between them. Then Helen opened her mouth; she was unwilling to lose Ben.

"Ben, I'll move to Montana," she said grudgingly. "But we have to get married in California. You have to come out and meet my family. They're going to love you."

In the year since he'd met her, Ben had never met Helen's family. She spoke of them frequently, especially her father, Johnny. He pictured a cozy house in Northern California. Although he had never been to California, he imagined the northern region was full of redwood forests and lots of foggy days.

When Ben pulled up to the house in Napa, his eyes bulged. The vision of the cozy cottage amidst the redwoods melted as his truck crunched down the gravel drive. The house had

been made with incredible attention to detail.
The cornices and the columns on the porch had
tiny flowers carved into them. The porch was
freshly swept and adorned with baskets of bright
flowers.

Ben gathered his bags and stood
awkwardly on the porch. He felt a pang of regret
that he had not stopped to change into nicer
clothes before he got there. The woman who
answered the door looked him up and down, her
caramel face lined with disapproval.

Ben spent Easter week with the Prince
family. He found them to be an odd,
mismatched bunch. Johnny Prince was a busy
man who barely acknowledged Ben's presence
in his home. His silver head was always bent
over some paperwork or he was in his office at
the back of the house, making phone calls.
Several times, Ben heard shouts of anger
coming from behind the closed office door. Ben
was not used to Helen's shrieking young sisters;
he only had one brother, Andy, and a dead little
sister, Arlene, who died before he was born. He
was not used to the level of noise the family
produced and frequently wished he was back in
Montana, alone in his quiet house.

Easter dinner was a loud and long affair.
Several rectangular tables were set up in the

front living room. Ben was astounded when all the children and the grandchildren started pouring through the door on Easter morning. It seemed unending. Soon, the house was full of people. Helen was dragging him from one little knot of people to another, proudly showing him off. He kept his brown eyes straight ahead and smiled politely. When Astoria found out Helen was planning to move to Montana, she became distraught.

"You've been looking at houses while you have been in the state?" Johnny inquired.

"No, sir. I've been looking at houses in Montana."

Astoria looked aghast.

"Helen, you never told us you were planning to move so far away," Astoria said, clearly hurt.

Helen looked at her full plate guiltily and said nothing.

Johnny looked across the wide table at his wife.

"It's so soon after Michael," Janice began furiously.

Johnny silenced her with a look. An uncomfortable silence hung over the table. After dinner, Johnny invited Ben to have a drink with him on the porch. Ben declined.

"Suit yourself," Johnny said as he poured himself a brandy. "Come with me out here on the back porch."

Ben followed reluctantly. Johnny settled on the wicker porch swing and indicated that Ben should sit in the chair across from him.

"Now, as you can imagine, Helen didn't tell us that you all were planning to move so damn far away."

Ben nodded. Johnny paused, took a sip of his brandy, and smiled in satisfaction. His thick, silver hair fell over one black eye, and he tossed his head like a stallion.

"Ben, I'm not sure my wife is too keen on the idea," Johnny said casually, examining his glass. "I think we need to remedy the situation. Don't you?"

"Ah," Ben stammered. He was a business man; he was used to making deals and coming out on top, but he dealt with farmers, not men like Johnny Prince. Ben didn't have the negotiating skills to tangle with Johnny Prince and win.

Johnny smiled in satisfaction. His black eyes never left Ben's face.

"I knew you'd see reason. So here's what I'm proposing, I know you got yourself a little business out there in Montana. I know you're making some decent money out there. I would hate for you to have to start all over in California. So, why don't you draw up a business plan and I'll bankroll it."

Ben stared at the man. Calculating. Johnny Prince took a sip of his brandy and waited for Ben to say yes. Ben dropped his brown eyes to his boots, unsure of how to proceed.

Johnny Prince leaned forward. "I'll tell you what Ben, You just give me a number. A rough estimate. We'll work out the details later."

"A million," Ben said instantly, looking shocked at the sound of his own voice.

Johnny smiled knowingly.

"Everyone has a number, Ben," he said easily.

Ben said nothing, put his hands in his pockets.

"I guess now you know mine," he said.

"My wife doesn't need to suffer needlessly. She's already had two children die. If she wants Helen in California, she'll have it."

Ben sold his house and his business and ignored the feeling of remorse in his bony chest. At the wedding, Johnny presented him with a cashier's check for one million dollars. Ben stifled a gasp when Johnny put the check into his hands. He fought the exclamation bubbling up in his throat.

"Well," Johnny said blithely, sipping his drink. "Congratulations."

Ben was unsure if he was being congratulated on the marriage or the check.

They moved into a large, suburban neighborhood in Marin County. Ben spent most of his time on the road, selling farm equipment. Helen quit her job at the jewelry store and started keeping house as she waited to get pregnant. After two years she was still waiting, and then Rhys came to live with them.

"Here's that check I promised you," J.J. said in the waiting room of the hospital as he handed Ben a clean, white envelope. Ben nodded and slipped the envelope in his jeans pocket. They had been waiting for half the day for the baby to be born. Ben's frustration showed in his clenched fingers, his shuffling feet. Finally, after midnight, he insisted they go back home.

"What if we miss it?" Helen whined.

"They'll call us," Ben said. "Ain't no use sitting around that place. This is ridiculous."

"Okay," Helen said primly.

"I have been thinking of names though," Ben said.

"Oh?"

"Want to name him Acel after my father. Acel Smith," Ben said proudly.

"Well, Ben, honey," Helen picked lint from her dress. "If we name the baby Smith, then he won't be entitled to any inheritance when Mother and Daddy pass. It's a provision Daddy built into the will."

Ben frowned. "At least the first name then."

Helen quickly hid a grimace. "I'll talk to Janice."

Janice refused to change the baby's name but Helen never told Ben. Ben called him Ace, but everyone else, including Helen, called him Rhys.

Once the child was in his house, Ben found he didn't want it. He didn't want his fate to be immeshed with the Prince family, either. Since the day he sold his business in Montana, a quiet unyielding resentment sat on his stooping shoulders. The over-bright California days strengthened this resentment. He hated Marin County; he hated his father-in-law's knowing smiles. The pitying glances from the Prince family penetrated his thin, white skin.

Ben began to dream of leaving. He had come to hate the grand family parties, the excess, the waste, the sheer audaciousness. The Prince family lived as if no one and nothing else existed. Theirs was an exclusive club, and Ben knew he was not a part of it. He was tired of their wagging tongues and penetrating black eyes.

He started to make plans. He would go back to Montana. He would build himself a house. He would be a farmer, like his father had been.

Ben grew up in Iowa. His father, Acel, had been a large, gruff man. He'd had gray hair for as long as Ben had been alive. Ben had no memories in which his father looked youthful; he could still picture his gnarled hands fingering the crops. His brother, Andy, had been the spitting image of Acel: heavily muscled arms and trunk, square jaw, his hands horny and knotted from working in the fields.

Ben favored neither of his parents. His father called him a beanpole and insisted he carry the heaviest loads. "You need to put some muscle on you, boy, so you don't look like a sissy your whole life."

While the child in his house went from a red, screaming burden to a laughing, overindulged toddler, Ben was quietly planning to leave his wife and her suffocating, emasculating family. He sat at those overblown parties in Napa, bitterness growing inside him like rotten seed. Helen would squeal and titter watching the black-haired boy tear around the lawn with all the other Prince children as Janice would sit under the shady willow called Astoria's Tree, holding her own black-haired baby, ignoring her husband, and watching Rhys, longing stamped in her hematite eyes.

Despite her family, Ben did love Helen. When Helen looked at him, there was worship swimming in her plain face. He was exalted in her eyes and he knew it. He didn't want to give her up. Maybe he would let her come with him to Montana. He knew she would go, with Rhys' tiny hand placed firmly in her own.

After they adopted Rhys, things had changed. Helen divided her attention between Ben and Rhys, but slowly, her attention focused more on Rhys and less on Ben. She had the bassinet in their room. She said it would make it easier on her when Rhys woke in the night. Then she moved him into their bed. She placed the squalling child between them and Ben rolled over swiftly. After a few weeks, Ben insisted Rhys stay in his own room. Rhys screamed all

night long for two nights in a row. Helen moved
Rhys back to their bed, and Ben started sleeping
in the guest room. For two years, he'd been in
the guest room.

When Johnny Prince died, Ben almost
fell to his knees to give thanks to God. He
thought briefly of his own father's death. Acel
died near the end of winter, in the South Pasture.
They found him late that night, after he failed to
come home for supper. Ben thought of his father
lying dead among the horse shit and frozen soil.
His hands curled up inside themselves; his
brown eyes staring at nothing. Those eyes had
taken his measure the very morning he had died
flicking over him in obvious contempt.

"You ought to be married, Benjamin.
You ought to have a wife by now. You're
twenty-nine years old, and you still live here."

Acel smirked. "If I didn't know no
better, I'd think you was queer."

Ben thought of Johnny Prince, collapsed
on his Oriental rug. Those dancing, gloating,
black eyes finally stilled.

Helen immersed herself in her grief.
Rhys was quiet for once; he seemed to sense the
somber mood of the family. Ben tried to avoid
the whole situation by spending as much time
on the road as he dared. When he came back the

day before the funeral, he found Helen on the kitchen floor. She was in a stained, white nightgown. Rhys played next to her, oblivious to Helen's abnormal behavior.

"Helen?" Ben asked tentatively.

Helen's head lolled to one side. Ben crouched before her and took her face in his hands.

"Helen?" he said again loudly. Her black eyes were glassy. She raised her hand and caressed his face clumsily.

"Mama?" Rhys asked, mimicking Ben. Ben spared him a glance. Rhys crawled across the floor and began to climb into Helen's lap.

"Not now, Ace," Ben said impatiently as he pushed Rhys onto the floor. Rhys looked up at him.

"Helen, come on. Get up," Ben said as he pulled at her doughy arm. Helen got to her feet, unresisting. He led her down the hall to her bed. Rhys followed behind as best he could, hollering gibberish.

Ben tucked Helen into bed. He noticed a pill bottle on her bedside table. Valium. He took the pill bottle and stalked into the kitchen, stepping over Rhys as if he were a pile of horse dung. He threw the pills into the sink and stood there, running the water, until they disappeared down the drain. He ignored Rhys' constant stream of chatter.

The day he closed the deal on the house in Montana, Ben left work early.

"Helen!" he called.

There was no answer. He went into the kitchen where the sink was piled with unwashed dishes. He shook his head in disgust.

"Where in hell are you, Helen?" he hollered.

He found her in their room, laying in the bed and clutching at Rhys, who was trying to squirm out of her arms.

"What in hell are you doing?"

Helen regarded him with slitted eyes. Tears streaked down her face. Ben sniffed the air; it was rank with the smell of unwashed flesh.

"Hey, girl," he said from the doorway. "You need to get up out of that bed. The time to grieve is over."

The boy squirmed out of her arms and started crawling across the bed.

"I sold the business today. We're moving back home."

"I am home," Helen said confusedly.

"Montana," he clarified.

"Ben!" Helen sat up in the bed, the springs in the mattress groaning. "We can't just up and leave. What about my family? What about Rhys?"

"That's another thing," he said sternly. "That child will be sleeping in his own bed in his own room once we leave California."

"What?" Helen cried, dismayed.

"You heard me. I've had enough. You're going to turn him queer, if you haven't already. He's too damn old to be sleeping with his mother, and I want my damn bed back!"

Helen looked at Rhys, who was sitting on the bed regarding Ben solemnly, as if he understood what Ben was saying.

"You think now your sister is married and your father dead, she's not thinking about taking that kid away from you? Of course she is!" he scoffed.

"No, Ben, she wouldn't do that. It would kill Mother. Jan knows better."

"Ha!" he spat. "She'd find a way. You know she would."

Helen stared at him, nonplussed.

"The only way to protect him is to take him away from here," Ben said gently. "I'm doing this for you, Helen."

Helen saw the way Janice watched her son. She knew Janice was not above taking him. As she prepared to move, Helen avoided her family as much as she could. She had never been a good liar. She felt the weight of her untold news circling her, lying next to her in bed at night. A lie of omission is what Astoria would have called it. Helen purposefully waited as long as she could; she had half the house packed before she called J.J.

"J.J. it's Helen."

"Oh," he said, sounding distracted.

"I hate to call you at work," she began.

"It's alright," he murmured.

"Ben and I are moving."

"Oh?"

"Yes," she paused, "to Montana."

"What?" he asked, sounding more alert.

"Ben's got a wonderful piece of land out there and he wants to try his hand at ranching. It would be a wonderful opportunity for little Rhys."

"Helen," J.J. said, his voice tight with anger. "I thought this was a non-issue. Dad already took care of this before he died. You can't leave. It would break Mother's heart. What about Janice?"

"What about Janice?" Helen asked uncomfortably. "She has her own family."

"Don't think there isn't going to be a fallout from this. There will be," he warned.

Helen sighed deeply. "I was hoping you could handle it."

"Really?" He was amused, but not surprised.

"Yes. Maybe you could tell everyone. I just couldn't handle the stress," Helen whined.

"When do you plan on leaving?"

"Next week."

"Next week! Helen, have you lost your mind? Our mother and sister are going to be devastated."

"That can't be helped, John," she said stiffly.

"Uh huh." He wasn't buying it. "I know exactly what you are doing, and I won't do your dirty work, Helen. You are a grown woman; you deal with the consequences of your actions."

Helen was outraged.

"You can't be serious!"

"I am," he said with finality.

In the end, she had Ben do it. He tried to keep the satisfaction he felt from his voice as he called each member of the family. He was quick and perfunctory; he never gave anyone the chance to say anything back to him. He saved Astoria and Janice for last.

"Hello, Mrs. Prince?" Ben said into the phone as Helen watched him anxiously.

"Yes, it's Ben Smith. How are you Ma'am?" he asked politely. Helen glanced at Rhys in his highchair. He blew spit bubbles at her while he played with his SpaghettiOs.

"I know. It's been tough on Helen too," he said rather brusquely. "Listen, the reason I'm calling is because-" Ben paused. "Well, because Helen and I are moving to Montana. I've sold the business and bought a ranch, and I think it will be better for us in the long run."

Helen squeezed her eyes shut and waited for Ben to hang up.

"Ah, Helen can't come to the phone right now. Migraine," Ben said swiftly. "I'll have her call you soon."

Helen watched Ben glance at the pad beside the phone and punch in more numbers. Her hands twisted as she waited for Janice to answer the phone.

"Hello? Janice?"

He paused. Helen stood beside him wringing her hands anxiously.

"Can I speak with her?"

He paused again, rolled his eyes at Helen. The maid, he mouthed at her.

"Uh, yes, Janice. This is Ben Smith."

Helen could hear her sister clearly and dearly wished she couldn't.

"Last on the list am I?"

Ben sputtered.

"How dare you call me? How can you do this to my mother so soon after my father's death?"

Janice was furious. Helen closed her eyes.

"Janice, I admit the timing was not great," Ben started.

"Really?" she laughed an ugly, mirthless laugh. "Seems to me your timing is just perfect."

"Listen," Ben raised his voice. "We got every right to go where we want."

"Who's paying for that ranch, Ben? I know just where your money comes from. Don't you forget that, you fucking hayseed."

Helen put her hand to her mouth. Ben was shaking with anger.

"You listen here," he began sternly.

Janice cut him off. "No, you listen. I'm not Helen. Don't you even think about speaking to me that way. If you do this, I will find a way to make you pay. Please know," she said silkily, "I will break you, Ben Smith. I will ruin you. Stay here in California and you'll be taken care of. You know that. But out there in Montana, well... Is this all clear to you?" she asked lightly.

Ben gripped the phone tightly.

"Perfectly," he said through gritted teeth.

The noise was audible as she slammed down the phone. Ben replaced the phone on the cradle and looked at his wife.

"It's done, Helen. Now we are free. Truly free."

Helen nodded, her eyes frightened. Ben didn't know the Prince family; he didn't understand them. There was no telling if Janice and J.J. would forgive them for leaving. Astoria would eventually, but Helen's brother and sister were another story; they never forgot, rarely forgave.

Helen and Ben drove their new Chevy from California to Montana. Rhys sat in the back in his car seat and chattered loudly. Ben's temper slowly intensified as the hours passed. Helen tried to shush the child as she watched her husband's brown eyes while the scenery whizzed by. They arrived at the ranch early in the morning. The sky held onto a pinkish glow as the little family exited the truck. There was a great deal of land, flat and grassy. The house was a prefabricated log cabin. Helen stifled her disappointment. She got Rhys from the car and he immediately took off across the long, whipping grass.

"Rhys! Come back here, honey. There could be wild animals out there!" Helen called.

Ben chuckled.

The first year in Montana was idyllic. Ben raised chickens for Tyson. Row after row of chicken coops littered their ranch. Helen soon grew used to the smell, but Rhys couldn't stand it.

"Smell yucky," he'd say if they went too close to the chicken sheds.

They had a small farm with a few cows, pigs and sheep. Ben was happier than Helen had ever seen him. He rose before sunrise and tended his animals. Helen spent her days playing housewife to Ben: cooking, cleaning and playing with Rhys.

Rhys was a charming child, outgoing and flirtatious by nature. He was loud, rambunctious, inquisitive, and intelligent. He seemed to enjoy the outdoors a great deal and would often attempt to wander outside. Helen kept him under her watchful eye, making sure he didn't hurt himself.

Helen was disappointed Ben did not take an interest in the boy. She thought, over time, he would get used to the child and accept him as his own, but he had not. Ben maintained a careful detachment from Rhys. He rarely acknowledged him, and, when introducing him, he never called the child his son.

Helen, who had grown up with so many people surrounding her, was suddenly alone. Her world shrank to three people: herself, Rhys, and Ben. Her sisters rarely called. Neither Janice nor J.J. ever called her. Astoria called occasionally.

On the days her mother called, Helen locked herself in the bathroom and cried. On Rhys' fourth birthday, Helen took the pictures from his party and put them in an envelope, intending to send them to Janice. But Ben found them and shook his head. "Bad idea, Helen," he'd said.

The holidays, which were once packed with people and filled with the joyous shrieks of children and the contented laughter of her siblings, became small and quiet, a shade of what they used to be. She tried to ignore the way Ben cut his brown eyes to Rhys.

When Rhys came of school age, it was Ben's idea to teach him at home. Helen had argued this, telling Ben that Rhys needed to be with kids his own age.

"No," said Ben. "Do it the old-fashioned way. That's what my parents did with us."

"But," Helen bit her lip.

"I said no. It's settled."

Ben's mother had been a plump, comforting woman. Ben remembered her bustling around the farmhouse, always cleaning or cooking or baking. He had been Olga's favorite. She used to sneak into his room, after his father had whooped him.

"It's only 'cause he loves you, Benjamin," she said, pulling him into her warm arms. He'd rest his head on her ample chest and clutch her with his small, white hands.

She'd gotten cancer when Ben was sixteen. The doctor pronounced there was nothing he could do for her. They moved her from the bedroom she shared with Acel to the back bedroom; Matilde, Andy's wife, would come and sit with her while Ben, Andy, and Acel worked the farm. At first, Ben visited his mother often. He read her passages from the Bible, stumbling over the words, his voice

445

stilted. Andy and Acel avoided her. It was rare for Ben to see either one of them in her room. The weeks piled on top of one another, and Ben began to avoid her as well. As the cancer ate at her, she began to moan in pain. She started to look like she had been in a concentration camp, a barely breathing skeleton. Ben couldn't bear the sight of her; she sickened him. She had ceased to look human; her plump and comforting figure was sucked away. In her last weeks, Ben rarely went to see her. When Matilde and Andy went home to their own house, Ben and Acel were left with her. They ignored her, letting her languish slowly in the cold back room. Ben only went in when he could no longer ignore her moans. He would administer the morphine, while trying not to look at her.

"Please," she begged him. "Please kill me. Just give me more," she whispered. "Just give it all to me."

He couldn't do it. He couldn't kill her. She died alone, on a windy day. Andy, Ben, and their father were already in the fields. When Matilde arrived, she went to see if Olga needed her and was met with the blank, glassy stare of death.

When Helen announced she had cancer, Ben almost vomited. Visions of his mother, repulsive, hairless, practically an animal, swam before his eyes.

"Boy, you go on and git now," Ben said harshly to Rhys, who was playing with his toys in the living room. Rhys got up slowly, a confused look on his face.

"No, Ben, I want him here with me," Helen protested.

"Ain't no time for a child to be around," he said gruffly.

Rhys stared at him.

"I said git on up to your room, Ace," Ben hollered.

Rhys scampered past him, and Ben swatted at the air behind him for good measure. Helen sat down on the brown leather couch. Ben looked at her plump body and wondered how much longer she would have it. Helen felt an unnatural calm settle over her. She was surprised; she had no ability to handle a crisis. She always fell apart. Yet, she was oddly calm. Ben remained standing, his body rigid, as if he were poised to run.

"It's stage one," she said.

"What's that mean?"

"It means that they caught it in time. Best-case scenario. Chemotherapy should take care of it."

"How long?"

"What do you mean?"

"How long until you... What I mean to say is," Ben paused.

"A few months and we'll know if it's gone."

Ben swallowed hard.

Helen called Astoria, who wept, and said she would be on the first plane out to Montana. "No, Mother, it's not that bad," Helen said, again surprised at the calmness she felt. "I'll call you if I need you. I promise."

About half an hour after Helen hung up with Astoria, the phone rang again. Ben, who was sitting in his den staring blankly at the wrestling match on TV, reached out and answered the phone.

"'Lo?"

"Ben." It was Janice. Ben cringed.

"Where's Helen?"

"Helen!" he yelled out from his chair.

"What?" she called from the kitchen.

"Phone for you."

"Hello?"

Ben knew he should hang up the phone, but he didn't.

"Come back home," Janice demanded.

"Jan?" Helen's voice cracked.

"I've had it with your crap, Helen. How in the hell are we supposed to help you when you are in Mon-fucking-tana? You need to come home. All of you."

"You don't care about me," Helen sniffed. "You probably hope I'll die just so you can get your hands on my son!"

"Don't be ridiculous," Janice said harshly. "You need your family right now. I am certainly not going to plot to take away your child while you have cancer."

"Ha!" Helen said.

"I've had friends go through chemo, Helen. It's very ugly. Very difficult."

Ben pictured his shriveled mother; she had been senseless in her last days, too much morphine. She thought she saw dead people. He remembered finding her hair all over the house. She dropped it in their food, clumps of it in the bathroom.

"You really think Ben can run your farm and nurse you and take care of Rhys," Janice was saying. "You're delusional. You need to come home."

449

"The doctor said we caught it very early. I barely have cancer," Helen said.

"That's the stupidest thing I've ever heard you say," Janice said, exasperated.

"You just want to get your hands on my son! I know how you work, Janice. Manipulating everyone! Always have to get your way. Always have to have everything. Always need to be in the spotlight. I will be fine. My husband will take care of my son. Don't you worry about me."

"Fine," Janice snapped before she hung up on Helen.

Ben put the phone down quietly. He decided the first thing in the morning he would hire a nurse and a housekeeper.

"What about Rhys' schooling?" Helen asked. The calmness she felt from the day she had been diagnosed was gone. Her hands were shaking in her lap. She couldn't keep them still; they kept twisting around each other. Twisting and twisting.

"What about it?"

"I can't very well continue teaching him when I'm ill. Should we enroll him in school?"

Ben considered this. "No, I can do it. He just has to do a bunch of papers right? Colors and numbers and letters?"

As the chemo wreaked havoc on Helen, Ben put his energies into schooling Rhys.

"Get them papers done and then you can come and help me on the farm," Ben ordered.

Rhys contemplated him.

"What're you looking at boy?"

"Daddy," the boy said tentatively.

"Call me Pa or Dad," Ben ordered swiftly.

Rhys' brow furrowed. "Dad, I'm also supposed to read from one of those books for a while too."

"You're five, what can you read?" Ben said dismissively.

Rhys grabbed the book eagerly. "I can read pretty good," he said proudly. He opened the book and began to read.

"So?" Ben was unimpressed.

"Mama says I'm really good for my age," Rhys said grinning uncomfortably.

"Too much of that bullshit. You need to be outside, learning the farm. You have any idea what I was doing when I was your age, Ace?"

Rhys shook his head.

"Finish them papers, then you come outside with me."

"What about the book?" Rhys asked.

Ben grabbed him by the shoulders and pushed him down into the chair. Rhys was startled.

"Don't back-sass me, boy," Ben said sternly.

Ben saw little of Helen during her illness. He moved her to the guest room and tried to ignore her retching in the toilet. He pretended not to see the clumps of hair around the house. Once, he entered her room and her head was uncovered.

"Why aren't you wearing that scarf thing?" he'd asked startled.

"I got hot."

"Put it back on," he said gruffly.

One day, he found Rhys in bed with Helen. He was reading in his childish voice, stumbling over some words, grinning up at Helen. Helen leaned against the headboard tiredly; she tried to pull Rhys closer.

"What the hell you doing, boy?" Ben asked.

"Reading my book to Mama. I know you didn't like me to read to you, but Mama likes it." Rhys smiled.

Ben strode over to the bed and yanked the boy out roughly.

"What are you doing?" Helen asked, alarmed.

"Git out of this bed and leave your mother alone. She's resting," Ben said as he pulled the boy out of the room by his arm. Rhys twisted in his grasp, and Ben looked down to see tears in his eyes.

"Don't you cry like a sissy, boy."

"I said it was okay!" Helen called after them. Ben ignored her. He pulled Rhys into his room and shoved him toward the bed.

"You leave your ma alone, you hear? She don't feel good. She needs her rest, and you climbing all over her ain't going to make her feel better. You hear?"

Rhys nodded, his green eyes shining with unshed tears.

"I catch you in there again, you'll get a whooping," Ben warned.

Astoria arrived on a cold November day. Morgan and Disby were in tow. They stepped out of the black rental car and surveyed the flat, grassy farm. They assessed the log cabin briskly. Ben, who was out on the farm, had seen the black car inching its way up to the house. He correctly assumed it was Helen's family and decided they could see themselves in.

The three women walked slowly up to the house. Helen had tried to take some of the starkness out of Montana by planting bright yellow flowers in the window boxes hanging from the porch. But the flowers were all dead, brown stalks. In the back, she tried to build a garden like her mother's and managed to fail spectacularly. The ground was frozen. Everything had died. Disby hauled the luggage up the porch while Morgan held Astoria's arm. Both women were reminded of their mother's age during the trip to Montana. She'd needed help getting up and sitting down. Her once vivid red hair was threaded with gold. She gripped the porch railing hard as she ascended the steps.

As they opened the door, a blast of heat rushed over them. The potbellied stove in the center of the room was crackling red with fire.

"Who are you?" Rhys asked alarmed. He was sitting in the kitchen eating a bowl of soup.

"Don't you remember us, honey?" Morgan asked gently.

"No," Rhys raised his green eyes to the ceiling. "Maybe. Are you my grandma?" he asked Astoria.

Astoria inclined her head. "I am."

"Okay," he said charmingly. "I remember you."

Disby and Morgan exchanged glances.

"Are you here to see Mama?" he asked, wriggling in his chair.

"Yes," Disby said. "I'm your Aunt Disby and this is your Auntie Morgan."

"Mama's going to die," he said blackly.

"No!" Morgan rushed over to Rhys. Her heels scuffed the floor as she came to him.

"Mama is much, much better, darling."

"Oh," Rhys said, though he clearly didn't believe her. "Don't read her any stories, even if she asks you to," he warned darkly.

Ben came in from the farm a few hours after the Prince women arrived. Disby and Astoria were cooking in the kitchen and Morgan was playing with Rhys on the floor of the living room. He grunted a hello and went to the bathroom to wash up.

They stayed for a week. Ben made it clear there was not enough room on the farm for them, so they stayed at a hotel in a nearby town. Each day, when Ben came in from the farm, he would find something new in the house: an afghan, a vase of dried flowers, a rug. Morgan gave the housekeeper and the day nurse the week off, and the three women took turns cooking meals and taking care of Helen. Ben ignored them, spending his time out on the farm or in his den.

Helen's mood improved noticeably; by the end of the week, she was on the sofa in the living room, having gotten out of bed for the first time since her chemo began.

"What in God's name is she doing out here?" Morgan hissed as she poured herself a drink.

"A little early for that, no?" Disby nodded to the drink.

Shut up and give me a cigarette," Morgan demanded as she shook out her bushy, red hair.

Disby sputtered.

"Come off it," Morgan said exasperated. "Mother's sound asleep in her room, and I know you smoke."

Disby reluctantly handed Morgan a cigarette and lighted one of her own.

"It's two thirty in the afternoon," Disby protested as Morgan poured more bourbon in her glass.

"Please, after this week? Helen's cancer ridden, her husband is a weirdo, and poor Rhys doesn't even know who we are. Are we going to talk about that house? How can she live there? No wonder she got cancer. It's so depressing."

"It is pretty bad," Disby agreed, taking a drag.

"I say, while Mother's napping, we go on a little shopping spree," Morgan suggested.

"You think you're going to find decent clothes in Montana?" Disby asked in disbelief.

Morgan laughed.

"You mean Mon-fucking-tana?" she asked, mimicking Janice.

Disby reddened. "Please, Mother is in the next room. Don't swear."

Morgan rolled her eyes. "Not for me."

"I don't think Ben likes your little contributions to the house," Disby ventured.

"You're right about that. No, I was thinking about poor Rhys. He's so lonely out there. No friends from school. No cousins to play with. He barely has any toys. How does the child amuse himself? Go out on the farm and watch the chickens shit out eggs?"

Disby smothered a giggle. "I'm sure they don't shit them out," she paused. "At least I hope they don't."

"Come on," Morgan grabbed the keys.

When the three Prince women left Montana, there were many hugs and tears flowed freely. Ben stood back and watched. They threw piles of gifts at Rhys, whose green eyes grew wider and wider as he opened each package. Morgan and Disby squealed delightedly and silently congratulated each other on their successful shopping trip. When the women had gone and Helen went back to bed, Ben surveyed the toys strewn about the new rug in the living room.

"You don't need all this," he said. Rhys, who was playing with his new yellow dump truck, barely looked up.

"I said you don't need all this crap. You'll become a spoiled brat," Ben declared. He went out into the shed and came back with a box. He started throwing the toys in the box. Rhys finally took notice of what Ben was doing.

"Dad? Why are you doing that? Where are you taking those?" Rhys jumped up alarmed. "Those are mine! My Aunties gave those to me!"

"Already acting like a spoiled brat," Ben confirmed to himself. "You can keep that one," he said, nodding to the dump truck. "The rest go to the church for poor kids."

Rhys pressed his lips together and tears gathered in his eyes.

"Oh, you're gonna cry, huh?" Ben mocked.

The tone in his father's voice caused the tears to spill over onto Rhys' cheeks. Ben watched the tears coursing over Rhys' face, walked calmly over to the boy, and spanked him soundly.

When Helen was declared cancer-free and her hair began to grow back, she moved her things back into the bedroom she shared with Ben. He seemed surprised to see her.

"Oh," he said as she slid into bed next to him.

"Aren't you happy to see me?" Helen asked shyly.

"Of course," Ben said jovially.

During her illness, Ben had shied away from her. He rarely went to her room to see her and, after he hired the nurse, she was the one who drove Helen to chemo. Helen thought it was because she lost her hair. He kept his eyes on the floor when he saw her; he couldn't bear to look at her. Now that she was better, she expected him to start looking her in the eyes again but he did not. If her feet grazed his in bed, he pulled them away swiftly, even in his sleep. Although he was having a hard time getting reacquainted with her, she was delighted that Ben was spending more time with Rhys. She believed her illness had brought father and son together. Ben took Rhys out on the farm with him in the afternoons after his school sessions. She noticed Rhys was reluctant to go but she said nothing. Then one day he came in with tears running down his white cheeks.

"What is it? A wild animal?"

Helen was always concerned about wild animals. Rhys shook his head.

"Honey, tell Mama what happened."

"Daddy spanked me," Rhys said with great gasping breaths.

Helen studied him. Her parents had never spanked her or any of her brothers and sisters, but she knew it was not uncommon.

"Were you a naughty boy?"

"Daddy, I mean Dad, said I was. He said I back-sassed him but I didn't," Rhys said in a rush.

Helen dried his tears with her skirt. She tucked her short hair behind her ears.

"You must watch what you say, Rhys. You can have a smart mouth, you know."

Rhys hung his head and Helen felt a pang in her heart. Still, if Ben was taking a more active role in Rhys' life, she supposed that included discipline too.

The following Christmas, when she'd been cancer-free almost a year, Helen wanted to

go visit her family in California. She had
thought they'd go back all the time to see her
family, but they hadn't been back once since
they moved. Morgan and Disby called her,
begging her to bring her family out to California
for the holidays. Even Janice called.

"I'm going to buy the plane tickets
tomorrow," Helen told Janice excitedly.

"I'll send you the damn tickets, Helen,"
she said testily.

"No, no, I have to clear it with Ben first,
but we can afford it."

When Helen broached the subject with
Ben, he stared at her for a moment before
informing her they'd been invited to Iowa to
spend the holiday with Ben's brother. His
brother hadn't attended the wedding and Ben
told Helen they'd had a falling out when their
father died. Helen was surprised at the
invitation. She called Disby at the Napa house
knowing when Janice found out they weren't
coming, she was going to flip out.

Helen couldn't wait to meet Ben's
family and see the house where he grew up. She
and Andy's wife would swap stories of being
farmers' wives. On the drive to Iowa, Helen
envisioned a cozy, old farmhouse and a great
family gathering. She didn't really like the quiet

and lonely holidays they had in Montana. She was glad to spend this Christmas surrounded by people. Rhys would have children to play with; Andy had six kids. Ben refused to fly, so they'd driven the fifteen hours to Iowa. Helen stifled the rising need to be with her own family as she ignored the fact that her husband still couldn't look her in the eye.

She thought they had been isolated in Montana, but Andy's farm was in the middle of nowhere. They had passed the last town about forty miles ago. Everything was white. Snow covered the fields and the road. Though the interstate had been plowed, the dirt road that led to the house had not. Ben put the truck in four-wheel drive and pushed slowly down the road. Helen felt disappointment blossom in her chest. Then the house came into view. It was not the cute, little red farmhouse she had imagined, but a weathered, ugly, gray building. It was in a serious state of disrepair. The front door hung from its hinges. One of the attic windows had been broken and was covered with plywood.

The family gathered on the sagging porch as she, Ben, and Rhys struggled to get their bags from the car. Snow crunched beneath their feet as they approached the porch. The brothers were awkward with each other, shaking gloved hands stiffly. Helen swallowed her immediate reaction of dislike when she saw the wife. Matilde was a tall reed of a woman, with graying, stringy hair and a pinched face.

The inside of the house was worse than the outside. The floors were terribly old and had not been cared for; they were arrested with deep grooves and scratches. The green wallpaper was peeling in spots. The curtains were badly made; the furniture was worn and stained. The place had a peculiar smell to it.

They all stood awkwardly in the foyer and Helen tried to envelop Matilde in a hug. She held out her arms and came toward Matilde. Instead of stepping into the hug, Matilde held out her own arms, as if to ward Helen off. Finally, Helen dropped her arms and stood there smiling shyly. Ben introduced Rhys as "the boy," and then told his brother's family his name was Acel.

Helen stared at him.

Andy, a bulky, homely man, assessed Rhys.

"Why don't he look like you?"

Helen started again.

"He got a lot of Helen's side."

Andy nodded, smirked, as though the lack of resemblance reflected Ben's lack of prowess.

"Acel, turn around, boy. Let me look at you."

Rhys fixed his green eyes on the man and did not move.

Ben prodded him.

"My name is Rhys," he said very clearly. "My Daddy calls me Ace."

Andy frowned as the boys nudged one another; one of them said "Daddy" in a falsetto voice.

"Don't he know his own name? You know you were named for your Granddaddy," Andy said loudly, as though the child were hard of hearing.

"Yeah, what is he some kind of retard?" Andy's eldest, Gunnar, mocked.

"Gunnar, hush up," Matilde admonished.

Ben chuckled. "His Ma's the only one who calls him Rhys, really." He turned to Rhys. "Your name is Acel, you hear?"

Rhys observed him with his almond-shaped eyes and said nothing.

The first days were uncomfortable. Andy barely spoke and referred to his wife as 'Ma.' When he did speak, it would come out in grunting fits and starts; his grammar was atrocious. Matilde spent most of her time in the kitchen. Helen shoved her bulky body on the bench at the kitchen table and tried to engage her sister-in-law in conversation. Her vision of comparing funny farmers' wives stories faded as the days went by. Matilde pushed out wan smiles and pushed back her stringy hair and said little. After a few days, Helen stopped trying. Andy found it amusing that Helen was from California.

"Can't believe you lived out there, brother. Palm trees and swimming pools and queers and hippies," Andy snorted.

"It's not really like that," Helen said primly.

Andy pinned her with his brown eyes before he demanded Matilde fill his plate again. The food, much like Matilde, was tasteless, gray and stringy. Helen enjoyed eating. It was one of the few and rare pleasures she indulged herself in. Food and jewelry were her two passions. She had noticed Matilde's gaze caress her silver bangles lingeringly and was glad she'd gotten her sister-in-law the earring and necklace set for Christmas.

Andy's six children were all boys, save the youngest. The boys, ages thirteen to nine, were big, brawny, blond kids. They were all older than Rhys and he didn't like playing with them. He wasn't socialized by any standards, but he had no defenses for these mean, callous boys. They were rough and violent; Rhys was not used to their kinds of games. As a consequence, Rhys spent most of his time playing with Jessie, Andy's sallow, mealy-mouthed daughter. They were the closest in age and seemed to get along well. Ben didn't like Rhys playing with his niece. "He'll turn queer. Go outside, Ace."

"It's snowing," Helen protested.

Helen spent the first three days of the trip dreaming of her mother's food and obsessively watching Rhys to make sure the Smith boys didn't hurt him.

"Acel," the eldest said, laughing. "Sounds like Asshole to me."

The other boys hooted and yelled Asshole at him. Rhys had never heard the word and he asked his mother what it meant. Helen glowered.

"Where did you hear that?"

"Leif said Acel sounded like Asshole and then they all started calling me Asshole. Is it a bad word?"

Helen bit into her cheeks, hard. She stroked her son's black hair.

"You just ignore those boys," she advised. "We'll be home soon."

"This is the worst Christmas ever," Rhys commented, laying back against her on the sofa. Stuffing bled out of the exposed arm. "I bet Santa doesn't even find me."

Rhys tried to ignore his cousins but it was nearly impossible. They treated him cruelly, peeing in his suitcase and pushing him into walls. He said nothing to his parents because the boys had threatened him. After the Asshole incident, Helen went to Matilde and told her what her sons were calling Rhys. Matilde lifted a weary hand as if to say, what do you want me to do about it? Helen crossed her meaty arms and insisted on speaking with the boys. Helen sat the five blond boys down and explained to them that they needed to be kind to their young cousin. The boys listened quietly and then, with angelic smiles plastered to their faces, they asked if they could take Rhys outside to play.

Once they had him in the barn, they shoved him to the ground and forced him to eat horse dung.

"You ever seen a pig slaughtered?" Gunnar asked him. Rhys shook his head. "If you tell anyone, that's what we'll do to you, Asshole," he sneered. "We'll hang you up from your ankles on the tree outside, and then we'll slit your fucking throat."

"Don't fuck with us," Lief added menacingly.

They let Rhys up from the cold barn floor and laughed as he spat and then vomited.

"You better clean that up, Asshole. If our Pa sees it, he will clean your fucking clock."

On the fourth day, Gunnar and Leif forced Rhys' head into the toilet and smeared poo on his toothbrush while the other boys watched. On the fifth day, as Rhys walked past the bathroom, Gunnar called to him.

"Hey Asshole," Gunnar said. "Saw your mom naked today. She's one ugly bitch."

"Yeah." Leif joined in, "She looks like a big rat. Maybe we should get the rat lady some cheese!"

Gunnar stepped in front of him.

"Where you think you're going? You ever drink piss? You're gonna drink my piss," Gunnar said as he undid his pants. He smiled maliciously. He stood in front of the stairs, blocking Rhys' only escape.

Rhys took note of the fact that Gunnar was standing in front of the top step. He took a breath and ran at him at full speed and pushed the older boy down the stairs. Gunnar tumbled, blond head over black shoes, and landed in a heap at the bottom of the stairs.

"Hey!" Leif cried out.

Rhys turned to him. "You want to fuck with me?" he asked menacingly, mentally wincing at the swear word. He'd never heard such words until they had come to Iowa, let alone said them.

Leif glanced at his unmoving brother and shook his head. Helen and Matilde rushed in from the kitchen where Helen had been attempting another stilted conversation. Helen saw the towheaded boy crumpled at the bottom of the stairs. She looked up at Rhys, who was standing at the top of the stairs looking at the body, an astonished look on his face.

"Andy!" Matilde called out, alarmed.

Andy and Ben ran in from the TV room.

"What in hell happened in here?" Andy demanded.

"It was him." Leif pointed a chubby finger. "He pushed Gunnar!"

The four adults glanced up the stairs at young Rhys who was standing very still, slightly shocked at what he had done.

"That true, Ace?" Andy demanded.

Rhys still did not move, stared at his uncle.

"Answer him!" Ben yelled, his face a mottled red.

Rhys nodded, his eyes on the floor.

"Son of a bitch, he ain't awake!" Andy thundered. "We're going to have to take him to a hospital. On Christmas Eve! Jesus Christ!"

He charged up the stairs and grabbed a startled Rhys by his green sweater.

"You have any idea where the nearest hospital is, you little-"

"Ben!" Helen cried.

Andy gave Rhys a hard look and let him go abruptly.

"Get the damn truck, Matilde," he ordered.

Andy and Matilde gathered the semiconscious Gunnar into their truck and headed out toward the hospital. Helen went up the creaking stairs to her son. She was unsure of what to do. Those boys had been bullying him all week. She could hardly blame him if he pushed one of them down the stairs. Helen debated on a suitable punishment and finally pulled a worn, wooden stool over to the corner of the kitchen. The rest of the Smith children, oddly quiet, assembled in the kitchen and watched Rhys on the stool. They whispered to one another.

"Maybe he killed Gunnar?'

"If he did, Pa will kill him."

"What the hell is he doing?" Ben asked as he came into the kitchen.

"He's in time-out."

"What the hell is that?"

"It's his punishment."

"Ha! That's not a punishment, Helen," Ben said angrily as he yanked Rhys off the stool roughly. "You come with me, boy!"

He pulled an unresisting Rhys into the living room and tossed him on the couch like a rag-doll. Helen followed quickly behind. The Smith children sauntered in behind her, eager to watch the proceedings.

"What are you doing, Ben?"

"Something that needs doing," he answered grimly. He put his hands on his belt buckle, the big one that read Smith, and removed his leather belt as he faced Rhys. "I don't know what the hell happened up there, and I don't care. You do not go around pushing people down the stairs. You could have killed that boy!"

Rhys stared at his father, his eyes on the black belt in his hand. He was silent, still.

"Ben! Ben, what are you going to do?" Helen asked alarmed. Ben kept his back to her, waved her off.

"Ben! No! Ben, don't!" Helen's voice pitched higher.

Ben sat beside Rhys on the worn, brown couch. "This hurts me to have to do this," he said placidly.

The Smith children watched with great interest, the boys silently snickering and elbowing one another. Jessie, watching with dead eyes, put her fingers in her mouth.

"Drop your drawers," Ben ordered.

Helen stepped back; tears ran down her face. She knew what was going to happen to Rhys, yet she felt powerless to stop her husband. Rhys turned his green eyes up to the ceiling. His eyes shone with the knowledge of what was about to happen to him. He got up from the couch slowly and put his hand in the button of his pants. Ben waited, glowering.

Rhys dropped his pants to his ankles.

"Them too," Ben said, nodding to his underwear.

Rhys looked at all the kids watching and then looked down. He lowered the back of his underwear until his rear was partially exposed.

The Smith children giggled. Helen wrapped her arms around herself.

"Now bend over the arm of this couch," Ben said calmly.

Rhys did as he was told. He was facing his cousins who eyed him meanly. Leif smiled knowingly as Ben positioned himself behind him and snapped the black leather together. Rhys jumped at the sound, and Helen cried, "No!"

Then he struck. The belt hit Rhys full force across the buttocks. He felt a searing pain and he started to cry.

"What a baby," said Leif, smirking.

Rhys lost count of how many times his father hit him. He only knew the burning pain. He wept, clutching the couch arm beneath him.

He did not realize when Ben had stepped away, only vaguely remembered Helen was there as she scooped him up and took him upstairs. There was blood running down his leg.

They left the next day, before Christmas lunch was served.

"Sorry about this mess, Andy."

"Shame you don't have more control over that boy of yours," Andy said.

"He'll learn his manners."

Chapter 18

The cabin in Montana became a dark place, a black place, an evil place. Rhys became a careful child. He tiptoed around the house, hoping his father wouldn't notice him. Helen cried all the time. Her hands trembled, even when it wasn't cold. In the last year, she'd gotten very fat. Ben hit Rhys more often, drew blood more often. When the welts and cuts healed, they left scars. Rhys kept his head down; he did his chores. He didn't back-sass. Still, his father found reasons to punish him.

In the last few years, Ben's face had become pinched. They weren't getting the subsidies from the Prince trust anymore. J.J. cut them off. Helen had no money of her own, and the money Ben made from Tyson was just enough to keep them afloat. Ben was tired; he was overworked. He was difficult to please, and Helen's nerves were frayed from having to anticipate his needs, his moods.

On his eighth birthday, Helen allowed Rhys to go to the rodeo with his friend from Sunday school. In his excitement, he forgot to feed the pigs before he left.

It was dark by the time he got home. Ben was waiting for him.

"Well, I hope you enjoyed your time at the rodeo," Ben said quietly.

"I did!" Rhys shouted exuberantly. He was too wound up to read Ben's mood correctly.

"Did you? That's good," Ben nodded. "I'm sure them pigs enjoyed not eating all day too."

Helen looked up from her needlepoint. Her hands were shaking. She put the needlepoint down and stood up.

"Ben, honey, it's his birthday," she reminded him haltingly.

Ben looked at her and wrinkled his nose, as if she smelled.

"Well, boy?" he said to Rhys.

"I- I- I'm sorry," Rhys stammered. "I forgot."

"Uh huh," Ben adjusted his overalls. "You need a lesson. Maybe you need to go a day without eating, see how you feel."

"Okay," Rhys said quickly.

"It's not that easy, Ace," Ben said, drawing out the S sound.

"Ben, it's his birthday," Helen said. "I made a chocolate cake. He's only eight. Can't we just let it go?"

Ben surveyed his wife coldly. "No," he said shortly. "Go get that long-handled spoon out the pantry, Acccce."

Rhys shuddered. He hated the wooden spoon. Once Ben hit him so hard it broke and they'd had to buy a new one, and this one was harder than the last one. It stung more. He started to turn toward the kitchen, but then he stopped.

"What?" Ben asked.

Rhys turned back to Ben. Helen's face was a mask of shock. Her hands shook even harder. She mouthed the word No and shook her head.

Rhys remained silent. He fixed his green eyes on his father's musty brown eyes.

"Go get the damn spoon!" Ben thundered, not used to being defied.

Rhys was still silent. He clenched his small fists.

"Boy, if you don't get that spoon," Ben warned.

"What? You'll hit me? Aren't you going to hit me anyway?"

Ben reached back and slapped his face. Rhys felt the sting and fell to the floor. Ben had never hit him in the face before. He tasted blood. He touched his mouth and his hand came away red. Ben stood over him as he lay curled on the wooden floor.

"Ben, no!" Helen cried.

"Sit, woman!" Ben yelled.

"Don't you touch my boy! Not again!"

She rushed behind Ben and tried to pull him away. He pulled his arm out of her grasp and struck her on the face as well. Helen turned white and reached up to her hot cheek. While she stood there in shock, Ben loomed over Rhys and pulled him up by the collar of his plaid shirt and slapped him again. Rhys felt the sting again as his neck snapped to the side.

"That'll teach you to disobey me. Now, you get that spoon," Ben said quietly.

Rhys lay on the pine floor, whimpering. It felt like the side of his face had exploded. His green eyes were wet with unshed tears.

"Benjamin! No!" Helen recovered from her stupor and again pulled on Ben's arm.

"I'll do as I damn well please! He's my son, ain't that right, Helen?"

Helen stood nonplussed for a moment. Then she said something Rhys didn't understand.

"No, he's not," she said, her voice wavering.

Ben stared at her. Rhys pulled himself up off of the floor and watched his mother. Helen kept her hand on her red cheek.

"No, he's not," she said in a stronger voice.

"Then take him the hell out of my house," Ben said, low and calm.

Helen gathered Rhys off the floor and hastily grabbed her purse. She piled him into the Chevy, all the while glancing over her shoulder, waiting for Ben to come and stop her. The Montana night was stifling in its stillness. Helen heaved herself up into the cab of the truck and turned the key. Rhys watched her warily.

"What about all our stuff?" he asked once they were safely ensconced in a hotel in Billings.

"We'll just get some more," Helen said, putting ice above his right eye. "Who wants that nasty old stuff anyway?"

Rhys regarded her solemnly. "What are we going to do now?"

Helen's lips twitched, as if she might cry. Her hands twisted around each other, but they no longer shook.

"Let's get you to bed," she said.

"Mama?" he asked when he was tucked into bed. She'd taken his bloody clothes off and told him to sleep in his underwear.

"What honey?"

"I never had a birthday like this before in my whole life."

Helen looked at him helplessly. When she was sure he was asleep, she picked up the phone and made a collect call.

"J.J.," she said upon his answering. "I need to come home. Now."

"What the hell happened out there, Helen?" J.J. asked, all traces of sleep gone from his voice.

"I don't want to talk about it right now," she said importantly.

"Is Rhys with you?"

"Yes, I have Rhys with me. Will you send me two plane tickets for the first flight out tomorrow?"

"You don't need three?"

"No."

"Are you sick again? Is there some kind of trouble with Ben?"

"I'll explain when I get there. Thanks, J.J. Good-bye."

She hung up before he could ask anymore questions.

Helen shook Rhys awake very early. It was still dark out. She dressed him in his bloody clothes and hustled him out of the door. She looked quickly around the parking lot of the hotel. She grasped Rhys' hand tightly, part of her waiting for Ben to pop out of the shadows and grab them both.

"Where are we going?" Rhys asked. His voice seemed unnaturally loud to Helen and she fought the urge to shush him.

"Home," she said.

He flinched.

"No," she said, seeing his face. "My home. California, where you were born."

"I don't remember California." Rhys pulled his hand from Helen's and examined it.

"No, I don't suppose you would. We're going to stay there forever, and you can see all your aunts and uncles and play with all your cousins."

Rhys nodded. "Dad's not coming?"

"No," Helen said firmly.

"Mom?" he asked hesitantly.

"Yes?"

"Is it true? What you said last night? Is Dad not really my dad?"

Helen grimaced as she put him in the cab of the truck.

"Yes.

"Are you my mom?"

"Yes," Helen answered promptly. "Yes, I am."

"So where's my real dad?"

"Let's talk about it later, okay?"

"But you'll tell me?" he persisted.

"Yes, someday. I promise."

Helen and Ben had never told Rhys he was adopted. She had the legal adoption papers somewhere in the house in Montana. She remembered signing them, looking the papers over for Janice's name, but J.J. had covered her tracks well for her. No one would ever know Janice's terrible secret.

When they were about to land at SFO, Helen pulled out her compact and tried to cover up the bruise on her cheek. She wondered if she should put some powder on Rhys. Although J.J. was sending a car, she knew he would expect to see her and Rhys sometime that day, and, if he saw the cut above the boy's eye and the swollen mouth, she did not know what he would do.

Helen grabbed Rhys' hand and stepped into the airport, looking for a driver with her name written on a placard. Instead she saw J.J. and Janice barreling toward them.

"Helen!" J.J. waved.

"Rhys, darling!" Janice shouted.

Helen felt fear tug on her.

Rhys tugged on her hand. "Mama, who's that?"

"That is your Aunt Jan and Uncle John."

"The ones who send me the big Christmas presents every year?"

"The very same."

"I like them," Rhys smiled, then winced a little at the movement. His lip was already scabbing over.

Janice and J.J. looked like movie stars. Rhys had never seen people who looked like his aunt and uncle did; the two of them seemed to sparkle and looked like they hadn't a care in the world.

Janice and J.J. were almost upon them. Helen started to feel panic. Once they were there in front of them, Janice reached for Rhys, who walked willingly into her thin arms.

"Hello, darling!"

"Hi," Rhys said charmingly. "You're my Aunt Jan."

Janice hugged him. "Yes, darling. I certainly am!"

"Are you crying?" Rhys asked, focused on her face.

"Oh," Janice sniffed. "I'm so very happy to see you, darling! We've all missed you so much!"

At this she shot a pointed look at Helen. Rhys touched her mouth lightly.

"We have the same mouth," he said delightedly.

Janice sniffed again. "Yes, we do. We get that from your Grandpa."

"Where's Grandpa?" Rhys asked excitedly.

"He's in Heaven, darling."

"Oh," Rhys was clearly disappointed. Then he looked at J.J. "You're my Uncle John."

"That's right, young man," J.J. smiled at the boy.

"You gave me that big truck for Christmas! It's my favorite!"

J.J. looked surprised. "Oh, well, I'm glad."

"Rhys, darling, what in the world happened to your face? It's cut and bruised. Did you fall somewhere on that farm? Get tangled in some barbed wire? Have you had all your shots?"

Rhys looked at Janice confused. Then he looked at his mother questioningly.

"Yes, and you seem to have fallen as well," J.J. said to Helen. She blushed and looked to the ground.

Understanding dawned on Janice's face and she clutched Rhys so tightly he cried out.

"Oops, darling!"

"Let's go get your bags," J.J. said.

"We have none," Helen said stiffly.

"I see," J.J. focused his steely eyes on Helen's beady ones. "Let's get to the car then."

Janice sent Helen murderous glances over Rhys' black head as they walked through the airport. Rhys leaned his head on Janice's shoulder and yawned.

"You've had an ordeal, haven't you darling?" Janice asked tenderly. "Don't worry, Auntie Jan is here now, and nothing bad will happen to you again. I promise."

Rhys lifted his head and looked into her eyes. "You promise?" he asked, very solemnly.

"I do," Janice said firmly. "Why don't we get you some ice cream, darling? What's your favorite? Mine's strawberry."

"Mine too," Rhys said happily.

Rhys put his head back on her shoulder comfortably, and Janice shot another look at Helen. The child's dirty shoes swung against her Chloe skirt with each step she took, but Janice didn't notice; she was intently focused on the boy in her arms. She breathed in and was incensed to find he smelled like Helen. A little dirty, slightly unwashed. Janice wrinkled her nose. She could smell the desperation rolling off her sister like waves of fog.

"We were going to send you out to Napa directly but under the circumstances, I think we'd better go to Jan's house," J.J. was saying. "If we go to mine, Olivia will have the whole family knowing everything before sundown."

"Whole family? Try the whole city, J.J." Janice said drolly.

J.J. laughed.

Helen entered Janice's house, the house that Johnny Prince was so proud of, with her head hung low. She barely looked around; she didn't like seeing the place the way it was. She preferred to remember it as it had been when her father had been alive.

"Go into the kitchen and Maria will fix you a snack," Janice said, releasing the boy for the first time since she picked him up in the airport. "Very soon, your cousins will be home from school, darling, and then you can all play together," Janice called after him. Then she turned to Helen, ready to scratch her eyes out.

"You let that monster beat my son," Janice accused in a low growl as she advanced on her sister.

"Shh!" J.J. said. "He may be able to hear you."

"What the fuck went on out there Helen?"

Helen bowed her head. Her tongue darted out to touch the corner of her mouth nervously.

"Did he beat you too, Helen?" J.J. asked, all business. Only Janice, who knew him so well, could sense the fire beneath his calm words.

"Not me," Helen said and then clamped her hand over her mouth.

"Not you, just Rhys you mean!"

Janice grabbed Helen by her meaty shoulders and started to shake her. "Not you until last night, right? That's when you decided to leave! Not before then!"

Helen tried to maintain her balance while Janice gripped her with ringed hands and shook her heavy bulk.

J.J. grabbed Janice and wrenched her away. She stood, breathless, a black-haired Fury. Helen twisted from her gaze. Her hands shook.

"I didn't, I mean... We were all alone out there and he was different."

"All alone. Who's fault was that Helen? Huh?" Janice lighted a cigarette.

"What happened?" J.J. asked.

"I don't know," Helen wailed, fat tears sliding down her round cheeks. "I thought I was stuck. I had messed up badly by leaving and I knew you two would never forgive me. I didn't think I could come back. I really didn't. He had all the money. When you stopped sending the checks, I had nothing! What was I supposed to do? It wasn't my fault!" Helen put her hand to her mouth.

Janice looked Helen over with cold, black eyes. Helen had gained so much weight since she'd left California. Her hands shook badly. Her black eyes darted around, like a cornered animal.

"What have you done to that child, Helen? What have you let happen to him? Have you seen his eyes? Have you looked at his face? Do you have any idea what you've done, you desperate, stupid bitch."

This last was delivered with such naked hatred, both Helen and J.J. flinched.

"You let your goddamn freakish desperation for a man ruin a child's life. You let it happen because you couldn't bear to be alone. Damn it, you're all alone now. How does it feel to ruin a life like that, with absolute blatant disregard for someone you're supposed to be protecting?"

Janice berated Helen but turned the words inward to herself. She had let this happen. She should have kept her son.

Ben Smith lost his wife. He had lost his farm and his business. The Prince family had torn into him with steely precision and unmitigated hatred. When the pit bull attorney they'd hired was through with him, Helen had everything he owned; he had nothing.

He went back to Iowa and moved in with Andy and Matilde. He had developed an ulcer during the divorce. His already thin frame became gaunt. When he looked in the mirror, he saw his mother's face, in her last days, that barely breathing skeleton. Finally, the pain got so bad he went to the doctor, who informed him he had stomach cancer. Ben's brown eyes clouded over as he thought of Helen and his mother, forgotten in that back room. It was his turn now. When Ben died, Janice threw a party and drank champagne until her head was spinning. When her friends asked her what she was celebrating, she smiled sweetly and said, "Justice."

Kirsten Langston

Chapter 19

John had a lot of time to think while he was at
the Redwoods. In fact, all he did was think. John
thought about his cousin, more than he thought
he would. Back when he was fifteen, he was
fascinated with Rhys. Rhys, with his long hair
and tattoo, the winking silver hoops in his ears.
Rhys was so cool. When he saw his cousin at
the family parties, standing in the shadows,
handsome face twisted in wry amusement, he
wished fervently that he could be like Rhys.
Nothing anyone ever said seemed to have any
effect on Rhys. He bore the polite suggestions
and outright accusations with the same satirical
smile, until the well-meaning or suitably
outraged party moved on, disappointed, shaking
their head.

Rhys was only a few years older than
John, but they might as well have been light

years. They used to hang out when they were kids, but around the time Rhys was twelve, they'd stopped. Rhys had no interest in the things they used to do. Instead of playing softball or tag with the other kids, John would find his cousin off in a corner, a walkman jammed in his pocket, head moving to an unknown rhythm. Rhys waved John off without a second glance. John had seen his cousin smoking cigarettes in the deep recesses of Granny's house, watched the glowing tip as Rhys inhaled and wondered how he got away with being so bad.

John found out Rhys was coming quite by accident. He was on his way upstairs after dinner when he heard his mother's rapid-fire whispers coming from behind a partially closed door.

"Are you fucking kidding me? Now she wants me to take him?" Janice half whispered into the phone. His mother was crouched over the desk in the study. Her back was to him; she did not see John behind her, hovering in the doorway.

"Are you sending Helen to some place discreet? If this gets out," Janice paused. She stayed quiet for a long time, then she sank down on a caramel-colored leather chair.

"I don't give a good goddamn," Janice said quietly.

John's eyebrows shot up; he'd never heard his mother swear like this before.

Janice was quiet for a minute, then she nodded her head subtly.

"Of course I will take him," Janice said. "What do you take me for?" she asked bitterly.

John spent the next week pacing the cherrywood floors, agitated. He was restless and short tempered. It was such unusual behavior for him that even his sister noticed. John walked into the living room. His mother's decorator had just been through the place, and he was still not used to the tiny, delicate tables shyly clinging to the corners or the bold, threadbare throw rugs scattered around the floors. He thought they looked old and ratty; his mother gave a little laugh and said it was a good thing he was not the decorator, as he clearly had no taste. He tripped lightly on one of the rugs. His baggy pants scraped across the bare wood as he deposited himself on the leather ottoman with a large, exasperated sigh.

"Jesus, John! What the hell is your problem?" Sarah yelled.

"Nothing! God!" he spat.

He stomped and sighed his way through the week, earning exasperated looks from his sister and causing his mother to question if his video games were too violent. Then, on a foggy and unremarkable Friday, he awoke, and he could feel the energy buzzing in the walls. He dressed quickly and pounded down the old stairs, jumping over the last two. His mother always screamed at him when he did that; she hated it. This morning she didn't even notice.

As John rounded the corner to the living room, he saw her gesticulating to Maria, the housekeeper. Maria stood, short and stocky, in her gray uniform and nodded her head as Janice spoke rapidly to her. John could sense, with that preternatural sense all teenagers have, that he should stay out his mother's way. He dragged his feet past the living room and down the hall to the kitchen.

Once in the kitchen, John pulled some bread from the fridge for toast. The white kitchen door swung open and his mother, wearing a black dress, sailed through it.

"What on earth are you wearing?" Janice demanded.

"What?" John glanced down at his body. "What?" he repeated, nonplussed.

Janice tossed her head like a filly. She eyed her son critically.

"You know I hate those pants. There's no way you are wearing those to school."

He glanced down at himself again. He was wearing a dark-blue, striped, oversized polo shirt and some jeans.

"What's wrong with the pants?" he asked.

Janice threw her perfectly manicured hands in the air.

She threw her head back and shouted: "They are twelve sizes too large. That is what is wrong with your pants! Not to mention they are hanging off of your behind! I can see your underwear. Why aren't you wearing your uniform?"

John shrugged. "It's free-dress day today."

"March upstairs and put on some decent clothes. I am not playing around today. I do not have the time!" Janice stated imperiously.

"Why?" John asked.

"Your cousin is coming today."

"Who?" he asked, knowing the answer.

"Rhys." The answer was short and clipped, and her tone spoke volumes. "He's coming to stay with us for a short time."

Sarah came into the room suddenly, pushing open the kitchen door forcefully.

"What?"

"Oh, for God's sake, Sarah. I don't need this right now!" Janice threw up her hands again.

"You weren't even going to tell us, Mother? I mean, that creature is coming to live in this house, and you weren't going to say anything? I live here too, you know!" Sarah screeched at her mother, tossing her backpack on the floor.

"Don't you speak to me in that tone, young lady," Janice ordered.

John rolled his eyes. His mother and Sarah were always at each other's throats lately.

"What were you going to do? Just not tell me until I walked in the house and found him here? How can you let him in this house? He's so distasteful."

Janice's eyes snapped and she clenched her hands at her side.

"He is misunderstood, and quite frankly, it's none of your business. I can assure you, Sarah," Janice said, saying her name like it left a bad taste, "Rhys will not disrupt your life in any way. That's the end of this discussion," Janice said to Sarah before she turned to John. "Now, will you please go and change!"

Janice pulled on his arm, and John reluctantly but obediently went upstairs to change.

Rhys made his debut in the Prince house Saturday morning. The sun was high and the beaming light came through the wavy glass windows. The white kitchen door opened abruptly and Rhys came through it, scratching his head. He was shirtless, wearing only blue, plaid pajama bottoms. His black tattoo sat proudly on his chest, the skeleton grinning at John. His blue-black hair was long, touching his shoulders, and his bangs hung in his almond-shaped, green eyes.

He slumped into a kitchen chair and put his elbows on the table and put his head in his hands. He rubbed his eyes.

John watched Rhys, captivated. Rhys took his hands away from his face.

"Hey, what's up?"

"Nothing, dude," John pushed out, hoping he sounded cool.

"Where's the bowls?"

497

"Over there." John pointed to the cupboard behind Rhys.

Rhys nodded. He sat there and ate a bowl of cereal. He did not speak to John, and John did not dare speak to him. Silence permeated the room. John felt it sitting on his shoulders, but he said nothing. He watched the silver hoops in Rhys' ears catch the light. John watched the blue black hair fall over his eyes and waited for Rhys to shake it away, but he never did. When Rhys was finished, he got up, put his bowl in the sink, and walked out. He did not see Rhys again for the rest of the day.

The first week of Rhys in the house passed quickly and quietly, and that Sunday, Janice decided to have a family dinner. John was laying in his room listening to NWA on his CD player. He had his headphones on because if his mother heard what he was listening to, she would flip. Janice stepped into his room. She crossed the floor to the window. He removed his headphones.

"What are you doing?" he asked as she opened his window.

"It smells in here," Janice said as she wrinkled her nose in distaste.

"It's cold outside," John complained.

"It's San Francisco; it's always cold outside."

"Mom," John said, rolling his eyes.

"Just for a few minutes," she insisted. John shrugged.

"We're having family dinner tonight. Maria's making enchiladas. Rhys said it was his favorite."

"Okay." John shrugged again and made to put his headphones back on.

"John Prince, I expect you in your chair at seven." Janice inclined her black, perfectly coifed head at her son.

"Okay." He lowered the headphones on his ears.

Janice tapped him on the shoulder. He lifted one side off his ear.

"Don't wear those pants."

John found it odd that his mother wanted a sit-down family dinner. She used to have dinner parties, and she'd throw open the double doors that enclosed the dining room, announcing dinner was served. These affairs always fascinated John and Sarah. Of course, they were never present for these dinners, but they would watch from the stairs, anxious for their mother to throw open the doors. The table was always set with the best silver, china, and crystal, stuff Janice wouldn't even let them touch. She would usually have some interesting, exotic centerpieces. The room was lit with candles only, and John and Sarah used to watch the laughing guests in the gold glow of the candlelight, entranced.

This dinner was nothing like those theatrical expositions he remembered from his childhood. It was an awkward and self-conscious affair. Rhys kept his head down, his shiny, black hair falling in his face. He kept his eyes on his plate and didn't speak. Sarah was also silent. She still wasn't speaking to Rhys, and she would only speak to Janice in clipped, short sentences. An uncomfortable tension began to build; the room filled with the sounds of chewing and the clinking of silverware on plates.

John felt sorry for his mother; she was making a strong effort to engage Rhys, but he obviously wasn't receptive. For the duration of the meal, she kept trying to draw Rhys into a conversation, and he kept giving her one-word answers. The repeated attempts made John uncomfortable and he longed to stand up and shout to his mother to shut up. Instead, he too kept his head down and didn't look at anyone. As soon as he was finished, Rhys got up and walked out. Janice looked angry, but held her tongue.

The San Francisco fog lingered into April and May. The sun showed itself sporadically. John plodded through finals, remembered not to wear those pants in front of his mother, and made a stealthy career out of shadowing his cousin around the house. He didn't know what was wrong with Auntie Helen; nobody would talk about it and he was afraid to ask Rhys.

In the two months Rhys had been there, John learned almost nothing about his cousin. John lurked around the house, lingered outside Rhys' door, studied him plaintively as he ate his breakfast, and loitered in the hallway as he brushed his perfect white teeth. He held his breath when Sarah's friends would come over. Tall, short, skinny, chunky, pretty, attractive and downright ugly, none of them were immune to Rhys. John watched his cousin, pulsing with that curious vitality, casually turn down every single girl.

He did his best to be as cool and uncaring as Rhys. He trailed behind him like an eager puppy, gauging his cousin's mood as best he could and trying to match it. He started leaving little things around for Rhys to find: an

NWA CD, a skin mag he copped from Ryan Sutton, a condom he'd gotten from a machine in a gas station. He hoped these treasures would convince Rhys he was cool. Rhys barely noticed him.

At the end of May, the sun finally came out. The frigid waters of the bay sparkled dazzlingly, and that formerly retiring tide inside Rhys turned and thrust itself full on at John. Suddenly, Rhys' blinding focus was turned on him.

One of Gus' kids was graduating college and there was a big party for him at the Napa house. When John got in the car, he was surprised to see Rhys in the passenger seat next to his mother. In the last few years, Rhys had stopped attending most family functions. John wondered why he was going to this one.

"Where's Sarah?" John asked. She was the one who usually got the front seat.

"She's staying with Aimee. It's just the boys tonight," Janice trilled.

Rhys did not speak the entire ride. Rhys usually wore black, and tonight was no exception. John had begun to emulate his cousin's style and was also clothed in all black. Last week, his mother had asked him, "Why are you wearing so much black? You look like an undertaker."

"Because Rhys wears black all the time and John wants to be just like his favorite cousin," Sarah had mocked meanly.

When they arrived in Napa around five o'clock, the sun still sat prettily in the sky. Cars were parked haphazardly in the long drive. Janice pulled the white Lexus in behind Morgan and Rick's SUV. The air was fragrant with flowers, and the fruit trees were covered in white and pink blossoms. Even from the driveway, John could hear his cousins running around in the back. No doubt a game of tag was going on down by the pond. When John and Rhys were younger, their games of tag always ended with someone, usually John, being pushed into the pond. Sometimes John would corral the younger cousins and start a kickball game, but not tonight. As Janice walked swiftly and gracefully up the porch stairs, Rhys pulled on John's black T-shirt.
He looked over to John and said, "Come on."

They navigated the white porch, Rhys ducking his head to avoid the baskets of bright flowers that hung from the eaves. As the sun lowered itself in the sky, it turned everything in its path golden with waning light. John heard the stentorian voice of his Aunt Minnie and the quieter tones of his cousin Trina as he and Rhys walked around to the back porch. All the windows of the house were open and the sounds of the party poured out of them. John could pick out a voice here and there.

"I said more ice, Rick. I'm not Morgan." That was Aunt Minnie.

"So, I said, 'What do you want me to do? I'm going through a divorce.'" Said quietly, but with a slight edge. Aunt Jane.

"I'll get it out in minute, Miss Astoria." Geraldine.

"What do you mean you lost the numbers? I don't have time to deal with this kind of incompetence." Uncle John, on his new cell phone.

The kids raced around the green lawn, feet stamping mercilessly on the delicate blades, their white faces alight with innocence and flushed with pleasure. Rhys ducked into the house and came back out with two cold, long-neck bottles of beer. He set the beer at his feet, leaned against the white railing on the porch, and took out a pack of cigarettes. He lighted one and looked around, his green eyes taking in the scene before him. John also leaned against the railing, trying to look nonchalant. He wondered if the second beer was for him. He hoped so. He had only been to a few parties where people were drinking, but he'd never had more than a beer. He was too afraid his mother would find out he'd been drinking.

"Looks like Jimmy's gonna have a helluva party," Rhys commented.

"Yeah, um," John said. "How come you're not having a party?"

He could've bitten his tongue. It was a stupid thing to say, but Rhys just laughed shortly.

"I dodged that bullet. Aunt Jan wanted to throw me a party bigger than this fiasco. I managed to talk her out of it."

"Oh," John said, surprised anyone could talk his mother out of anything.

Rhys took a drag on his cigarette.

"Hey, can I have one?" John asked.

Rhys laughed.

"No. These things'll kill you, dude. Besides, you're not the type."

"Dude, come on. What do you know if I'm the type or not?"

"Fine. Here."

Rhys pulled the pack out of his pocket. John had never smoked in his life. He placed the cigarette carefully between his pointer and middle fingers, getting used to the weight of it. Rhys watched him carefully, head cocked toward the house, listening. John put the cigarette in his mouth and lighted it. He took an experimental puff. It really wasn't that bad. He took another. He was halfway through the cigarette before he started to feel sick. Rhys took one look at his green face and laughed again.

"C'mon," Rhys said as he pulled the cigarette from John's fingers and tossed it to the ground. He stepped on it. John waited for his stomach to stop churning, hoping his cousin didn't think he was a total loser. Rhys picked up the butt and tossed it into some nearby bushes.

He led John down toward the vineyard at the edge of the property. They ducked into the rows of glaucous leaves and Rhys used his lighter to pop the tops off the beers. They sat in the dwindling sunlight, drinking their beers in silence, listening to the distant screams of the cousins as they chased one another on the velvety lawn. John accepted the beer Rhys passed to him with affected nonchalance.

"So you like rap huh?" Rhys asked him.

"Oh, yeah." John took a long swig from the brown bottle. "Don't you?"

"Sure, some of it, anyway. Aunt Jan doesn't know what kind of music you listen to?"

"Hell no, man," John was starting to relax.

"She'd flip out, huh?"

"Yeah."

Rhys drained his beer and lighted another cigarette.

"You want to go grab us another couple of beers?" Rhys asked him.

Fingers of fear tugged at John's black sleeve; if anyone saw him taking beers, he would be in deep shit for sure. He didn't even want to think about what his mother would do to him.

"Yeah, sure," he said eagerly. "No problem."

John got up from the dirt and brushed off his pants.

"Don't get caught," Rhys warned.

John ignored the furious whispers of apprehension in his head and wove his way through the laughing children. They seemed so young to him as they whisked past him with their chubby arms and gap-toothed smiles. He invaded the kitchen stealthily and opened the pantry. He spotted a six-pack of beer. He heard footsteps approaching. He grabbed the beer and thrust his black sweatshirt over the top. He dashed out of the kitchen, his heart beating madly. When he returned to their spot in the vineyard, he thrust the six-pack at Rhys, like a serf giving an offering to a king. Rhys grinned.

"You got a six-pack?"

John shrugged modestly. Rhys took the beer and broke a can off the plastic ring.

"These are warm, Johnny Boy," Rhys declared.

John felt his cheeks stain crimson with a dull heat. How could he have gotten warm beer?

"Never mind," Rhys said genially. "I could give a fuck if it's warm."

"Yeah," John said, relieved. "Me too."

They sat there and drank the warm beers, one after the other, in the waning light; when the sky was that particular shade of purple that Granny called the gloaming, John heard the adults calling the children inside. The bugs were eating him alive, but he had no intention of leaving Rhys' side.

"You got a little girlfriend, Johnny? You never bring any girls home," Rhys commented.

"Neither do you," John pointed out.

"Nah," Rhys said, lighting another cigarette, "the girls I fuck with aren't the kind you bring home, you know what I mean?"

John heard his name being called by his mother. He glanced back toward the house and rose unsteadily to his feet.

"Whoa, Johnny, are you drunk?" Rhys asked with a mixture of amusement and disbelief.

"No," John mumbled.

"Holy shit, Aunt Jan is going to kill you," Rhys commented.

"I'm fine," John said as he staggered out of the twining grape leaves and into Granny's yard.

Rhys put a hand on his shoulder.

"Dude, take this," he handed John a breath mint. "For Christ's sake, you better be able to play this off. I can't believe four beers got you drunk."

"What, aren't you even a little buzzed?"

"A little, but you, Johnny Boy, you're smashed." Rhys threw back his black head and laughed deeply.

Jesus, his cousin was so freaking awesome.

As the summer unfolded like a decadent dessert, Rhys started letting John hang out with him. When he saw John hanging around outside his room, he invited him in. John was amazed to see the room was very neat and littered with books. Sometimes Rhys would go into John's room and they'd play video games together. John was in; he belonged.

Rhys entered his room after a quick knock. "Listen, I have a few T-shirts I don't really want anymore. I thought you could use them. Get you out of those damn polo shirts."

"Yeah," John said eagerly.

Rhys tossed the shirts on his bed. They were mostly black, emblazoned with names of bands he had never heard of. Some of them had weird pictures on them. John tossed off his baby blue striped polo and pulled on a black T-shirt with the word Christdriver on it.

That night, Rhys asked John to go out with him. Janice had already left for some party and Rhys was headed out the door when he spotted John watching TV on the couch.

"What're you doing, dude?"

"Nothing, just watching TV."

"Want to come out with me?"

"Seriously?"

Rhys suppressed a grin. "Yeah, seriously."

"Cool," John said as he jumped up from the couch. "Where we going?"

"House party in Oakland."

John hesitated.

"She won't even know you're gone," Rhys said impatiently. His pager went off and he rolled his emerald eyes. "C'mon, let's go."

From then on, when Rhys went out, he took John with him. They went to all-ages shows where the kids threw themselves into the crowd with calculated violence. They went to places like the Mission and the Tenderloin, hands jammed in their jacket pockets, walking the cracked sidewalks swiftly. They went to rough-looking places where the people spoke in a clipped unfamiliar vernacular. John wore the T-shirts Rhys had given him everywhere. His polo shirts hung unused in his closet.

The people Rhys introduced him to were an odd assortment of characters. Hippie kids who played hack-e-sack in Berkeley, dudes who rapped on street corners in Oakland, goth and punk kids who wore powder on their faces and thick, black eyeliner and the same shirts that now hung in John's closet. They were unlike any kids at John's school. John threw himself into those summer nights with all the passion he had. He bathed in the newness of it; he reveled in the strangeness of the cold city.

There was somewhere to be every night of the week. Janice barely even noticed they were gone. At one point, she caught them both going out the door at nine o'clock on a Wednesday night. The warmth of the day had melted into a cool and breezy San Francisco night.

"Where are you two going?" Janice asked from her position on the couch.

"Nowhere," John said quickly.

"Uh huh," Janice said as she closed her magazine and stood up.

"To a friend's house, Aunt Jan," Rhys said smoothly.

Well, it wasn't a lie, John reasoned. They were going to see some of Rhys' friends.

"Where?"

"Berkeley."

"Hmmm. How long will you be out?"

"Be back by midnight," Rhys said easily.

"You're looking out for John? Keeping out of trouble?"

Rhys shrugged. "He can take care of himself."

"That's not the answer I'm looking for."

"I'll make sure he stays out of trouble," Rhys said, green eyes flashing.

"Alright. Be safe."

Janice returned to her place on the couch and John exerted some effort to keep his mouth closed. It was never that easy with his mother. Usually she required phone numbers and the guarantee that an adult would be present.

"Don't go to Oakland," his mother called out as they stepped out the door.

They went to a house party in an old Victorian house in the hills. The party mirrored all the others Rhys had taken John to in the last month. There was an unending supply of cheap beer and the air was thick and blue with smoke. The house was crawling with hot girls. The girls loved Rhys. He would stand on the wall and smoke cigarettes and drink beer and, one by one, the girls would just come over to him. Preening and tossing their hair, each one would try to outdo the other. Rhys, unimpressed, usually ignored these girls. Every so often, one would approach and Rhys would be interested; John could tell because Rhys would incline his head toward the girl, and, when he spoke to her, he would lower his head and put his mouth right next to her ear. When he did that, John knew his cousin would disappear somewhere for a while. When he reappeared, he would be alone. Rhys didn't share tales of his exploits like the guys did at school. John was too shy and embarrassed to talk to many girls. Sometimes, after a few drinks, he would talk to one or two cute chicks, but he never disappeared with them like Rhys did.

As July rolled into August, one party drifted into the next, one day dissolved into another. John took his cues from Rhys and his friends, and soon he was smoking cigarettes and drinking beer every night. If Rhys rolled a joint, John would smoke it. On more than one occasion, Rhys disappeared into the bathroom with a few people. John knew they were doing something in there, but he wasn't sure what. Another time, he saw Rhys take a pill with his beer.

"What is that?"

"It's called MDMA and you can't have any, so don't ask."

John regarded him blankly.

"'Don't go to Oakland,'" Rhys said in such a perfect imitation of Janice that John laughed until beer came out of his nose.

One night, John had too much to drink. After vomiting profusely, he passed out on the soothing, cool floor of someone's bedroom. When Rhys found him lying there, he poured a cup of water on him. John had been embarrassed, but Rhys just laughed at him.

It did not occur to John that he was exhibiting the same behaviors that made the family so disapproving of Rhys. The very things he was doing were the things his aunts would whisper about in disgust. "Rhys is going to kill his poor mother," they would say. "He's shameful, disgusting, the way he's acting," they'd whisper.

One night, John sat on the railing of a house in Santa Cruz and breathed in the salt-tinged air. Rhys leaned against the railing, watching the party as it raged around him. John, too, watched the laughing people surrounding him.

"My name is Cindy. You got a light?"

She was short, blonde, and had huge breasts. John stared. "Sure."

Cindy and her abnormally large breasts ushered him into manhood that night. On the hard bathroom floor of a beach house owned by a guy named Guy, John lost his virginity. Afterward, he stumbled out of the bathroom with Cindy's pager number and a silly grin. When he found Rhys, it was near three.

"We have to get home, dude," John said.

Rhys was reclining on the grass, his back against a tree, a beer in one hand and the other on some girl's bare thigh. The girl had dark eyes and short bangs. She glanced at John, uninterested.

"Johnny, we won't make it home tonight," Rhys said, shrugging.

"Huh?"

"I can't drive, too drunk. Why don't you go find that Kewpie doll you were talking to?" he suggested.

"But if we don't get home..." John trailed off, unsure of what might happen if they didn't make it home that night.

Rhys shrugged again. "She doesn't even notice when we're gone anyway."

John pondered this for a moment. It was true; his mother had been mostly oblivious to his and Rhys' comings and goings.

Rhys woke him around five, and John stumbled out to the car, still drunk. When they arrived home, he saw the porch light on, gleaming dully in the bright gold morning light. The San Francisco air was crisp when he got out of the car, and he inhaled sharply, aware that he was still slightly drunk.

Before they could set foot on the porch, the door swung open. John felt his heart drop to his feet and he wanted to throw up. There on the threshold, like a wraith, was his mother. She was tying her black silk robe; each tiny movement betrayed her emotions. She was furious. She stared hard at them both.

"In," she growled and she pointed a long, pink-tipped finger at them. They both walked in the house. John hung his head, plainly afraid of his mother. Rhys walked through the door and just kept walking.

"Rhys," she said.

He stopped just in front of the stairs, but did not turn around.

"Helen will be home in two weeks," Janice spat out.

He nodded and walked up the stairs.

Janice turned on John. "You," she said quietly.

John stared at his toes, afraid if he spoke, she would see he was still drunk.

"You pack your bags."

John looked up at his mother; her eyes were snapping with electricity. Her mouth was set in a grim line. He realized she was restraining herself with much effort.

"Why?"

"Why?" she repeated.

The single question lit the fuse, and he watched his mother's face flush an ugly red.

"You want to know why? Let me tell you, young man!" Her hands shook; she raised and lowered them several times, as though she wanted to slap him. "Your behavior is completely appalling. I shouldn't have brought Rhys into this house! I knew it would bring nothing but trouble! Where in the hell have you been? How could you stay out all night long and not even call me? I thought you were hurt or dead! But no, you two were out having a grand, old time, weren't you? My fifteen-year-old son should not be spending all night out at some horrible drug party! That's where you were, wasn't it? Drugs, alcohol, what else, John Prince? What else have you been doing?"

John swayed slightly.

"You're drunk!" Janice nearly swooned. "Damn him, damn you! I can't believe this! My son, my baby boy. Are you trying to put me in an early grave? Are you?"

Janice grabbed him by the upper arms and shook him. "What is the matter with you?"

John tried to shrug off his mother's hands, but she held fast.

"I am well aware," she said quietly, her face inches from his, "that everyone is entitled to a mad season now and then, but this has gone too far. You are going to stay with your father. The car will be here to take you to the airport in half an hour."

John paused at the top of the stairs in front of Rhys' door, but he did not knock. As he

left the house, he knew when he returned Rhys
would not be there.

Chapter 20

The day after she returned home from her daughter's wedding, Geraldine went to the hospital.

"Ah, Mrs. Prince will be so happy to see you. You're her best friend, I take it?"

"Yes. How is she doctor? One of her girls told me about her taking bad pills. She's going to be okay?"

Dr. Thompson nodded. "It's a terrible thing what Dr. Millen did. We've obviously let him go. Mrs. Prince will clear up in a week or so and then she can go home."

"No end of life stuff?" Geraldine asked him with anxious eyes.

"No, I should say not. Mrs. Prince is healthy and almost healed. She'll be fine."

"I shouldn't have left," she said to Astoria when she saw her.

"Nonsense," Astoria said in her hoarse croak. "Next time bring pictures for me to see."

"I will. I'm just glad you're going to be okay."

"Me too," Astoria said quietly.

"I don't want to upset you," Geraldine began hesitantly. "Did you know Disby left the Napa house?"

Astoria nodded. "Painters."

"Yeah, painters, that's what J.J. told me too. Except I haven't seen any damn painters. I went in the house this morning. It's sparkling clean, so somebody's been in there to clean it, but nobody's painted it."

Astoria felt a shadow cross over her soul. She felt a sudden and unwelcome dislike for John Junior. He was too much like his father.

Geraldine pursed her lips. "He's up to something. I don't want to see you lose your home."

"You care too much about me," she said, reaching out for Geraldine's hand.

"Well, somebody has too. I'm sorry Miss Astoria, but you raised a pit of vipers. No good vipers!"

"They do the best they can," Astoria said slowly. "Anyway, the doctor said I can go home in a week. I can sort it out then."

"It will be sold by then. They'll put you in some home, just like this one," Geraldine said gently. "Junior's been visiting here. What do you talk about?"

"I don't recall," Astoria said, alarm bells ringing in her ears. Fear stabbed her stomach.

"Did you sign something?" Geraldine asked quickly.

"No," Astoria answered. But had she? Had John Junior really been in her room or had she dreamed it? She had a gauzy memory of John Junior standing in her room with a man, a lawyer. He told her it was the best thing for everyone and she had agreed. He meant not selling the house, of course. Or had he meant selling the house? Did she sign something?

Aris knew she was dreaming. She was lying lengthwise across the guest bed in the second bedroom; the choking heat that occupied the room invaded her dreams and she was back in the valley.

She looked down and saw her body covered in a long, white, cotton nightgown. Her hair was long and curled softly around her shoulders. She looked out at the too-bright light. She was in Gram's garden; the sun was sickeningly dazzling. It looked so close, Aris thought, if she put out her hand, it would come away blackened and burnt. The garden was dusty and dry; the plants had withered in the heat. The tomatoes and corn grew high, taller than she, but they were dead. The corn was black, the tomatoes pulpy, overripe. The place reeked of decay. Behind her, she could hear rustling. She turned.

Gram, wearing her gardening clogs, lavender shorts, and white blouse, smiled grimly. Though Aris could feel no wind, Gram's straw hat blew back off her head, exposing her beauty queen blonde hair. She was dragging something behind her through the corn.

"You need to help me with this," she said.

Although she knew she was dreaming, Aris nodded. "Of course."

She hurried through the dying garden to her Grandmother.

"Let me get that; it's much too heavy for you."

Gram heaved a tired sigh as Aris held out her hand. The light was white and blinding; the sun hung low, devilishly hot. The dusty air permeated every orifice. A fine layer of powdery earth covered her white nightgown, coloring it brown.

Gram placed a hand in Aris' hand. It was not Gram's hand; it was attached to the body Gram had been dragging through the garden.

Aris accepted the hand without surprise. Gram stepped to the side and revealed Laura's dead body encased in the outfit in which Aris had last seen her.

"We should bury it," Aris said.

Gram nodded.

"Aris."

Her mother's mouth moved, mouthed her name, but it was Janice's voice.

"Aris."

Aris opened one violet eye to find Janice standing over her.

"Wake up."

Aris slowly awakened. Janice was indeed standing over her, dressed in tennis whites. Her black bob shivered as she titled her head.

Aris sat up slowly. Janice took her measure, and her cold black eyes narrowed.

"John is sick."

Aris blanched. She looked up at Janice mutely. Janice looked down at her, black eyes unreadable. Aris realized she was stark naked, her golden flesh exposed, her brown nipples hardened in the air. She tried to feel shame, thought about covering herself, but she did not move. Janice's lips thinned, peeled back into a tight humorless smile.

"John has requested to see you, though God only knows why he would want to."

At that, Aris sat up. She did not speak to Janice, but continued to stare mutely.

"Get off that bed. Get dressed," Janice ordered.

Aris obeyed dully. She walked as though she were in a trance. She went slowly past Janice and into the hall. She entered her bedroom and glanced once at the rumpled, soiled coverlet where she and Rhys had fucked last. Janice followed behind her, pushed past her, and yanked open the closet doors. She threw out a black sundress.

"Here, wear that."

Aris picked up the sundress and pulled it over her head. Janice threw her some white espadrilles; Aris sat down and pulled those on as well.

"For Christ's sake, Aris, put on some underwear."

Aris nodded. Janice walked into the master bath and began yanking open drawers until she found a hair brush. She positioned herself behind Aris and pulled the brush roughly through the short, golden-blonde tresses. Janice tossed the brush onto the distressed white dresser and walked back to the vanity in the bathroom. She pulled out a lipstick and tossed it on the bed.

"Put that on too. You look like hell."

Aris mechanically applied the pink lipstick. Janice glanced disdainfully at the wrought iron bed, as if she knew what had happened there only a few days before. She swept out of the room like a tiny, well-muscled hurricane. Aris slowly rose from the bed and followed behind her. Janice was waiting at the door with Aris' purse in hand, her house keys jingling.

"Lock the door."

Aris took the keys and purse from Janice, careful not to touch her mother-in-law's skin. Janice stepped out into the sun and waited for Aris to pull the door shut and lock it. Janice's silver Lexus was parked in the small driveway. Across the street, the rusted Camaro sat, its occupant asleep in the front seat. Aris stared at it numbly. It had not been parked there for weeks; Aris repressed a shudder as her hands fluttered up to her mouth. Janice glanced at the car and her eyes showed distaste. She practically shoved Aris in the passenger seat and slammed the door.

Aris was unable to focus; her vision was hazy, and every noise she heard had an underwater quality. She thought dimly that perhaps she had gone crazy, then realized the prospect was not unappealing.

Janice did not speak the entire ride to Sonoma County. The scenery changed from familiar to foreign. Finally, all she saw were trees and farms and the occasional small vineyard. Janice embarked onto a series of small, winding roads. The trees got denser, almost blocking out the sun entirely. Then they turned off onto a gravel road; Janice glanced at Aris.

"We're going to The Redwoods. It's a mental hospital, Aris."

Aris did not respond. The grounds of the place opened up before her. There was a great lawn that flanked either side of the road; beyond that were the woods. Dominating the landscape was a large, white, stucco building with a red tile roof. Janice pulled the car into a small parking lot on the left side of the building.

Aris pushed open the car door. Janice followed her, jumping out of the car neatly, as though she were a woman half her age. She

came up behind Aris and grabbed her arm. Aris
automatically pulled away, but Janice held firm.

"I thought about paying you off," Janice
eyed Aris speculatively. "Just giving you money
to leave my son alone."

Janice tightened her grip until her fingers
drained of blood, and a sharp pain shot down
Aris' arm. Aris again tried to pull away, but
Janice was stronger.

"I don't want your goddamn money."

"You make me sick," Janice said, low,
and with such venom that Aris recoiled. "I know
what you've done with Rhys."

Aris recoiled. Janice raked her black
eyes over her, her mouth curled in contempt.

"Everyone knows. You've sabotaged
yourself. John will never marry you now. I'll
never allow it."

Janice released her arm abruptly and
began walking in her clipped manner toward the
hospital. Aris had to run to keep up. The whole
situation felt like a dream to her, as if she had
never woken; she felt like she was still back in
Gram's garden. The roasting sun blazed
overhead, casting its radiant light on the
waiting, white building. John was in there
somewhere.

She obediently followed Janice up the concrete stairs and through a set of double doors. She was in a small waiting room. Directly in front of the main entrance was another entrance. Those doors were obviously locked. On the walls hung inoffensive pictures of nature scenes. In the corner by the main entrance were some potted plants. A cat wandered the lobby. To the left of the locked set of doors there was a small desk behind a window. The woman looked up behind the window and gave a benign smile of welcome. Janice walked up to the window.

"Hello, Janice Prince for Dr. Sidney Fitzsimmons."

The woman inclined her head and picked up a white phone. A few seconds later there was a buzz and the double-doors opened. A handsome older man motioned them in. He smiled a reassuring smile and leaned in to kiss Janice on her white cheek.

"Hello, Sid," Janice smiled.

"Aris, this is Dr. Sidney Fitzsimmons. He's the director of the hospital and a very dear friend of mine. Sid, this is John's..." Janice trailed off. "Aris."

Sidney stuck out his hand. Aris mechanically put her hand in his. She did not speak. The doctor shook Aris' hand quickly.

The walls were white; the lights overhead were long, florescent tubes. The small group of people made little noise as they processed down the carpeted hall. Sidney stopped in front of a large, wooden door and opened it.

"My office. Please, come in. Ladies, you'll be pleased to know John is doing much better. We have seen quite an improvement since he's been here."

Two weeks! Aris almost screamed. Surely it had not been that long.

"Now, Janice, Monique is waiting outside the door for you. She's going to take you to visit with John."

Sidney smiled and held open the door for her. The door shut with a click.

"She's devoted to her son, you know. She visits him often," he said. "John has requested to see you. Honestly, I'm a little surprised you came."

I didn't have a choice, Aris thought through the dull haze of dreaminess.

"Alright then, Aris," he offered her his hand. "Let's head out."

Aris ignored the doctor's hand as she got up; she cursed the shoes on her feet. Janice had picked out shoes she didn't wear much and her toes were pinched. She followed Sidney down the empty hallway. Aris' heart skipped a beat and her breath stilled as she realized she was about to see John for the first time since he had discovered her with Rhys. Sidney stepped into a room and motioned for Aris to follow him in. She could not make her feet move. Finally, she put one pinched foot in front of the other and crossed over into the room. She expected to see John, clad in pajamas, sitting in a wheelchair, drooling. The room was empty.

She looked around.

"I'm just going to go and get John and we'll be back in just a minute. Have a seat."

Aris nodded and sat down on the long, brown leather couch. Her eyes clouded and she tried in vain not to think about the last time she saw John.

Aris was unsure how she managed to go to Rhys each morning and return home to John without a quiver of conscience, but she had. How easy it had been for her to separate the two lives. When she was with Rhys, she felt a zipping, almost thrilling, sense of guilt; when she was with John, which wasn't that often, she felt nothing. She waited for the hot, sticky days and Rhys' hard, demanding arms. Sex with Rhys was varied: coarse and hurried, or languorous and intense. Rhys had an uncanny ability to make Aris giggle, breathless, girlish. She loved making Rhys laugh. His laugh was like a balm that lay itself neatly across her soul, filling in spaces she didn't even know were there. Rhys' painting had become frequent and frenzied. The abstracts became faces, the faces became familiar. It was Aris in ten different shades.

The day John caught them together, all she really felt was relief; now she didn't have to tell him.

The week John was in New York, Aris stayed with Rhys. He would take her to dim, rough clubs or to see old movies. She did not relish the idea of returning to her neat cottage in Larkspur; it was like returning to another life.

It was mid-afternoon. The heat swam through the loft like a lackadaisical fish. There was a black fan aimed at the bed where Aris was laying naked, golden limbs on display, nipples standing up proudly. Rhys was painting. It was a large canvas, deep burgundy, covered with eyes. Black eyes. She did not like it and he knew it. He knew why, though they never spoke of it. It made her uncomfortable, but Rhys just laughed. "I'll turn it around," he said.

She was lounging in the bed, loving the sensuous feel of the cool white sheets, eating an apple, her nails making crescents in the green skin.

"You know I hate it when you eat in my bed," he growled.

Aris smiled saucily. "So?"

Rhys came slowly from behind the painting. Even at that distance, she could see his flashing, green eyes darkening.

He approached the bed and looked down at her. He was streaked with paint and she knew, when he grabbed her, she would be covered in red. He was quick, striking like forked lightning. She felt him tug the apple from her hand and throw it across the room where it landed with a thump. He kissed her, with a slow, delicious mouth. She felt the red paint seep into the white cotton, opened her eyes for a second, saw the red streaking the pristine sheets, Rhys' eyes filling the whole world. Her hands clutched at the hot skin of his back. Then all she knew, all she wanted, was Rhys.

In the press of flesh upon flesh, between the moans and little breaths, reality intruded. John, in the doorway, Rhys lifting her off of him. The three of them frozen in a little tableau. In medias res. The phrase surfaced in Aris' mind; she continued to turn it over in her head, like a tongue probing a sore tooth. She couldn't leave it alone. In medias res.

"You should go."

When she left Rhys, her hands had been shaking; they fluttered around her eyes and forehead like moths.

The door opened. Aris looked up. Her heart leaped, then plummeted. She had expected some drooling, unrecognizable figure, head lolling around on a wheelchair, but as John came through the door, she saw he looked the same, only thinner. He was dressed in clothes she did not recognize. His usually dancing eyes were dead. His movements were slow, measured, as if he had to concentrate to control himself.

Sidney led him into the room. Janice was not with them. John followed Dr. Fitzsimmons like a little boy. The doctor sat in a brown leather chair to the left of the sofa. He gestured for John to sit. John, barely glancing at Aris, sat down on the sofa opposite her.

The handsome doctor cleared his throat. Aris looked at John; he stared back at her, his eyes flat. Neither spoke.

John did not speak. He continued to stare at Aris. She wanted to drop her eyes, hang her head like a shamed dog, but she could not. How had they gotten here, staring at each other across the room in a crazy house?

John jumped up from the sofa suddenly and turned his back on Aris. He walked behind the brown leather sofa and stood with it between them. He crossed his arms over his blue polo shirt. He did not look like the star quarterback now. All that confidence that was so attractive to Aris was gone; her betrayal had drained him of it. His shoulders were no longer proud, but stooped. For the first time she noticed how pale he was, how he seemed to curl into himself. Seeing him like this, she could take it no longer.

"John, I'm sorry," she said simply, quietly. The minute she said it, she knew it was not true. Not precisely true. She was not sorry she had been with Rhys; she was not even sorry for what it had cost her. She was sorry for causing John pain.

John laughed an ugly laugh she had never heard before.

"You're sorry?" he asked in disbelief.

Aris stared at him.

"Fuck!" he said excitedly. "I don't even know where to begin. I picked you up out of the gutter," John began.

Aris was taken aback.

"I gave you everything. I bought you clothes, a house, a car. I made sure you got your hair and nails done, that you wore the right make-up. I introduced you to major power players! And you? You fucked my cousin," he said bitterly. "I'm so glad you're grateful," he said sarcastically.

"I don't know what to say," she said, and then she did hang her head like a punished dog.

"I've got an idea," he yelled sarcastically. "Why don't you tell me all the lurid details! Why don't you tell me how it all happened? I've got nothing but time here, Aris."

Sidney cleared his throat but did not speak.

"What the fuck?"

He drew the sentence out slowly and Aris flinched at the vulgarity.

"What did I do that was so goddamn wrong, Aris? I still can't believe that you did this to me! Me! After everything I did for you. Everything I did to make you better!"

John glared at her from across the room; she could see the tears shining in his eyes and instantly wanted to run to him and comfort him.

"I loved you. Why wasn't I enough? I would have given you the world. Why wasn't I enough?" This last was said brokenly.

Yes, John was enough. Yes, John gave her what she needed, but Rhys had given her something she hadn't even known she wanted. How could she explain that to John?

"You were enough," Aris said tiredly, rubbing her violet eyes with her hand. "Of course you were enough. I don't know what I was doing. I wasn't thinking."

"Oh, please. I make your car payments. I bought you the house in Marin County. Where would you be without me?"

"You were the one who wanted me to have a BMW! You were the one who said we should live in Marin! I never cared, John. I really never cared. Love is not money."

John snorted. "But it makes life a hell of a lot easier, doesn't it?" he asked her bitterly. He continued without waiting for an answer. "Maybe you liked lying down with trash. Rhys is trash, you know. He is. Maybe you were so used to trash, you couldn't help yourself."

"You're ashamed of me," she accused.

"You think he isn't?" John paused, his hands working at his side. "How do you think it felt? All those people asking me where you were from and asking about you, your family. Your parents. Everyone wanted to know where you came from, what you were doing. They thought you were a gold digger! I had to persuade them you were more than white trash. It was embarrassing. But, damn it, Aris, I defended you. Every time, I defended you."

"All those people. Your family. Your precious, snobby family."

John glared at her.

"How do you think I felt? All the while knowing they were talking about me. Knowing they thought I wasn't good enough for you, or them? You didn't want to tell me what they were saying about me but I knew, John! How could I not know? God, it's no wonder Rhys and I ended up together."

John blanched at the name.

"It's not an excuse," Aris said. "I know it's not an excuse."

John came around the sofa and smoothed his khaki shorts before he sat down.

"I don't want to fight," he declared.

Aris smiled mirthlessly.

"Who does?"

"Maybe we need to go to a therapist, someone to help us work through this," John said.

"What are you saying?"

"If we're going to get past this, we're going to need some help," he said logically.

"So," she said slowly, "you want to stay together?"

"Yes. Don't you?" he asked.

Aris was silent.

"Don't tell me you don't know," John said, warningly. "Don't tell me you have to think. I know Rhys doesn't want you. He just wanted to play one of his little games. You understand you were a game for him, don't you? He would never really want you."

"I need to think," Aris said, panicky.

"What's there to think about?" John asked her. "I'm the only one, don't you get it, Aris? I am the only one for you. I am willing to take you back. I am willing to forgive you. I know Rhys doesn't want you. I know he used you. God knows what kind of shit he said to you to get you into bed. No doubt he lied to you. He probably told you all sorts of horrible things. I don't even want to think about it. I know it wasn't totally your fault. You can't help it, Aris. You're a follower, not a leader. He led you right off a cliff. I wasn't there to protect you. I should have been."

Aris sat still; she felt very confused. John said it was her fault, now he was blaming Rhys and himself? She rose to her feet, because she could think of nothing else to do.

John rose as well, his classically handsome face flushed red with emotion.

"Good. I'm glad. You made the right decision. We'll get past this. I know we will."

"John," Aris said.

"No!" he said quickly. "You don't have to say anything. I'm the kind of guy that you don't have to say anything to, not a word. You don't need to explain."

Sidney cleared his throat again. "It sounds to me as though Aris has not made up her mind yet."

"Sure she has," John said and he turned and walked out of the room without looking at her.

Chapter 21

Rhys threw the rest of the chicken feed and ran off. He slid stealthily into the woodshed and tried to make himself as small as possible. Small and quiet as a mouse. Quieter than a mouse. Footsteps came closer. Rhys closed his eyes.

"Goddamn kid. Thinks he can run off on me. Well, he's got to come home sometime."

Dad laughed a harsh laugh as he stepped into the woodshed. Rhys popped open one green eye. His father's denim-clad legs were directly in front of him. His back was to the woodpile. If he turned around and looked down, he would surely see Rhys. Rhys held his breath. Quiet, like a mouse. Invisible, like a ghost. He was a nothing. He was a nothing and Dad couldn't see him. He was a nothing and Dad couldn't see him.

Dad turned around slowly as he puffed his pipe. The scent of tobacco wafted over the woodpile. Suddenly, Dad started taking his black leather belt off. Rhys cringed. It was the one with the wide buckle that read Smith. Dad crouched low, right in front of him. But he was invisible. He was a ghost. He was a mouse. He was a nothing. He wasn't there.

"Get out from behind there, Acccce. Don't make me drag you out."

Reluctantly, with lead feet, Rhys crawled out from behind the woodpile.

Rhys awoke with a start. The white sheets were damp with sweat and tangled around his legs. It had been years since he'd had that dream. He slipped out of the bed and lighted a cigarette. The summer night whispered its hot breath on him and he shuddered.

Rhys had returned to Northern California, sickened by the world, disgusted with himself and the sycophantic hangers-on that filled his life. He craved solitude and the hot, dry California summers. When Rhys came back to California, he set up shop far away from anyone else in the family. He thought maybe Oakland or Berkeley, but in the end he chose an obscure little town in the East Bay. He was there for two months before he decided to announce his return.

He was searching for something, though he did not realize it. He found himself looking forward to seeing his family, those pretty people who touted their halcyon lives as if nothing bad in the world ever happened to them. He appeared at Astoria's house during the family reunion with expectations lining his pocket; now that he was a success they would stop treating him as an outsider. They'd all stayed away from him, as if he were a disease. Only his mother, Aunt Janice and Granny deigned to speak to him. The rest of the family eyed him surreptitiously, and those who did speak to him did so haltingly, even fearfully. He decided to leave, wondering why he'd come in the first place. That was when he saw her.

The first time he saw Aris from the gleaming white porch of Astoria's house he was fascinated. She was a thin whip of a girl; long arms and a long neck made her look like a foal. Her skin was that golden tone only true blondes possess. He could hardly see her face from where he stood. She moved clumsily, her gestures quick and unsure. Even from far away, he could see she was all nerves. There was no grace about her; she was made of long limbs and awkwardness, like a fourteen-year-old girl.

He stayed and watched her all that day; he couldn't stop watching her.

Then he saw Johnny walk over to her, put his arm around her. Johnny's girl. Rhys left the house in Napa and locked himself in his studio for weeks. Johnny left messages on his voicemail:

"Hey man, it was really good to see you the other day. We should get together. Call me."

"Hey, it's John again, you should come over for dinner, meet my fiancée Aris. Give me a call."

Then another voicemail. Frat boy voice, Johnny: "So I hear that you're a famous artist. Dude, that's awesome! How come you never told anybody? Call me."

Then he got another message:

"Rhys honey, it's Mama. There's a little to-do for the family in Napa next week. Black tie. I think it would be nice if you came. Everyone will be there. I love you, honey."

Napa. The party. Aris: golden skin, fuck-me red dress, hair almost completely shorn off. He'd wanted to come up behind her and strip that dress from her golden skin, inch by languorous inch. He didn't stop himself from

walking up behind her, so close, he was almost
touching her. He kept his hands clenched in his
pockets so he wouldn't reach out and grab her.

He felt Aris respond to his closeness, the
sound of his voice in her ear. She'd been all
nerves and fluttering hands. She hadn't known
what to do with herself. He drank in her
uncertainty, her skittishness, would rather have
died than still those fluttering hands. He loved
the slope of her long neck and those beautiful,
perfectly crooked teeth. Janice cornering him in
the den.

"So Marie and Sarah tell me you're some kind
of famous artist. Is that true?"

Botoxed brow slightly furrowed, pouty lips
pursed, hope at the bottom of her hematite eyes.
He nodded shortly, aware of just how much she
needed him to be something.

The house was crowded with people
swathed in couture and tuxedos. Johnny, golfing
lawyer, former quarterback, still followed him
around with adulation lurking in his black eyes.

The days were made up of the slick heat,
eating at them all slowly like a cancer, and Aris'
liquid, languid, violet eyes. He drank until the
heat slid over him sickeningly and Aris had
faded in his mind's eye. Aris in the loft, the light
from the back doors completely illuminating

her, like a Madonna. Beads of sweat running down her back, nimbus gold hair, flushed with heat. Katrina, brown eyes smudged with hurt. "Go home," he said shortly as he gently pushed her out the door.

And then that day. The violence, the sticky warmth of her. He'd wanted to take Aris with all the ugliness he had in him. His need for her was tinged with mania. He wanted to absorb her and sink into her at the same time.

He saw Aris trying to bend to the collective family will, and he knew it was futile. He knew she was unhappy, though it seemed Aris had no idea she was unhappy. She was trying to fit herself into a puzzle in which she did not belong. Any fool could see she would never be a Prince. She had a wistfulness about her that the Prince family didn't understand or tolerate. Rhys thought of his rigid cousin and his quixotic fiancée. Johnny couldn't possibly know who or what she really was.

He watched her trying so hard and failing so miserably. He saw Johnny's disappointment, which he tried to hide. Aris' control was held so tenuously; he enjoyed watching her snap.

Helen called him and told him primly that she knew what had happened.

"Hello?"

"Rhys."

"Mom."

"I know what's been going on," Helen said tentatively.

"What?" he asked. He'd been painting and looked for a rag to wipe his hand on.

"Between you and John's girlfriend," she said plainly.

"What?"

"You heard me," she sniffed. "I am so embarrassed."

"What for?" he asked shortly.

"What do you mean? The whole family knows; John had to be dragged from the Napa house, stinking drunk. They took him to The Redwoods."

She could never bring herself to call it the asylum or even hospital. It was always The Redwoods.

"They did?" Rhys tried to keep his voice casual. So, he'd sent his cousin to the asylum.

"How can you be so callous?" Helen cried.

"Mom," he said quietly.

"I just can't understand why you can't just be normal and nice. Why must you be so difficult and make so much trouble? Ever since you were a young boy, it's been one thing after another. You disappeared for years! Years, Rhys! With not a word, not a phone call. How could you do that to me? Then you come home and start an affair with your cousin's fiancée! I am humiliated," Helen moaned.

"Helen," Rhys said harshly and could almost hear her mouth shut. "What I'm doing in the privacy of my own bed is none of your business, or anyone else's for that matter. I told you when I came back. I'm not discussing anything about where I've been or what I've been doing. I honestly don't give a damn if you're humiliated. This has nothing to do with you. Nothing," he repeated.

"I-"

"I've got to go," he cut her off.

Rhys buried his head and painted.

When Janice pulled into the driveway of the purple house, Laura was lounging against the garage door, smoking. Janice almost hit her.

"Who on earth is that?" Janice asked.

"My mother," Aris said absently, oblivious to the shock in Janice's black eyes.

Laura grinned at them and sauntered over to Janice's window. She tapped on the glass. Janice ignored her.

"You must be Miz Prince," Laura shouted in her jovial, welfare lady voice.

Janice gripped the wheel tightly.

"Hey!"

Laura was pounding on the window, leaving dirty handprints all over it. Aris glanced at Janice and quickly exited the car.

"Mama," Aris said as Laura tapped madly on the glass. Janice started to pull away and Laura began walking beside the car as it moved. Aris felt a glancing blow of pity. Finally Laura stopped and Janice pulled smoothly away.

"Snobby bitch!" Laura screamed after the car.

She walked back up the drive and assessed Aris.

"You look like shit."

Aris blanched.

"So maybe you loved him after all," Laura mused. "Listen, I'm out of money."

Aris sagged against the garage door, as her mother had moments before.

"Your fiancé, that guy? He gave me some but I'm out now," Laura began.

"When did you see John?" Aris asked sharply.

Laura blushed. "Listen kid, I was real angry at you. I maybe did something I shouldn't have."

"He paid you to tell him," Aris said faintly. "And you drank all the money and now you need more."

"I been following you and that other guy," Laura said somewhat sheepishly.

"You fucking piece of shit," Aris said softly.

"Now, you just wait a goddamn minute! Who the hell do you think you're talking to? I'm your Ma."

She hadn't been talking to her mother, though. She'd been talking to herself.

Laura blustered in front of her. Something inside her broke in that moment. She knew then that she would never marry John, that if she did, she would be miserable.

"Hey, you're better off," Laura was saying to her, smiling benignly. "I married the wrong guy once. I seen the way that lady looked at me; you shoulda heard how that hot-shit man of yours talked to me. They never would have accepted you, you know," Laura told her confidently.

"You're right," Aris said.

Laura looked surprised. Aris rummaged through her bag. Laura stepped closer to her.

"Here," Aris said as she thrust The Ring out.

Laura's muddy eyes flashed.

"What?"

"Here," Aris said, her eyes full of pity and pain and self loathing.

Laura reached out and took The Ring in her dirty hands.

"Pawn it," Aris said.

Laura looked at her uncomprehendingly. "A ring like this has gotta be worth a lot."

"I know."

"Wait," Laura said. She twisted one of her rings from her finger and held it out to Aris. "Here, you take that. I pawned a lot of shit of mine, but this I've had since forever. It's a family heirloom. It used to be Ma's."

Aris took the chunk of silver and turquoise.

"Maybe I could come in," Laura said hopefully. "It's hot out here."

"No, Laura," Aris said, and she did not sound like herself. "You and I are done now."

Laura's eyes watered. "I ruined your life, didn't I?" she asked in a self-pitying voice.

Aris ignored her and went inside the house.

Astoria was dreaming. Her husband was sitting in the corner of the room. He looked as handsome as he ever had.

"You're not going to make it back there," he said.

Astoria frowned. "What are you talking about? I'm getting out of here in two days. I healed quickly, like a woman half my age," Astoria said proudly.

"Still, you're dying."

"Now?"

Johnny paused and smoothed back his hair, his beautiful black hair.

"Yes."

"But I can't! I think Junior is trying to sell the house! I have to stay alive to stop him."

"Why?" Johnny shrugged indolently.

"What do you mean? It's our house; it's our children's house."

Johnny shook his head.

"We're going to sort this whole thing out and I'll be back home in no time," Astoria said stoutly.

Johnny shook his head and pursed his lips.

"You were never this stubborn when I was alive."

"You might've liked me more if I was," Astoria said.

"Maybe."

"What are you even doing here?"

"I told you, you're dying. I'm here to help you."

"Ha! Help me die? Don't bother; they kill people left and right in this place."

"Help you let go," Johnny said gently.

"But," Astoria faltered, "I can't. If I die, he'll sell the house. I can't die!"

Johnny shook his head, "Baby, I don't think you're going to make it."

Chapter 22

Laura decided to drive to the valley. She decided to go see Ma.

Her mother's car was not in the driveway. Laura got out of the rusty Camaro slowly, the door creaking loudly. She walked up to the green and white stucco house. The paint on the house was peeling, like it always had been. The trees shuddered as a hot breeze ripped through them. She peered around the back and noticed the garden her mother had tended to lovingly for all her life was wild and overgrown.

She decided to walk next door to Mrs. Nelson's house. She rang the doorbell and a Mexican lady answered the door.

"Where's the lady that lives next door?" she demanded.

The woman lifted a shoulder.

"No woman there."

"What the hell are you talking about? Who lives there?"

"No one live there."

Laura scratched her wizened cheek and peered around the lady, who was quite fat. The living room was gaily lit and there were two fat kids playing on the floor.

"Mary Dunn," Laura said loudly.

"Quien?"

"My fucking mother," Laura said slowly.

"No se. I don't know, lady."

A man came to the door.

"What is going on here?" he asked in a heavy accent.

"I'm looking for my mother. She lives next door."

"No one live next door," he said clearly.

"Well, where the fuck did she go?" Laura asked rudely.

The man said something to the woman and she left the door quickly.

"I think the lady die. I'm not sure. You go now," he said plainly, and he firmly shut the door.

Laura backed down the steps and went over to her mother's house. She sat on the porch with a sigh and started pulling at the peeling white paint. The neighborhood was quiet. She heard the sound of the Mexicans' TV and a few crickets. Laura laughed bitterly. Her mother was gone and she was back in the valley with nothing but a stolen car and an empty bottle of gin. Well, she did have a lot more money than she was used to. Damn it, she should have asked the pawn shop guy for more. She knew she didn't sell that ring for enough money.

She got up and tried to peer into the windows of the house, but it was too dark to see inside. She could live here. Laura pictured the house: the worn floorboards, the scrapes and grooves in the worn wood made by their dog, Lincoln, the orange easy chair where her father spent every evening, the blue tiled kitchen. She could almost smell her mother's peach pie.

Without realizing what she was doing, Laura slunk around the side of the house like a thief. Dead leaves crunched under her cheap heels. She ran her stubby nails along the peeling stucco, stuck her face on the cold, wavy glass and tried to see inside. She decided she didn't want to sleep in the Camaro. She was going to sleep in her house. She could just break a window and slip inside until someone gave her the keys. She threw a rock at the window next to the back door. The tinkle of the breaking glass made her jump.

"S'cuse me? Ma'am?"

It was a policeman. Christ, the Mexicans had called the cops. She hoped Old Max hadn't reported the car stolen.

"Yeah, I lost my key," Laura said as she turned to face him. He was a tall, skinny, white guy, couldn't have been more than twenty-five. She could see him donning his authority. It did not come naturally to him.

"This is Mrs. Dunn's house," the officer stated, shining his flashlight in her face.

Laura put up her hands.

"What are you doing? Trying to blind me?"

"Come back from the door, Ma'am," the officer ordered.

"I live here, okay? I'm Mrs. Dunn's daughter. You wanna see my I.D.?" Laura asked.

"Yes," he said.

"It's in my purse," Laura said snappily.

She handed it to him, and he looked at it under his light.

"You are Mrs. Dunn's daughter, you say?"

"S'right."

"Your last name is different," he commented.

"My married name. Not married anymore," she said, almost sheepishly.

"Mrs. Dunn doesn't live here anymore, but she still owns the house. I'm sorry, but you can't stay here," he said.

"Right, fine," Laura said shortly. "I'll just find a hotel or something."

The officer escorted her to the car and watched her drive away. She drove the streets, searching for her old hangouts, but they were all gone.

"Yuppy trash," Laura sneered at the little cafes and wine bars that had taken their places. Finally, something familiar. Red's.

Laura parked the car and went inside. The front of the place had a new coat of paint since she had seen it last. Inside, the layout was the same, but everything was brand new. The dirty, red carpet was now a shining, red tile floor. The nicked and stained bar had been sanded and glazed. The walls were lined with intimate, red leather booths. She didn't recognize anyone there.

Laura took a seat at the bar and waited for the bartender. A tall, bushy-haired guy about her age sauntered over; he handed her a menu. She turned it over questioningly.

"Wine and microbrews," he said shortly.

"I'll have a gin and tonic," Laura said as she pulled her cigarettes out of her purse.

"No smoking," the man said as he poured her drink.

"What the fuck?" Laura said. "Come on man, everyone used to smoke in here."

"Used to," the man said rudely as he deposited her drink in front of her. It was a tumbler. She took a sip; there was barely any gin in it.

"Hey," she called to the bartender, who was now on the other side of the rectangular bar. "This is bullshit, man. Put some fucking liquor in here!"

The man scowled at her.

"I'm serious. This is all soda," Laura complained.

He came over to her. "That'll be four dollars, lady."

Four dollars! At this rate, she'd be broke in an hour. She leaned in to the bar.

"You know, when I used to come here, the drinks were two dollars for something twice as big as this. This is a fucking rip off."

The man leaned closer to Laura's face. "Then fucking leave, you goddamn hag."

Laura grabbed the glass and twisted her wrist to let the clear liquid fall into her mouth.

"I'm gone," she said as she slipped off the red stool. She made her way through the crowd of valley hipsters to the ladies' room. A few young women were in there fixing their hair.

"This bathroom used to be a fucking hole in the floor; now the toilets flush themselves," Laura snorted.

One of the girls smiled politely at her. Laura looked at herself in the mirror above the sinks. She looked at the 22-year-old kid next to her. She looked at herself. Christ, she was old. She had a sudden vision of her parents when she was pregnant, her mother's blonde beauty contestant hair shot with silver. Her father's weathered hands. They couldn't have been that much older than she was now.

Another girl sauntered up to the sinks. She threw her long, blonde hair over her smooth, tanned shoulder. She pulled at the hem of her skirt. It was almost identical to the one Laura had on.

"I gotta get outta here," Laura said to her reflection.

Instead of leaving, Laura bought herself another drink. Then she bought a drink for the kid sitting next to her. "You yuppy kids have no idea what this place used to be like!"

The night became unexpectedly warm and shiny. Laura was beautiful; everyone loved her. She careened around the bar like she was on ice, talking to people here and there, buying drinks for them. She was telling anyone who would listen about how the valley used to be and what a big shot she was now. She was pulling handfuls of bills out of her cheap-looking purse.

Suddenly, the bushy-haired bartender was hollering for last call. Laura called him over for one last drink. He poured her drink and took her money, not bothering to make change.

"How about you take me home, honey?" she asked him, grinning lasciviously.

The man smiled at her and leaned on the bar until he was very close to her face.

"Now, why in the hell would I want to do that?" he asked meanly.

Laura's hand reached out for her glass of gin. She was going to fling it in his face. She drew back her hand and then glanced at the full glass. No way in hell was she going to waste good liquor on this asshole. She pulled her hand toward her mouth and downed the gin in one gulp. The man laughed shortly and moved passed her down the bar.

"I am so rich, you asshole!" Laura screamed after him. People fell away from her as she made her way out of the bar, as if they were afraid of touching her.

"Wasn't too good for you fuckers when I was buying your drinks, though, was I?" she yelled in her scratchy voice.

Laura left Red's and went across the street to the gas station. She got a bottle of gin and two packs of smokes. Fuck it. She was rich now.

Laura started the engine of the old Camaro and smiled; she forgot about the cruel bartender and started thinking how lucky she was. Old Max hadn't bothered to call the cops. Hell, he was probably so stoned he didn't even realize the car was gone. She had more money than she had ever had in her life. All those bills, just sitting in her purse. She was going to the fanciest hotel in town.

Laura laughed out loud. She gunned the engine and pulled out of the gravel parking lot, thinking how good her life was going to be from now on. Her luck was turning. Laura was so drunk and so intent on counting her blessings that she failed to see the semi bearing down on her until it was too late. Metal screeched, the smell of burning rubber filled the air, and Laura

Dunn's body sailed through the windshield, landing on the sizzling asphalt with a sickening crunch.

Chapter 23

She was going back to the valley. Back to the dust and the heat and the dirty little town that provided the backdrop for her youth. As Aris sat on the train, her thoughts swam in her head.

For years, the specter of her mother had haunted her. Aris spent most of her youth waiting for her mother to reappear and lay claim to her, if for no other reason than to spite her grandmother. Gram tried to assure her that it couldn't happen because it was all legal, but Aris knew there were other ways. She knew there was a reason Gram wouldn't let her walk home from school or play out in the front yard alone.

When she was a teenager, the fear had subsided and would only occasionally rear up in the form of hideous and terrifying nightmares. She would wake up, skin wet, in twisted sheets, shaking. When she'd gotten the phone call, she had a strange urge to laugh. Laura was dead. She died, ironically, drunk on the street in front of Red's.

When Aris got to the valley, the hot air slammed into her. There was no breeze; the heat simply hung in the air like smoke, thick and choking. The little green and white house was empty, had sat empty for over a year now. Aris could not bring herself to sell it. John kept trying to convince her to at least rent it, but she couldn't bear to have strangers in Gram's house. She told herself Gram was coming home someday, even though Gram had made scant progress in the last year.

It stood, as it had always stood, small, the paint peeling, the screen door hanging open. The street was quiet; the air was stifling. She paid the neighbor across the street to keep the front yard up, but Gram's garden had gone wild. The fruit trees, untrimmed these last years, were heavy and low to the ground with rotting fruit. The perennials had gone wild and taken over any open space. She pushed open the green gate and walked up to the white porch.

Somewhere in her head, she heard the echo of Laura's ugly laugh.

She knew she had to go to the morgue. She couldn't do it, didn't want to. She didn't want to see the body.

She put her key in the lock, heard the subtle click and pushed open the door to a thousand memories. The musty, unused smell, mixed with the smell of Gram, assaulted her. The place was practically the same. Aris had taken a few pieces of furniture for her and John's house.

"Secondhand junk," Sarah had whispered to Janice at the housewarming.

"Try third," Janice said shortly.

Aris wandered through the small house. Her flip-flops thwacked on the worn hardwood as she inspected the place. The back window was broken. She would have to get that fixed. She thought of Gram and wished she were there with such a sudden fierceness that she sank to her knees on a keening wail.

Aris sat on the floor for some time. She was not sure how long she'd been crying; she knew her violet eyes were red and puffy. She knew she looked like she had been through a war. She pulled at the ends of her hair, the pain spurring her into action. She got up from the cool floor, squared her shoulders, and strode purposefully to the door.

"No sense in putting off what needs doing."

That's what Gram would say.

John stepped out into the hot sun. Janice wrapped her thin, white arms around him.

"It's going to be okay. Everything will be okay now. Mother is here. Mother will get whatever you need," she crooned.

John shook her off.

"Aris didn't come with you?"

"No," Janice said carefully.

They got into Janice's silver Lexus. They were halfway home; Janice had been chirping in an animated monologue for the entire ride. John suddenly interrupted her.

"Did she know I was coming home today?" he asked.

"Well," Janice said slowly, "I'm not sure."

"What do you mean?" he asked. "Didn't you tell her?"

"Didn't you?" Janice glanced at him, almost nervously.

"No, I wasn't allowed phone calls. You know that. You were supposed to tell her. Didn't you?"

"Well, no then. I didn't tell her. I assumed you had. It doesn't matter anyway," she blurted. "Aris is gone. Her mother died"

"What?" John was shocked.

"I know, I know, a remarkable feat for someone who was already dead."

John ignored that.

"How did you know?" he asked. "Why didn't you tell me?"

"Why should it matter how I know? I just told you, didn't I?"

John ignored his mother as his fingers gripped the dash tightly.

Aris waited for the overweight balding man to pull out the freezer drawer. When he did, Aris stifled a gasp. It was undoubtedly her mother. Her body was covered with a big, white sheet; her face was uncovered. Even in death she looked trashy and cruel. Cuts and lacerations criss-crossed over her skin; there was still gravel embedded in her face.

Aris looked up at the man and nodded. He closed the drawer and directed her upstairs. There were papers to fill out. Aris went through the legal requirements mechanically, still unable to believe her mother was dead. There was relief, true, but also a sadness that hung around her head like a sick halo. She did not want to grieve for a woman she didn't know.

"There's a lovely mortuary on Third Street, dear," the kind-faced, old woman told her as she handed her the papers.

It struck Aris that she wanted to see her mother go into the ground. She wanted to go to the cemetery and stand there and see the coffin lowered into the dirt. She picked out a coffin at Serenity Pines Mortuary. The man there told her he would handle all the arrangements; all he needed to know was when she wanted to have the funeral.

"No funeral," she said. "Just a plot."

The man was confused. "You don't want a service?" he asked gently.

"No, no service, no prayers, no eulogies. You just tell me when to be there. I want to be there when they put her in."

"Of course," the man nodded.

Aris stayed at Gram's house in the old easy chair in the living room. She covered herself in a beach towel she bought at the Five and Ten. All the windows were open to let in the night air. She couldn't bring herself to sleep in Gram's bed.

When she woke, Aris pulled on some shorts. She was going to see Gram. She wasn't due at the cemetery until later in the afternoon. It was only nine and the heat was already filling up the house. It would be sweltering in just a few hours.

"Mrs. Dunn, you have a very special visitor," the nurse sing-songed as she led Aris into the room.

Aris was surprised to find Gram sitting up in her bed, her hair plaited. The TV was on.

"Hi Gram," Aris said.

Gram looked at her and blinked.

"Mrs. Dunn is able to use her right hand pretty good now," the nurse said. "And she can say a few words, too!"

"That's wonderful news, Gram!" Aris beamed. "How are you feeling?"

Gram blinked again and made a low sound in her throat.

"That means not so great," the nurse put in. "She has good days and bad days. I'll let you two visit."

The nurse walked out of the room and Aris pulled up a chair next to Gram.

"Gram, I have some news," Aris began.

Gram closed her eyes briefly, and when she opened them they were shining with tears.

"Gram, I've made a mess of my life," Aris felt tears forming in her own eyes. "I've

done something really stupid. I've betrayed
John, and I don't think he will ever forgive me. I
don't know what to do! I thought I loved him.
Now, I don't know. Rhys, he couldn't possibly
love me. I mean, I know he doesn't. I'm just
some kind of game for him, but John's family,
I've let them down, too. And, Laura, Mama...
She came looking for money."

At this, Gram's eyebrows shot up and
she began to make an urgent gurgling noise in
her throat. Her lips worked slowly.

Tears fell down Aris' cheeks, and Gram's
worked her right hand. Aris grasped the old
woman's hand and was surprised to find how
strong her grip was.

"Gram, you're going to be okay," Aris
said in shock as the hand gripped her tighter.
"My God," Aris said as a smile spread across
her face. "You're going to be okay."

Tears spilled over onto Gram's cheeks.
Her lips formed the word, okay.

"Yes, thank God. Yes," Aris closed her
eyes.

"I have to tell you something else, Gram.
It's about Laura. She had an accident last night,"
Aris said, pausing to search Gram's face for any
emotion. When the old woman showed nothing,
she went on.

"She's dead, Gram. I'm sorry."

Gram squeezed her fingers once and mouthed the word okay again.

"Okay," Aris said to her. "Okay."

Gram squeezed her fingers again and said, in a hoarse garble of words, "Love you. All okay."

Aris felt tears falling down her cheeks again. She rose to leave. "I have to go. I have to go to the cemetery but I'll be back soon. I promise. You just keep getting better and better, Gram!"

Aris drove through the big, rusty gates toward the back of the grounds. The heat sat upon her like a carrion bird. Sweat glittered her brow as she drove slowly through the empty graveyard. As she went deeper and deeper into the cemetery, she watched the rows of white headstones fly past. When she arrived at the plot, she was surprised to see an old man there. He was standing over the gaping hole, wiping his brow with a red rag. He looked up as she exited the car.

"Uncle Kirby?"

"It's me," the old man affirmed.

Inexplicably, she thought of her fifth birthday when he sent her all those presents. "Stolen," Laura had scoffed. The last time she had seen him was a Christmas when she was around twelve. Whatever he had done between now and then had broken him. He was stooped, balding. He had a large handlebar mustache covering his mouth. He wore blue bib overalls. His skin was an ashen gray; the pallor suggested an incurable and pervasive illness.

"Aris?" he asked.

"Yes."

"The old girl is really gone, huh?"

She was shocked to see him there.

Aris shrugged.

"Couldn't afford to bury her proper, eh?" he asked.

Aris looked about helplessly.

"I don't blame you," he continued. "She was a shit mother."

Aris gaped at the old man.

"She was. I ain't going to make excuses for her, now she's dead. No sense in it."

He had inherited Gram's sensibility and practicality.

"Them two boys is gonna push her in," Kirby gestured to the two youths, lounging in the background near a large oak. "If you're ready."

Aris nodded. She glanced down; the coffin was already positioned over the hole, held into place by some mechanism.

Kirby turned, "Alright boys, come on over here."

The two boys loped over and started messing with the contraption.

"Want to say anything?" Kirby asked her.

"No," Aris said, staring stonily at the shiny, gray box being lowered into the dirt.

Kirby nodded comfortably.

A throat cleared behind her. Aris turned.

It was John. He was dressed in a light summer suit and tie. She immediately felt inadequate and improperly dressed. He stepped toward her uncertainly. She gave an almost imperceptible nod. He came up to stand beside her. She watched as the coffin hit the bottom of the hole.

The second half of his show was taking place at Katrina's gallery that night. Rhys hadn't seen her since he'd asked her to leave his place so many weeks ago. The show was going better than he expected. He was going to make enough money for years to come. He was starting to gain a lot more attention from serious collectors.

He supposed he should feel a sense of triumph, but he didn't. He just wanted to go home. He was amused at himself. He'd worked so hard to get away from the Prince family all those years ago, and then he came back expecting something from them. It was a boyish idea that he'd clung to and knew he must now discard. Even if they knew the truth, even if they knew Janice was his mother, and Rhys suspected J.J. did, they wouldn't care. He simply wasn't like them and the more he saw them, the more he realized he did not want to be like them.

He could still remember the collective sigh of relief the family breathed when he left. When his mother lied and told everyone he'd gotten into NYU, he laughed at that. He didn't have the grades to get into NYU. In reality, he graduated high school, waited for his mother to get home from the mental hospital and when he saw she was stable enough, he left.

"Where are you going?"

Rhys shrugged indifferently.

"But you don't have any money," Helen protested.

"I have enough," he said grudgingly. "I'll be fine. Don't worry about me."

Helen had been beside herself. "What will I tell everyone?"

"Tell them whatever you want."

So she lied and told them he was going off to college. He left Northern California and meandered up to Seattle; from there he hit Santa Fe, Austin, New Orleans, and finally landed in New York. He was a wild thing; nothing could tame him. He constantly sat on a razor's edge, always feeling the teeth just beneath him. He lived as if he knew no fear, and yet, fear was all he knew. In those days, fear drove him. Under his placid exterior, his blood ran wildly. He had been a volatile creature, constantly searching. But he hadn't known what he was searching for. In the years just after he left California, he sunk himself into drugs, violence, and women. The dirtier, the meaner, the uglier, the more hurtful, the more he liked it. The more he wanted it.

When he surfaced from the sticky, warped web he had created, he hadn't recognized himself: his gaunt face, his filthy hands, his haunted eyes. He realized, in that moment, how much he hated himself and how many years he'd lost abusing himself.

Rhys left America and went to Europe. He'd always had a talent for painting; he would frequently have small shows in New York, just to make enough cash to fuel his self-destruction. In Italy, his passion for art began to push over him in waves. He set up a studio and began to paint obsessively. He became something of a darling of the Italian art world. Suddenly, people wanted a piece of him. At first, he basked in it. He loved the attention, so many people clamoring to be near him. After a while he felt drained. The adoration began to reek of insincerity; the compliments became too effusive.

The women were the same women: wild, coltish, easily hurt. He'd collected them like dolls on a shelf. He rarely acknowledged they had feelings, didn't care if he hurt them. Once he could smell the desperation on them, he got rid of them. He had no need, no desire, to be possessed. Something had been different with Aris; no matter how much she wanted him, no matter how much she reeked of need, it wasn't ever enough for him.

He had been abandoned by his biological parents a long time ago. His adopted parents stripped him of his childhood stupidly and callously. He spent his teenage years trying to feel something. He spent his twenties trying to destroy himself. He didn't have a place among those deceptively glittering people that made up his family. Aris gave him a place inside herself, whether she knew it or not. That was the place he wanted to be; that was the place where he belonged.

The fight they'd had was brutal and when Rhys left her place, he wasn't sure he wanted her back. He wasn't sure she'd really wanted him. Even when she spoke of love, Rhys was unsure. As the summer melted into a string of days and the light grew dimmer as autumn approached, Rhys knew he loved her. He knew it as he knew the cadence of her heart and the color of her eyes. He knew she would come to him.

He stretched his canvas, he mixed his colors, he picked up his brush, he waited for Aris.

Chapter 24

The death of Astoria Prince sent a shockwave throughout the family, in spite of her advanced age. Astoria died the day she was due to go back home, and her children, who had assumed the dangerously complacent attitude that the old woman would never die, descended on the stately white house with ferocious and zealous grief.

"I won't tell her," Disby muttered to herself. She had gone to the house. She'd seen it hadn't been painted, knew it never would be painted. She called J.J., who refused to directly answer any questions she had.

Disby walked the halls swiftly.

"You're early. Mrs. Prince might not be awake yet," the nurse commented.

"Mrs. Prince?" the nurse knocked on the closed door.

The nurse pushed open the door, and it was immediately evident that Astoria was dead. The nurse did not speak, and Disby stared at her with wild eyes. Suddenly, Disby pushed the nurse out of the way and went careening into her mother's room. The sight of Astoria, lying motionless in the bed, her weak and watery light extinguished forever, made Disby cry out. She threw herself on the bed. She clutched the body of her dead mother and cried. It had been years since Johnny Prince had passed away and Disby had forgotten the pain that had sliced through her then, but she felt it now, pressing down on her thin shoulders, shooting out to her long fingers, and gathering behind her dark eyes. But this was different than when her father had died and Disby knew it. Astoria had been the thread that ran through them all and made them a family. Without Astoria, they would fall to pieces.

The nurse, who was less experienced than her counterparts, watched Disby from the doorway with her mouth open.

"Excuse me, Ms. Prince?"

Disby ignored her.

"Ms. Prince, she's gone. You have to let go. We need to call the coroner."

"Get out!" Disby said tiredly.

The nurse looked at her, nonplussed.

Disby looked up, cradling the body. Tears ran down her cheeks unheeded.

"I said leave. You're dismissed, now get out and leave me with my mother," Disby said, sounding more like Janice than herself.

The nurse, startled, obeyed her and began backing out of the room.

"I'll just call the coroner," she said softly, placatingly.

Disby dropped her mother's body gently back on the flowery coverlet and got up from the bed.

"You'll do no such thing. You are dismissed. You are no longer needed here," she said as she came toward the woman slowly.

The nurse continued to back away, and Disby finally gave her a push out of the room and threw the lock. Disby climbed into the bed with her mother. She was stiff and cold.

There was a commotion in the hall. She heard shouting. A key slid into the lock and she heard more shouting. Then it all stopped and all Disby heard were her own sobs.

When Janice got to the home, she had
to beg Disby to let her in. Janice ordered,
cajoled, and hollered, and, finally, she begged.
Disby pulled back the lock and admitted her
sister, leaving the nurse to stand outside the
room, her nose pressed to the glass. Once inside
the room Janice flung herself upon the bed,
screaming in anguish.

Aris allowed herself to be led back to
Gram's house. Uncle Kirby declined to follow
them and instead, jerked his head to an old big
rig across the street.

"Gonna visit Ma before I get on to
Barstow. You did right, taking care of her all this
time, Aris. You're a good kid," Kirby said
affectionately.

The police had given her Laura's effects.
Aris took the battered, blue suitcase and threw it
in the trunk of John's car. She didn't want to
open it.

She allowed John to put her in his
Mercedes, handling her as if she were fragile
and childlike. Since he had appeared at the
burial, he had been nothing more than kind and
solicitous toward her.

On the long drive back to Larkspur, she
was mute, pressing her head against the cold

glass and looking out the window at the dry, fevered valley. As she watched the landscape change from houses to farms to nothing and back to houses again, she knew she didn't belong there anymore.

John knew she was going to leave; she could sense it. His dead eyes seemed to silently beg her not to go, not just yet. Her infidelity sat between them like an imposing stranger on a plane.

Aris waded through life like a sleepwalker. John resumed working; his black eyes focused on something in front of him. Something that Aris couldn't and didn't care to see.

Aris made John a ghost when she started her affair with Rhys, but now she was a ghost too, a forgotten and befuddled shade who wandered the small house in Larkspur rattling her chains of emotional distress as loudly as she dared.

On the day of the wake everyone was gathering at the Napa house. Slowly, the clan came together to mourn the staid and gentle Astoria. Relatives came from back east, dignitaries came from all over; the Prince family was wide and far reaching.

"Please, Aris," John said to her. "I need you to do this with me." This last thing for me were the unspoken words.

She'd been packing up the Larkspur house slowly. Boxes littered the rooms; John knew she was going. Neither of them spoke of it.

Aris and John joined the mass exodus from the city to the sleepy wine country. As John drove the black Mercedes up the gravel drive, Aris could see people dotting the grounds like pieces on a chessboard. They seemed small and motionless. Nothing moved but the black Mercedes crunching its way toward the house. The stillness outside was captivating. The late afternoon heat hung in the air like the stultifying perfume of bright and heady flowers. Cars lined the drive; more were starting to trickle in behind them. Aris inhaled deeply and caught the hot scent of manure. They walked slowly up the porch stairs, looking straight ahead of them to the open front door. Family was shoved into every crevice of the big, old house, yet it was silent. People spoke in the hushed voices required of death and grief. A pall hung about the place, as though the passing of Astoria had taken the life out of the family. There was a shriek of childish laughter and Aris jumped.

John, his blank drug-induced stare made only more blank by the shock of grief, led Aris into the house. She held her breath and prayed no one would say anything to her, though if someone did, it was no less than she deserved.

The heat was oppressive. Although the house was unusually cool, the more bodies that poured into it, the less air there seemed to be. As Aris entered the house, she could hear screaming coming from the back study. She glanced into Astoria's old room. The double doors were standing open, the bed made; a whisper of lavender hung in the air. Aris and John came in through the kitchen door and saw Paul Hodge sitting in the metal kitchen chair checking his Blackberry. He glanced up at them, the top of his bald head shining with sweat, his reddish hair circling the bottom half hung over his ears. He made a face and shrugged. John nodded and Aris stared. As they walked through the house, the screaming got louder and Aris heard the rumbling of J.J. As they made their way through the still heat, Aris noticed cousins sitting quietly in corners, checking mobiles, staring out windows.

The shouting grew louder, and Aris recognized Janice's throaty voice. John pushed the half-open door to the study and it swung open to reveal a small crowd.

J.J. was holding his mobile in his hand like a weapon; his dark brows hung heavy over his cold, black eyes. He spoke calmly, but his voice was gritty with anger.

"You are being unreasonable," he said.

Janice was in a fury; her black hair whipped about as she paced the room. She curved her nails like talons and bared her teeth like an animal.

"You go to hell, J.J.! You can just go straight to hell! You viper!" she screamed in his face.

Disby was standing by the fireplace, her head bowed.

"How dare you? How dare you? You had no right! You had no right, damn it, John!"

Sarah was sitting in a chair beside the fireplace, looking tired and staring at nothing. Before Aris and John moved into the room, Jane and Helen came between them through the door.

"What did you do, J.J.?" Jane was screaming.

"He sold the house! He sold the house right out from under us!" Janice screamed, her face red, her eyes black fire. At this revelation,

Helen collapsed against the door frame. John caught her bulky body and righted her.

"I have power of attorney, Jan," J.J. said, punctuating the words "power of attorney" by slamming his mobile into his fist.

"Well, how in the hell did you get that? You deceptive son of bitch!" Janice screamed.

"You knew about this, Disby, for Christ's sake! Don't act innocent!" J.J. yelled.

Janice whirled. "You knew?" she said menacingly. "You knew?"

Disby flinched.

"Did she know, J.J.?" Jane planted herself directly in front of him. "Did Mother know what you two vultures were planning?"

Disby sank onto the floor, white-faced. "I didn't know," she said. Nobody paid her any notice.

J.J. regarded his sister impassively. "She signed the papers last week. She was never coming back here. She knew that."

The room erupted. Jane's mouth was open, her face frozen in a scream that couldn't make it out of her body. Helen began to cry in earnest on John's arm, loud, ugly sobs that wracked her body. Janice was screaming.

"You killed her John. You killed our mother!" Janice accused.

"Oh my God! Mother! Mother!" Disby was shouting, torrential tears coursing down her face. "We killed Mother!"

Janice, who until now had been pacing the room, stopped in front of J.J., took one look at Jane's shocked face and pushed her out of the way. Less than an inch away from his face, she said, "How could you? How could you? She loves this house!"

"Loved it," said Jane. "She loved it."

Janice pulled back and slapped her brother with a force that snapped his black head back. Immediately, a red handprint appeared on his face. Still, he remained impassive and simply stared at Janice.

Helen wailed. Jane stepped over the sobbing Disby and shoved J.J.

He stumbled backward a few steps and regained his footing. Blank-faced, he watched his sisters, implacable Furies, whirl before him like the witches in Macbeth.

"Murderer!" Janice screamed.

Aris looked over at Sarah, who was still sitting in the wingback chair, looking as if she were at the theater and was waiting for intermission; she did not spare Aris a glance. Aris looked at John. He still had his arms wrapped around the voluminous Helen, holding her up. Aris slipped out behind them, leaving the old woman's offspring to battle over her bones. She went back through the house, the eerie quiet punctuated by the shouts coming from the study. She passed Gus and his wife in the living room with Marie. "It was the right thing to do; she was too old," Minnie was telling Gus and Marie in a hushed and solemn voice. She patted her short, black hair with her red-tipped hand.

Gus took a surreptitious bite from the potato chip in his hand and winced as Minnie shot him a disapproving look.

Aris passed the little group sitting on the blue sofa. They all glanced up to watch her go by, but no one spoke to her.

As Aris came back through the kitchen, Sarah's husband was still on his Blackberry, emailing someone. His stubby fingers flew over the tiny keys at a frantic rate. He didn't even look up as Aris went through the swinging door into the dining room. The air was stifling; all the windows were shut against the heat. Morgan was collapsed in a chair, drunker than Aris had ever seen her. Her bare feet swung sideways from the bottom of the chair; her knees were bent beneath her. She was clutching a tall glass of bourbon and weeping piteously into it. Ice clinked furiously against the glass as Morgan's

hands shook with tremors. Every so often, she
would say the word Mama wearily. Aris
shuddered, despite the sticky heat, and went
swiftly past the redhead, who didn't even realize
she was there. She went through the main foyer,
out the front door, and into the suffocating heat.
Sweat ran down the backs of her thighs. The
porch was empty; she shaded her eyes from the
glaring sun and watched the people milling
about the grounds. The house sagged with the
wretched sorrow of its inhabitants, and she
longed to be away from the place. She walked
slowly, her steps hushed, toward the back of the
house to Astoria's garden. The rowdy blossoms
rose up in the thick heat and the branches of the
willows rustled gently, as if not to disturb the
mournful gloom that shuttered the old place. As
she pushed open the weathered wooden gate, the
breeze strengthened, the lament it carried with
it, unmistakable.

Chapter 25

The shouts in the study grew louder. Aris could hear them from her position in the garden. Janice was threatening to murder J.J. Helen was still crying. The door to the side porch opened and Aris recognized Marie and Sarah's voices.

"I can't believe she showed up here," Marie said in a shocked voice.

"I can't believe my brother brought her here. What was he thinking?" Sarah fumed.

"She's clearly been manipulating him from the beginning," Marie said.

"Of course she has. I never bought that innocent, country girl crap from her. I knew better. Mother knew she was a gold digger from the minute she laid eyes on her. We tried to tell John but he wouldn't hear it. He thought she was so sweet and innocent. Tell me, does sweet and innocent jump into bed with your cousin?"

Marie laughed harshly. "She thought she had us all fooled."

Aris stiffened. She thought about confronting them.

"Rhys of all people. Talk about disgusting."

"He is rather good looking," Marie threw out tentatively.

"Oh, please," Sarah said dismissively. "He's such trash. They belong together."

"But John took her back," Marie said. "You have to accept it."

"Like hell I do. Mother already said she was going to cut him off if he took her back. She'll leave him when he has no money. That's all she was after in the first place."

Aris wondered if part of that was true. Was Janice right? Was it impossible for her to separate John from his money? If he weren't wealthy, would she still be here?

Marie and Sarah went on talking; Aris stole out of the garden, not caring if they saw her. She began to walk down the gravel drive alone, unsure of where she was going or what she was doing. She felt their eyes, their accusatory black eyes, on her still. She shook herself, trying to rid herself of the guilt she felt. The sun was starting to set. The sky was radiant with gold and pink, but to Aris, it seemed out of place.

Aris left John in Napa, not caring how or if he got home. She climbed into the Mercedes and drove to Larkspur. She entered the house; Laura's battered suitcase sat in the corner of the hallway. Aris shuddered and moved to walk past it. Then she stopped and opened it. She heard the echo of her mother's gravelly voice.

Aris peered into the open suitcase. The heat pulsed around her. The smell of cheap perfume and cigarette smoke wafted up to her. She poked through the filthy clothes until she found the pile of papers.

Dear Aris.

Aris' violet eyes widened. They were letters, pages and pages of letters and they were all addressed to her. They dated back years.

Dear Aris, I met this guy and I married him. He would've been a good dad, I think. He loved me. But then I fucked it up like I fuck everything up...

Dear Aris, I got a new job today. I'm really going to do it right this time. No more booze, no more powders or pills or anything else. I'm going to do it real good and maybe I'll come see you.

Dear Aris, I was close to the valley today, closest I've ever been anyway in a long time. I thought I'd come see you but then I got into a fight with this guy I was with. You're in high school now I think. I wonder sometimes if you look like me. If you act like me.

On and on they went, pages filled with the minutiae of Laura's life. Strange anecdotes, odd recollections, some of the letters were a pure stream of consciousness, almost as if Laura had forgotten she was even writing to someone.

Aris left the letters scattered on the floor. She realized she was crying. She went to the guest room and stood in the hot shower until her skin was blotched with red.

Surrounded by the unreal night, she got into her car and turned the key. She drove slowly through the streets, with all her windows down so she could smell the summer on the air. She got on the freeway and gloried in the hot wind as it caressed the tan leather interior. After a while, she got off the freeway and drove slowly through the industrial wasteland that Rhys called home. She did not think of anything but the sounds and smells and sights of the unmoving night.

She parked in front of his place. She exited the car and went to the blue door. The high, yellow moon glowed in the black sky. She put her hand to the knob and felt it turn under her fingers.

The door opened slowly, and Rhys was there on the stairs. His black hair hung in his face and his green eyes threw back the moonlight. He stared at her and she stared back. A calm settled over her and she felt strength coursing through her veins. Rhys quirked an elegant brow at her, and, at once, she understood he saw the change in her. He did not make any sardonic gestures or sarcastic remarks; he simply stood there and waited.

The night seemed to sparkle around her as she stepped through the doorway. She inhaled, and he smelled so intoxicating, her mouth began to water. She could feel the heat of him shimmering just over her skin. Everything was slow, crystalline, and perfect. He was shirtless, wearing only unbuttoned black jeans. She stood as close as she could to him in the

narrow, dark hallway. She met his green eyes
with a fierce challenge. Her own eyes flashed as
though he were delectable prey and she were a
wildcat about to pounce. Still, she did not touch
him. She slid past him and walked slowly and
purposefully up the stairs. Aris could hear his
steady tread behind her. When she reached the
loft, she stopped. The full moon peered in the
windows and the silvery light filtered into the
room.

Aris turned and faced him as he came up
the last stair. The longing she had felt in her
vivid and terrible dreams welled up inside of her
and spilled out on a deep breath as she exhaled
his scent. Her lips trembled and parted. Rhys
was no more than five feet from her. He
watched her in the clear shafts of light; his
muscles tensed. She watched his pulse jump in
his throat; she memorized his face. She could
feel her heartbeat; her head was light. She took
careful note of his face, his eyes, his lean body.
Her stomach began fluttering; her fingertips
tingled. The energy between them was so
intense, Aris felt her knees shake.

Rhys picked up his bare feet and moved
slowly toward her; Aris felt her own feet
moving as well, though she was not conscious
of walking. They met on the polished wood

floor, between the bed and the stairs. The air was dull with heat. He had the door open downstairs; she could smell the fresh air winding its way toward them. Aris' hand reached up and came to rest on his cheek. His pulse leapt in his throat. They were practically kissing, they were so close. Her other hand reached up and caressed his left cheek. With each breath, she trembled; she could practically taste the salt on his skin. He reached out and ran his long fingers through her hair. Aris' hands slid down his face to his chest. She felt his heart beating its familiar, quick staccato under her hand.

His gaze moved from her purple eyes to her lips. He looked at her with undisguised hunger. A smile curved its way across her mouth; it was knowing and sexy. Rhys shattered the stillness with sudden violence, and pulled her by the waist until she was pressed against him. His mouth possessed hers with gentleness she had not known he was capable of. His arms encircled her roughly, rearranging themselves on her skin as he ripped at her shirt savagely. She had worn no bra, and the feel of his hot skin on her own made the need twisting her bones surge. They kissed lazily, slowly, as their hands and arms laid claim to each other feverishly and possessively. The smell of soap and mint and sex meant Rhys, and she inhaled and drowned in it. She tasted the salt in his mouth and on his skin, and it made her move her hips against him. Her hands moved over his chest and face and back as if she could read him through touch.

How long they stood there, half naked and kissing in the moonlit heat, she did not know. Her need, her longing, was so great, she wanted to fuck him until her skin was saturated in him, until her mouth tasted only of him, until every time she breathed, she breathed him like oxygen.

She kissed him as though she would never get enough of him. The moon shone through the high windows as their hands slid over torsos and legs and arms and necks, tugging on silky hair and brushing over raised nipples.

She pushed him back on the bed and pressed her forehead against his. She felt the delicious slide as she sank down. Her eyes closed, her need finally assuaged, her desperation finally quelled.

Aris stayed with him until the sun began to rise. She wrapped herself in the white sheet and walked quietly downstairs. She knew he was awake, but he made no move to stop her.

His green eyes followed her silently. She slipped out of the rear door and into the early morning. The light was purple; the trees were black silhouettes, mere hints of reality. She could see the glimmer of the sun from across the marsh. She sat, wrapped in the sheet, on an old wooden bench and waited for the sun.

She heard Rhys come behind her, but she did not turn to him. He sat beside her on the bench. His hips were wrapped in a red blanket. He threw an arm around her and drew her close. Aris tucked her head into his shoulder. The sun slowly rose and they watched the shadowy things of night become the ordinary things of day.

When the sun was high over the horizon and the tentative chirps of birds became loud and raucous chattering, she rose. She had memorized his face, his taste, the feel of him. She knew she would dream of him no longer.

"Where are you going?" he asked quietly.

"I'm not sure. Away from here, from all of this."

He was able to read her easily, as he always had been able to.

"So," he said, "why'd you come here?"

"To say goodbye."

"You could've called," he said ruefully.

"What would be the fun in that?" Aris asked, sadness under her light tone.

Rhys looked down, his green eyes dull. He pursed his lips and took a deep breath. His beautiful hands gripped each other in his lap. She watched him and let out a breath. He wanted her to stay; she could feel it dancing between them, the possibility of happily ever after.

But she had already tried happily ever after.

"I have to go," she said to him.

Rhys kept his green eyes on the creek and said nothing.

She turned to leave him, sitting there in the early morning, the breeze lifting his hair and making it dance across his handsome face. He watched her go, his emerald eyes following her until she could see him no longer.

As she got into the car, she did not have to look up to know that, from somewhere inside, he was watching her.

As she drove, she thought of the Princes: John waking up alone in his bed, unsurprised, eyes focused on the phantasm of disgrace that loomed in front of him; Janice, melancholy and angry all at once, a force of nature, surviving on her own particular brand of malice and entitlement; Helen, forever seeking out prolonged and invasive physical contact; Morgan teetering on her heels, drunk yet impossibly steady; The Whisper Sisters, Marie and Sarah, huddled in a corner and smirking. She saw them all, in her mind's eye, expensive and pretty pets, muzzled to the world, savagely baring fangs to one another.

As the car gained speed and the wind whistled through the windows, she detected the barest hint of autumn tumbling in under the hot summer air.

Kirsten Langston

Kirsten Langston is a lifelong resident of northern California. *The Mad Season* is her first novel.

www.kirstenlangstonauthor.com

Kirsten Langston

CPSIA information can be obtained at www.ICGtesting.com
Printed in the USA
BVOW05s0359090514

353023BV00001B/29/P